Camp Firwood

D1526520

Boris Bacic

1
The Choosing

"Are you worried?" Michael asked Bill as they sat on the lonesome tree stumps.

The sky was grey, and the rain was expected to start at any moment, but that didn't stop the counselors from going forward with The Choosing. The campers had just had their breakfast, and most of them were sitting in front of the main lodge with forlorn expressions on their faces, some talking to each other but most quietly staring at their feet.

Bill shrugged, pursing his lips.

"Maybe a little. There's a lot of campers. What are the odds that we'll get chosen?"

Truth be told, he was extremely nervous. He felt it in his stomach, knots twisting and making him sick. But he couldn't let his friend know. Even though Michael was a good friend despite knowing him for a short time, he could never know if he would go telling the other campers sensitive things. That exact thing happened to Alex, who snuck a cigarette inside the camp but was later ratted out by someone, which resulted in Alex having to do wood-chopping for a whole week.

Bill barely managed to eat a couple of bites of his toast and scrambled eggs for breakfast, spending the rest of the breakfast time playing around with his food on the fork, until Assistant Counselor Dwight forcefully nudged him and told him it was time to leave the cafeteria.

Bill noticed that the other kids hadn't eaten much either, save for maybe Barrel Mark. They called him that way because he was the most obese teen in the camp. He ate his own food and even asked Javier for his, to which Javier slid the plate to him absent-mindedly. Bill wondered how Mark was able to eat on such a day but then figured that Barrel Mark probably didn't understand the severity of the situation.

He remembered how Mark constantly complained about being hungry for the first few days of camping when they arrived, even going as far as to ask Lunch Lady Daisy for seconds. And then, all of it just stopped. Other campers warned Mark not to go asking for extra food; otherwise, he'd be in trouble. He probably listened to them - and good thing, too. If any of the counselors heard him, especially Dwight, he'd be in a lot of trouble.

"So, what do you think happens to the ones who get chosen?" Michael asked.

Bill shrugged.

"I dunno. Complete the trial and go home, I guess."

"Do you really think they complete the trial with the Firwood Wraith roaming around?"

"Oh, come on. Not that shit again. We don't even know if those stories are true."

The Wraith of Firwood.

The campers had been talking about it ever since day one. Bill wasn't even sure who started the story or what exactly the wraith was, but the campers seemed terrified of it. Apparently, there was a ghost right outside of the summer camp, roaming the woods at night. It would prey on campers who dared to escape from the camp and would kill them.

A story went around that one camper tried running away from Camp Firwood last year and died in the woods. The counselors never said it was the Firwood Wraith, but a lot of the campers jumped the gun and stated that it was. Bill himself wasn't an enthusiast or believer of the paranormal. However, now that The Choosing was almost at hand, he was more open-minded. He even thought he heard some screeches a few times during the night since he arrived, but he chalked it up to his imagination going wild over the other campers' tales.

What do you think the wraith looks like? How do you think it kills the campers? Do you think it uses a weapon like an ax? Has anyone ever survived the encounter?

Then, there were the exaggerated rumors that kept spreading like wildfire.

Legend has it that the Firwood Wraith used to be a camper who got killed and is now stalking the woods. The wraith comes out only during summer when the campers are present. The wraith only hunts bad teens.

"Of course the stories are true," Michael retorted, snapping Bill back into reality. "What do you think happened to Brian and Omar? They never came back."

"Well, maybe they were sent home."

"You heard that whistle in the woods a few nights ago."

"That was an animal," Bill scoffed.

"No fucking way. I think Brian and Omar are dead."

"Well, why would they pick some campers to send them home and others for... whatever it is they choose them for?"

Michael shrugged.

"Maybe they don't send them home at all."

Bill nodded, staring at his feet. He didn't want to talk about the Firwood Wraith anymore. He drew a line with his foot in the dirt and dragged his shoe back and forth across it, making it clearer with each drag. All this talk about The Choosing and the wraith didn't make him feel any less nervous. If anything, it only made him even more anxious. He remembered hearing once that the only reason why we feel afraid was because we fear the unknown. In this case, he had no idea what, exactly, the Choosing was, save for what the counselors told them.

The Choosing occurred every two weeks, and since Bill had been in the camp for only a week and a half, he never witnessed it taking place. All he knew was it terrified the other campers so much that they did their best to avoid getting into any trouble and getting negative points added to their names. The counselors never clarified The Trial, either. Jim once asked about it, to which the counselors smiled and told him that it wouldn't be so special if they revealed the surprise.

"I still think the trial is not as dangerous as you guys think," Bill said, unable to let Michael have the final word.

"Maybe," Michael shrugged bemusedly.

The fact that he didn't want to argue back irked Bill, but he figured that now was not the time for fighting.

7

The crowd of campers around the main lodge was ominously quiet today, which was understandable. Those who believed in the Firwood Wraith were scared shitless. And those who didn't were either starting to believe the rumors or they were nervous about spending a few nights in the woods alone.

Bill glanced toward the entrance of the lodge just in time to see Dwight and Head Counselor, Mr. Adams, emerge. The two of them faced each other and spoke, but they were too far away for Bill to make out any of the words. As if on cue, the campers closest to the entrance scrambled to their feet and rushed in a stampede to line up in front of the counselors.

Others seemed to become aware of the commotion and clambered to their feet as well, leaving clouds of dust behind them as they loped to join the ranks of the other campers who lined up like soldiers.

"Come on, Bill!" Michael grabbed Bill under his arm and helped him up.

The two of them rushed to the five lines which the campers now formed, one behind the other. Bill hurriedly sprinted to the fourth row, squeezing himself between Michael on his left and Steve on his right.

The pounding of footsteps on the ground all but stopped, except for one, which joined in seconds later. It was Ethan, and he rushed to the back of the line with panting breaths, trying to squeeze in between two campers.

"Come on, guys, move; give me some room!" he shouted, desperately trying to make his way into the line, but the other campers wouldn't budge.

They couldn't budge now, especially since the counselors' eyes were on them. Dwight stuck two fingers in his mouth and whistled loudly, pointing his index finger at the back where Ethan was.

"Looks like we got one here, Mr. Adams!" he said with his croaky voice.

"No, I'm in the line!" Ethan shouted with a high-pitched and trembling voice, sounding like he was on the verge of tears.

"Camper, get over here!" Mr. Adams curled his index in a motion to call Ethan to get closer.

"Mr. Adams, I'm in the line, please!"

"Camper," Mr. Adams lowered his chin and raised his eyebrows.

Ethan hung his head down and, with a defeated sniffle, made his way around the back of the line and all the way to the front, looking down at his feet the entire time. Dwight shook his head and clucked his tongue as Mr. Adams flipped a paper on the notepad he was holding. He clicked his pen a few times and looked at Ethan before putting it to the paper and asking, "What's your name, camper?"

"Ethan," Ethan responded timidly, still looking down.

Dwight took a menacing step toward Ethan with his hands on his hips. Ethan slightly recoiled before Dwight's towering figure but refused to look up.

"Camper, when the counselor addresses you, you look up, and you respond with respect! Is that understood?" Dwight was so close to Ethan now that his spit probably defiled the poor camper's face.

Bill couldn't see his face, but he imagined eyes glossy from tears. Ethan was the slowest kid, and so far, he'd always make it in the nick of time. But today, he was not so lucky.

You chose the worst day to be late, Ethan.

Ethan looked up and nodded briefly in short, energetic head motions. Mr. Adams put his hand on Dwight's shoulder, which seemed to defuse the assistant counselor. Dwight stepped back and allowed the head counselor to take over.

"Now tell me again, camper, what's your name?"

"Ethan, Mr. Adams," Ethan responded, more bravely this time.

Mr. Adams produced an *mhm* sound as he politely nodded and wrote something down in his pad. A moment later, he looked at Ethan with a smile and said, "Alright, that makes it four points for you. Back in line you go, camper."

Ethan needed no further motivation. He began running forward, but Mr. Adams raised his index finger and said, "Tsk, tsk, tsk. What did we say about going back in line, camper?"

Ethan froze, staring at Mr. Adams in confusion. An eerie silence filled the air as Ethan glanced at his fellow campers, desperately seeking help with his eyes before turning back to the senior counselor.

"Um…" he started, swinging his hands back and forth while looking down again.

Go behind the counselors when returning to the line, not in front of them!

Bill wanted to scream at Ethan, but he couldn't. Any sign of insubordination would earn him the same kind of reward that Ethan just got for himself. He remembered on the second day how Michael ran between Dwight and the line of campers to quickly get back in line after his watchtower duty, and Dwight was nowhere near as tolerant as Mr. Adams was.

Needless to say, all the campers who witnessed Michael receiving such harsh backlash from Dwight didn't dare even think about cutting in front of the counselors again.

"Give him another one, Mr. Adams!" Dwight spat, frowning at Ethan.

Mr. Adams tapped his pen on the pad, staring at Ethan the whole time.

"Camper," he said, which made Ethan raise his head and lock eyes with Mr. Adams. "We said you should never go between the counselors and the line of campers, didn't we? Now go on, run *behind,* and get back in line."

He pointed behind himself with his thumb while grinning widely. Ethan quickly obliged, jogging around Mr. Adams and Dwight and hastily making his way to his designated spot in the fourth row.

"You should have given him another one, Mr. Adams. These maggots never learn," Dwight spitefully said, shaking his head.

"Now, Dwight. Don't be so harsh." He turned to the campers and bellowed, "Good morning, campers!"

"Good morning, Mr. Adams!" the camp roared in unison.

"Come on now, campers, why the long faces?" Mr. Adams asked. "Today is a big day! No need to be so gloomy!"

He threw his hands up in the air with a wide grin. His politeness never ceased to amaze Bill. To this day, he couldn't figure out if Mr. Adams was just morbidly polite because he enjoyed the somberness of the situation or if he was simply oblivious to what was going on. The latter would explain why Dwight was such a dick to everyone tenfold when no other counselor was around.

"Alright, I can see no one is in the mood today. But we have to recite the core values of the camp," Mr. Adams said with a smirk. "Campers, recite!"

All campers, forty-something of them or so, began chanting in unison.

"Discipline is the mother of all values. Discipline is the bridge between goals and accomplishments. By following the rules of the camp, I will become a disciplined and better person. Discipline is the core value of Camp Firwood. Discipline is the core value of life."

The recital went smoothly. The first few days, the recital was messy with unsynchronized and wrongly chanted words. Now it sounded like a well-prepared orchestra.

"Let's do a roll call, and then we can go to the choosing stage," Mr. Adams said.

He spent the next couple of minutes calling on campers numerically, starting with cabin one and ending with cabin five. Everyone was present, so when he checked off the last camper on the list, he clicked his pen multiple times and shouted.

"Aren't you all good today! Start walking toward the Choosing Grounds and take your seats there. I will see you there in…" — he looked at his wristwatch — "fifteen minutes, so that will be exactly nine-twenty-five."

"You heard the man, let's go! I don't wanna see anyone lagging behind!" Dwight annoyingly clapped his hands together.

Immediately, the campers turned right and started moving in the direction of the Choosing Stage like a herd. Bill glanced to the right and waited for his friend Michael to catch up with him since they didn't need to stay in line when walking. As soon as they put some distance between themselves and the counselors, the campers started talking to each other.

"Oh man, poor Ethan," Michael said with a defeated sigh.

"Yeah, well, we warned him a million times to be ready. He knows he's not fast, so he should always be ready for lineup before the others." Bill shrugged.

The two of them went along with the rest of the campers, suddenly aware of how loud their voices were in comparison to the rest of the group. On any other day, the campers' murmurs would drown out their own voices, but today, everyone was gloomy. It felt like walking to the gallows.

"Say, did Ethan ever try telling any of the counselors to, like, take it easy on him? I mean, because of his health and all," Bill asked.

"He did." Michael nodded. "But the idiot told Dwight."

"Ouch," Bill responded.

"Yeah. And Dwight doesn't like whining. He immediately put Ethan on bucket duty for the whole day."

"Bucket duty? He had to lug buckets full of rocks all the way from the cabins to the rock pile?"

"Yep," Michael sighed.

"Damn. Dwight's a psycho," Bill shook his head.

"Quiet," Michael retorted, looking to his right as if to see if Dwight would magically appear next to him.

He looked back at Bill and said in a more hushed tone.

"That guy has eyes and ears everywhere. I wouldn't be surprised if some of the campers reported directly to him."

They had just gotten off the main beaten path between the buildings and onto the narrow gravel trail, which took them between thick rows of pine trees.

"Why would they report to him?" Bill asked.

Michael shrugged.

"I dunno. Privileges? Better treatment?"

"Better treatment from Dwight? Do you hear yourself, Mike?" Bill frowned.

He and Michael stared at each other for a moment before they both burst into laughter. It massively contrasted the gloomy atmosphere of the other campers quietly walking. Bill half-expected one of the counselors to yell at them to shut up, but no warning came. Still, that reminded him to keep his voice down, to avoid any unnecessary punishments, especially now when The Choosing was about to begin, even if it did help alleviate his anxiety a little bit.

The gravel road curved slightly to the right, but Bill couldn't see where it ended. He hadn't attended The Choosing before, so he had no idea how far it was or how it looked. He wanted to ask Michael about it, but before he finished that thought, he started seeing the end of the road.

It curved to the right and then straightened, leading directly into a large meadow surrounded by tall pine trees that stretched over the view. At least, it looked like a meadow at first, but the closer they got, the more details became discernible to Bill. There were dozens of tree stumps evenly cut, looking like rows of chairs. At the very front was a wooden podium elevated a little higher than the stumps.

"Is that it?" he asked Michael, already knowing the answer.

Michael silently nodded. His mood seemed to suddenly drop like an ax in water as did the moods of the rest of the campers, no matter how impossible that seemed. Some of the campers murmured with worry in their tone, asking their friends what would happen to them if they were chosen or simply staring directly at the meadow, wide-eyed. Only a few campers seemed nonchalant about the whole thing, or at least, they didn't show any signs of worry on their faces.

Tough Norton, as the other campers called him, seemed the most indifferent – even relaxed - about walking toward the Choosing Grounds. He got his name on the first day of camping. Bill wasn't there to see it since he arrived a few weeks after the others, but this was what the other campers told him.

Dwight, it seems, took a special *liking* to Norton and led him to the old outhouse toilet, telling him he needed to finish cleaning it by the end of the day or face wood-chopping duty for a week. Even though the outhouse seemed like it hadn't been used or maintained for years, Dwight clearly just wanted to give Tough Norton something that would break him or humiliate him. Tough Norton, despite being two years younger than Dwight, responded by shoving the assistant counselor inside the outhouse and dropping him upside-down inside the pile of shit.

Tough Norton didn't look tough at all, to begin with. He was short and skinny, save for his forearms, which were bulky and veiny from years of working with his folks on the farm. At any rate, when the other counselors rushed to see what the fuss was all about, they restrained Norton and sent him somewhere. He returned a week later, saying he was given detention and had to do some mundane chores, but he didn't seem to mind.

He even told the entire story with a shrug and a smile, the detention clearly having had no effect on him. Bill wondered how Norton managed to get away for so long in the camp without being severely punished, but he guessed that years of hiding things from his stern father taught him how to get into trouble just enough to avoid getting into *serious* trouble. The Choosing was something unfamiliar to him, too, though, and Bill assumed that Tough Norton was simply not aware of the potential danger of the situation. Or didn't care.

The first droplet of rain fell on Bill's nose, and he looked up, starting to feel tiny cold droplets momentarily stinging his face.

"Oh no. Here comes the rain. Disgusting," Clean Ryan said worriedly from somewhere in the front.

Bill knew exactly who each camper was before even seeing them. This seemed to be something shared among all the campers since they spent so much time together during the day. They not only recognized each other based on their voices but by just looking at their silhouettes in the distance when it was dark.

Clean Ryan was a germaphobe, a skinny kid who was afraid of getting dirty in every sense of the word. Bill once had to do some digging with Barrel Mark and Ryan, and Ryan spent the time doing no work at all most of the day, stating that there were millions of harmful microorganisms in the dirt. When Mark reminded him that there are microorganisms literally everywhere, including his face, Ryan grew visibly agitated. He wanted to excuse himself to the bathroom, but with Dwight watching them like a hawk, taking breaks was next to impossible.

"Well, come on, let's hurry up and get this over with, then!" another camper shouted, which seemed to urge the entire group to move faster.

Bill started walking faster to keep up with the quickened pace of the campers in front. The campers behind him started fast-walking too, practically forcing Bill and Michael to hurry up, even stepping on the backs of their shoes a couple of times. Within minutes, they reached the meadow and then the messily strewn stump-chairs.

Bill saw the wooden podium more clearly now. It was basically a bunch of planks put together and elevated about four feet above the ground with a small set of stairs on the right side leading up to the podium. The group in the front stopped in front of the rows of stumps. The campers who were in the back got around their peers, curiously peeking at the sight before them.

"What do we do now?" Camper David asked.

Tough Norton shrugged.

"The same thing we always do. Just take a seat and wait for those assholes to arrive."

It was just like back in school. No one wanted to sit in the front seat, so students usually rushed to grab the seat furthest away from the teacher's. The case was the same here, and luckily for Michael and Bill, they managed to take two seats next to each other somewhere in the middle. It really didn't matter where they sat, though, because it wasn't like they could quietly talk amongst each other. When the counselors climbed the podium, they'd be able to see everyone anyway.

The commotion lasted for a minute or so until everyone found their own seat. The front row seats remained mostly empty, save for a few campers who were too late and had to take those seats – Ethan being one of them. The somber murmurs of the campers permeated the air, and Bill could feel the tension on all sides. They were all worried. The rain was still meager with only a few miserly drops falling here and there. No one was paying attention to the rain, though.

"Who got the most points?" One of the campers asked in a somewhat hushed tone, much to the indecipherable whispers of other nearby campers.

The next few minutes were spent counting days amongst the campers. In the end, they concluded that Tough Norton broke the record with a whopping nine negative points. He seemed indifferent when he talked about it, shrugging it off as something unimportant. Others exchanged how many points their fellow campers got, and no one seemed to be nearly as high as Norton. Ethan and a few other campers had four. David and Javier got three, and the rest only had two, one or zero.

After they were done discussing that, they went on to talk about who the best-behaved camper was. There were a bunch of candidates who got no extra points for The Trial, so chances were they might get picked to leave earlier. Barrel Mark seemed to be the luckiest one since he not only had no extra points added, but he never seemed to get in trouble either. Some campers even started calling him Lucky Mark; however, the name didn't stick.

"So, what will you do if they pick you for The Trial?" Bill asked Michael.

Michael pursed his lips and shrugged.

"No idea. I don't even know what this is all about. But we probably won't see each other again if one of us gets chosen."

Bill suddenly felt a surge of unfamiliar emotions that he likened to fear and sadness. He didn't want to be chosen, but he didn't want Michael to be chosen, either. Of all the campers he got to know so far, Michael was his closest friend. The thought of having to spend another day in this hellhole without his new best friend terrified him.

"Hey, let's make a deal," Bill said.

This caught Michael's attention. He looked at Bill and asked, "Alright, what kind of deal?"

Bill leaned forward on his knees.

"If either of us gets chosen, we'll find the other person."

This brought a meager smile to Michael's face.

"Deal," he said and put his hand forward.

They shook hands.

"Quiet, they're coming!" Clean Ryan said in a hushed tone.

Bill turned around and looked over the shoulders of the campers behind him, who also happened to be looking in the same direction. Dwight, Mr. Adams, and a dozen other adults were walking down the gravel path toward the Choosing Grounds.

"Don't look!" another camper said in a whisper.

By now, most of the campers had turned to face the podium. They had been taught that they had to look straight when the counselors or anyone of authority was nearby. They were to be quiet, and they were to address the persons of command only when spoken to.

"Either way, this will all be over soon," Michael's voice came from next to Bill.

Bill dared to turn his gaze toward his friend and realized that Michael was staring straight in front of himself like a soldier.

"Here we are, campers!" Mr. Adams' jovial voice came from behind, which reminded Bill to look straight.

A rustle of soft footsteps upon the trimmed grass filled the air to the right, and soon the entire group of camp counselors made their way up on the podium.

"Put it right here, Dwight," Mr. Adams pointed to the podium.

Seconds later, Dwight climbed up, lugging two backpacks over his shoulder before slumping them in the middle.

The supply backpacks.

Dwight walked over to Mr. Adams and said, "Backpacks are in place, Mr. Adams."

"Thanks, Dwighty-boy." Mr. Adams patted Dwight on the shoulder, who retreated to the back of the podium along with the rest of the staff. "Now we just gotta wait for the others to arrive."

The others?

Bill quickly gave a once over to the present counselors and deduced that everyone was there, save for Nurse Mary, Lunch Lady Daisy, and Groundskeeper Andy.

17

"Ah, here they come," Mr. Adams said a second later. "You'd better be on your best behavior, Dwight."

More rustling resounded on Bill's right, and he sneakily turned his head in that direction, straining to see who was coming. Two tall, bulky men stepped into his view, walking side by side. They were wearing sunglasses and had marine-blue uniforms. The thing which caught Bill's eye right away was the guns they had in their holsters. At first, he thought the men were police officers, but then he saw the word *SECURITY* on their backs.

Armed security guards? In a summer camp?

The guards stepped onto the podium and joined the line of camp staff members on the left end. The fact that armed security guards were present in the Choosing made him all the more nervous. What was so important about the Choosing that they had to be here?

Mr. Adams glanced around in random directions, casting contemptuous glimpses at the campers. This lasted for a few grueling minutes. And then, Bill heard the sound of a car engine approaching from behind. He instinctively turned his head, as did the rest of the campers. A black car was approaching the meadow, leaving a cloud of dust behind it from the gravel and dirt.

"Eyes in front!" Dwight shouted, and the campers immediately turned back to face the podium.

Moments later, the car pulled up to the right of the podium, coming to a halt. The engine sputtered out of life, leaving the entirety of the Choosing Grounds in silence and anticipation. The campers, including Bill, stared at the car but couldn't see inside due to the dimmed windows. A few soft murmurs of the campers rose in the air, and Mr. Adams had to reprimand them for staring at the car. Once everyone finally managed to avert their gaze from the mysterious vehicle, Mr. Adams grinned.

"Good morning again, campers!" he raised his hand with a smile.

"Good morning, Mr. Adams," the campers replied unanimously in their trained fashion with a few of them slipping in an 'again' in between.

"Thank you all for coming here today," he said.

18

Not like we had a choice.

Bill angrily thought to himself.

"We have a special guest who wanted to attend today, but unfortunately, he is too busy, so we will have to do this faster. Thanks to him, we were able to organize everything that we have today. *And* he is the one to thank for financing all the activities you get to enjoy here at Camp Firwood. Please give your applause for the director of Camp Firwood!"

Mr. Adams gestured a hand toward the car, and the campers began clapping loudly. Bill took this as a sign that it was okay to look at the car, at least for the moment. Once the clapping started dying down, he turned to stare at the guards, who seemed motionless like statues. They held their hands clasped in front of themselves, staring forward, but Bill couldn't tell if they were watching the campers or staring somewhere else. Moments later, the clapping stopped entirely, and Mr. Adams continued speaking.

"I am really sorry to bring all of you here on such short notice, but as most of you know, we host The Choosing every two weeks or so in order to give you guys the chance to prove that you've learned something in the camp. So today, we will be choosing two campers for The Trial and one for Departure - like we usually do. I know you're all eager to start, so before we begin with The Choosing, I would like to ask you all one question."

He paused for a prolonged moment, silence lingering in the air in anticipation.

"Do we have any volunteers?"

The question came like a knife to an already open wound. What little sound remained of campers shuffling in their seats before Mr. Adams' question was now replaced by complete and utter silence. The occasional chirping of the birds was heard here and there. Bill wished more than anything right now to be a bird, without a worry in his life, hunting worms, feeding his fledglings, and having the freedom to fly wherever he wanted. But he wasn't a bird. He was Bill, and he was stuck in Camp Firwood.

"Anyone?" Mr. Adams repeated, glancing from camper to camper.

Everyone stared down, avoiding his gaze. If you don't look at him, he won't call on you. Everyone knew that rule from school. When the teacher asked you a question, you just avoided making eye contact with them, and you'd be safe.

"Come on, campers, this is a great honor to be chosen for! Plus, if you complete The Trial, you get to go home! Show that Firwood spirit!" Mr. Adams said in a comically enthusiastic manner, swinging his hands up as if to raise the energy of the audience.

When, again, no one responded, he pursed his lips and nodded in disappointment.

"Alright. I guess we'll just choose from the list. Let's see here…"

He looked at his notepad and tapped the pen on it rhythmically while grimacing. He flipped to the next page, glancing at it for a long moment before returning to the previous one as if contemplating between two things on the pages.

Come on, just call out the names already.

"Okay, so we're going with this one and this one. And let's see, who else…" Mr. Adams mumbled to himself, marking something on the notepad with his pen.

A moment later, he complacently looked up at the campers and said, "Alright, the honorary Departure camper who gets to go home earlier is…" he furrowed his forehead and looked at the campers with his chin down, carefully observing them from left to right with a curious glance.

Bill looked to the right and noticed Michael's color draining from his face. He was staring wide-eyed at Mr. Adams, probably as stressed as Bill himself was.

Come on, just say it!

"Camper Scott, cabin one," Mr. Adams enunciated and raised his chin, staring at the group of campers.

Murmurs of disappointment filled the air amongst the campers. Bill knew the chances of him getting picked for that were low, but he still had some meager hope.

"Finally," a voice behind Bill muttered.

Scott made his way between the campers, holding his hands up in the air like an athlete who just scored a goal. He climbed on top of the stage and stopped a few feet from the head counselor. Mr. Adams motioned to the security guards and said, "Officers, please escort camper Scott to the main lodge." He looked at Scott and said, "Congratulations, camper Scott. Would you like to stay to say goodbye to your fellow campers?"

"Nah… I mean, no, Mr. Adams." Scott looked like he could hardly contain his excitement.

The two guards menacingly strode to Scott. One of them outstretched his hand in order to turn him around, but Scott was already facing away from them and making his way down the stairs.

"Adios, fellas," he said to his fellow campers as he hopped down the stage and left with the guards as his escorts.

They walked over to the black car, and one of the security guards opened the back door and motioned with his head for the camper to get in. Scott happily obliged, and the door slammed shut as soon as he entered. The guards got into the car too (one on the passenger's side, the other next to Scott on the other side), and moments later, the vehicle's engine roared to life. With finesse, it spun around and drove off the Choosing Grounds toward the main grounds in the same reckless manner as it did when it first arrived.

Mr. Adams waited for the commotion to settle, and once silence ensued again, he said, "Alright, now on to the main event."

Everyone settled down, visibly more distressed again. Mr. Adams looked at the notes and said, "As I said, we will be choosing two campers for The Trial. The first one is…"

Bill felt cold sweat overwhelming him in anticipation. This effect seemed to transfer to the other campers as well since they stared at the stage blankly.

"Camper Victor, cabin one."

Bill felt a wave of relief wash over him momentarily. He instantly began darting his eyes around the sitting area to see where Victor was. Victor was sitting in the center, pale and wide-eyed. All the other eyes were already locked on him, and he probably knew that there was no way to avoid this, so he stood up without any defiance.

He timorously sauntered between the campers and climbed on top of the Choosing Stage.

"Stand over there, camper." Mr. Adams pointed to the right side of the podium.

Mr. Adams followed Victor with his gaze until the camper stopped on the right side of the stage before looking down at his notepad again.

Come on, just one more.

Bill felt guilty for hoping that someone else would be chosen, but he really didn't want to go to the woods with the Firwood Wraith or whatever the hell that thing was. For all he knew, maybe it wasn't even a wraith - maybe it was just a cougar. He pondered for a moment which one would be worse to encounter.

"Okay, the final camper for the Survival Trial is..."

Come on already!

"Camper William, cabin four."

Bill felt something drop to the pit of his stomach, and his legs cut off. No, that can't be right. Mr. Adams must have read it wrong. There were fifty or so campers; there was no way his name got pulled out.

"William? Where are you, William?" Mr. Adams called out, glancing from camper to camper with his chin up.

Heads started turning toward Bill, and there was no way he could hide now. He looked at Michael and saw that he was equally pale. He thought he'd be relieved not to have his name read, but he was wrong.

"Are you William, camper?" Mr. Adams pointed at Bill as he crumpled the piece of paper and put his hands on his hips.

Bill timidly nodded.

"Well, come on up here, camper." Mr. Adams motioned for him to get there.

But Bill couldn't move. He was frozen in place. This couldn't possibly be happening.

"Come on now, camper. Unless you don't want this duty. Because if that's the case, not a problem at all! We can always choose someone else to replace you. They'd automatically be assigned double negative points, but you'd get to stay in the camp," Mr. Adams said with a conniving smile, albeit more sternly.

No, I want it! Bill thought to himself.

He willed himself to stand up. He locked eyes with Michael, silently pleading for his help. But there was nothing Michael could do.

He made his way to the right between the rows of turning heads. Even as he climbed onto the podium, he couldn't believe this was happening. This was a dream, and he was going to wake up soon, he knew it. It had to be.

Bill stopped next to Victor and looked down at his own feet. Mr. Adams took a step closer to the campers and leaned on his knees to be on the same level as them. He looked directly at them and said, "Campers. This is a great honor at Camp Firwood. Making it through The Trial will not only give you a certificate, but you'll also be able to go home earlier. Doesn't that sound great?"

Neither of the two campers responded.

"But... what about the Firwood Wraith, Mr. Adams?" Victor finally asked timorously.

Mr. Adams threw his head back and guffawed.

"Nonsense, those are just rumors."

"But we hear something at night sometimes. I-I even saw someone at the window a few nights ago," Victor insisted.

"Just rumors," Mr. Adams sternly said. "There's nothing dangerous in the woods. Now, come on, let's get you ready. Dwight!"

Mr. Adams snapped a finger at the assistant counselor. Dwight ran up to the backpacks and picked them off the floor before loping to the campers and shoving each backpack into their hands violently. He then retreated to his spot again.

Mr. Adams said, "In your backpacks, you will find a number of supplies. Remember to use them wisely, campers. Try not to eat the MRE unless you absolutely have to. Try to make shelter, find some food and a source of water. Understood?"

"Yes, Mr. Adams," both campers chanted unanimously.

"Alright then, campers," Mr. Adams said the next moment with a grin, straightening his back.

He motioned one of the counselors and said, "Mr. Baldwin, you can escort the campers to the designated location."

A bald, buff-looking counselor stepped forward and approached the campers with such long steps that Bill thought he was going to punch them in the face. He put his hands on the campers' shoulders and turned them toward the stairs. Bill looked at Michael in desperation. His friend stared at him, and it was visible he wanted to say something, but his hands were just as tied as Bill's were. The next thing he knew, he and the other camper were nudged toward the edge of the woods on the other side of the stage.

"Move," the counselor groaned with enmity.

Bill turned around long enough to scan the plethora of heads for Michael's face. Although he was far away, he could still tell that his friend was staring at him. The counselor took menacing steps toward Bill and Victor, effectively forcing them to retreat deeper into the woods. Bill forced himself to turn around and walked between the trees where the rays of sunlight were already blocked out by the lush leaf-covered branches. With each step he took, he went farther from the camp's safety and into the unknown of the wilderness.

Despite having some doubts about the existence of the Firwood Wraith, he had no idea just what kind of hell he was about to witness in the woods.

2
The Arrival

"Kevin, straighten your shirt," Kevin's mom told him as she stared at him with a penetrating gaze from the front car seat.

Kevin glanced in her direction and ignored her, continuing to stare out the window. He pushed the earbuds a little further inside his ears and continued listening to *Rise Against*. For hours now, he'd seen nothing but endless rows of pine and fir trees stretching in every direction. He continued staring at the trees, avoiding his mother's gaze, although he could feel it on him.

"Listen to your mother, Kevin," the stern voice of his father bellowed from the driver's seat.

Kevin glanced at the rearview mirror and noticed that his dad was glowering at him with an unblinking gaze. The next thing he would do is warn him. And then he would stop the car and teach him manners. Kevin knew that his dad's patience was not to be tested. With a wrinkled nose, he grabbed the bottom of the shirt and tugged it down.

"There, now you look presentable," his mom said, turning back toward the road even though straightening the shirt did nothing to eliminate the already hard-present wrinkles.

Not that it mattered how he looked anyway. It was a goddamn summer camp, not a graduation ceremony. For all he knew, he could show up in a potato sack, and the camp staff wouldn't care. He reckoned he'd get his own uniform there anyway. He looked down at his phone and tapped the button to change the song. *Soldier Side* from *System of a Down* started playing, and he turned up the volume to drown out the noise of the car engine.

He watched as droplets of rain began falling from the grey sky and onto the car window, sliding sideways and down from the speed. With his peripheral vision, he saw his mother turning to face him and mouthing something that he couldn't hear. Lethargically, he pulled out one earbud, tentatively holding it close to his ear, ready to plug it back in.

"We'll be there soon, Kevin. Now, remember what we talked about, okay, sweetie? Behave there, especially if any of the counselors are nearby," she smiled, stretching out her bright-red lipstick-stained lips.

"I don't understand why you're making me go to camp. I don't want to go there," Kevin said with annoyance, letting the hand holding the earbud drop into his lap.

"Because it will be good for you," his dad said.

"Summer camp is for kids. It's fucking stupid," Kevin retorted angrily.

"Language!" his dad shouted back, even turning around to give his son an angry look.

Kevin put his head down, aware that he crossed the line. But he wouldn't apologize, no way. There was nothing his dad could do to punish him. Not now, anyway. His dad looked back at the road and said, "The camp we signed you up for is for teens your age. You're already sixteen, and you need to learn some valuable skills and knowledge. Camp will teach you that."

"Like what? That bullying is not nice? That good campers always share with friends? That drugs are bad for you?" Kevin sarcastically said with a higher tone.

"That's enough, Kevin," his father said tersely. "We are not going to argue over this again."

Kevin gritted his teeth and put his earbud back into his ear. A slow, sad song he didn't recognize began playing, and he couldn't help but shake his head at the irony of having the song match his sudden mood drop.

The good thing about being at the bottom is you can't sink lower, he thought to himself with a weird sense of comfort. His mood was bad already, ever since his mom barged inside his room at 5 a.m. and forcefully shook him awake. After this argument with his father, though, his mood plummeted even lower.

He glanced at the rearview mirror in time to lock eyes with his dad and then looked away at the rows of trees outside the car. The steady rain turned into a downpour, further dampening Kevin's mood. In the past few hours of driving, he saw no signs of civilization anywhere. Not even landmarks, which made him wonder how his dad even knew about this place. He wondered about the camp and how it would look upon his arrival.

He imagined a massive dirt area surrounded by wooden cabins and, beyond that, rows and rows of thick trees.

The camp, called Camp Firwood, was apparently a place where teens between the ages of 14 and 17 could go to spend their summer productively. He didn't read the pamphlet his mother left in his room, but from what he was able to see on the front page, some of the activities included art classes, kayaking, swimming, learning about the history of the camp and the surrounding areas, botany, and at least a dozen other interests. Based on the happy counselor he saw on the pamphlet, he expected some overly friendly people to welcome him when he arrived.

None of that interested Kevin. Although he was happy to be away from his parents, he planned on doing it on his own terms. Amy already told him he could crash in her place whenever he wanted, despite her incredibly strict stepfather. He had known Amy for about a year, ever since he met her through his friend Henry. He took a liking to Amy almost immediately, and things started stirring between them pretty soon. He wanted to ask her out on a date multiple times officially, but he either chickened out, or they weren't alone.

Her invitation to stay over was a perfect opportunity for him to start something with her. But then his parents had to come and ruin his plans by signing him up for Camp Firwood against his will. Amy seemed to be as devastated as Kevin was and assured him that the offer still stood when he returned eight weeks later. They had a heartfelt goodbye the night before he left. He wanted to kiss her, but he wasn't sure if she wanted the same thing, so he opted for a hug instead.

Now that he knew he was going to be gone for eight weeks, the regret he felt burned hot like fire. He wondered if she liked him less now because he didn't kiss her. He wanted to text her while on his trip, but the signal seemed to be pretty bad out here. He hoped that Camp Firwood had better internet access.

"How much longer until we arrive?" he asked his parents as he pulled out one earbud.

"Shouldn't be longer than an hour," his dad somberly said.

Kevin held the earbud close by, waiting to see if his dad would offer any follow-up information. None came. The tapping of the rain on the roof and the roaring of the engine uncomfortably penetrated the air. Kevin placed his earbud back in and leaned against the back seat. Maybe it was the weather, but he suddenly started feeling a little sleepy.

He listened to *Eminem's Not Afraid* on low volume as he started drifting to sleep.

***

A smack of his head on the car window jolted him awake. He opened his eyes and realized that the car was turbulently jumping up and down. He glanced through the windshield and realized that the steady concrete road turned into a miserly pothole-filled dirt track. The trees were now right next to each side of the road, some of them encroaching on the road and obscuring the meager beams of sunlight, which gleamed through the branches.

"We're almost there, Kevin. Just a few more minutes," his mother said, turning toward Kevin enough to give him a courteous smile.

Kevin rubbed his eyes, trying to fight his urge to close them again. He glanced down at his phone and realized that the earbuds still plugged in were dangling limply down the edge of the seat. They must have fallen out of his ears while he was sleeping. When he unlocked his phone, he realized it was a little past 11 a.m. He'd been sleeping for about an hour.

"Make sure to grab everything before you get out, Kev," his dad said, keeping his eyes on the road.

Kevin looked left and right at the seat to see if he misplaced anything. He put his phone and earbuds in the pocket of his jeans and rummaged through the rest of the items. He picked up his half-empty bottle of water and drank a few sips before tossing it back onto the seat.

The road, if it could be called that, steeply curved to the left and then gradually began ascending. Within minutes, it flatlined, and the trees close to it started thinning out. The sky became visible once again, sending annoying beams of sunlight directly into Kevin's face. He shielded his eyes, reveling in the split seconds when the taller trees would come between him and the sun.

"There it is," his father suddenly proclaimed with a hint of cheer in his voice.

Kevin looked ahead and saw something in the distance. At the far end of the road was a big arc with a wooden sign above. He couldn't discern what the sign said, but he assumed it must have had the camp's name on it. As they got closer, he saw some lodges and cabins behind the sign, but most of the camp seemed to be obscured by the tall trees. It looked as if the designers of the camp used the trees to their advantage to make a wall.

Kevin wondered why a summer camp was so far deep in the Oregonian forest in the middle of nowhere and why it had no landmarks for miles before that. Anxiety suddenly started overcoming him at the thought of entering this place and spending the next eight weeks in it, surrounded by strangers and with no moments of privacy whatsoever or chance of leaving at his whim.

He wanted to plead with his parents to turn the car around and take him home. He wanted to tell them that he would do all the extra activities on his own, double if he had to, that he would find a job and take any classes that they wanted if they would just not leave him in this place.

But that would never work. Kevin was too proud to beg his parents. He would never show them his weak side. He never talked about emotional things with them, and he sure as hell didn't plan on doing it now. Not that it would make a difference, anyway. His dad would just tell him that this was good for him and that it was not up for debate. So he chose to be quiet instead. He would suck it up. He would spend eight weeks in camp, and then he would come back home and continue his life as he normally would.

"Remember to behave during your stay, Kevin," Kevin's mom faced him and said with the same annoying grin from before. "And make sure to listen to the counselors at all times. Oh, and brush your teeth at least twice a day. And if they happen to need any help with anything, make sure to offer to assist them. And be nice to your fellow campers. Don't get into any fi-"

"Relax, Helen," Kevin's father shot a judgmental look in her direction, which immediately shut her up.

For once, Kevin was grateful for his father's interjection.

"I'm just saying," his mom insisted. "If he's going to behave in the camp like he did at home, then we might as well-"

"*Relax*, Helen." Kevin's dad emphasized the first word with a lot more seriousness in his tone.

Kevin had been listening to his dad scolding him and occasionally his mom for long enough to know that this was the tone he used only when he absolutely had to. The last straw before he took some drastic measures. Kevin had only once crossed that line and saw what measures those were.

He was eight years old and was running around the house, screaming and talking loudly while playing with his then-best friend Harris. His father, who had just returned from work, politely asked them to be quiet. Kevin and his friend got a little carried away and continued being loud, to which Kevin's father warned them to lower their tone immediately. Being the rebellious kid he was, Kevin started screaming at the top of his lungs, just to annoy his dad.

His father stood by and kindly asked Harris to leave, stating that 'Kevin can't play anymore.' As soon as Harris was out of the house, Kevin's dad then calmly asked his son to bring all of his favorite video games and comic books outside. He asked in such a polite tone that Kevin hadn't even suspected what was about to happen. At the back of his mind, though, he knew that he probably should have anticipated something bad.

As soon as he brought out some of his favorite things (he didn't want to bring out all of them for fear of what his father would do), his dad took the pile and put it in the fireplace. He gave Kevin some matches and a lighter. He pointed to the bunch and told him to light it up. At first, Kevin was confused, and when the utter realization hit him that his father wanted to make him destroy all his favorite things, he began crying and pleading. His dad wouldn't hear of it. He grabbed Kevin by the wrist and said that if he didn't do it, he would.

After minutes of unsuccessful pleading and promises that he'd be good, he was forced to burn his favorite things. Not only that, but he had to stand there while watching them burn. And then he had to clean up the ruined mess. While cleaning, he kept wiping his tears and desperately tried salvaging something from the pile. But nothing could be saved. It was all burnt to a crisp or melted beyond recognition.

Although this specific memory didn't actively come back to Kevin when he heard his dad scold his mom, he still knew at the back of his mind that he shouldn't push his luck with him. And although the bad memory of burning his favorite things long since faded, especially since he knew that he was wrong to scream despite his father's demands, he never forgave him for such a cruel punishment.

They were close enough to the wooden sign now, and just as Kevin suspected, it said CAMP FIRWOOD with large, pointy letters. Beyond the entrance arc, he saw something that looked like a small parking lot and, behind it, a big, two-story lodge.

Oh god, I hope not everything is gonna be made of wood in here.

Kevin's dad slowed the car down and looked around for a place to park. There were only four parking spaces, and only one of them was occupied by a black car. Moments after he parked the car, someone walked out through the entrance doors of the big lodge.

Kevin suppressed laughter as he looked at a comically tall and skinny man smiling at their car. He had a thin mustache, which, in Kevin's opinion, made him look like a rapist. He wore shorts that seemed to be pulled up uncomfortably high with the belt reaching way above his waistline. His green socks were pulled almost all the way up to his knees, and Kevin couldn't help but wonder if the guy had been bullied in school for dressing like that.

31

The car engine sputtered out of life, replacing the noise with uncomfortable silence all of a sudden. Even the hammering of the rain had stopped entirely by then.

This is it. Time to go, Kevin thought.

His mood, which had previously risen to an acceptable level, now dropped again like a rock in the water.

"Alright, we're here," his dad said and opened the car door.

Kevin hesitantly followed, seeing that the man from the camp immediately started approaching them with long stork-like steps.

"Hi, there!" he said in a jovial tone, stopping right in front of them. "I'm head Counselor Adams!"

Kevin noticed that he had a nametag hanging around his neck, which said *Head Counselor* and, under that, the name *Marvin*.

"Hi. We made a reservation for our son," Kevin's mom said with a fake smile.

It was the same smile she gave whenever she wanted to leave a good first impression on someone. She had been giving that smile in front of other people so much that she eventually started using it with Kevin and his dad, too. The transition was visible, and Kevin told her about it multiple times, but she'd always respond by shaking her head and saying, "What do you mean? This is me, this is who I am," and then she'd continue smiling.

"Ah, I recognize your voice," the counselor said, raising his index finger. "You made a reservation for…"

He pointed his index at Kevin and said with a smile, "Kevin. Am I right?"

Kevin looked away in bemusement, a gesture which he was sure neither of his parents appreciated. To quickly mend that, his mother jumped in and said, "Um, yes! We reserved it for Kevin. Do we need to sign any papers, or…?"

"No, that won't be necessary, ma'am. We can get him in right away. I'll give you some time to say goodbye, and then when you're ready, Kevin, I'll be right there inside." The counselor looked at Kevin and pointed behind himself at the big lodge.

"That won't be necessary, counselor," Kevin's dad said. "We will be on our way right now so you can get him prepared. Oh, and if you have any trouble with him, don't hesitate to call us on the provided number."

You fucking asshole, Kevin shot his dad an angry glance, but his father didn't look his way.

"I'm sure that won't be necessary, sir," Marvin said with a wide smile before looking at Kevin. "Alright, Kevin, if you're ready, let's get you inside then."

"Kevin, don't forget your clothes!" his mom said, turning toward the car.

"He won't need them, ma'am. We provide uniforms here," the counselor said with one hand raised in a stop sign, grinning unnaturally.

"Oh," Kevin's mom said and approached her son with a few swift steps.

"Let me give you one last hug before we-"

Kevin didn't wait for her to finish her sentence. He scooted past her and Marvin and strode inside the lodge. He found himself in a pristine hallway where, to his dread, everything was made of wood. He heard his parents talking to Mr. Adams outside in a muffled tone.

"Alright, well, don't worry. He's in good hands here," the counselor said.

He was already beginning to annoy Kevin, and he hoped that he would be assigned some other counselor if there were any. The cacophony of indecipherable voices continued outside, and Kevin put his back against the wall on the left, looking around and wondering what his life was going to be like in here. He hoped he wouldn't need to get up too early every day, although he assumed it wouldn't be later than 8 a.m.

A barrage of heavy footsteps echoed in the hall from the left, and Kevin turned his head to face the direction of the sound. Two bulky men in security uniforms had appeared at the far end of the hall, walking toward the exit. A teen wearing the camp's uniform, similar to the counselor's, was walking in front of them with a grin plastered on his face.

They strode to the exit without so much as batting an eye in Kevin's direction. As they moved past him, Kevin noticed that the security guards were armed with handguns. He frowned, wondering why the fuck they would need security guards in a camp full of teens in the first place, let alone armed with firearms.

Is that boy in some kind of trouble? he wondered with a raise of his eyebrow.

Moments later, the noise of the voices of his parents and the counselor outside became muffled by the sound of car doors opening and shutting, followed by the engine starting, and finally, the car driving off.

Kevin's parents said something in a muffled tone that he didn't understand, but he heard Mr. Adams' reply clearly, indicating he was closer to the door now.

"Thank you. Have a safe trip back home!"

Approaching footsteps a moment later warned Kevin that the tall, hunched-over figure of the counselor was returning. He smiled from ear to ear and said, "Alright, you ready to begin your adventure, camper?"

He said it similarly to the intro of *Spongebob Squarepants*, giving the impression that Kevin's response should be an enthusiastic *YEEESSS*, but he simply shrugged.

"Alright, well, follow me, then," the counselor patted Kevin on the shoulder with his overly long arm and started walking down the hall.

Kevin went after him, putting his hands into his pockets, not feeling enthusiastic in the slightest. They walked past a few rooms along the way, some of which included the counselors' break room, storage, and a bathroom.

"My first name is Marvin, by the way. But the campers address me as Mr. Adams," the counselor said. "Make sure to remember that, alright?"

He turned toward Kevin enough to give him a courteous smile. Mr. Adams led Kevin up the wooden stairs to the second floor. Another counselor walked past them, and the two staff members greeted each other, Mr. Adams contrasting the other counselor's low energy.

"The other campers are out learning how to set up tents right now. They should be back soon, and then you can all go to lunch together," he told Kevin as he turned left at the far end of the corridor and opened a door on the left side.

"Mr. Adams, good day," a rough voice came from inside the room.

"Hi, Phil. How's it going? Come on in, Kevin!" Mr. Adams spoke to the person inside before shouting for Kevin to join them.

Kevin tentatively entered the room and realized he was in a sort of laundromat. Laundry machines and drying machines were lined up in rows all over the room, the entire room illuminated by the bright neon lights above. The machines were currently not turned on, and Mr. Adams stood in the middle of the room, talking to a tall, overweight, and bald man. He was nowhere as tall as Mr. Adams, but he still towered above Kevin in both height and width.

"We have a new camper. Need a uniform for him," Mr. Adams said, looking toward Kevin.

Phil scratched his cheek and approached Kevin with a pant, bending down as if to inspect him. Kevin smelled his warm, stale breath but refrained from making any visible grimaces. The man pulled out a yellow folded tailor tape. He forcefully put one hand on Kevin's shoulder and said, "Hold still." Kevin froze in place, too afraid to budge around this mountain of a man.

"Boy! Get over here!" he croaked so loudly in Kevin's ear that he flinched for a moment.

Seconds later, a tiny teen around Kevin's age with glasses rushed in from the backroom, stopping in front of the laundryman.

"Yes, Mr. Phil?" he asked with a high-pitched voice.

"Grab a piece of paper. Write down the measurements."

"Right away, Mr. Phil," the boy recited and turned on his heel.

"Hurry, boy! I don't have all day!" Mr. Phil shouted, mumbling some incoherent numbers to himself with each measurement he took.

Seconds later, the camper boy returned with a pad and pen and said, "I have it, Mr. Phil."

Phil measured Kevin from various sides, spinning him forcefully, stretching out his arms, and so on, all the while dictating numbers to the camper.

"You get it all, boy?" Phil asked sternly.

"Yes, Mr. Phil," the boy said and repeated all the numbers that Mr. Phil wrote.

Once that was done, Mr. Phil leaned on his knees and straightened his back with a groan. He put a hand behind his back, probably to alleviate the pain, and pointed to the backroom while ordering.

"Go find him a uniform for those measurements. Hurry boy, you got other work to do!"

Why does this kid stand for this? I'd have told them to fuck themselves and left long ago.

"You go on there with him," laundryman Phil said tersely.

Kevin waltzed over to the backroom door, tentatively standing at the threshold. The backroom was considerably darker than the main laundry room, and it took Kevin's eyes a moment to adjust to the dark. The smell of laundry detergent filled his nostrils, and when he entered, he realized he was in a room full of uniforms. Huge white baskets of freshly washed and dried uniforms were lined up. Neatly folded clothing occupied the shelves and tables with another bunch of dried piles resting next to the ironing board. On the other side of the room were baskets full of dirty uniforms and piles of neatly sorted shoes.

The camper from before vigorously read the paper where he wrote Kevin's measurements and glanced intermittently toward the shelves with stacked clothes. He lifted one pair of pants and pulled out the one underneath it. He put it on top of the neat pile he prepared beforehand and turned to face Kevin.

"This is your uniform. Try it out to see if it fits you." He'd said it so quickly that Kevin barely understood every word he uttered.

Kevin sighed in response and approached the table where the picked-out clothes sat.

"It'll be fine. I don't care." He threw his hand up dismissively.

"No, you have to put it on now," the kid said fast again, scratching the back of his head.

Kevin shook his head and started taking off his shirt.

"Fine, whatever."

He picked up the green t-shirt and observed the logo on the chest. It was a white fir tree with multiple trees in the background inside a big circle. *How creative.* He put the shirt on and then tried out the brown shorts. Aside from the two main pockets, the shorts had back pockets and side leg pockets, similar to cargo pants. Although Kevin hated wearing shorts, he found the abundance of pockets with zippers to his liking.

At least, I don't need to worry about dropping my phone somewhere along the way.

"Are they comfortable? Can you walk around a little bit, try to stretch out?" the camper asked, and Kevin shrugged, now already a little more comfortable with the kid's speaking speed.

When the camper opened his mouth, probably to remind him that he had to flex around to see if it worked, Kevin interrupted him by jumping a couple of times and raising his arms up at the same time.

"There," he said.

The shirt felt rough against his skin, but he didn't care. A t-shirt was a t-shirt.

"Okay, we need to get you some shoes," the camper said.

He turned around and took hurried steps to the back of the room where the shoes were. He asked Kevin what size he wore, and after Kevin informed him, the camper brought two pairs of brown sneakers. Or were they shoes? They looked so ugly that Kevin couldn't decide. He took off his sneakers and slid inside the shoes, taking a few steps around in them.

They were heavier than his sneakers, and the soles seemed too flat, so he tried the other pair. A little better, but still not ideal. He really didn't want to go trying out different shoes of the same bad quality, though, so he dismissively waved.

37

"Which ones work better for you? I gave you one number bigger because, that way, you'll avoid shoe bites," the kid recited quickly.

"Shoe bites? What exactly am I gonna be doing here? Running a marathon?" Kevin chuckled.

"Boy! You done in there yet?" Phil's voice bellowed from the other room.

The camper turned to face the direction of the voice and shouted back.

"Yes, Mr. Phil! I just gave him the uniform and shoes!" his voice, although still fast, seemed more frightened when speaking to Mr. Phil.

"Why do you let them treat you that way?" Kevin asked in a hushed tone. "You're not their servant."

The camper turned to face Kevin and suddenly looked as though all the color was drained from his face. He glanced over his shoulder and then turned back to face Kevin.

"Le-let's find you um... a spare u-uniform," he said and rushed over to the shelf with clothes.

Kevin frowned. He wanted to tell the camper that he didn't need to be afraid of the counselors overhearing them talking, but somehow, he thought a timid kid like him wouldn't listen. He then suddenly started thinking how he probably didn't want to be here, just like Kevin, and felt sorry for him being stuck in a laundromat with a grumpy asshole like Phil.

"I'm Kevin, by the way," he finally introduced himself, deciding to be more polite.

The camper kid tentatively looked at Kevin before looking away. He then turned to face him again.

"Camper George," he uttered in a hushed voice.

"*Camper* George?" Kevin raised his eyebrows. "How come you're not with the other campers?"

"Everybody has duties. This week, I'm on laundry duty," George said while folding a pair of shorts and a t-shirt on top of each other. "Last week, I was on toilet duty."

"Toilet duty? Are you serious?" Kevin winced disgustedly.

George gave him an expressionless look while holding out his spare uniform set.

"Campers. You done here, yet?" Kevin turned around to see Phil's omnipresent figure standing at the doorway with his bulky hands on his hips.

"Y-yes, Mr. Phil. He's good to go," George said.

"Did you give him the pajamas and the towel, too?"

George's eyes widened in palpable fear as he quickly rushed over to one of the shelves, shouting, "N-no, Mr. Phil. Right away, Mr. Phil!"

He snatched a light-blue shirt and a pair of pants as well as two pairs of underwear, two pairs of socks, slippers, undershirts, and a towel. He quickly put everything on the same pile where the uniform was and froze in place, staring at Mr. Phil in anticipation.

The old man shook his head as if disappointed before looking at Kevin.

"Alright. Take your things and follow Head Counselor Adams," he croaked, turning around and heading back into the laundry room.

Kevin took the extra uniform set and pajamas and put them on the table next to the clothes he brought from home. They weren't folded even remotely close to the scrupulous manner as his uniform was, but he stacked all of them together on top of one another and picked them up.

"Bye for now. Thanks for picking out the uniform for me," Kevin said on his way out.

But George didn't respond. Kevin glanced at him to see if he heard him, but George seemed to be looking at his feet.

Fine, whatever.

Kevin walked out into the laundry room to see Mr. Adams and Mr. Phil talking to each other about something he couldn't quite make out. By their tone and the surprising smile he saw on Phil's face, he figured it was something unrelated to their work.

When he stepped closer, Mr. Adams, who had been facing Kevin, glanced at him and said, "Look at you, all dressed up and ready to join our camp. Alright, come with me, camper," he gestured and turned toward the exit. "See you later, Phil."

Phil raised one hand full of stubby fingers in response. Kevin followed Mr. Adams outside to the corridor and then left, in the direction the counselor had gone. They got to the end of the hall, and Mr. Adams pulled out a keychain from his pocket with a jingle. With an unfamiliar tune that he began humming, he picked out one key and stuck it in the keyhole.

Once the door was open, he entered and gestured for Kevin to follow him. Kevin obliged, entering the small-looking office. It held a low desk with a chair and a door in the back of the room. Mr. Adams sat down on the chair, looking like a grasshopper by the desk with his knees pointing upward. He opened a drawer and pulled out a piece of paper.

He took out a pen that was attached to his front pocket and annoyingly clicked it a few times. He gently placed the paper on the desk while Kevin stood awkwardly in silence, holding the stack of clothes. Mr. Adams began humming the same tune from earlier, and Kevin suddenly found out that the counselor could become even more annoying. Mr. Adams flipped the paper to the other side and then back before putting his pen to it and writing something down.

The sound of Mr. Adams' scribbling on paper reverberated through the air while Kevin impatiently switched his weight from one foot to the other. He transferred the weight of the clothes into his left arm and used his right hand to pull out his phone. He still had thirty-five percent battery life, so he had time before he had to charge it. He tapped on the wi-fi signal and waited for it to scan. He saw results from places he'd been to earlier, but nothing in close proximity to the camp.

"Marvin, do you have wi-fi on the campgrounds?" he asked casually, looking up at the counselor.

The counselor stared directly at Kevin with a stern look, contrasting the perky mood he was in up until now. He was tapping his pen on the paper, unblinkingly staring as if in anticipation.

"What?" Kevin asked with a frown.

"*Mr. Adams,*" the counselor emphasized. "And no, we have no internet here. We believe that campers need to experience Camp Firwood to the fullest without technology. Speaking of that, we also don't allow campers to use personal items. I will need you to give me everything you brought from your home, and we will stow it away in our storage. That means *that* too."

He pointed at Kevin's cellphone.

"What? That's bullshit! I'm not giving you my phone!" Kevin retorted, suddenly feeling insulted by this request.

To leave all his personal belongings? That was absurd. How did they expect him to spend the whole day without scrolling through social media and texting?

Mr. Adams threw his hands up with pursed lips and said, "Kevin, it's only for eight weeks. Trust me, the activities here are going to keep you so occupied and amused that you'll have no time to play on your phone. You will never have a dull moment in Camp Firwood."

"I'm not giving you my phone," Kevin stuck to his guns as he shook his head.

Mr. Adams nodded, his lips still pursed. He looked down at the paper in front of him and tapped his pen on it a few times. A moment later, he shot up and said, "Alright, not a problem, Kevin. I'll call your parents and tell them to come pick you up." Then he started walking toward the exit door.

"Wait, what? Why?" Kevin asked, now frustrated to the point that he'd punch the counselor if he weren't so tall.

Mr. Adams was already at the door, but he turned around to face Kevin and shrugged.

"Well, I can't sign you up in Camp Firwood if you don't leave your personal belongings with us. Those are the rules. I'm sorry. I didn't make them."

Kevin sighed deeply, gritting his teeth. He looked at his unlocked phone screen. No internet, no signal, low battery. With another sigh, he slammed the phone on the desk. He then placed the clothes next to the phone and fumbled through the pocket of his jeans underneath the uniform. He pulled out his charger and earphones and messily put them next to the phone.

"You won't regret it, camper. Trust me," Mr. Adams said as he put his elongated hand on Kevin's shoulder.

He made his way back to the chair by the desk and continued writing something. He then began questioning Kevin about his full name, birth date, and other personal information. The questions seemed normal at first but got weird toward the end. Mr. Adams asked Kevin things like what his religion was, what his stance was on politics, how important he thought obedience and discipline were, and more. Kevin gave the questions no second thought and just answered them absent-mindedly, not caring the slightest about the philosophical bullshit.

Once the final question was done, Mr. Adams clicked his pen and placed it back in the front of his shirt. He put the paperback in the drawer and stood up with a grin, saying.

"Alright. Let's just take your personal things here and place them in the storage. Pick up your camp things."

Kevin grabbed his spare uniform, feeling how light it was to carry without his extra clothes and sneakers. He watched as Mr. Adams took his 'civilian' clothes and technology and carried them to the back room. He heard a distinct sound of a locker opening and some rummaging before it was closed. Having his phone taken away felt like losing a limb. He suddenly felt naked, vulnerable.

Mr. Adams returned to the room seconds later and said, "Alright, you're pretty much all set. Just a few more things, and you're good to go. Come on."

He walked out of the room, and Kevin followed him. He had to walk abnormally faster than he usually did to keep up with Mr. Adams' superior steps. They went down the stairs and out of the building through the back entrance. In front of them was a more open area with big, precisely made dirt roads that led in various directions.

Several buildings were lined up on both sides of the main dirt road. On the far right, separated from the main grounds and across a grassy field, was a row of cabins, which Kevin assumed was the place where campers slept. The road wound behind buildings in some places, so it was impossible to tell where it ended. The entire campgrounds were surrounded by tall fir trees like a wall, clearly outlining where the camp territory ended and where the forest began. Off the campgrounds in the distance, nestled among the thick trees, protruded a wooden tower high above the sea of firs. It looked like a fire lookout tower, and Kevin assumed that the camp used it exactly for that. He felt a little claustrophobic at the sight of the camp being enclosed in what was probably hundreds of miles of nothing but forests but pushed that thought to the back of his mind.

"Let's get you to the infirmary first," Mr. Adams said, making his way to the left.

"Infirmary? Why? I already had a pretty annoying and thorough medical check before I came here," Kevin said, taking a few hurried steps to catch up with Mr. Adams.

A week before, he had to undergo a full medical checkup, including blood tests, pulmonary tests, and even a psychological evaluation. The whole thing took over five hours, and he hated every second of it.

"Need to give you some shots for your immune system. We've had campers come down with sicknesses here and there, so we started giving shots as prevention," Mr. Adams said.

"I don't need a shot," Kevin protested. "I haven't been sick in years."

"You have to take your shot, camper. You're in the great outdoors right now, and you never know what you may or may not be susceptible to." Mr. Adams stopped long enough to turn around and face Kevin before continuing his walk.

Kevin knew that arguing would do him no good, so he decided to bite the bullet and take whatever bullshit vitamins he needed. They crossed the dirt road and approached a wooden building with a red cross above the door. Mr. Adams opened the door and allowed Kevin to step in first.

They entered a small hall that held a bench, which made Kevin assume that this was the waiting room. There were two doors on

43

either side of the room, and the one on the right, where a female voice was coming from, was open.

"What were you thinking, jumping down the watchtower steps like that?" the feminine voice retorted somewhat angrily. "You're lucky you're still alive, let alone come off with only a sprained ankle."

Mr. Adams walked into the room, which Kevin took as a cue that he should follow him. This seemed to be the patients' room because the first thing that Kevin saw were beds lined up on both sides of the room with curtains obscuring most of them. A few campers were inside from what he could see, and the woman who spoke earlier, a nurse in her late twenties, was scolding one camper, who was lying on the bed with a bandage wrapped around his forearm.

The camper had a look of guilt on his face as the nurse stood above him, checking his bandages and sighing. She appeared to hear the footsteps behind her, so she turned around and smiled when she saw Mr. Adams. Kevin couldn't help but notice how pretty she was with her curly hair, blue eyes, and enchanting smile.

"Counselor Adams, hello." She focused all her attention on the counselor, completely neglecting the boy in the bed.

"What can I do for you today?" she turned to face him and asked politely.

"Hi, Mary. Looking good today. Did you lose some weight since the last time we spoke?" Mr. Adams asked with a grin.

"Oh, you flatter me, Mr. Adams," the nurse giggled and twirled her hair.

Kevin felt like puking at this display of flirtation between them. *Can you, like, try to bang her in your off-hours, dude?*

He shot Mr. Adams a contemptuous glance, but the counselor was too busy staring at the nurse. The two of them made some small talk a little bit while Kevin stood as a decoration on the side.

Eventually, Mr. Adams switched the subject back to business and said, "Well, listen, we've got a new camper here today." He put his hand on Kevin's shoulder as if to present him.

The nurse and Kevin locked eyes for a moment. He smiled courteously, but she ignored the gesture. She looked back at Mr.

Adams and said in a somewhat more serious tone now. "A new camper? I see. That is… unexpected."

Mr. Adams shrugged with a smile.

"This will take around ten minutes. Can you wait outside?" Nurse Mary asked.

"Yep." Mr. Adams nodded and turned to face Kevin. "I'll take your spare uniform, camper. You go on with the nurse."

He collected the clothes Kevin was carrying and made his way out into the waiting room.

"Come with me, young man," the nurse said in a stern tone now.

Kevin first thought that she was talking to the camper in bed, but when he looked in her direction, he realized she was staring at him impatiently. He followed her through the doors, which led to another room. It seemed to be the main examination room, as Kevin saw a desk with a computer and various medical supplies and tools used for basic checkups.

Nurse Mary got behind her computer and said while staring at the screen, "Take off your clothes down to your underwear." Then she began clicking on the mouse furiously as the bright screen flared to life and lit her face.

Kevin took off his shirt, shoes, and pants, putting them on top of the examination bed. He immediately felt cold, so he rubbed his arms in hopes of warming them up. The nurse continued clicking, still staring at the screen.

"So… are you the only nurse in the camp?" Kevin asked, hoping to strike up a conversation.

He wasn't trying to flirt with her or anything, but she did seem polite enough when she talked to Mr. Adams, and the deafening silence that suffused the air felt awkward.

"Step on the scale over there," she responded, pointing to a scale next to the examination bed.

Kevin scratched his nose, feeling awkward about his question being ignored. He did as she asked, and she asked him what number it displayed. He read it to her, and she typed it on her keyboard, each button clicking loudly.

Who the hell still uses mechanical keyboards?

Mary stood up, walked over to the stadiometer, eyeing it with a frown, and adjusted the top.

"Stand over here," she said, still staring at the device.

Kevin found it amazing how she was able to go through the entire communication so far without making a moment of eye contact with him. He stepped on the stadiometer, and the nurse measured his height before running back to her computer and typing it in. She continued clicking and scrolling for a brief moment before hovering her fingers above the keyboard and asking Kevin, "Your date of birth."

This was followed by questions related to his medical condition, history, and whether there was any mental illness in his family. Kevin answered all of them annoyedly with the same kind of half-assed answers he gave Mr. Adams back in the administration room or whatever it was. After the questions were finished, the nurse stood up and walked over to the drawer behind.

"Sit on the bed," she said while pulling out various items that he couldn't see from there.

He hopped onto the bed, which squeaked in response.

"*Gently.*" The nurse looked over her shoulder and, for the first time since they entered the examination room, made eye contact with Kevin. "That thing is fragile."

"Sure," Kevin dismissively said, leaning on his palms.

The nurse raised a filled syringe and tapped on it a couple of times. She placed a cap on the needle, picked up an alcoholic wipe, and approached Kevin with both in her hands. "Try not to move."

She wiped his shoulder, which felt uncomfortably cold at her touch. The nurse removed the cap from the needle and said, "You'll feel a small sting."

Kevin looked away from the needle and stared in front of himself. He wasn't afraid of needles, but the sensation of getting pricked was uncomfortable, nonetheless. He braced himself, and the prick came, slightly less painful than what he expected. The nurse put gauze on the place where she injected him and said, "Hold this for a minute or two."

Kevin held the gauze firmly on his shoulder as the nurse grabbed the items she just used and tossed them into a bin. She strode back to her computer, the screen illuminating her face again.

"What was this for?" Kevin asked, looking in her direction.

"Immune system," she simply said and started typing something again.

She clicked the mouse a few more times and stood up, making another meager eye contact with him.

"You're done here. You can continue with Counselor Adams now."

"Uh, alright. Thanks," Kevin said as he hopped off the bed with another loud squeak.

The nurse shot him a judgmental glare, and he was sure that she would scold him for it. A second later, she walked out, into the patients' room. Kevin removed the gauze and checked to see how much he'd bled. There was barely any blood on it, so he shrugged and tossed it into the bin. He slid into the uncomfortable camping uniform, feeling relieved to be warmed up by the rugged texture of the shirt and shorts.

Mr. Adams was sitting in the waiting room. Once he saw Kevin step out, a smile stretched across his lips, and he slapped his knees, shooting up into a standing position.

"All set?" he asked, looking down at Kevin.

"Yeah," Kevin somberly said.

"Alright. Well, let's show you your room then. Here's your uniform," he practically tossed it to Kevin, who reacted quickly enough to catch it before it could fall.

Once they walked out of the infirmary, Mr. Adams took the lead and began striding toward the line of cabins on the far left end of the main grounds. He glanced at his watch and said to Kevin, "Right on time. The other campers are almost back from the field. They'll be thrilled to meet you."

"How many campers sleep in the same room?" Kevin asked, suddenly worried about sharing space with a lot of people.

"Ten per room, give or take," Mr. Adams briefly responded.

Shit, that's a lot. He was hoping it would be two, maybe three, max. But ten? *Oh, well. I'll tough it out these eight weeks, I guess.* The area with the cabins was enclosed by trees more so than the rest of the campgrounds, which effectively obscured the sunlight from gleaming through and giving it a further encroaching feeling.

The five cabins were identical and lined up with perfect width apart from each other, fulfilling every OCD person's dream. There weren't even numbers on the cabins or anything, so there was no way of telling them apart. In front of the cabins were a couple of wooden benches and tables, probably used by the campers between activities to relax or take a short break.

"You'll be staying in cabin number four, which is this one," Mr. Adams said, making his way up the short steps of the fourth cabin from the left.

He stomped on the top step with his feet a couple of times and turned to face Kevin.

"Make sure to always clean your shoes before entering the cabin, alright? Otherwise, your fellow campers who are on duty will have extra work to do, alright?"

"Yeah," Kevin replied lifelessly.

"Yeah, what?" Mr. Adams raised his eyebrows, eyeing Kevin suspiciously.

Kevin sighed and rolled his eyes.

"Yeah, Mr. Adams." By this point, he was too tired from the trip and the whole recruitment, so he just wanted to slump into a bed, no matter how uncomfortable it was, and take a nap.

Mr. Adams opened the front door and got inside the small foyer-looking room. Kevin mimicked Mr. Adams' movement and kicked the dirt out of his shoes before walking inside. There was a door on the left, which was left open, portraying a small restroom. Kevin peeked inside and saw five urinals along with a long sink in front of the mirror. It looked cramped as it was, which made Kevin think of the next question.

Where is the shower? And how do all the campers use this one tiny fucking bathroom?

Directly across the foyer was another door, which presumably led inside the sleeping quarters. He bit his tongue and avoided asking any questions until later, hoping there was more to the cabin than what he saw. Mr. Adams pointed to a low shelf by the right wall. Stickers with numbers ranging from one to ten labeled spots on the shelf.

Mr. Adams said, "Always make sure to clean your shoes and put them over here before entering the sleeping quarters. You're going to have a specific number for everything, so try not to mix them up, okay? You're number nine. That means you put shoes on number nine, you sleep in bed number nine, and you stand ninth in line. Alright?"

Mr. Adams lowered his chin, observing Kevin carefully.

"Yes, Mr. Adams," Kevin said with a fake grin.

Mr. Adams ignored this gesture and put his hands on his hips. He pointed to the sleeping quarters' door.

"Alright. Well, you go on inside now. Wait for the other campers to come back, they should return in about ten minutes or so. Once they're back, they'll instruct you about further rules before lunch."

"Yes, Mr. Adams," Kevin repeated.

He wrinkled his nose, suddenly realizing how much he sounded like George from the laundry. Mr. Adams was already out of the cabin, and Kevin was left with a silence that he didn't even know he missed so much. He took off his shoes and messily threw them onto the shoe stand. They fell on number nine, and Kevin sardonically thought to himself that he should have gone for a career in the NFL.

He opened the door of the sleeping quarters, revealing a long, simple wooden room, not unlike every other fucking room in the camp. Ten beds were lined up, five on each side. Each bed had a number on the front of the wooden frame and was made so perfectly that not a single wrinkle showed on the sheets. The bedsheets were tucked under the mattress so tightly that it looked to Kevin like he could jump on it and bounce up into the ceiling.

Each bed had a small blue locker next to it. Everything was so identical in this room that it made Kevin's head spin. He found the bed labeled with the number nine, which was on the right side, second to last in the row. He put his spare uniform on top of the locker and slumped into the bed, regretting it immediately when he felt how hard it pressed against his back. He put his hands on the back of his head and stared at the ceiling, which happened to have the exact same appearance as every other wall and floor in the camp.

"Fuck this place," he said with no particular reason.

He closed his eyes. He thought about being at home and playing video games. He thought about loudly blasting music in his room while he lay in bed. He thought about hanging out with his friends in Henry's usually smoke-filled room. He thought about going out on a date with Amy and finally confessing that he liked her. He lingered on that thought for a moment.

He'd hoped he'd at least be able to text her while he was here, but he told her to expect no response from him, depending on the signal and internet. He thought about Henry, Rick, and Luis and wondered what they were doing now. Henry was probably still sleeping. He'd be waking up in a few hours, around 2 p.m. Kevin smiled at the thought. Rick and Luis? Who knew? They might be staring at the ceiling too, listening to music until they met up later.

Kevin suddenly felt left out.

He thought about how much he was missing out at home while his friends were probably having fun. He wondered if they'd remember him from time to time. He wondered if he'd still be welcome as a friend in the circle. Why did he have to be in this stupid, fucking place? Why couldn't he just stay home? He could have just slipped out of the house last night and suffered the consequences later. Fuck.

Muffled voices carried through the air outside the cabin. Kevin jolted up and perked up his ears. The voices were indecipherable but were getting closer by the second. In moments, the front door of the cabin swung open, and a group of campers around Kevin's age barged inside, loudly talking while taking off their shoes and scrambling into the room.

"No, you have to make the tent stable," one of the campers said to another one. "Did you see mine? It was so firm that even when Counselor Jones shook it, it didn't fall apart."

The campers began walking into the room one by one, and as soon as they laid their eyes on Kevin, they stopped and stared at him wide-eyed and silent. Kevin clambered to his feet and awkwardly pulled up his shorts.

"Come on, move!" One of the campers from the back shouted, pushing his way through.

As soon as he saw what was going on, he stopped and went silent as well.

"Uh. Hi," Kevin raised one hand to greet them. "I'm Kevin. I just arrived here."

A few campers exchanged confused glances with each other, still not uttering a single word. Moments later, a drumming of footsteps resounded in the foyer, and a tall figure walked inside. At first, Kevin thought it was Mr. Adams. However, this was a different counselor, a buff, bald man in his thirties.

"Alright, alright. What's the holdup, campers?" he asked, shoving the campers to the side.

When he saw Kevin, he snapped his fingers and said, "You must be the new kid. You got everything you need?"

"I dunno. I just got here," Kevin shrugged.

The incessant stares of the other campers made him feel really uncomfortable, and he hoped that he wouldn't be the center of attention once he was left alone with them.

"Got your camping gear?" the counselor asked sternly.

"Just my uniform and pajamas." Kevin shrugged.

"I see," the bald counselor said, rubbing his perfectly shaved chin.

He pointed his finger at a chubby camper and said, "You. Take the new camper to Groundskeeper Andy. Tell him the new kid needs all the gear and other essentials. You got that?"

"Yes, Mr. Baldwin."

Baldwin? For a bald guy? Kevin ran his hand across his mouth to hide the smile forming on his face. Mr. Baldwin turned around to leave and shouted.

"The rest of you pack up your stuff and be in front of the mess hall at exactly one o'clock."

"Yes, Mr. Baldwin," the group chanted in unison, which took Kevin aback.

What is this shit, everyone being so goddamn obedient to these rude-ass counselors?

As soon as the counselor was out, the chubby kid ran up to Kevin and said, "Come on, let's find the groundskeeper."

3
The Groundskeeper

The chubby camper gestured for Kevin to follow him. Kevin slid into his shoes and followed him outside the camp, past the prying eyes of the other campers. Relief washed over him when the incessant stares were away from him, and even then, he felt them burning a hole in the back of his head through the doors.

"The groundskeeper should be close by." The chubby kid bounced down the steps, pulling his uncomfortably small-sized shirt down to cover his exposed lower back. "I'm Mark, by the way. But most people call me Barrel Mark."

"Barrel Mark?" Kevin frowned, a little taken aback by the notion of being verbally bullied in a summer camp.

Then again, he saw, himself, the way some of the guys in his school would come down on the vulnerable new kids on their first days like packs of hyenas. Nothing should be surprising with teens.

"Yeah, but not in a bad way. Most of the campers have a nickname. We got Tough Norton—he's the strongest one in our group. We have Nerdy Van—you can guess why they call him that. We have Slow Ethan because he's always the last in everything. But some campers have no names. For example, Javier is just Javier."

Kevin wondered what his nickname would be and whether he would like it.

"Well, nice to meet you, Mark," Kevin said, deliberately leaving out the Barrel nickname as he walked alongside him. "What exactly do we need to do here?"

"We need to get you a backpack with all the essential items like rope, flashlight, tent, and so on."

"I see," Kevin said, striding to keep up with Mark.

For a kid his size, he moved quite fast.

Is everybody here a fast walker?

They made their way to the right, between the infirmary and a big unmarked building across the main lodge. Kevin glanced to the left through the building's windows and realized he was looking at rows of tables and chairs. Just when he realized what he was staring at, Mark pointed at the building and said, "That's the mess hall. The food can be great sometimes, but not always. Lunch Lady Daisy never gives seconds, though. I don't know why since there always seems to be an abundance of food left."

"What kind of food do you usually get?" Kevin asked.

"Depends. We rarely know what it is unless we're in contact with the kitchen duty campers. Today, some guy from cabin one is assisting the lunch lady on the food line, and apparently, he told his camping buddies that we'll have burgers. Oh boy, can't wait for that. It's been weeks since I've had a burger."

"Weeks? Why?"

"Well, I've been here for a couple of weeks, and I didn't eat a burger for at least a week before that."

"So, the campers don't all arrive at the same time?"

"Right. The first batch arrived… I think around eight weeks ago? I arrived in the batch with Michael and Bill. But Bill is no longer with us in the camp." Mark turned around long enough to look at Kevin before facing the way they were going again.

"I see," Kevin bemusedly replied.

They reached the back of the buildings, and Kevin beheld a vast meadow in front of him, stretching at least five hundred yards in all directions before being halted by the formed treeline, which acted as a wall.

"There," Mark pointed at the treeline over yonder.

A few hundred yards diagonally to the left, nestled near the treeline, hidden in the shade of trees, was a small cabin. The gravel trail Mark and Kevin stood on morphed into a dirt path, which went in an arc and led directly to the cabin. The entire area leading up to the treelines in all directions was an empty grassland, save for

54

the small trail leading up to the cabin and one grey concrete building far to the right.

Mark took point down the path toward the cabin, and pretty soon, Kevin saw someone outside of it. A hunched-over figure stood in front, doing some kind of work, which Kevin couldn't see from here, but it looked like mowing the lawn or something. A moment later, Kevin realized that mowing the lawn here would be ridiculous without a big vehicle or machine, so he concluded that it must have been some other work the person was doing.

"A couple weeks, huh? So you'll be leaving in what, six more weeks?" he asked Mark as they stepped onto the dirt path and started making their way toward the small cabin.

"Six weeks?" Mark asked as their footsteps started sounding much more muffled. "No, the camp doesn't end for at least seven or eight more weeks."

"Wait, what?" Kevin stopped in his tracks.

Mark didn't seem to notice this at first, so he continued walking a little farther before realizing that Kevin was falling behind. He turned to face him and said, "Well, yeah. The camp is ten weeks, but the counselors said they might prolong it to twelve if everybody liked it."

"No, no. That can't be right," a dread started washing over Kevin.

He took a step closer to Mark and said, "I was told it's only eight weeks."

Mark looked down as if thinking. He shrugged and said, "I dunno. Maybe everyone stays here differently. My parents said I would stay for ten weeks, but maybe everyone gets signed up differently. I did arrive a few weeks after the others, and you arrived a bit after us, too."

As quickly as it appeared, Kevin's dread slowly started leaving him, replaced by tentative relief. The skepticism remained in him, though, so he took a mental note to check with the counselors later.

"Yeah, I guess that makes sense," he scoffed, continuing to lope down the trail.

Mark went on with him, and they spent the next minute in silence, the chirping of the birds and their own footsteps the only sounds interrupting the quiet. As they got closer, Kevin started to see more discernible features on the figure in front of the cabin. It was a man wearing overalls. He looked thin, skeletal even. Not as much as Mr. Adams, though, but close enough.

The man seemed to be doing something with a hoe, his movement with his arms repeatedly going slowly forward and then dragging the hoe across the ground backward. It soon became apparent that the man was much older than the rest of the counselors, maybe in his fifties. Although his top was balding, he had long, unkempt hair on the rest of his head. He was facing sideways to the two campers, so Kevin caught only a glimpse of his bushy beard.

The man stopped to wipe the sweat off his forehead with his forearm and looked in the direction of the boys heading toward him. He turned back to the hoe and continued doing his work, not giving any signs of actually noticing the campers. Kevin and Mark got close enough to hear the sound of the hoe being dragged across the ground with a scraping noise. They stopped right next to him.

"Good afternoon, Groundskeeper Andy," Mark politely raised his hand to greet the man.

The groundskeeper continued steadily dragging the hoe, not bothering to look in Mark's direction. He was still turned sideways, so Kevin figured the groundskeeper might have simply not heard them. He was old, after all.

"Um. We have a new camper, and he needs the basic gear," Mark uttered, fiddling with his fingers uncomfortably.

The groundskeeper ran the hoe across the ground three more times and then straightened his back and wiped the sweat off his forehead once more. He turned around, opposite the boys, and headed toward the cabin before disappearing behind the corner.

"Uh..." Kevin started, looking at Mark.

"Wait," Mark interrupted him with a hush.

They stood quietly while the sound of a creaking door came from behind the cabin, followed by a clatter. Then another creak and the sound of a door shutting. Moments later, the groundskeeper came back without his hoe and turned to enter the cabin. He shut the door behind him, and for a long moment, he and Mark stared at each other in silence. Then, he heard the muffled sound of keys jingling from inside, and the groundskeeper swung the door open, stepping outside and striding toward the campers. His steps seemed so menacing that Kevin couldn't help but recoil a little bit.

Just as the groundskeeper reached them, he went past them and continued trundling down the dirt road, back toward the campgrounds. Mark and Kevin exchanged looks, Kevin more confused than Mark.

"Come on, let's go with him," Mark whispered with a gesture of his head.

He turned around and started walking behind the groundskeeper, and Kevin followed. The groundskeeper was walking slowly, so this time, Kevin had to walk slower than his usual speed. What transpired was a few minutes of awkward silence as the campers paced behind the man.

Serves me right for complaining about their walking speed.

Mark, who struck Kevin as a talkative person, was awfully quiet all of a sudden, which he took as a sign that he was just as uncomfortable around the groundskeeper as Kevin was. He glanced in Mark's direction a couple of times, but the boy seemed to be focused on the path in front of him.

Groundskeeper Andy led them back to the main lodge, not uttering a single word the whole time. They walked through the main hall where one counselor walked past them.

"Hi, Andy," he nodded to the groundskeeper, who, in turn, seemed to ignore him.

What a grumpy guy. That's badass, Kevin thought to himself with a smile, wishing that he could go through life not caring about being polite to other people.

He then wondered if the groundskeeper was like that because he really wanted to be that way or because some bad experience shaped him that way. His thoughts were interrupted when the old man grabbed a specific key from the keyring and, with a jingle, unlocked a door on the left that said *STORAGE*. He stepped inside, leaving Mark and Kevin in front of the door, waiting like uninvited guests. Kevin leaned toward Mark and whispered.

"You sure we were supposed to follow him? Maybe he just didn't hear us."

"I'm sure," Mark whispered loudly enough to be heard by the entire hall, not only the groundskeeper who was a few feet away. "Groundskeeper Andy is… just like that. He works in a specific way. You don't talk unless you have any questions, and he doesn't talk unless he has something important to say."

"Okay, I guess." Kevin shrugged.

A sound of items being rummaged through reached them from in the other room. This lasted for a minute or so before the groundskeeper came walking out of the room with a backpack in his hand. He shoved it into Kevin's hands, practically making him stumble backward from the sheer force. Kevin couldn't tell what the groundskeeper was thinking due to the lack of expressions on his face, mixed with the inability to clearly see his mouth from the thick beard.

"Okay, then," Kevin said, looking down at the backpack.

He then remembered that he probably should have said something like, "Okay then, Mr. Groundskeeper," but luckily, the man didn't scold him or anything. Without a word, he went around Mark and Kevin and disappeared down the hall.

"Well, thanks, I guess," Kevin said to no one in particular, eyeing his backpack.

"Let's check if everything is inside," Mark said, eagerly snatching the backpack from his new camping buddy and unzipping it.

Kevin let him have it and waited patiently while Mark, digging nearly shoulder-deep to comb through the contents inside.

"Okay, so you have the flashlight," he pulled out the hand and held a small black flashlight.

He flicked it on, flashing it directly in Kevin's face. Kevin shielded his eyes with his hand before Mark apologized and flicked the flashlight off.

"You also got two packs of batteries here," he said as he stuck his hand back inside the backpack. "But make sure not to lose any of them even if they don't work. Slow Ethan lost one pack and got into a lot of trouble with Dwight."

"Who's Dwight?"

"Oh, right. I forgot to tell you about him," Mark said, now in a somewhat quieter timbre.

He glanced over his shoulder as if expecting someone to be standing behind him. When he was sure that the coast was clear, he said, "Dwight is the assistant counselor. He's the youngest counselor here, but everybody hates him. He likes to exert power on the campers when other counselors aren't around. Make sure not to get on his bad side, Otherwise, you'll get all sorts of difficult duties."

"He sounds like an asshole. But if he thinks I'm going to let him bully me in any way in a camp I voluntarily decided to join, he's sorely mistaken," Kevin retorted, raising his tone for the last few words.

"Shh, quiet." Mark pulled his hand out of the backpack to put his index finger to his mouth, looking over his shoulder again. "Listen, Dwight is a real psycho. You don't want him to catch you saying anything bad about him. Some of the campers here got stuck on toilet duty for over a week over smaller things than badmouthing. Not to mention you get negative points added for the Trial."

"The Trial?"

"Yeah. Basically, it's a sort of final test you need to pass before leaving the camp. Every two weeks, the camp organizes The Choosing, and there they get to choose two campers for The Trial. The worse your behavior is, the more difficult The Trial becomes. You pass, and you're out. But um..."

"Yes?"

"Ah, nothing. Never mind. I'll tell you more about the trial later," Mark shook his head.

Kevin dismissively waved his hand in Mark's direction.

"Whatever. I'll deal with it when the time comes. And as for Dwight... I'll deal with Dwight if he decides to pick a bone with me. Anyway, what else you got in there?"

Mark grabbed the backpack with both hands now and stared directly into it rather than rummaging through it with his hand.

"Well, you have a first aid kit, in case it really happens to be an emergency."

"First-aid kit? I don't even know how to use that," Kevin chuckled.

"I'll show you later. They gave us a lesson in first aid during the first week. You also have a rope and a rolled-up sleeping bag. And there are some personal hygiene items like a toothbrush, soap, and other similar things."

"So, I guess we'll be spending some time outside the campgrounds, huh?" Kevin took the backpack when Mark handed it to him.

"Here and there. We do some activities deeper in the woods, but most of the chores are conducted on the campgrounds."

"What kind of chores?" Kevin asked, not liking where this was leading.

He did not sign up to do any stupid fucking chores. If that was the case, he could have just stayed at home and washed the dishes or something. Mark shrugged.

"Depends. Kitchen duty, infirmary duty, toilet duty, wood-chopping duty, watchtower duty, cleaning duty, laundry duty, you name it. There's always work to be done around the camp."

Mark started walking down the hallway, but Kevin seized him by the arm, perplexed by his words. Mark jerked his head in his direction, confusedly staring at him. Kevin let go of his arm, realizing that he may have been a little too rough.

"Wait a second. I thought this camp was for some activities," Kevin said. "Like art, sports, surviving in nature, that kind of thing."

Mark looked uncomfortable. Kevin could see clearly on his face that his new friend didn't know what to say. Mark cleared his throat and said, "Um, well. We usually have training in the morning. And we do have some activities that we do between duties afternoon or on the weekends. Like, you can sit in front of the sleeping cabins. Or you can take a nap instead if you prefer."

"How much work do campers actually have to do here?" Kevin asked.

Mark opened his mouth, but another deeper voice bellowed from down the hall.

"Campers!" Both of them looked in the direction of the sound and saw Mr. Adams standing menacingly in the middle of the hall with his hands on his hips, his boney elbows prominently sticking out. "Did you get the gear for the new camper?"

Mark quickly shot around, wide-eyed and visibly more nervous now.

"Yes, Mr. Adams," he said. "We did."

"Alright. Well, head on back to the cabins until lunch is ready," Mr. Adams replied and continued standing in the same position.

"Yes, Mr. Adams. Right away!"

Mr. Adams turned around to leave only when Mark addressed him by his name.

"Come on, let's go back. Lunch is almost ready," Mark said with a shaky voice, putting his hand on Kevin's shoulder and steering him in the direction of the exit.

With hurried steps, they exited the building, Mark walking faster than Kevin. Kevin couldn't understand why Mark was so nervous around the head counselor. Was he just shy talking to adults? Kevin could somewhat relate to that because his friend Rick was like that.

Rick would be a loudmouth the entire time when they hung out with the gang, but the moment Henry's dad or mom walked in, he'd clam up and assume this personality of a well-behaved kid. Henry's mom would always be especially nice to him, and Henry even said that his mother said once that Rick was the kind of kid every woman with a daughter would want for their son-in-law. If she knew how much weed he smoked and what kind of rap lyrics he listened to, she surely would have changed her opinion. Rick's shy behavior seemed to take place around any adults, not just Henry's parents, which caused all of them to perceive him as a polite, well-mannered teen.

Kevin decided it was probably not a good time to pry or badger Mark about being so timid around the counselors, so he kept quiet on their way back to the cabins. Once they were a good distance away and only the sound of the birds and their own hasty steps surrounded them, Mark seemed to calm down again. Kevin gained enough courage to ask the important question that had been bugging him for the past fifteen minutes or so.

"Hey, Mark? I wanna ask you something."

"Sure, what's up?" Mark asked.

"Why did all the campers stare at me like that when they first saw me?"

Mark continued walking but frowned while staring at the ground.

"What do you mean?" he asked.

"Oh, come on. You can't tell me you didn't see them staring like that at me," Kevin retorted with a snicker.

Mark pursed his lips and shook his head, staring at his feet as he walked forward.

"I dunno, honestly. I guess they were probably surprised to see a new camper join. We've all been here for weeks, and we weren't expecting someone to just join in the middle."

"That's a hell of a reaction for a new camper who just joined."

"Well, we spent a long time here, seeing only familiar faces. It's always the same people. The campers who share your cabin, the campers next cabin, the same staff members… It's not like we see a new face pop up every day, you know?"

"Right."

Kevin didn't find the topic interesting anymore. He continued walking with Mark in silence for a while, the cabins in the distance slowly getting bigger the closer they got. He saw a bunch of campers scattered in front of the cabins, some sitting by the tables, some lying on the grass, some on the steps, some standing and talking to each other. The whole group seemed quiet, though, unlike the typical teenage spirit usually seen during recess.

"Camp activities must be tiring, huh?" Kevin asked, glancing in Mark's direction.

"Sometimes. I think kitchen duty sucks the most."

"What? Really?" Kevin asked with a chuckle. "Don't you, like, get to at least eat as much as you want?"

"No way," Mark shook his head. "Lunch Lady Daisy is very strict about any of the food going missing. There's a specific number of all products for all the campers, so if even one goes missing, someone will remain hungry."

"That doesn't sound like effective management. What if something just gets, I dunno, misplaced?" Kevin shrugged.

Mark chuckled.

"There's no way it can be misplaced. The food is counted by the counselors after being taken out of the storage, and then after the campers deliver it wherever it needs to be taken, it gets counted again. If it went missing between the two counts, you're in trouble."

"That's bullshit," Kevin said, feeling a bit of anti-authority enmity boiling inside him. "You're helping them with duties. They should be rewarding you with extra food there."

"Well, there are ways to work around that, sometimes," Mark said with a conniving smile, which implicitly said that he had something naughty to share.

"Oh, yeah? Like what?" Kevin asked, intrigued to find out what this nice, seemingly adult-fearing kid could have done that was so wrong.

Mark lowered his tone and started talking with the cunning smile still on his face.

"Well, this one time, we had dessert after lunch, and it was a mini roll. Another camper and I had to slice each roll into three equal pieces. So what we did was we sliced each roll into *four* pieces – one very small and three equal ones so that it wouldn't be noticeable. And then we ate each of the small rolls. Piece by piece, and we couldn't even eat lunch later."

He let out uncontrollable laughter before snorting. Kevin stared at Mark with raised eyebrows in disbelief. Then he started laughing as well at the pure genius of the scheme.

"Oh, and this one time..." Mark continued. "There's someone from our cabin they call Ninja-"

"Ninja?" Kevin couldn't help but be amused by the peculiarity of the camp's happenings.

"Yeah. He got his name the first night when he snuck out of the window and roamed the campgrounds, all the while avoiding the patrolling counselors."

"Wait, what?" Kevin shook his head.

Each sentence Mark uttered became increasingly more bizarre.

He felt like he entered some alternate reality where nothing made sense.

Mark continued. "Yeah. At night, there are counselors who patrol the premises to stop campers from wandering into the woods. Mr. Adams said that a few years back, one kid sleepwalked out of his cabin and into the woods. He was found dead a few days later, but ever since then, the camp started having patrols for the campers' safety. He said his death was an accident, but everyone in the camp knows it was the Firwood Wraith."

"The what now?" Kevin frowned, his surprise surpassing his own expectations yet again.

"The Firwood Wraith," Mark said as if it was the most obvious thing in the world. "It's a ghost that roams around the woods at night and kills unsuspecting travelers."

"Is… is that a real thing?"

"That's what the campers think, at least. And there are often sounds coming from the woods near our cabins at night."

"You're bullshitting me."

"I'm not. It's something that- Nevermind, doesn't matter. Coming back to the previous story," Mark continued with a dismissive wave. "So, Ninja worked in the kitchen once with me. I was on dish-washing duty; he was in the bakery. So anyway, the food storage is always locked, but this one time, the lunch lady left it unlocked while she went to take some things to the big pot. I was in the locker room at that time, and the next thing I knew, I saw Ninja running in with his hands full of all sorts of goods."

He was barely able to finish the sentence before he started laughing uncontrollably again, and at this point, his contagious laughter passed on to Kevin until they were both laughing. Mark regained his composure, wiped the laughing tears from his eyes, and continued talking, now loudly, despite starting the mischievous story with a whisper.

"There were juice boxes there and tuna cans and chocolate milk, and he gave it out to everyone. We had to end up putting all the trash inside a bag, and then Ninja snuck out one night again to hide it in the woods."

"Didn't anyone find out about the missing items?" Kevin asked.

"Not that we know of. If they did, they never blamed it on us," Mark said, wheezing out the last remnants of his laughter.

This made Kevin happy. Good on the campers for getting extra food on their own. He hated authority and obeying the system. Fuck these counselors and the camp for thinking they could treat their campers how they wanted.

His mind did get stuck on the story of the Firwood Wraith, though. He wondered if it was an animal the campers heard or the counselors' way of scaring the campers into staying put and obedient. He decided he'd ask some of the other campers about the wraith.

They were close enough to the cabins to hear the murmurs of the other campers. There must have been a few dozen of them at least, and Kevin felt a little anxious at the thought that all those eyes may be pointed at him.

"So, there are five cabins. Are there fifty campers here?" He asked Mark to try to look in front of the others like he was having a natural conversation.

"Not exactly. Maybe forty, give or take," Mark said. "There were more, but they completed the final trial and got sent home earlier."

"I see," Kevin said, subtly glancing around at the other campers.

Some eyes started staring at him but quickly lost interest, to his relief. They made it past the majority of the campers, the murmurs now getting audibly silent. Kevin did his best to ignore the eyes that he felt on him as he asked Mark, "So um... what do we do now?" he asked as he followed Mark to the steps of cabin four.

"Now, I show you how and where to keep your gear," Mark said, opening the door and stepping inside.

Kevin followed closely and closed the door behind him to shut out the remaining few faces that stared at him.

I hope they forget about me soon.

66

Mark got to Kevin's locker next to bed number nine and opened it. There were two empty shelves just below the drawer on the top and an empty locker space under.

"Let's first see about your uniform," Mark said, staring at the messily splayed heap of clothes on Kevin's bed.

He stole the shirt from the pile and said, "This won't do. If they see any wrinkles, they'll give you hell. Here's how you do it."

He gently placed the shirt on the bed and neatly folded one sleeve and then the other. He then clasped the top of the shirt and folded it across itself.

"There," he said, pointing with an open palm toward it as if presenting it.

It was a perfect rectangle of a shirt.

"Damn. That's impressive," Kevin whistled, scratching his head and wondering if he could imitate the movement.

Back at home, he used to throw all his dirty clothes on what he called *the chair*, which was essentially a computer chair he never used for anything except piling dirty clothes. Mark gripped the shirt by the collar and yanked it up, completely ruining the perfect fold, much to Kevin's horror.

"Now you try it," Mark said, stepping aside.

Kevin shook his head, feeling pretty stupid for having to do something like this. Mark assisted by verbally guiding him when he was stuck. The end result was much sloppier than Mark's was, but the camper encouraged him by saying he would get better in a few days. He then proceeded to show him how to fold the pants, and once both pieces of clothing were satisfactory in their meager rectangle shape, Mark showed him how to squeeze them inside the locker on the shelf.

"You have to put the pants in first, then the shirt, and then the shoes, and then the towel on top of that. Let's grab the towel from your backpack."

Kevin reached into his backpack and pulled out a small green towel. He handed it to Mark, who proceeded to fold it while saying.

"This one is simple. Just fold it like this and put it on top of the shirt. It needs to line up like this," he neatly placed the folded towel in the locker, presenting the three equally folded items, which lined up perfectly with the edge of the locker shelf.

"Remember, there can't be any wrinkles, or you'll be in trouble," Mark said.

"Who gives a shit about that? I'm just gonna toss it in. It's my locker, anyway," Kevin annoyedly responded.

"You can't do that," Mark shook his head. "Sometimes the counselors have a surprise inspection, and if you haven't done your things properly, you get in trouble."

Kevin laughed, not believing what he was hearing.

"What is this? A fucking military boot camp? Come on!"

Mark shrugged. There was a moment of silence before he took the backpack from Kevin and said, "Alright, as for your hygiene items, you can leave them in the top drawer."

He pulled out a toothbrush, toothpaste, toilet paper, soap, needle and thread, and other things that were messily thrown inside the backpack.

"Why do I need the needle and thread?" Kevin asked.

"If you tear your uniform anywhere, you have to repair it."

Kevin opened his mouth to ask if he was serious, but he already knew the answer. He closed his mouth and allowed Mark to do his thing. Mark grabbed the backpack and stuffed it into the lower part of the locker.

"You can keep the backpack here. That one doesn't need to be placed neatly."

"Halle-fucking-lujah," Kevin said.

Mark chuckled before straightening his back.

"As for the pajamas, put them on the shelf here, above the uniform. Also, fold them neatly. Try it."

Kevin did his best to fold the pajamas as well as he could, and even though it wasn't as good of an attempt as Mark's, it was close enough. Once he had it, he placed the pajamas neatly on the top shelf above the uniform.

"You can put the rest of the things on top of the pajamas; no need to fold those," Mark pointed.

Kevin groaned and did as Mark told him.

"Anything else I should know?" he asked, bracing himself for more surprises.

"A few things here and there. But I'll explain things as we go. Just do what the others are doing, and you'll be fine."

Mark went past Kevin and said, "Come on, let's go outside so you can meet the others. It's almost lunchtime, anyway."

Kevin wasn't exactly thrilled by this thought, but it was inevitable, so he may as well do it now. He scratched the back of his head awkwardly and followed his new friend outside. Mark walked over to a nearby bench where five other campers were sitting. The ones facing him looked in his direction, and the others soon followed their gaze.

"Barrel Mark. Come on, man, sit down. You haven't had a break yet," the tiniest of the bunch with short, messy, dark hair perkily said and scooted to the left, leaving space on the bench.

"Thanks, Ninja," Mark responded and looked behind himself at Kevin.

A few eyes moved in his direction, but no one continued staring at him.

"Guys, this is Kevin," Mark said theatrically. "He's the new guy."

"Hi," Kevin raised his hand briefly before putting it down.

He stood in one place while the others looked in various directions, avoiding his gaze. Except for one visibly taller and bulkier camper by the table, who was staring directly at him with an unblinking gaze.

"Well, come on and sit down, new guy," Ninja said.

He scooted further to the left, effectively pushing the camper with glasses to his left to the edge of the bench.

"Move over, my dude," Ninja said to the guy, leaving enough space for him and Mark to sit.

Mark sat down first, and Kevin followed, squeezing himself in between Ninja and Mark. The camper who stared at Kevin was still gazing at him with what looked like an angry look on his face, so Kevin stared back.

"Am I really that interesting?" he asked the camper.

The boy continued staring at him for a solid two seconds or so before slamming his hands on the table and getting up. Kevin thought he was going to start a fight, so he mentally braced himself, but the camper just stepped around the bench and walked away.

"He must really like me," Kevin said sardonically to no one in particular.

He knew that he probably shouldn't be making enemies right off the bat, but he was annoyed and tired, especially from the staring. The other campers were looking in the direction of the boy who just left before slowly turning back to the table, one by one.

"That's Michael. Don't mind him," one of the campers said. "I'm Steve, by the way."

He started pointing at each camper by the table and introducing them.

"That's Ninja. We call him like that because he likes to jump around and do some stunts and shit. You already met Barrel Mark. This little fucker next to me is Tough Norton," he pointed to the camper next to him. "He's the strongest in the camp."

He definitely didn't look extremely strong. He had veiny and muscular forearms, but he looked somewhat skinny. Maybe he was one of those resilient kids who did a lot of physical labor in his life and didn't look tough but was strong enough to wrestle a bull.

"And the guy next to Ninja is Nerdy Van," Steve introduced the camper with thick glasses and braces. "We got more in our group, but they're somewhere else right now."

He looked around and pointed to a group of three a little farther in the distance. They were sitting on the grass, forming a circle and talking to each other.

"That's Javier, Clean Ryan, and Slow Ethan," Steve said.

"Some of you guys have names, but others don't. Why's that?" Kevin asked.

Steve shrugged.

"I guess we're not special enough in any way. If you're worried about your own name, wait a day or two, and you'll see what people start calling you."

Kevin nodded, staring at the table. To kill the awkward silence, he asked, "So what fun activities do you guys get to do here at camp?"

Kevin noticed Steve's mouth opening in confusion. He looked at the rest of the campers and realized that they, too, appeared perplexed. Steve looked at Mark and formed an *O* with his mouth before a loud voice barked from the middle of the campgrounds.

"Alright, you maggots! Line up!"

Kevin looked in the direction of the sound and saw a counselor swiveling his head from left to right. This one was much younger, though, maybe a couple of years older than Kevin. *He can't be more than eighteen,* Kevin thought to himself. The counselor visibly just recently got out of puberty – his acne-covered face a testament to that. He was much larger than any of the campers, though, easily towering above some of them by a whole head.

"Alright, lunchtime. Let's go," Ninja said and, with an elegant move, hopped over the bench he was sitting on.

All the other campers on site started swarming the area in front of the young counselor, lining up like soldiers.

"That's Dwight," Mark said to Kevin in a rush while following the stampede of campers.

The campers started forming up in five lines, and when Kevin saw all of his cabin mates forming up in the fourth line, he followed them.

"New kid, you're here," Steve grabbed Kevin by the shoulder and directed him to the edge of the line. "Number nine."

Kevin mimicked the movement of the other campers and stood in line, leaving an arm's length between himself and the next camper on each side. In seconds, Michael, the camper who stared at Kevin by the table, rushed over to Kevin's left side. He stared in front of himself, at the back of the camper who was standing in front of him.

The commotion finally stopped moments later, and Kevin looked around, impressed by the aesthetic line-up that the campers formed. There were five rows, each row formed by ten campers, perfectly aligned with precisely measured distance between each of them. Some spots were left empty, however, which made Kevin assume those campers had some camp duties. The young counselor paced around, shaking his head, his lips turned into a thin slit as if to express disappointment.

"Too slow, campers. Too slow. If you continue like this, I'll have to file a recommendation for the reduction of food. You wouldn't want that, would you?"

The air was silent as everyone stared in front of themselves with no expressions on their faces.

Who the hell is this asshole?

"What? No one has anything to say? Huh?" Dwight asked angrily, spreading his arms as if to challenge them.

He slowly began walking between campers while shouting, "Some of you have been here for over three weeks now, and you're still too slow for lining up. You're a disgrace!"

Kevin looked to the right and saw that the counselor was walking between the rows of campers numbers three and four. He then started walking left, carefully observing each camper he'd pass by. Kevin felt a tension in the air coming from everyone. This was bullshit. Why in the hell did they all stand there and take this kind of treatment? The counselor continued.

"You're here to do as you're told, not fuck around. This isn't a picnic."

"This isn't the fucking army either, asshole!" Kevin snapped, unable to contain his anger.

Whoever this asshole on a power trip thought he was, he was *not* going to treat Kevin like that. As soon as Kevin shouted that sentence, the counselor stopped and turned his head to the right with a wild glower in his eye.

"Who said that?!" He shouted, his spit visibly flying on some unfortunate camper's face next to him.

"New kid, shut up!" Steve muttered through his teeth, but Kevin ignored him.

"*I* did, you zit-faced douchebag!"

Suppressed laughter broke out among the campers as Kevin put his hands on his hips, leisurely shifting his weight on one leg, contrasting the rest of the campers, who stood still like robots. The counselor was practically fuming from his ears as he got all red in the face and shouted at the group.

"Stop laughing! What's so funny?!" the laughter stopped immediately, and Dwight turned his attention to Kevin.

He strode over directly in front of him with menacing steps, but Kevin refused to budge.

If I flinch, he'll think I'm scared.

He continued holding his hands on his hips, even as the counselor was right in his face. Kevin saw clearly the cliffs forming on his face from the acne. It was even uglier up close than from afar.

"New kid, right?" Dwight asked with a conniving smile, even though it was visible from his erratic head motions that he was pissed. "I don't think you're acquainted with the rules here. So I'm going to teach you."

Kevin stared at Dwight bemusedly, trying to put on his *I'm bored* face as best he could. He saw that the other campers were just dying to look at him but were too afraid to take a direct glance. Dwight took a deep breath and stepped back as he shouted.

"Alright, move out to the mess hall, you little shits! You all got sweeping duty thanks to the new kid, so you can show your gratitude to him!"

There were a few disappointed groans and moans before Dwight silenced them and said, "Hey, don't blame it on me. Someone here needs to learn some manners. And what better way than to spend the afternoon sweeping the main lodge?" He stared directly at Kevin with a malicious smile.

"Fuck you. You can't force us to do that," Kevin said, feeling anger growing further inside him like slow-boiling water.

"Force you? Oh, I'm not forcing anyone," Dwight said and turned around.

He started pacing toward the front of the line as he shouted at the top of his lungs.

"Does anyone here *not* want to do sweeping duty?" he stopped and looked around with his hands behind his back.

Everyone was silent. Kevin looked around at his fellow campers and realized they were all still staring in front. Dwight's expression changed into a stupid grimace as he continued shouting.

"Anyone? Anyone at all who doesn't want to do sweeping duty? No one?"

He shrugged and smiled widely, revealing crooked teeth, before he said, "Alright, then! Get your asses to the mess hall, and after that, I want to see every one of you in front of the main lodge at exactly"—he looked at his wristwatch—"one-forty p.m."

He put his hand down and leaned forward.

"MOVE IT!" he shouted, a bulging vein appearing on his forehead and neck.

The campers lethargically started walking around the assistant counselor. Kevin suddenly felt like shit. The campers were probably already tired, and now he earned them some extra work. They were probably going to hate him even more now. He hadn't been in Camp Firwood for more than a few hours, and he was already making enemies out of both the counselors and the campers. He scolded himself for allowing his anger to get the better of him, despite Dwight being an asshole.

He followed the other campers, trying to stay at the back as much as he possibly could to avoid the even more awkward glares now. When they were halfway through the meadow, someone from the crowd shouted.

"Where's the new guy?"

Kevin froze in his tracks, dreading what was to come next. All faces turned toward him, and a moment of stillness filled the air. And then someone jumped in front of Kevin, firmly grabbing him by the shoulders with a vice-like grip.

"Dude, that was awesome!" It was Tough Norton, and he had a facial expression that portrayed utter happiness. "Did you see the look on his face? I mean, his zit-faced face."

He and a few other campers broke out laughing. The majority remained somber and stared at Kevin with judgmental glares. Steve stepped forward and said, "That wasn't awesome, Norton. He could have put us in serious danger," he said and turned to face Kevin. "You can't ever do that again, got it? You have no idea what these people are capable of."

Kevin slapped his hands against his sides and shook his head.

"What are you talking about? We're in a summer camp. They can't make you do anything you don't want to. If they don't like it, they can just kick us out."

Everyone went dreadfully silent, some continuing to stare at Kevin, others looking at their feet or awkwardly glancing around.

"What?" Kevin asked, scanning the other campers.

Steve stared at him with a face that said, *you don't know something that I do*. His suspicion was confirmed when Steve shook his head and said, "Mark didn't tell you anything about the camp, did he?"

Kevin was taken aback by this question momentarily before scoffing and responding.

"What's there to know, Steve? I'm in a summer camp called Camp Firwood, and that's that."

Steve licked his lips and looked over Kevin's shoulder, probably to see if Dwight was coming.

"Oh, you're wrong, Cocky Kevin. You're so wrong; you have no idea how wrong you are."

Kevin stared at Steve, expecting a further explanation.

"Why?"

"Ever heard of The Trial?" Steve asked.

This caused a few campers to exchange glances with each other momentarily. Kevin shrugged.

"Yeah, Mark told me. You host The Choosing, then have a final test, get some negative points, blah-blah-blah."

"You have no idea what danger you might put yourself in. The Trial is already bad enough as it is. And if you get enough negative points... well, let's just say you probably don't wanna be out in the woods for too long at night."

"Why? Because of the scary Firwood Wraith?" Kevin raised his hands and made the final two words sound scary.

The campers awkwardly exchanged glances with each other.

"Oh, come on, are you guys serious?" Kevin scoffed. "A ghost in the woods killing people? Do you hear yourselves?"

"He's right, though," one of the campers said. "It's pretty stupid to believe a ghost is killing the campers."

Steve ignored him. He looked over Kevin's shoulder one more time and said, "Dwight's coming. We need to get to the mess hall. We're already late. Come on, people!"

One by one, the campers started moving in the direction of the mess hall while Steve continued staring at Kevin. He looked over his shoulder and then leaned closer to Kevin and said in a hushed tone, "You're lucky we only got the sweeping duty."

With that, he turned around and followed the group of campers, who were now well ahead of them.

"What do you mean? Just wait a second!" Kevin shouted, but Steve ignored him.

What the fuck is going on here?

Kevin thought to himself as he watched the other campers put distance between himself and them. A soft voice came from his right.

"Well, I warned you, Cocky Kevin," Mark said.

Oh great, I guess that's my name from now on.

Mark and Kevin jogged to catch up with the other campers, after which they followed at the back of the group with a slow-paced walk.

"Mark, what's going on here? Why is everyone so secretive and afraid?" Kevin asked.

Mark sighed, looking at the back of the feet of the camper in front of him.

"I haven't been fully honest with you. I couldn't because I knew you wouldn't believe me."

"Believe you about what?" Kevin asked with a higher tone than he wanted to.

Mark put a finger to his mouth and produced a *shhh* sound.

"Quiet!" he said. "You don't want to be so vocal about these kinds of things."

Kevin scoffed and shook his head impatiently. This was getting ridiculous. He started to think that the whole camp was just playing an elaborate prank on him to get him to shit his pants.

"Well, then why don't you tell me?" Kevin asked.

Mark sighed and stopped. Kevin stopped along with him and waited. Mark looked like he was thinking about carefully choosing his words. Kevin silently stood by, not wanting to interrupt him and possibly make him change his mind about opening up.

"Okay, look," Mark finally said. "The camp, The Trial… all of this is way more dangerous than you think. This isn't just an ordinary summer camp."

He stopped as if waiting for Kevin to give him a response.

When Kevin gave no indication that he was about to interrupt him, Mark continued, "The counselors say it's a survival trial in the woods and that the campers get to go home after they finish it, but..."

"But?" Kevin was becoming impatient.

"Like I said, there are these strange noises coming from the woods at night. The campers think that... we're being sacrificed to the wraith."

Now Kevin was more than sure that this was all just a big prank.

Mark continued, "Look, I know it sounds crazy. But just think about it. Do you think any of us would stand for this kind of abuse? I mean, take Tough Norton as an example. He was brought here *because* of his behavior!"

"Mark, stop fucking with me. I am already in a bad mood about having to be in this shithole. You're not helping." Kevin was on the verge of losing his patience.

"I'm not fucking with you, I swear! Look, I can't talk about it right now, but if you think I'm joking, go ahead and try to leave the camp. Ask for your things back. Ask to make a phone call home. Ask to be escorted out because your grandma died. Ask anything you want, and tonight when we're all in the cabin, if you still want to know, I'll tell the others to confirm it for you."

"You know what? I *will* ask to leave the camp! Right after sweeping duty is finished, and that's only because I don't want to leave you guys with a thing *I* fucked up," Kevin retorted, throwing his hands up.

"Alright," Mark said reticently and turned to follow the rest of the campers.

I don't know who these assholes think they are, but I'll get my phone, call my parents, and leave this fucking place by the end of the day, he thought to himself confidently.

And yet, despite knowing that the campers were probably screwing with him, he couldn't help but feel a sense of dread slowly growing inside him.

4
After dinner

The campers formed a long line in front of the mess hall, which started at the food line inside the building and wound like a snake through the exit and around the wall. It was cabin two's turn to be first in line while cabin four was third.

Most of the campers were shifting their weight from left to right, obviously agitated or impatient – or just plain tired. Kevin himself was starting to feel hungry. He hadn't even thought about food until he stepped near the entrance and smelled something good cooking inside. He couldn't tell what it was, but his guess was something with seafood.

"Oh, man! No burgers," Barrel Mark's disappointed shout from the front confirmed that there were no burgers like he hoped earlier there would be.

The line slowly moved forward, and Kevin stepped over the threshold, glancing at the interior of the mess hall. The clattering of silverware against plates and murmurs of the campers filled the air, and he saw a bunch of teens chowing by the tables. Counselors Baldwin, Adams, and another one Kevin didn't recognize were observing the mess hall. Kevin glanced at the table closest to his left, where a few campers were sitting, and happened to see their plates. They had fish and chips on their plates, not burgers.

Kevin was indifferent about seafood, but the smell which infiltrated his nostrils made his mouth water. He peeked behind Steve's shoulder and saw that there were still a dozen people being served on the line. He saw a big woman behind the food line, wearing a chef's cap, apron, and yellow gloves that went all the way up to her meaty elbows, slapping food on plates with tongs and sliding them on the line for the campers to take.

Next to her was a boy in white clothes and a white hat, assisting her clumsily and erratically. He looked scared as he darted around the various foods in front of him, messily throwing them on plates in a desperate attempt to prevent the line from getting cluttered by the campers. He was around the same age as the campers, so Kevin assumed he was indeed a camper on kitchen duty.

When it was Kevin's turn to get his food finally, he took the plastic platter from the stack and clumsily picked out a knife and fork from the silverware section. He proceeded to take the plate of food, which was handed to him by the angry-looking lunch lady. The fish and chips looked a little watery, but he was too hungry to care.

"Thank you, ma'am," Kevin politely responded.

As rebellious as he was, he knew his manners. She didn't so much as look at him before proceeding to put food on the next plate. Kevin grabbed two pieces of rock-hard bread, comically tapping them on the platter to see how old they really were.

Fresh from three days ago, nice.

He made his way past the timid camper on kitchen duty, who was transfixed on the food about as much as the lunch lady was but with less intensity.

"Over here, Cocky Kevin," Steve gestured with his head while holding the platter with both hands.

Kevin was surprised that Steve displayed a friendly attitude despite the earlier hostility, but instead of saying anything, he followed him to a nearby table where Javier, Nerdy Van, Slow Ethan, and Barrel Mark were sitting, already eating their lunches.

"I thought you were sad that there were no burgers, Barrel Mark," Javier said in his prominent Mexican accent as he put a piece of bread into his mouth and, with a yanking motion of his head, tore one bite off.

"He's never sad when he's eating, are you kidding?" Steve responded, making his way onto his seat.

Kevin sat next to him, garnishing brief glances from Ethan, Van, and Javier.

"You guys haven't met Cocky Kevin yet," Mark said with his mouth full, his cheeks bulging from the amount of food he stuffed inside his mouth.

"We haven't, but we already know who you are," Javier said and introduced himself.

"That was pretty brave, telling Dwight that thing back there," Nerdy Van responded, waving a piece of fish on his fork before putting it into his mouth.

"Ah, it was nothing really," Kevin said, as he dug into his own food.

The fish was too bland and the chips too salty, but he assumed there was no other food to be eaten for lunch.

"Hey, is there a vending machine or something for chocolate bars around here?"

Steve sneered, glancing in Kevin's direction.

"Even if there was, what would you buy it with? Flower petals?"

"No. I just thought... yeah, okay," he realized how silly his question must have seemed to the rest of the campers at the table, so he shut up and continued eating instead.

"So, Mr. Adams gave you an extra hour of tent-setting up, huh?" Javier asked Slow Ethan.

Ethan nodded.

"Yes. I'll have to do it in front of Dwight tonight after dinner."

"What was wrong with your tent, anyway?" Steve asked.

Ethan shrugged.

"It wasn't stable enough, and I was too slow setting it up."

"Surprise, surprise," Steve responded. "Well, at least you didn't get any toilet duties."

"That's Stan's duty this week. I heard he pissed off Dwight real bad," Ethan stuck his fork into one piece of potato and stuffed it into his mouth.

"What did he do?" Mark curiously looked up.

"I think he left a wet floor, and Dwight slipped on it."

"Ay, too bad he didn't break his neck," Javier scoffed.

Kevin tuned out at this point. He quickly finished his food and continued playing with the remaining pieces of bread, stabbing them with the fork, leaving various holes in both the crust and the soft part, which was equally hard as the crust. He was thinking about what the campers told him earlier. The conversation he had with Mark about not being able to leave the place worried him way more than he wanted to admit it to himself.

He tried telling himself over and over that this was all either a prank or that the campers had been intimidated into believing they needed to do everything the counselors told them. Either way, he would go to Mr. Adams as soon as sweeping duty was over and ask to be escorted out of camp.

A scenario ran through his head of the way his parents would be angry with him.

We signed you up for eight weeks, and you couldn't last a single day, his father's voice echoed in his head.

But he didn't care. He was supposed to *learn* something, not do hard physical labor. And he'd get to see Amy and the rest of his friends. The thought of going home to the ones who really cared about him overwhelmed him with a homesick feeling. Images started popping into his mind. Henry embracing him in a bear hug, Rick asking him about the 'chicks in the camp', Luis patting him on the back and telling him he did the right thing. The whole gang sitting in the abandoned trailer park and listening to Kevin's experiences in the camp, him sitting close enough to Amy to feel the warmth of her body…

"Come on, campers, hurry it up!" Mr. Adams loudly clapped a few times, waking Kevin up from his daydreaming. "You got work to do! No schmoozing after lunch like old ladies, come on!"

Most of the campers seemed to ignore Mr. Adams, but a few stood up with their platters. They carried them over to a window on the left side of the mess hall where someone took them and disappeared. Kevin didn't feel like sitting anymore, but he didn't feel it was right to get up and leave first among the table crew.

It was like the tradition in school that started years ago. If you got up to leave before the others, you were uncool, so you had to wait until everyone unanimously decided to return to class. This seemed to carry over from elementary school to high school, and it felt the same in this case. So, he instead waited until someone decided to give the sign. He expected that *someone* to be Steve, who seemed to assume a silently agreed-upon leadership position, and sure enough, he was right.

"Alright, I guess it's time to go," Steve said a minute later after everyone was done with their food.

Everyone except Slow Ethan, who stuffed the remaining food into his mouth to catch up with everyone else who just stood up. With their platters, the campers who sat by the same table – including Kevin – tentatively followed Steve. One by one, they approached the window on the left side and left their platters on the extended sill. A teen dressed in all white, just like the one on the food line, was rapidly snatching the platters and placing them somewhere in the room behind him. Kevin couldn't see clearly what was there, but he guessed it was the dish-washing room.

"How's the kitchen duty going, Max?" Steve bent down to face the camper through the window.

"You know. Same shit like every day," the camper on the other side of the window rolled his eyes.

"Well, just don't let Lunch Lady Daisy get on your nerves," Steve straightened his back and headed toward the double doors leading outside.

The campers still had a little time to relax, probably until everyone was out because the ones who finished their meals were standing in front and talking to each other. Kevin separated from the rest of the crew, feeling like he needed some time alone. It wasn't that he didn't like spending time with people, but he spent way too much time with people today, and he felt like he needed a break now.

"Hey," a voice called behind him, and he instantly recognized it as Mark's.

"Hey," he said back, not wanting to tell him to go away.

He didn't want to alienate Mark just because he was in a bad mood, especially since Mark seemed like such a cool and friendly guy.

"How's your first day going so far?" Barrel Mark asked him, looking way more content now that he had his lunch.

Kevin shrugged.

"It's shit. I fucking hate this place already. Good thing I'll be leaving soon."

He eyed Mark, hoping he would try to give him a reason why he wouldn't be able to leave, but nothing like that came, much to Kevin's disappointment.

Wait, why am I disappointed by that? I'm supposed to be happy that he isn't stopping me.

It then dawned on him that Mark may have been omitting information and that that's why he wasn't saying anything. That feeling of dread started growing in him again, so he pushed the thought back down by trying to change the topic.

"How are things going for you? You've been here a while now, so what are your thoughts about this place?"

"Hate it," Mark replied before Kevin even finished his sentence.

He was dead serious when saying that, which would have been funny to Kevin in any other given situation. Here, it only intensified his dread.

"What exactly do you hate about it?" Kevin shifted his weight from his right leg to the left.

Mark looked over yonder and said, "Everything. The work, the food, the counselors. But the thing I hate the most is the fact that I can't see my little sister. Only the campers are good. I made some really good friends here. I could never do that in school."

"Why not?" Kevin frowned.

Mark shrugged shyly.

"I dunno. Because I'm fat," he pursed his lips.

"Well, that's a stupid reason not to be friends with someone. You're a pretty cool guy to hang out with," Kevin winked.

This seemed to catch Mark's attention as he chuckled and tentatively looked Kevin in the eye.

"You mean that?"

"Yeah, man. Hell, I'd invite you over for gaming night with my buddies. Which part of Oregon are you from, anyway?"

Mark squinted suspiciously and told him, "I'm actually from Idaho."

"Wait, what?" Kevin's jaw dropped. "Why did they drive you all the way to Oregon for a summer camp? Don't they have any camps in Idaho?"

"I guess my parents just thought Camp Firwood would be the best fit for me." Mark dismissively waved his hand.

"Hm," Kevin nodded.

After a moment of silence, he asked, "You said you have a little sister? How old is she?"

"Four. Her name's Sherry. To tell you the truth, I'm not very happy about not being there to take care of her."

"Why's that? Your parents are there for her, right?"

Mark nodded.

"Yeah. But she's really attached to me. Can't really go too long without seeing me. Can't even fall asleep unless she's sure that I'm in the same room."

Kevin nodded. He couldn't relate to the feeling of taking care of a sibling since he was an only child, but he admired Mark's protective attitude nonetheless. The crowd in front of the mess hall was much larger now, and pretty soon, Mr. Adams and Dwight stepped outside, discussing something. Mr. Adams carried a paper pad and explained something to Dwight with vigorous hand gestures while Dwight stared at him and nodded fervently.

Moments later, Mr. Adams turned to face the campers and took a deep breath, his chest heaving up.

"Line up, campers!" he shouted at the top of his lungs.

Those who were standing began rushing in front of the counselors, while those who were sitting clambered up to their feet and rushed to join the ranks. Just like last time, everyone lined up in five rows, and it didn't take Kevin long to figure out where he was supposed to be standing. He was still much slower than most of the other campers, though, as they seemed to already have it in their minds which spot they were supposed to run to before any line was even formed.

Only seconds later, the commotion stopped, and silence began reigned. It was even more intense now than the first time around when Dwight was the only person in command who was present. But why was everyone so afraid? Mr. Adams seemed like a nice counselor. Annoying, yeah, but nice. He didn't look like the type to raise his tone at all. Kind of like Kevin's history teacher, Mr. Milton, who gave the students too much freedom, and they took advantage of it, pushing their luck as much as they could without getting into trouble. Here at the camp, nobody seemed to be pushing their luck.

"Alright," Mr. Adams theatrically proclaimed. "I hear we've had some problems today. Anyone care to tell me what happened?"

He smiled at the campers, swiveling his head slowly from left to right in anticipation.

"Anyone? No?" he darted his eyes around more fervently this time.

A moment later, he sighed and looked down at his notepad. He took the pen out of his front pocket and annoyingly clicked it a few times before placing it on the paper.

"Dwight, which cabin was responsible for the incident?" he asked.

"Cabin four, Mr. Adams. But all of them laughed when the incident occurred," Dwight responded with a docile tone, which clearly said that he had no power or equality with Mr. Adams.

Mr. Adams nodded and scribbled something down while saying, "Well, we can't put all of them on sweeping duty, can we now? We need someone in the main lodge and someone to relieve the watchtower camper, and someone to assist with the logs. Or maybe you thought that was all being done by ghosts?" he cackled at his own joke as he looked at Dwight, who wore a disappointed look on his face.

"Well, no... I didn't think that, Mr. Adams. I just thought that this would be a fitting punishment for all of them," Dwight mumbled out timorously.

"Don't think too hard, Dwight. You'll hurt yourself. Plus, that's not your job. So here's what I want you to do. Take cabin one for sweeping duty around the main lodge. Cabin two for sweeping around the mess hall and infirmary. Cabin three for log duty. Cabin five for an extra hour of starting a campfire. Aaaaaand as for cabin four - you guys get to take a break while the others work."

Groans came from the majority of campers (everyone but cabin four) until Mr. Adams raised his index finger scoldingly and shushed them.

"Ah-ah-ah. I don't wanna hear complaints. Unless you guys are okay with someone sleeping out in the woods tonight." He turned down his lips and raised his eyebrows.

With that expression, he lifted his chin and glanced around at the campers to see if anyone would complain. It suddenly got eerily silent, which seemed to please Mr. Adams. He clicked his pen and put it in his pocket with a smile as he said, "Alrighty then. Dwight. Get the campers to work. Cabin four, get back to your cabin."

He grinned toothily and glanced specifically at the cabin four campers, making sure to keep longer eye contact with Kevin. This sudden change of Mr. Adams' polite and irritating mood into passive-aggressive was shocking. It was like a completely different person was speaking than who Kevin met when he arrived.

Maybe I was wrong about him after all.

Kevin saw all the campers from cabin four turning to the left, and not wanting to be left behind; he mimicked their movement. He watched as Michael started walking forward and then turned left to walk around the campers from behind.

"Follow Michael," Kevin heard Steve say behind him.

He hurriedly caught up to Michael and followed him all the way around and behind the campers from cabin five, eventually heading in the direction of the cabins. Kevin stepped out of the line and glanced back at the two counselors. Mr. Adams was standing with his hands behind his back, smiling as he observed the campers. Dwight waved his hand and shouted for cabin one to follow him.

Kevin started walking toward Mr. Adams and immediately heard a hushed and panicked voice behind him.

"Kevin! What are you doing?!" it was Mark.

Kevin ignored him and continued walking by the right side of the campers. Cabin one was already out of line and following Dwight somewhere. Even as Kevin got close to Mr. Adams, the counselor seemed to be oblivious to his approach. Even when he stopped a couple of feet away from him, enough for the counselor to see him with his peripheral vision, Mr. Adams outright ignored Kevin.

"Mr. Adams?" Kevin asked, feeling the eyes of the other few dozen campers on him.

Mr. Adams jerked his head in Kevin's direction and smiled as he turned to face him.

"Camper. What is it?"

Now that he had to ask a question in front of all the other campers, he felt embarrassed. It reminded him of the time he was in a school play a few years ago where his classmates and their parents came to watch the kids performing. He felt so nervous back then that his stomach was twisting into knots and was glad he didn't tell his parents about the play. That would have stressed him out even more, knowing their judgmental eyes were watching from the crowd. Now that he stood in front of the head counselor, he felt the same kind of nervousness as back then, minus the knots.

"Well, um..." he started, not even knowing where to begin, "I need to use my cellphone."

"Your cellphone?" Mr. Adams asked, his smile subtly fading away but still etched on his face.

"Yeah," Kevin said more confidently now that he caught some momentum. "I want to call my parents to pick me up."

Mr. Adams' smile completely dropped, and he frowned with a confused stare.

"You want to leave Camp Firwood? You don't like it here?"

"No, sir. I don't like it here one bit. I want out," Kevin retorted, his defiance kicking in now, giving him the courage to say a fraction of the things that were on his mind.

If he were to fully express himself, it would have sounded something like, *give me back my fucking phone and let me out of here, you elongated asshole.* Mr. Adams scratched his chin, eyeing Kevin for a moment before he made a vacuum-like sound with his mouth and said, "Is there anything I can do to change your mind?"

"Sorry, no. I really just wanna leave," Kevin said, wanting to at least pretend to be polite to the counselor.

Mr. Adams nodded.

"Well, if you're sure about it... but right now, everyone is too busy with camp duties to go and fetch the cellphone for you. But here's what we can do. After dinner, you come find me, and I'll give you your cellphone. Then you can call your parents, and they can pick you up in the morning; how does that sound?"

Kevin was too hyped to consider disagreeing. It's not like Mr. Adams would leave the campgrounds and escape with his phone before dinner. So Kevin nodded, agreeing to Mr. Adams' proposal.

"Alright. After dinner, then," he confirmed.

"Alright, then. Now go back to your cabin mates," Mr. Adams grinned once again, but the sentence sounded like a polite order.

Content but not happy, Kevin turned around and returned to his fellow campers from cabin four, who all had curious looks on their faces.

"What?" Kevin asked as he spread his arms.

Most of them looked away, and they continued walking back to the cabin.

***

According to the other campers, they had an hour of free time, and most of the campers decided to take a short nap during that time. Kevin watched in awe as each of the sleepy campers neatly put the blankets over their bedsheets and lay down on top of them.

"Can't lay on your bed in your uniform," Mark said as he adjusted his pillow to be puffier. "It might get the sheets dirty. So most campers, when they get to take a nap in the afternoon, they sleep in their uniforms on the blankets since it takes way too long to get into your pajamas."

"That's stupid," Kevin snorted.

"Give it a few days and see if you still think that," Ninja said, throwing himself onto the bed, which squeaked loudly.

"I'm not gonna be here that long," he said.

No one said anything to that. Since most of the campers seemed to be getting ready to do their own thing, Kevin figured he might as well try to take a nap to pass the time a little.

"What time is dinner?" he asked Mark.

Mark had already slumped into his own bed and made himself comfortable on his side.

"Seven-thirty," he said through a yawn.

Still some time until then.

Kevin followed the ritual with the blanket, just like the other campers, by tossing it across the entire bed. He didn't want to get the campers in any more trouble for the short stay here. As soon as his head hit the pillow, his eyelids became heavy, and he started to realize just how tired he really was.

***

He was woken up by voices outside the cabin. They were cheerful but somewhat jaded voices. Teenage voices, which took Kevin a long moment to recognize as those belonging to the campers of the other cabins.

They must have returned from their duties, Kevin thought to himself as he forced his eyes to open.

Some of the other campers from his cabin were already up and buzzing around the cabin. Mark was folding his blanket when he looked at Kevin.

"Good, you're up," he said. "We have afternoon class soon. Get ready for it."

Kevin clambered to his feet with a groan. He felt groggy, but he didn't want to sleep anymore.

"What time is it?" he asked with a hoarse voice.

"A little after three. We have to be in the study hall at four."

"Wait, what exactly are we gonna do there?" Kevin frowned and inadvertently closed his eyes, having trouble keeping them open.

"Study. We have classes like nature, survival, equipment, camp history, and so on. Like you asked," Mark grinned.

He neatly patted his folded blanket and bent down next to the bed. He grabbed the sheets from under the bed frame and began tugging them, going from one end of the bed to the other, effectively removing any wrinkles on the top.

"Jesus, I thought this camp couldn't get any worse than it already was," Kevin groaned.

Mark finished all four sides of his bed until the bed was in such a flawless and wrinkle-less condition that it looked brand new.

"We gotta fix your bed up, too," Mark said.

Kevin stood up and looked back at his bed. He removed the blanket and stared at the wrinkled mess he left on the sheets. It still didn't look bad, though. No edges were untucked, so Kevin didn't really see the big deal.

"I mean, it's not so bad like this, right?" he asked.

"It's very bad," Mark said as he knelt and started doing the same sheet-tucking motion from the foot of the bed. "It has to be completely tucked so that there are no wrinkles whatsoever."

"Yep, now I'm sure I mistakenly joined the army," Kevin joked.

Mark didn't seem to find his joke amusing as he simply continued tugging the edges of the sheets from under the bed frame with a focused expression on his face, his tongue sticking out of his mouth.

"There," he said moments later as he stood up, admiring his masterpiece.

The bed looked like it was a completely different one than the one Kevin slept on just a minute ago.

"Wow. I'm impressed, Mark," he nodded.

"You can thank me later. Come on, let's get ready for the lecture," he said and headed outside the cabin.

On their way out, Mark proceeded to explain about the lectures they had five times a week.

"So, mornings are essentially used for either assigned duties or training. Like learning essentials about survival in nature, giving first aid, that kinda thing. Afternoons are for duties and lectures. Make sure to pay attention because we'll be given a final exam in a few weeks. If you pass, you get a certificate or something. Weekends are just for work."

"Man, this camp blows," Kevin disappointedly pointed out.

The campers outside looked tired, contrasting the ones from cabin four, most of whom were looking fresh and well-rested. Kevin was given a few contemptuous glances, but he did his best to ignore them deliberately. He still felt guilty for pinning the extra work on them, but he would have said the same thing to Dwight if he could turn back the clock. He happened to glance in Michael's direction and noticed that the camper was staring at him. When he realized Kevin saw him, he quickly moved his glance away and pretended to adjust his shoes.

"Seriously, what is that guy's problem?" Kevin asked Mark. "I know I messed up and all, but he seemed to dislike me right from the start."

Mark shrugged.

"I guess Michael's just like that. Probably not very friendly toward new faces or whatever."

Kevin scoffed. He looked away from Michael and decided to pass the time by talking to Mark. They exchanged tidbits about their lives back home, what they liked doing, that kind of thing. Although both of them were usually busy with school and homework, Kevin mentioned that he enjoyed spending time with his friends away from home since he wasn't on great terms with his parents. He told Mark how he'd often listen to rock on his earphones in his locked room when he was home or would simply blast it on the speakers, just to avoid any interaction with his parents.

He didn't share any details about his parents but instead asked Mark to talk about his own life. Mark was a food enthusiast, which was visible on him – as he put it - and his parents used every opportunity they could to remind him of that, even going as far as comparing him to his much skinnier peers. This put a lot of stress on him and instead caused him to eat even more. He didn't have any friends, so he spent a lot of his time reading and playing video games as well as with his sister Sherry.

Listening to his story, Kevin almost felt grateful for the life he had back home. His parents weren't great, sure, but at least they weren't belittling him like Mark's parents did.

"Hey, when this is all over, I'll come visit you and Sherry in Idaho. Or you two can come visit me in Portland," Kevin patted Mark on the back. "We can play some Call of Duty if you want."

"No, I'm bad at Call of Duty. Or any other first-person shooters. I mostly play single-player games," Mark somberly said, looking at his feet.

It was visible from his gradual tone change that he was feeling blue, but Kevin couldn't tell if it was homesickness or just the fact that he reflected on his life the way he did.

"Okay. How about some fighting games? Mortal Kombat?"

Mark's gloomy expression changed when he turned his lips up and said with a weak smile, "Deal. But be warned, I've played Mortal Kombat for years now. I mean, I didn't have a chance to play with people much, but the ones who went up against me lost. Except for Sherry," he quickly added. "I usually let her win."

"You're a good brother, Mark. Alright, you got yourself a challenger, then," Kevin smiled.

Talking about the things they would do together once this was all over felt good. It brightened Kevin's bleak mood in this god-forsaken place and reminded him about the good things at home. His moment of respite was short-lived, though, because the next thing he knew, Ninja clasped his hands around his mouth and shouted at the top of his lungs.

"It's three forty-five! Move out!"

"Well, time to go, I guess," Kevin tentatively stood up along with Mark.

***

The study hall was right next to the main lodge and partially across the mess hall. Although it looked somewhat the size of the main lodge on the outside, it felt much smaller on the inside. It was a one-story wooden building, not unlike the rest of the structures in Camp Firwood. It consisted of one narrow corridor, which had six rooms – five classrooms and one unmarked door. Cabin four campers were to enter classroom four, which was the second door on the left.

The classroom had a blackboard, a teachers' desk, and ten student desks, all neatly lined up in two rows of five desks each. A small TV, which looked like it had been there from the 90s, sat in the corner of the room on a metallic cart with wheels, which Kevin assumed would be used for educational purposes.

"Where do I need to sit?" Kevin asked as they entered the classroom.

"Doesn't matter. As long as you're here," Mark said and took up the front seat.

"Wait, why don't we sit in the back?" Kevin pointed to the seats that were already being taken up by other campers.

"It doesn't matter. This isn't like school. You have to pay attention, and you can't speak," Mark shrugged.

"Pfft," Kevin puffed at the absurdity of yet another rule in the camp.

He sat at the desk left of Mark, shaking his head at the irony of spending his summer in a school chair. Minutes later, another counselor, Kevin hadn't seen before, waltzed inside, and the murmurs of the campers immediately stopped. It wasn't like back in school when the students gradually stopped speaking because some of them simply didn't see the counselor walk in.

This was an instantaneous silence that immediately shredded the room. Kevin didn't want to stick out like a sore thumb, so he followed the other campers' examples and kept silent. The counselor was older than Dwight but younger than Mr. Adams, maybe in his mid-twenties, and looked like a typical pretty-boy with well-combed hair and blue eyes, which girls would be falling for. He also looked fit, and Kevin couldn't help but feel somewhat jealous. The counselor took off his side backpack and gently placed it on the table.

"Good afternoon, campers," he softly said as he sat down.

"Good afternoon, Mr. Owens," the campers chanted unanimously, too fast for Kevin to do it along with them.

Dammit, Mark, you should have told me.

Counselor Owens unzipped the backpack and pulled out a notebook. He took out a pen that he held tucked into his front pocket, much like Mr. Adams, and clicked it (only once). He opened the notebook and stared at the pages, tentatively flipping them one by one. Eventually, he found the right page and placed the pen on the paper.

"Camper Norton," he called out and glanced up at the class attendees.

Tough Norton raised his hand and roared.

"Me!"

Mr. Owens continued by calling on the other campers one by one. When he got to number nine, he said, "Camper William."

He looked up, and when no one responded, he called out again, this time more loudly.

"Camper William isn't with us anymore, Mr. Owens," Steve said.

"Oh, right," the counselor looked down at his notebook and, with swift motions, scratched something out. "We have someone else instead of William now, right? Camper Kevin."

"Me," Kevin said, raising his hand.

The counselor looked at him and nodded before looking down at his notebook and jotting something down briefly. He clicked his pen and tucked it back into his pocket before slamming the notebook shut and shoving it back inside his backpack.

He did everything with such finesse that Kevin couldn't help but start feeling an ember of hate forming inside him toward the counselor. He couldn't tell why exactly he felt that way until it hit him – because everything about Counselor Owens felt shallow. He was practically perfect on the outside, but what was in his head? What was he like as a person? Did he care more about having perfectly combed hair for the day than actually doing something good, or was his personality as good as his looks? Was he able to run a mile without getting winded, or was his fit appearance just there to look good? How confident or judgmental or kind was he?

Those questions raced through Kevin's mind until the counselor looked back up at the campers and leaned in his (much more comfortable) chair and said, "Well, campers, you already learned the basics of building a campfire and starting a fire with the equipment you have, but you still haven't learned how to start a fire *without equipment*, so that's what we'll learn today."

He stood up and approached the blackboard, turning his back to the campers.

Even the uncomfortable uniform looks so well-tailored on him.

The counselor began writing something on the blackboard.

This would be a great time to talk to others, Kevin thought to himself, but when he looked at Mark and then left at Javier, he realized that all the campers were paying careful attention, staring directly at the blackboard.

"I'm right here. Where the hell do you think you're looking, camper?!" the counselor's voice roared so fiercely that it startled Kevin.

He looked at Mr. Owens in time to see the counselor angrily staring at him. Once he realized that he'd grabbed Kevin's attention, he turned back to the blackboard and continued drawing something with the chalk. The ember of hate, which previously formed in Kevin, sparked into a full-blown fire.

"So, as I was saying. You have a spindle, which you will use for friction…" Owens continued.

Kevin continued staring at the blackboard but tuned out.

Just a little longer, and I'll be getting the fuck out of this place. He gritted his teeth and used every chance when Mr. Owens was turned around to sneak a peek at the clock on the wall.

***

"That was even more boring than my history teacher's classes," Kevin sighed to Mark once they were out of the study hall two hours later.

"Well, you never know when this stuff may come in handy," Mark responded.

"So why aren't we taking any notes or anything like that?" Kevin asked.

Mark shrugged.

"I guess they want us to memorize it. We have most of it in practice in the woods, too."

"That's the one upside of this fucked up place. I always wanted to learn something related to survival in nature. I just didn't know it was so boring," Kevin said.

"Not me. I hate going outside," Mark said.

As they made their way past the mess hall, they saw the groundskeeper sweeping around it. He gave Kevin a brief contemptuous glance before continuing to do his work.

"I thought the campers did the sweeping earlier," Kevin frowned, glancing behind himself at the groundskeeper.

"The groundskeeper still needs to sweep up the remainder of the fallen leaves. I guess the campers made his job easier for him, huh?"

They returned to their cabins and had another hour to kill before dinner time. By then, the blue sky had already been replaced by orange color, slowly bringing about the end of the day. Kevin hated sunsets. For some reason, they always filled him with a sense of profound sadness. He preferred winters where the orange color could be entirely skipped and replaced by the star-riddled sky.

By this time, he was impatiently tapping his foot on the floor, waiting for the time to pass so that he could find Mr. Adams and call his parents. He contemplated doing it now instead, but he didn't want to bother the counselor in case he was busy with some other work, as much as he wanted out.

At 19:15, Dwight came to the cabins and lined up the campers. He personally led them to the mess hall and decided on the order of cabins, making sure that cabin four was last in line. It was a personal fuck you to Kevin for talking to him with disrespect earlier, but he didn't mind.

They had rice with meat and mushrooms, which was a downgrade from what they had for lunch. Kevin couldn't even tell which animal the meat came from or even what the meal itself was until he took a closer look. Combining his disgust with the fact that he wasn't feeling too hungry, he gave Mark his meal. Mark happily took it from him and wolfed down both bowls, making sure to ask Kevin a few times between bites if he was sure about relinquishing his meal.

Kevin looked around to see where Mr. Adams was, but he was nowhere in sight. Dwight was there, and so was another counselor he hadn't seen earlier, but not Mr. Adams.

"I'll be back in a sec," Kevin said and jumped out of his chair.

He approached the new counselor, who was observing the situation around. The man became aware of him immediately but only glanced at him briefly before continuing his surveillance of the campers.

"Excuse me, have you seen Mr. Adams?" he asked.

"He's not available at this time. You can talk to him in the morning," the man briskly said, not dignifying Kevin with a glance.

"No, he told me to find him after dinner," Kevin shook his head. "Is he in the main lodge?"

"You can talk to him in the morning," the man responded disinterestedly.

Feeling frustrated with this counselor's lack of help, Kevin turned on his heel and exited the mess hall. He was the first one to be outside, and by this time, night had already fallen, and the sounds of crickets filled the air. Kevin made his way to the back entrance of the main lodge but found it to be locked.

That's... strange.

He started to feel a knot turning in his stomach, but ignoring it, he made his way around the building and to the main entrance. Before he even rounded the corner, he heard two voices chit-chatting with each other. He got to the front door and saw two young counselors standing in front, wearing smiles on their faces while gesturing and talking about something. As soon as one of them saw Kevin, his smile dropped, and he raised his hand with a shout.

"Hey! You there, camper! Where do you think you're going?"

The two of them took menacing steps forward until they were towering right in front of Kevin.

"I'm looking for Mr. Adams. He told me to find him after dinner," Kevin said, all confidence drained from his voice.

The counselors exchanged glances with each other before the one who shouted asked, "Do you have a duty that Mr. Adams assigned to you?"

"No. He told me to find him after dinner so I can call someone to pick me up," he said, the knot in his stomach twisting with more intensity now.

The counselor sighed with a disappointed expression on his face. He scratched his cheek and said, "Mr. Adams isn't available during these hours. You'd best go back to your cabin. You can talk to him in the morning."

Kevin shook his head, pointing his index finger to the ground.

"No, you don't understand. I already asked him earlier today to give me my cellphone, but he said he was busy. And then he told me to-"

The other counselor repeatedly tried interrupting Kevin.

"He told me to find him after dinner. Now let me in so I can talk to him!"

"Okay, that's enough!" the first counselor said. "You get your ass back to the cabin, or I will drag you to the detention house, you understand?"

Detention house?

Kevin seriously contemplated punching the counselor in his groin, but he could tell from his facial expression that he was serious. They eyed each other for a long moment, and the counselor looked like he was ready to jump on Kevin.

"Fine," Kevin finally said, turning around and starting the way he came.

"Ronnie, go escort him back. Make sure he doesn't do something stupid," the counselor said, pointing to his quieter partner.

Kevin was fuming by this time. An imaginary scenario played out in his head where he kicked the counselor in the groin and then punched him in the face while he was keeled over, effectively knocking him out. He turned around and shot the counselor an angry look, weighing whether actually fulfilling his fantasy would be worth it.

"What? You got a problem, camper? Get your fucking ass back to your cabin. Now. Before I give you a whole week in detention," the counselor said, now more authoritatively and with a higher tone.

Feeling angry but powerless, Kevin turned around and stomped away with the other counselor's steps following closely behind. They walked in silence until they reached the back of the main lodge.

"Your friends are still in front of the mess hall. Go join them," the counselor said, pointing to the group of people in front of the mess hall.

Not willing to argue anymore, Kevin made his way toward the group, bearing the curious glances of the other campers.

"Hey, Dwight!" the counselor shouted, grabbing the attention of the assistant counselor right away.

"What?" Dwight shouted, and just then, Kevin saw him emerge from the shadowy part under the mess hall.

"You got a problematic one. Keep an eye on him until he's back in his cabin, will ya?"

Dwight shot an angry look at Kevin before scoffing and turning back to the other counselor.

"Sure, you got it."

The counselor who escorted Kevin turned around and left while Kevin started walking toward the middle of the crowd, trying to blend in, despite most of the faces being turned in his direction.

"Hold up, camper!" Dwight called out to him.

Kevin stopped in his tracks and made an angry grimace before turning around to face Dwight. The assistant counselor stood with hands on his hips, staring down at Kevin with a malevolent look on his face.

"What do you want?" Kevin asked.

Dwight took another step closer so he was merely inches away from Kevin's face. He leaned closer to his ear and, with a low tone, said, "You'd do best to watch your fucking mouth, camper. You're not home anymore. And you're gonna be here for a looong time. So you'd best get ready to take orders."

He stepped back with a contented smile before turning around and shouting, "Alright, shitstains! Back to your cabins! NOW!"

He turned to Kevin and said with a smirk, "That's one extra point added to your Trial," with that, he left.

The campers immediately started moving like a herd back toward the cabins. Kevin stood, feeling defeated for a moment, waiting until he had blended with the middle of the crowd. He then started walking along with them, holding his head down the entire time. The knot twisting earlier in his stomach was gone now, and he was instead left feeling drained of all energy, devoid of any willpower. He was too tired to even fight back. Once he was back in his cabin and he sat down on his bed, he started processing what just happened. This was a dream. It had to be. He couldn't possibly be a prisoner in this camp, could he?

"Now, do you believe me?" Mark appeared next to him with a bland facial expression.

Kevin lethargically looked in his direction, still deep in his thoughts, only half-processing what Mark said.

"What?" he asked confusedly.

"You can't leave, can you?" Mark asked.

Kevin realized just then that all eyes in the cabin were directed at him. The campers were standing around his bed and staring at him with expressionless faces.

"No, I can leave. It's just... Mr. Adams is busy tonight is all," Kevin said, looking down.

"Sure, he is. Just like every night," Ninja said. "And then when you talk to him in the morning, he tells you he forgot and promises he'll give you your phone after dinner. And if you argue, you get detention."

"So what... you're trying to say that the parents didn't know they were signing us up for a prison? And for what purpose?" Kevin jeered with ironic laughter.

Mark made a grimace, which vocalized *ummm* instead of him. Other campers just exchanged glances awkwardly.

"The Firwood Wraith," Steve said. "Campers are being sacrificed to it."

"Oh, come on, Steve. Not this shit again," Clean Ryan said annoyedly. "There's no such thing as ghosts!"

"Well, then what happened to the other campers, Norton? Why did they go missing?" Steve asked.

"They didn't go missing! They left! They completed their trial and left!"

Voices broke out, some confirming Steve's statements, others disagreeing and saying it was nonsense.

"Something *is* out there!" Steve finally said and silenced the others. "If it's not the wraith, then something else."

Utter silence fell on the room.

"Are you guys serious?" Kevin raised his eyebrows. "So you wanna tell me that the camp punishes the campers by sacrificing them to some Boogeyman in the woods? Come on!"

He shot up from his bed and said exasperatedly, "I gotta say you had me there for a moment, but the story is too far-fetched. Gotta hand it to you guys, though. You really organized the prank well."

He laughed while the other campers stared at him in silence.

"We're not fucking with you, Kevin," Tough Norton said, sitting on his own bed. "You think we wanna be here? You think we wanna do as these pricks tell us?"

"Norton's right," Steve said. "None of us wanna be here."

Clean Ryan interjected. "That doesn't mean we're prisoners here. Don't listen to them, Kevin. They didn't tell you that in addition to picking campers for The Trial, they also pick one well-behaved camper to go home earlier!"

"What? Is that true?" Kevin asked.

Steve hesitated.

"Well, yes, but that doesn't take away from the fact that campers who are picked for The Trial need to go to the woods to survive a number of days, based on how many negative points you got. And not to mention that most of us have been here much longer than we should have been."

Kevin remained silent, not knowing what to say in response.

"Norton," Steve called out to him. "How long have you been here?"

"Eight weeks," Norton nonchalantly said.

He was splayed on his bed like on a beach, on his elbow and with one leg stretched out.

"And when were you supposed to leave?" Steve asked.

Norton kept quiet for a moment before answering more somberly this time, "Two goddamn weeks ago."

"And why did they send you here?" Steve asked, staring at Kevin.

"Behavioral correction, or some shit like that."

Kevin glanced at Norton and then back at Steve. Steve put his hand on Mark's shoulder and asked, "Mark, you've been here for almost two weeks now. Why did they send you here?"

Mark scratched his arm and looked down shyly.

"My parents said it was a weight loss camp. They said it would last ten weeks."

"Javier, what about you?" Steve looked at the camper.

"Eight weeks. Sent for cultural awareness training. Was supposed to leave last week," Javier recited, giving Kevin a contemptuous glower.

Steve threw his hands up as if to show he proved a point and said, "See? We were all sent here for different reasons. So by all rights, each camper should have different training here, right? But we all do the same shit. And most of us were already supposed to leave. But we can't leave. And we can't talk to our parents under some excuse that it would break the immersion."

"Bullshit!" Kevin retorted angrily. "Your parents would have arrived here by now. The police would have come to investigate. Your story has holes in it."

Steve shook his head.

"That's the thing. Nobody is coming to check up on us. I know this sounds hard to believe, but it's the truth."

Nerdy Van jumped to interject.

"I honestly think you guys are blowing it out of proportion. We were clearly sent here for some improvement, yes, but I don't think we're actual prisoners. And I sure as heck don't believe that the Firwood Wraith as anything more than a figment of our imagination, blown out of proportions by the circulating stories."

"Then why aren't our parents coming to pick us up?" Norton asked with a hint of frustration in his voice.

"Because if they told us the camp lasted longer, we'd object," Nerdy Van said, "Think of it this way. Maybe the camp has a job to fix something about us that our parents requested or maybe not. Maybe they just want us to be more disciplined, more obedient, and hard-working. If they told us that they were sending us to the camp for those reasons, most of us would rebel and come back from the camp worse off than we were before we joined."

Kevin's head was spinning. He didn't know what to believe anymore. A prisoner in a summer camp? A murdering ghost?

"So then, why don't you just leave? There are no walls or anything to stop you from running; you could easily just leave the place."

Steve shook his head before Kevin even finished his sentence, further elevating his frustration.

"Haven't you been listening to what we just said? Most of the campers are afraid of stepping near the woods because of the Firwood Wraith. Even if they were brave enough, they wouldn't last long enough. Who knows how far these woods go."

Javier interjected.

"The counselors here don't even need to have eyes everywhere since no one will try to escape. It would be suicide. Last year, a camper tried it and died in the woods."

"It's true," Mark nodded fervently. "The counselors always remind us how there are dangerous animals and bear traps set all over the place. They said if you step into one of those, it'll break your leg, and you're as good as dead."

"Yeah, it might take you days to reach any place where other humans live," Slow Ethan responded.

"We're in Oregon, it can't be that far, right?"

"Do you have any idea where exactly we even are?" Steve asked.

"I dunno, Deschutes National Forest? Williamette? Ochoco? Shit, I dunno, man. No idea which direction we even went in."

"Exactly. You could be stumbling for days and end up nowhere," Steve said.

Kevin rubbed his eyes. He felt frustrated, confused, angry, and many other negative emotions he couldn't recognize. This couldn't be happening. He was home yesterday. He talked and chilled with his friends and planned what they were going to do when he returned home. And now he was a prisoner in Camp Firwood with no way to escape? No, the campers must be wrong. He would prove them wrong.

He pointed his finger to the ground and angrily. "So let me just get this straight. Campers here typically stay longer than usual, but they get to leave either by getting picked during the so-called Choosing to go home, due to good behavior or by making it through The Trial? And if I understood correctly, The Trial is basically surviving in the woods based on the number of negative points you were given?" Steve nodded and opened his mouth, but

Kevin raised his tone. "And you guys never get to see what happened to the campers after they get picked in The Choosing, so you believe that the campers who go through The Trial are getting killed by a wraith in the woods? And that we are prisoners in this camp?"

Steve looked at the other campers, but all of them remained silent. Kevin scoffed and shook his head before saying, "I'm leaving tomorrow, one way or another. And when I do, I'm calling the police and shutting this whole fucking place down. There's no way in hell I'm letting them abuse campers like this."

Steve sighed loudly and glanced down at his feet before looking back up at Kevin with a pitiful look in his eye.

"We should get ready for lights out. It's gonna be a long day tomorrow."

He turned around and made his way through the crowd of campers, back to his locker next to Kevin's bed. The other campers seemed to consider this the end of the discussion, so they, too, went to take off their uniforms and don their pajamas, after which they picked up their hygiene items from the top drawer.

They folded their uniforms in a similar fashion like the extra set that was kept in the locker, and they placed it on top of the drawer. Kevin mimicked their actions and put his own uniform on top neatly. The campers went to brush their teeth one by one in the tiny restroom they had. The biggest problem seemed to come from Slow Ethan since he spent way more time than the others in there. Once Steve was done, and it was Kevin's turn, he patted Steve on the back and asked, "Where are the showers?"

"There aren't any," Steve replied.

"What? So how do we clean ourselves?" Kevin shot him a wide-eyed glance.

"You don't. Once a week, the counselors take us to the showers, and we have ten minutes to wash there." Steve picked up his toothbrush and paste, making his way back to the sleeping quarters with the squeaking sound of his slippers with each step.

Wow. This just keeps getting better and better.

The campers spent some more time talking to each other or lying in bed. Nerdy Van was reading a book about survival in nature, which the camp so generously decided to give him. At some point during this time, Kevin glanced through the window on the left side of the cabin and saw a commotion coming from cabin three. All the campers lined up and were standing next to their beds, still.

Mark approached Kevin and told him, "Dwight will be here soon for a roll call. When he enters, just stand right here next to your bed and answer when he calls you."

Kevin nodded, lacking any more strength to ask or say anything back. Within less than a minute, the commotion in cabin three ended, and the main entrance of cabin four swung open. Dwight's punchable face appeared in the sleeping quarters. He was carrying a notepad similar to the one Mr. Adams was using.

"Line up!" One of the campers shouted to alert the others.

Everyone in the room shot out of their beds and stood up on the left side of their beds. Kevin was right across from Mark, so they were staring at each other face to face. There was a moment of silence until Dwight started calling on the campers one by one.

Once all ten were checked as present, he turned around and left the cabin without a word. Then the commotion came in cabin five, which Kevin was able to see from the window on his side of the wall. By this time, all the campers in cabin four got in their beds and covered themselves. Kevin did the same, trying to sleep on his side but unable to due to the narrowness of the bed.

He turned on his back, knowing he would probably have a hard time falling asleep in that position. The lights suddenly went out, leaving only the moonlight gleaming in through the window with a dark-blueish glow. Somewhere in the distance, music started playing. Kevin perked up his ears, trying to decipher what the music was, but it was barely audible. The more he listened, the more he recognized it, and with a sickening feeling, he realized that it was the same music that Mr. Adams was humming earlier that day.

A minute later, the music stopped. He thought about his friends. Right now, they could be sitting in Henry's place and drinking. He wondered if they thought about him or if they continued hanging out as if he was never even a part of their group. He saw Amy's smile in his mind's eye, and it gave him some comfort.

Despite being dead-tired, he couldn't fall asleep for another hour.

5

The communications building

Kevin was startled awake by the same anthem that played last night. This time, however, it was loud enough to wake up the dead. He opened his eyes and shot up from his bed to sit on the edge. He realized that the bright morning light illuminated the cabin, effectively blinding him in his groggy condition. The other campers were already hopping out of their beds and opening their drawers, grabbing their toothbrushes. Kevin yanked the covers off of himself and swung his feet to the left, hopping out of his own bed.

"Come on," Mark said raspily in the commotion. "We gotta brush our teeth, make our beds, put on our uniforms, and get ready for lineup."

Kevin shook his head, unable to utter any coherent words after the shocking wake-up call. He rubbed his eyes and, after clambering up to his feet, opened the top drawer of his locker, and snagged the brush and paste. He jumped into his slippers and made his way to the lineup of campers in front of the bathroom. One by one, they were finishing up brushing their teeth and rushing back inside the sleeping quarters. By this time, Kevin was still feeling hazy from waking up early, albeit a little less. He found out moments later that they were woken up at 7 a.m.

Mark waited for Kevin to finish up, and once they got back, they made their beds and jumped into their uniforms. Mark corrected the remaining blemishes on Kevin's bed and then straightened his uniform, correcting his collar and telling him to tuck his shirt inside the pants neatly.

"Remember, no wrinkles," Mark said.

"What, not even on my uniform?" Kevin said as he reluctantly stuffed the bottom of his shirt inside the pants on all sides.

111

"Yes. They don't take lightly to that."

"Well, fuck them very much," Kevin said, starting to finally wake up a little bit.

It was nearing twenty minutes past seven when Mark and Kevin got out in front of the cabins. Some of the other campers were already there, and the ones who were still inside were coming out one by one. The crowd was becoming larger and larger by the minute, but the lack of enthusiasm was apparent in the group.

By 7:30, Mr. Adams and Dwight arrived at the cabins. Mr. Adams was carrying his same notepad as yesterday, looking fresh and well-rested.

"Line up, campers!" he shouted jovially, and the campers needed no more pushing.

They quickly rushed into their memorized spots. Kevin remembered where he was supposed to stand and promptly got between Michael and Steve. He planned on simply sitting by the table on the side until he got Mr. Adams' attention, but he knew that that would probably only get the campers in trouble again. He would wait until Mr. Adams was done with his bullshit inspection routine.

The chirping of birds and Mr. Adams scribbling something on his notepad were heard for a while, mixed with the silent breeze blowing in the branches of the trees.

"Campers, recite," Mr. Adams commanded.

Immediately, the campers unanimously began reciting.

"Discipline is the mother of all values. Discipline is the bridge between goals and accomplishments. By following the rules of the camp, I will become a disciplined and better person. Discipline is the core value of Camp Firwood. Discipline is the core value of life."

Kevin listened, mesmerized, wondering if he had perhaps stumbled into a fucking cult, rather than a summer camp. He wanted to laugh but, again, refused to get the campers in more trouble.

"Dwight, go inspect the cabins," Mr. Adams said and clicked his pen.

Dwight nodded, mumbling a meager "Yes, Mr. Adams," before running behind the lined-up campers and into the first of the cabins. Mr. Adams then started the roll call, beginning with cabin one. The whole process took a few minutes until the list even reached Kevin. When Kevin shouted, "Me," Mr. Adams shot him a glance before checking him off the list, not showing anyhow that he remembered who he was or what he promised him yesterday.

Once everyone was accounted for, Mr. Adams lowered his notepad just in time for Dwight to return from cabin five. He made his way around the left side of the campers toward Mr. Adams.

"What have you got, Dwight?" Mr. Adams asked, placing his hands behind his back.

Dwight stopped next to Mr. Adams and read aloud, "Cabin two, bed seven. Not made well."

Mr. Adams mumbled an *mhm*, before looking through his notepad and taking out his pen, clicking it loudly three times.

"Cabin two, bed seven, camper Shane." He looked up at the first row.

One of the campers from the front row raised his head with a meager shout of *me*. Mr. Adams nodded and scribbled something down.

"That's four negative points already, camper Shane. What else, Dwight?" he turned back to Dwight.

"Cabin four, bed nine."

Son of a bitch.

Kevin gritted his teeth in anger. There was no way his bed wasn't made well; he and Mark made sure it was up to standard.

"Cabin four, bed nine, camper Kevin," Mr. Adams called out, raising his chin to get a better look at the back rows.

Kevin didn't respond but instead just stared at Mr. Adams. The counselor darted his eyes around the campers.

The fucker is pretending not to know who I am.

113

"He's the one, Mr. Adams!" Dwight impatiently pointed his finger at Kevin, glancing at Mr. Adams in anticipation.

Mr. Adams squinted at Kevin, pointing his pen at him.

"Are you camper Kevin?"

Kevin stared at him angrily, waiting for Mr. Adams to correct himself, but he instead found himself locked in a staring contest.

"Just say yes," Steve mumbled through his teeth.

"Yes," Kevin hissed.

"That's not how you address the head counselor, camper!" Dwight shouted, shooting Kevin a frown, furrowing his nose.

"Quiet, Dwight," Mr. Adams interrupted him as he glanced down at his notepad. "Why aren't you answering when called on, camper?"

He looked up from his notepad in Kevin's direction, staring him down for a prolonged moment. He sighed and looked back at his papers, tapping his pen upon the notepad.

"What was wrong with his bed?" he asked Dwight, not moving his eyes from the notepad.

"It was a complete mess, Mr. Adams," Dwight excitedly said. "The sheets were not tightly tucked in, and the blanket was not folded."

Kevin was on the verge of calling Dwight a liar, but he stopped himself at the last second. He didn't want to get the other campers punished again.

"Mhm," Mr. Adams said as he scribbled something down. "Okay, since it's only your second day, camper, I'm not gonna give you an extra day for The Trial. Let's see now…"

He tapped his pen on the notepad continuously, which made the air feel heavy in anticipation of what was to come. Finally, he looked in Dwight's direction and said, "Give him thirty minutes of bed-making."

Dwight stared at Mr. Adams obediently, not uttering a word. Mr. Adams continued, "Make sure you're there, watching him the entire time. And bring him to join the rest of the campers in the mess hall once you're done. You understand?"

"Yes, Mr. Adams. But who will take the campers to the mess hall?" Dwight looked concerned, although Kevin assumed that he just didn't want to spend the next thirty minutes teaching one individual camper how to make his bed properly.

"I will. Don't you worry about that, Dwighty-boy. Just teach camper Kevin how to make his bed."

"Yes, Mr. Adams." Dwight nodded energetically and immediately started making his way through the ranks of campers with hurried steps.

"Come on, camper! Move your ass!" he shouted at Kevin.

Kevin shot Mr. Adams one last angry glance, fuming on the inside, but the counselor was staring elsewhere. It felt like he was deliberately avoiding looking at Kevin. With utter hesitation, Kevin followed Dwight behind the lines of campers and toward cabin four. Mr. Adams' jovial voice bellowed from behind him.

"Alright, campers! Follow me!"

As soon as I call my parents and they're on their way here, I'll fuck you up, Counselor Adams.

"Get in," Dwight stopped next to the staircase and gestured with his head for Kevin to step inside the cabin.

Kevin silently obeyed, taking off his shoes in the foyer (all the while being hurried by Dwight) and swinging the door of the sleeping quarters open. He walked over to his bed, and the sight in front of him made him want to turn around, jump on Dwight, and smash his head on the wooden floor. The bedsheets were messily untucked from his bed on one side, and the blanket was left in a heap at the foot of the bed.

"What the hell did you do to my bed, Dwight?!" Kevin gestured to the bed as he angrily retorted to Dwight.

"That's Assistant Counselor Dwight, to you, fuckface. You got it?!" Dwight got into his face, staring down at him from the height.

115

Kevin relentlessly stared up at him, refusing to back down. If he backed down or looked away, Dwight would have the upper hand.

"Well, what are you waiting for? Start making your bed, camper!" Dwight leaned even closer, a gust of his rancid breath hitting Kevin in the face.

Kevin turned around and knelt in front of his bed, partially just to get away from Dwight's putrid breath. He began straightening the sheets and tucking them under the mattress. It took him a minute to undo Dwight's sabotage and adequately fold the blanket.

I'm getting the hang of this, he thought to himself with a mixture of anger and pride.

"There," Kevin angrily remarked.

"Let me see that," Dwight shoved him aside and stepped closer to the bed.

He bent down to look for any blemishes and then walked around the bed, carefully inspecting every nook and cranny.

"Okay. But we still have about twenty-five minutes," he finally retorted, grabbing the sheets and yanking them off the mattress. "Get to it."

The blanket on top of the sheets woefully unfurled on the bed as Kevin stared at the messy bed. He imagined grabbing the sheets and strangling Dwight with them, but there was no way he would be able to do that, of course. Dwight was much bigger than him. He could possibly throw a successful punch or two, but there was no way he could overpower this gorilla.

He did manage to beat one bigger guy in a fight once, back when he and the gang were hanging out in a secluded street basketball court. A group of three people was passing by, and one of them, a tall oaf, stopped by the fence and kept throwing comments in their direction, mostly insults directed at Luis. Luis said he didn't know his name, but he knew him from his school as a guy who constantly bullied others. Kevin didn't want to stand for that shit, so he called out the guy.

116

Pretty soon, the two groups were facing each other in the center of the court with Kevin and the oaf at the front, chest to chest. He was taller by at least a whole head and looked like he weighed double Kevin's weight, but that didn't stop Kevin from fighting back. He wasn't even going to start a fight, but when the fat oaf tossed a comment in Amy's direction about how he'd like to take her for a ride, Kevin's fist automatically flew up toward the fucker's face.

He knocked him down on his knee and, from there, landed another punch that toppled him sideways on the ground. The bully was suddenly no longer tough, but instead shielded his face with both hands and pleaded with Kevin to stop. Seeing this, Kevin got an even higher burst of adrenaline, and he ordered the bully and his two lackeys to get out of there before he beats up all of them.

The oaf scrambled up to his feet and began staggering out of the court along with his two friends, shouting something cliché down the lines of, 'This isn't over.' The next thirty minutes or so were spent with Kevin being the center of the attention, praised by Henry, Rick, Luis, and Amy as the hero of the group. Amy thanked him and gave him a kiss on the cheek, which made him burn with a pride he'd never experienced before. Luis later confirmed that the bully always looked the other way when they saw each other in school, much to Kevin's contentment.

Now that Kevin was with Dwight in the room, he tried to compare him to the oaf from Luis' school in his mind's eye. The oaf was just fat, and Dwight looked somewhat muscular, athletic even. There was no way Kevin could take him down even with a surprise punch.

No problem. I'll do as he asks. And then I'm outta here.

He bent down and started making his bed, more slowly this time. He knew that Dwight was going to revel in every minute of his punishment, so he may as well take it slower so that he doesn't need to make his bed so many times. The next twenty minutes were filled with grueling making and unmaking, coupled with Dwight's taunts and insults, calling Kevin a useless snail, an unsuccessful abortion, and a few other demeaning names. Kevin ignored all of them and silently made his bed, time after time, knowing that the end was near.

"Alright, you're done here for now," Dwight said with a hint of disappointment in his voice. "Get to the mess hall."

Kevin stood up, his knees painful from the kneeling, and went toward the exit.

"Not so fast, camper," Dwight called out from behind.

Kevin pressed his lips tightly together and turned around to see what Dwight wanted. The assistant counselor grabbed the bedsheet and yanked it, unmaking Kevin's bed. He then did the same thing to the other four beds in the same row and said, "Looks like your cabin mates didn't make their own beds. So you'll have to do it for them. Make sure they're nice and tight before you go to the mess hall." He pushed his way past Kevin with his shoulder with a smirk on his face.

A moment later, the sound of the entrance door opening resounded, and Dwight's voice came from behind Kevin.

"Oh, and, uh, you better hurry if you don't want to stay hungry because the mess hall closes in less than ten minutes."

Dwight shut the door, leaving Kevin alone in the room with messed-up beds. Kevin was on the verge of crying from anger. He kicked the leg of the closest bed, fuming. He inhaled through his teeth and exhaled with a hiss, staring at the mess in front of him. He thought about simply leaving without actually making the beds, but something in him pushed him to complete his camper's duty. It wasn't a camper's obligation.

It was an obligation to his peers.

It took him more than five minutes, and he was covered in sweat by the time he was done since he rushed to finish the job. Once he finally finished, he rushed out of the cabin and, with a sprint, made his way toward the mess hall. By the time he arrived, all the campers were already sitting outside, finished with their meals.

"Kevin, how was the-" Mark started with a look of curiosity on his face.

"Not now!" Kevin shouted, rushing inside the mess hall.

The building was empty, save for campers on kitchen duty who were cleaning the tables. The food line was unattended, and with dread, Kevin rushed to it, desperately looking for someone to serve him. There was still food there, from what he could tell. Scrambled eggs and low-quality looking sausages, although it was evident from the lack of steam and color that they had long since gone cold.

"Hello!" Kevin shouted, eagerly holding his platter and trying to glance behind the food line.

Lunch Lady Daisy peeked through the door in inquisitiveness seconds later. She waddled to the food line and jerked her head up at Kevin.

"What?" she asked.

"I had some duties. I just arrived for breakfast," Kevin said.

"Food line is closed. Come back for lunch," the lady emotionlessly retorted before turning around.

"No, wait. You don't understand. I just finished my duties. I couldn't come earlier. Can I please have some food?"

The lunch lady leaned on the counter and, with a frown, said, "Boy, if I say the food line is closed, that means the food line is closed. I don't make exceptions. Now get on out of here before I call the counselors!"

She waved her gigantic arms toward the exit door, her triceps wobbling furiously in the process. Was there a point in arguing with her? Probably not. He would just get himself or his fellow campers in more trouble. Kevin threw the platter loudly on top of the other platters and stormed out, feeling angry and hungry.

The campers were talking to each other and luckily didn't bat an eye toward Kevin, which he was grateful for. He didn't want to answer the questions he expected them to ask about Dwight and the punishment. When as he stepped out, a hand grabbed his shoulder.

"Hey Kev, you okay?" Mark asked him.

"I'm fine, Mark. Look, I really don't feel like talking right now, so…"

"Okay, just hold on a second," Mark bent sideways and reached into his pocket.

He glanced around in suspicion like a thief, and moments later, he pulled out something that looked like a sandwich, but upon closer inspection, Kevin realized it was actually a sausage between two pieces of bread.

"I figured you wouldn't make it in time, so I told Jeremy to sneak me another sausage on the line," Mark said, handing the food to Kevin. "Here, eat it before one of the counselors sees it."

Kevin lethargically took the sandwich, his mind absent. He was overwhelmed suddenly with a flood of emotions. Mark, the rule-abiding camper, snuck a sandwich out of the mess hall for Kevin because he assumed he would be hungry.

"Mark, I…" he started but couldn't find the words to express his gratitude verbally.

The most synonymous way to show his appreciation would have been to hug him, but he couldn't do it for a variety of reasons – being misinterpreted as emotional or, god forbid, homosexual. That would probably be a death sentence for both him and Mark in a place like Camp Firwood. But he also didn't have it in him to express his emotions adequately without cringing.

"Thank you. Really. I appreciate this a ton," he mumbled, sounding barely coherent.

"Don't talk; just eat. And eat it fast since the counselors will be here any minute. Our training starts soon. And make sure they don't see you, or we'll both be scrubbing the toilets for a week."

Kevin took a big bite. Despite the bread being old and crumbly and the sausage having a sinewy taste, it was an immensely enjoyable breakfast. He finished it within a minute, wiping the oil on his mouth with his forearm in case any evidence of his illegal food consumption remained.

Within minutes, Counselors Baldwin, Mr. Adams, Dwight, and three others, whom Kevin didn't recognize, came out, and the campers lined up. Mr. Adams hand-picked five random campers for wood-chopping duty, who Dwight proceeded to lead to the task. The counselors then divided their own duties per cabins.

"Alright, let's see," Mr. Adams said, reading off his notes. "Baldwin, you take cabin one for tent setup. Johnson, you're with cabin two, take them tooo…"

He annoyingly extended the final word.

"…campfire training. O'Brian, cabin three — packing things inside their backpacks. Get the campers to pick up their stuff from lockers. Torres, you take cabin four — primitive tool creation and usage. I'll take cabin five for… well, whatever they have."

The counselors started leading campers one by one in groups, and when it was time for cabin four, Kevin dared to step out of the line and approach Mr. Adams. Counselor Torres, a morbidly obese counselor with a furrowed brow, didn't seem to notice it in his focus of waddling alongside the line of campers and panting heavily.

"Mr. Adams," Kevin called out sternly, despite the counselors' gaze being focused elsewhere (on purpose, Kevin thought).

Mr. Adams snapped his head in Kevin's direction and grinned courteously.

Fake smile, Kevin thought to himself with disgust.

He wasn't entirely sure if the disgust was from the fake smile or from the sinewy taste that still lingered in his mouth from the piece of sausage stuck in his tooth.

"Camper. What can I do for you?" the counselor asked jovially.

"We talked yesterday. About me leaving the camp? I looked for you last night, but your counselors practically dragged me from the main lodge."

Mr. Adams listened attentively with a focused expression on his face before snapping his fingers and saying.

"Right, I remember. I already called your parents this morning, and I'm afraid I have some bad news for you. Unfortunately, they

121

decided that they really want you to stay in the camp until your time is over, so I promised I'd try to make you as comfortable as I can while you're here. Is that alright with you?" he asked patronizingly.

He already called my parents? And they said no, just like that?

Kevin found this suspicious. There was no way his parents, especially his father, would just tell Mr. Adams no. He would insist on talking to Kevin himself to give him a good lecture before sending him back to the camp. No, Mr. Adams was lying, the son of a bitch.

"Well, I would really like to talk to them myself if you don't mind," Kevin insisted.

Mr. Adams drew his breath in through his teeth, his face twisted into a grimace as if he was in pain, before saying, "I'm sorry, camper. I can't give you your cellphone while you're still technically a camper, I'd get into a lot of trouble for it. You understand, right?"

Kevin smiled courteously, already prepared for a comeback.

"Alright, not a problem. Then I'll just leave the camp on my own. I'll give you your shitty uniform back, but I want my stuff, and then I'm gone."

It felt good to say that as a small act of defiance. Mr. Adams' facial expression changed from a grimace to a serious look, which incessantly focused on Kevin.

"I'm sorry, camper," Mr. Adams said reticently. "But I have rules I need to follow. Your safety is my concern, and I can't just let you go. Not until your parents sign some papers. Now, if you'll kindly get back in line-"

"No," Kevin said, unwilling to budge. "I won't."

The campers from cabin five shifted in their spots nervously. Mr. Adams' lips turned up in a smile, but his eyes remained furious.

"Excuse me?" he asked.

"I said, I won't," Kevin retorted defiantly, too frustrated with Mr. Adams and this entire fucking camp.

He would take no more from any of the counselors. Mr. Adams' expression remained the same, but his face turned red.

"Mr. Torres!" he called out, still staring at Kevin.

"Yes, Mr. Adams?" Counselor Torres' rough voice bellowed from somewhere far behind Kevin.

"This camper *insists* on making a call back home. Take him to the communications center. Let him talk to his folks, and then bring him back to training."

"Yes, sir," Counselor Torres nodded, his double chin shaking vigorously.

He turned to the campers he was leading and shouted.

"You there, camper," he shouted, pointing at Steve, "lead the group to the designated training spot. You know where that is, right?"

"Yes, Mr. Torres," Steve said.

Kevin saw Mark's worried expression before the group continued walking in the opposite direction. He looked back at Mr. Adams, once again locking himself in a staring contest with him. He heard Torres' toddling steps approaching him before he felt a massive hand on his shoulder.

"Come with me, camper. This way," he said with a mixture of gentleness and authority, steering the boy to move to the right and forcing him to avert his gaze from Mr. Adams.

Only when he was forced to start walking did Kevin look away from Mr. Adams. On their way to the communications building, Torres didn't say a word, save for when he needed to re-steer Kevin in the right direction. They were headed down the road to the left of the main grounds.

They went past the main lodge and a couple of other buildings before turning left and following a small trail that stretched between the tall trees and ended in the distance in front of a lonesome building. Unlike most of the structures in Camp Firwood, this building was actually made of concrete, much to Kevin's surprise.

"Why's this building so isolated?" Kevin asked, looking straight ahead of him.

The cacophony of footsteps was his only response. He was sure that Torres heard him because there were only the two of them, but yet he ignored him.

Fine, don't tell me, asshole.

As they got closer, it became apparent that the building was actually relatively small, maybe no bigger than the campers' cabin. It had small, square-shaped windows, but Kevin couldn't see inside. There was one metallic door in front where the trail ended, serving as the entrance. Kevin started to feel a sense of suspicion growing within him. Something felt off over here, but he couldn't tell what. He ignored his gut instinct and tried pushing that thought to the back of his mind.

What are they gonna do? Imprison me and keep me here forever? My parents know I'm here.

As soon as they reached the building, Torres put his hand on Kevin's shoulder and effectively stopped him from moving forward.

"Wait here," he croaked before approaching the door.

He raised one meaty hand and knocked loudly. A moment of birds chirping filled the air with a mixture of eerie silence before the sound of the door unlocking echoed loudly from the inside. The door swung open, and a young counselor, maybe in his early twenties, stood at the entrance.

"Mr. Torres," he nodded respectfully to the counselor. "What can I do for you?"

Torres raised his hand and pointed with his thumb behind himself at Kevin.

"This camper wants to make a call home."

The young counselor looked in Kevin's direction with curiosity before turning back to Torres and nodding with equal respect as before.

"Yes, sir. Right away, sir," he said, motioning with his hand for Kevin to approach him. "Come on. In here, camper."

Kevin took a tentative step forward, even though every fiber in his body was screaming at him not to step inside. The relentless gazes of the two counselors put pressure on him, and step by step, he got closer until he entered the building. He found himself in a small office-like room with a bed in one corner and a desk in the other. Another young counselor was sitting by the desk, jotting something down, until he saw Kevin walk in.

He dropped his pen and stood up at attention. The other counselor, who still held the door, looked at Torres and said, "Don't worry, Mr. Torres, we'll bring him back as soon as he's done."

Kevin didn't hear Torres answer, but the next thing he did hear was the sound of the sturdy metallic door closing behind him and the lock echoing once more. His panic grew even more, especially now that he was trapped with these two counselors and no way of calling for help.

The young man who locked the door put his hand forward with a smile and said, "I'm Peter. This is Jordan."

Kevin tentatively shook his hand, doing his best to steady the shaking and hoping the counselor hadn't noticed it.

"Kevin," he mumbled.

"Well, Kevin. Nice to meet you," Peter said. "Now, let's get you to the phone, shall we?"

He walked over to the door on the other side and opened it for Kevin.

"Right this way."

Kevin tried to see what was behind the door, but it was too dark. He looked to the right at the other counselor, who smiled even more widely.

"Come on now, don't be shy. We have landlines in here," Peter said in a friendly tone.

"Why don't you go in first?" he asked.

"Sure," Peter smiled and strode inside with confidence, merging with the darkness.

Kevin slowly took a step forward, his heart thumping. He wanted nothing more than to run to the exit, unlock it, and get out of the building. He might make it. He might manage to unlock the door and make a break for it, but there was no way he'd outrun the counselors. In the end, what exactly would be in here that caused him such primordial panic? Maybe he was just paranoid, and the other campers' stories were starting to get to him. It was stupid.

With that thought, he stepped over the threshold, further squinting to see anything in the dark. He saw that he was in a corridor of some sort, but he couldn't see anything more than that.

"Right there," Peter said from somewhere in front.

"Where? I can't see an-"

Before he could finish the sentence, he felt a jolt of pain surge through the back of his leg. He found himself losing balance and falling on his knees. Another forceful impact on his side, and he fell sideways. That's when the pain in his leg came, searing and overwhelming. He felt more impact on various parts of his body and, through the dark, managed to realize that he was repeatedly punched (or kicked).

He shielded his face as his stomach, arms, legs, and head throbbed with pain.

"You don't like our camp, you little shit?!" one of the counselors shouted between hits with intensity.

The hitting persisted for a minute or so before they stopped; their panting filled the air.

"Alright, alright. I think he's had enough. Let's throw him into the cell."

6

Detention

Kevin's entire body was throbbing with pain. He managed to protect his face partially, but the counselors still succeeded in throwing a punch or two. He ran his fingers across his front teeth to see if they were still intact and breathed a sigh of relief when he realized that they were. He slowly got his bearings and, with a pained groan, got up on his feet. The first thing he noticed was the horrid piss-like smell. It was like a gas station bathroom. He looked around the room and immediately figured out what he should have realized long before stepping inside the building. This was no communications building.

The room was barely large enough for him to completely stretch his legs when lying down. A small bed, much smaller than the one in the cabin, was hanging off the walls by a pair of chains on either side. The mattress was so thin that the bed looked more like a street bench. If he had to stay here overnight, sleeping on that monstrosity was going to be torture. A rusty sink sat in the middle of the wall, the tap looking so browned that Kevin imagined it spewing shit-mixed water. On the floor in the corner, right next to the sink, was a ceramic plate with a hole inside and a moist-looking toilet paper roll beside it. Right next to the hole was a brown stain. With a shudder, Kevin realized that it was a literal shithole and would serve as his bathroom in case he had to go. It also explained the smell, which nearly made him gag.

The wall where the door was supposed to be was instead replaced by metal bars, looking out into the dimly lit corridor where he was beaten just before. Right across from his cell was another cell, and since the lights were on now, he realized that the entire corridor was a cell block. He couldn't peek through the bars outside, but he estimated that the whole block had five cells on each side. The cells in front of him were empty, giving him a feeling of claustrophobia. That feeling was drowned out by the anger that started to boil deep inside him.

He was angry at Mr. Adams. He was angry at the detention counselors for beating him up. He was angry at Dwight. He was angry at the entire camp. And most of all, he was angry at his parents for bringing him here.

Why did his parents do it? Why would they want to bring him to this hellhole? Did they not research this place enough before bringing him here? Was this some kind of secret organization that kidnapped teens and kept them imprisoned? What if his parents or the police never found him? What if he never saw his friends again? What if he never went on a date with Amy like he'd planned to? What if everyone he held dear to him eventually forgot about him? If he became just another missing person case that the neighborhood talked about in passing?

A million questions raced through his head, which began drowning his anger and slowly replacing it with fear. He wanted to scream and kick the bars, but he knew that would do no good. If anything, the counselors would be on him in seconds to beat him again. But he had to know how long he was going to be here and what to expect. Not knowing what was waiting for him scared him beyond words.

"Hey! HEY!" he shouted as he grabbed the bars like a caged animal, unsuccessfully trying to rattle them. "Let me outta here!"

A door somewhere on his right opened almost immediately, and a slow thudding of footsteps echoed in his direction. The counselor who had been sitting by the desk earlier, Jordan, stepped in front of Kevin's cell. He had a grievous expression on his face. He tapped what looked like a baton upon his own thigh, giving Kevin a warning glance.

"Shut the fuck up," he calmly said with a hint of relish in his tone.

Kevin stepped away from his cell, darting his eyes from the baton to the counselor's face.

"You better be quiet, or I'm gonna open this cell door. And trust me, you don't want me to do that."

He turned to the left to leave, giving Kevin a prolonged glance that distinctly said, 'Know your place, bitch.' The heavy door at the end of the corridor opened and closed, leaving Kevin in complete silence and with his own thoughts. He took a deep breath and sighed, trying to calm himself down.

Okay, calm down. Calm down. Here's what I'll do. I'm going to look for a way out. I'm not going to let them get to me. I'll look for a way out, either now or wait until they release me from detention. They have to release me sooner or later, right? If they don't, I'm going to find a way to break out of here, fake a seizure or something, and bolt for the woods.

"Guess you messed up too, huh?" an oddly jovial voice came from somewhere in the cell block, loud enough for Kevin to hear, but not loud enough to alert the detention guards.

Kevin paused, not sure if the voice actually came from the cells or if it was someone outside yelling.

"Yeah, you. The one they just brought in. I'm talking to you," the voice came again.

"Me?" Kevin dumbly asked.

He glanced around, beginning to realize that the voice was coming from somewhere to his left.

"Yeah, you. Right here. I'm your cell neighbor," the voice said again.

Two loud knocks thumped on the left wall. Kevin got closer and leaned his ear against the cold concrete.

"Who are you?" he asked, excitement surging through him.

The panic was gradually decreasing as the feeling of ecstasy overwhelmed him. He was not alone in here, after all.

"They call me Sneaky Rob. I got put into detention because I got caught stealing from the kitchen storage. But let me tell you, it was worth it. I ate better than I did in weeks since I joined here."

129

Kevin listened attentively, half-sure that the guy on the other end of the wall was just screwing with him. He wanted to say that his name was fitting for his punishment but decided not to vocalize it.

"What about you, neighbor?" Rob asked.

Kevin felt his anxiety slowly decreasing, enough to respond to the mysterious person on the other side of the wall.

"I'm Kevin. They call me Cocky Kevin," he said.

"Cocky Kevin? What'd you do? Punch a counselor in the face?" Rob chuckled.

Kevin found it surprising how perky his mood was, especially in a place like this one. Had he been here long?

"No, I didn't punch a counselor, but I wanted to. I disobeyed Mr. Adams' orders."

An impressed whistle came from Rob's side of the wall.

"What were you thinking doing that? Don't you know that Mr. Adams is the worst counselor to do that to? Are you new here or something?"

"As a matter of fact, I am. I just arrived yesterday," Kevin somberly said.

He leaned on the wall with his back and waited for Rob's next response. A moment of silence passed before Rob's voice was heard again.

"Well, I'm kinda glad you did what you did because it was getting pretty lonely in here. They just released Cowardly Adrian less than two days ago, and I didn't have anyone to talk to."

"So how long do you reckon I'll be here?" Kevin finally asked, feeling his heart thumping a little in anticipation.

"Hard to say," Rob tentatively responded matter-of-factly. "I think no longer than a few days. They need labor, and putting us in detention doesn't really make things easier for them."

"What's the longest anyone has ever stayed here?" Kevin uncomfortably asked.

"One week. Tough Norton."

Kevin felt a little relieved. Although he didn't know how long he was going to stay, he knew it couldn't be too long. His hopes did drop at one thought, though – getting out of the camp was definitely going to be a challenge.

A minute of silence ensued before Kevin spoke up once again.

"Hey, Rob. You still there?"

"Yeah, yeah. Still here. If you had called me a minute later, you would have missed me. I was about to go for a stroll around the camp," Rob cheerfully joked.

It took Kevin's overwhelmed mind a moment to understand Rob was being sarcastic, after which he started laughing. In a typical situation, he wouldn't have laughed at a silly joke like that, but his mind must have been in such a shock that it was looking for a way to cope. When he exhausted his laughter, he took a moment to relish the silence.

"So, when are you leaving?" Kevin asked, sitting against the wall where his cell neighbor was.

"In a day or two, I think. They never tell you how long you have to stay. But to tell you the truth, I think I'd rather stay in here."

"Why?" Kevin chuckled.

Rob's tone seemed to turn more somber.

"I get tired of the counselors' gawking. Especially Dwight. I sure hope to god someone pulls the same thing on him as Tough Norton did."

"What did Tough Norton do?" Kevin perked up his ears in curiosity.

"Oh, you don't know?" this seemed to pique Rob's interest, and his voice flared up again. "That guy's a legend around here, let me tell you. Even the batch of campers who arrived later know about him."

There was a muffled sound of something moving from the other side of the wall before Rob's voice started again, a little louder and closer this time.

"So, as soon as the first batch of us campers arrived by bus, around eight weeks ago, Dwight started throwing his weight around to show us how important and scary he is. I mean, we all see through him; we just can't tell him anything because he starts throwing a fit and giving us trouble."

Yep, that's Dwight, alright.

Kevin contemplated his first encounter with the oaf yesterday. He got angry really quickly. Rob continued.

Rob continued. "Anyway. I guess he could tell that Norton wasn't going to stand for his shit. At least not as much as the rest of us. So he decided to give Norton some work right off the bat. But not just any work. He wanted him to clean an outhouse toilet which isn't even used by the camp anymore."

Rob chuckled, but Kevin just shook his head. The fact that Dwight deliberately tried to be an asshole like that pissed him off.

"Long story short, somehow, Norton managed to throw Dwight inside the toilet."

"He what?" Kevin raised his eyebrows, not believing Rob's words.

"Yeah. He somehow threw the fucker inside *and* tried to walk away from it. Everybody heard Dwight's effeminate screams, so the counselors rushed pretty soon to see what was going on. They restrained Norton and pulled Dwight out. They gave Norton two extra days for the trial and sent him here to teach him a lesson – as if that would do any good for a tough nut like him – and for a week after he returned, campers were leaving messages around the camp that said things like *Dwight the Shite* or they would laugh and give naughty glances in Norton's direction whenever someone mentioned toilet duty."

Kevin found that amusing. Not only was the story funny to him, but it felt like karmic justice to have Dwight literally be bathed in a pile of shit.

"But, soon campers started getting into a lot of trouble for that, so they made the rules stricter, and the mocking eventually

132

stopped, unfortunately," Rob mournfully finished his story with a sigh.

Kevin nodded before he remembered that Rob couldn't see his face. He turned his head slightly to the wall and said proudly, "You know, I insulted Dwight yesterday."

"Shut up!" Rob said in disbelief.

"No, it's true. He was prancing around, showing off and shit, and I just couldn't have it, so I insulted him."

"Well, don't keep me on the edge of my seat! What did you tell him?" Rob asked, loudly and with audible excitement in his voice.

"I called him a zit-faced douchebag."

After a moment of silence, Rob burst into uncontrollable, hyena-like laughter.

"Come on, dude, it's not even that funny," Kevin said, a chuckle slipping out of his mouth.

Rob's laughter was infectious, and he, too, started laughing uncontrollably with him. Through breaths of laughter, Rob asked, "What was his reaction?"

"Oh, man. He was fuming. I could tell he wanted to strangle me, but I guess he had to control himself. Anyway, the entire camp got around an hour of sweeping duty because of me, so I shouldn't have done what I did."

"Are you kidding me? That was totally worth it! Ah, man, I wish I could have been there to see his face when that happened." Rob let out the remainder of his laughter before calming down and exhaling deeply. "Hoo, boy."

He took a moment to regain his composure before asking, "Did you get any punishment?"

"No, not me. Or my cabin. But all the others did."

"Which cabin are you in?"

"Four. Number nine."

For a while, silence stretched between them, and Kevin listened to the sound of something dripping in the distance. He hated the thought of having to be in a cell that had a leak. His nose had already started adjusting to the shitty smell, but every time he looked toward the squatter, he felt the sausage he had for breakfast climbing up his throat.

He wasn't sure what time it was when the cellblock door opened with a loud echo, and a pounding of footsteps approached Kevin's cell. Kevin looked up from his stone-hard bed and saw that Peter was standing in front.

"Get up," he motioned for him with his hand to do as he said.

Kevin obliged, but he did it slowly, to give a small act of defiance. He couldn't do more than that, seeing as the counselor had a baton in his hand. Peter pulled a keyring out of his pocket with a jingle and inspected the keys carefully, one by one, as if looking for the right one. Once he found it, he slipped it inside the keyhole and turned it. The lock echoed loudly, and the counselor slid the metallic bars aside. He took a step back and gestured with his head for Kevin to move outside.

"Where are you taking me?" Kevin asked, not budging from his spot.

Peter pointed the baton at him and said, "Move out, or I'll drag you out."

He didn't have a choice. Kevin stepped outside and turned toward the entrance door. Peter nudged Kevin, making him slightly stumble forward. As he made his way toward the exit, he saw a bucket and mop leaning against the wall.

"Not there. Stop," Peter said when Kevin started toward the exit, "Here."

He brought out his keys again with a loud rattle before opening the cell closest to the door, to the left of it. The number above it said '1'. It wasn't dissimilar to Kevin's own cell, possessing the same shithole, same sturdy bed, and same rusted sink.

"Take this, get inside, and start cleaning," Peter pointed to the bucket and mop next to the cell.

Kevin bent down and picked up the bucket, holding the handle of the mop so it wouldn't fall out. He stepped inside the cell, and the door slid behind him. Peter locked it and slammed the bars with his baton, causing an echoing, clinking sound.

"I'll be back later. I want this cell to be spotless. Got it?"

Before Kevin could answer, the counselor opened the door leading out of the cell block, stepped outside, and closed it behind him. A click echoed, indicating that the entrance was being locked, flushing all of Kevin's meager hopes of escape down the drain.

Well, I better get to work, he unwillingly glanced inside the bucket.

A sponge was resting at the bottom, alongside a floor-cleaning product. Kevin removed the contents and placed them neatly on the sink while putting the mop on the floor, leaning it against the wall. He positioned the bucket under the tap as best he could, forced to tilt it at forty-five degrees to fit it. The faucet had a valve on top that could be turned and no way of adjusting the temperature. Kevin turned it with some effort, as it was evident that it hadn't been used in a while.

Water started spewing in broken-up gusts before it stabilized and started filling the bucket. Once the water started spilling out of the bucket and into the sink, he placed it on the floor and opened the floor-cleaning product bottle. The smell of citrus immediately hit him, and he moved the bottle away. He hated citrus, lemon, and other fruity scents when they were in any form other than what mother nature gave them. Holding the bottle as far away from himself as he could, he bent down and poured the yellow liquid into the bucket, mixing it with water. And then it was time to start working.

Some of the stains inside the cell were stubborn, so he had to scrub extra hard to remove them. The sink was a lost cause, and despite scrubbing it so hard that his fingers were red and swollen, he couldn't fix the black and brown stains that seemed to become one with it. He was particularly proud of the way he managed to clean the floor, though. When he started, the cell looked barely fit for an animal to sleep in. Now, he figured it was clean enough for a human being to dwell in it.

He spent extra time scrubbing the shithole, and the end result was a pristinely white squatter (save for the few rusty stains that couldn't be removed). Although present still, the putrid smell was now mixed with citrus. However, Kevin was sure that in only a matter of hours, the citrusy smell would dissipate, and the cell would once again look like a pig's pen. Peter came around thirty minutes later, carrying two trays with food on them. He smiled when he looked inside cell number 1 as he said, "Well, look at you doing fine work over here. Alright, you can eat your lunch now."

Kevin hadn't even realized how hungry he was until he smelled the fried chicken and mashed potatoes. His mouth started salivating, and he quickly emptied the bucket of dirty water into the shithole before rinsing it and collecting the remaining items. Peter went over to Rob's cell and gave him one food tray, after which he returned to Kevin. He used one hand to hold the tray while he used the other to take his keys out and unlock the door.

He slid it aside. "Alright, today's menu is pretty good. Or I guess I should say, it *was*."

He lowered the tray for Kevin to see. There was a plate with a picked chicken bone and half-eaten mash potatoes. A piece of bread with a bitemark woefully rested on the side of the tray.

"Sorry. Jordan and I were feeling extra hungry, so we ate your lunch. You don't mind, right? I mean, ordering prisoners around is hard work."

He lowered the tray further down, and it slowly slid out of his hand. The contents fell on the floor with a loud clattering noise, the remains of food splattering all over the floor and adjacent walls.

"Oops," Peter said with a malicious smirk. "Well, too bad. Anyway, clean this shit up."

He patted Kevin on the shoulder and, with the camp's whistling tune, left the cell block, locking the entrance behind him. Kevin bent down to see if anything was salvageable. The bones were picked clean, and the mashed potatoes were ruined on the dirty detention floor. The bread would have been edible had it not fallen into a wet

136

splotch. Kevin's vision started to become red, and his ears started buzzing. He was angry, but he was holding it in. It manifested itself with tears forming in his eyes. Frustrated, he grabbed the platter and chucked it at the opposite cell door. It loudly banged, and Kevin expected the counselors to come back inside any moment.

Good, let them come back inside. He didn't care if they beat him, but he would fight back. He would punch them even if it meant that he had to spend two more months in this cell.

"Hey, Kevin!" Rob called out to him.

Rob's voice sounded like it was coming from a distance, but after the third call, Kevin registered his voice.

"Come on over here, Kev!" Rob called out to him.

Kevin sighed and stood up.

"Kevin," Rob called again.

"What?" Kevin asked, stepping around the food and heading to cell number nine on the left side.

Inside the cell was an entirely ordinary boy with no features that stood out whatsoever. He had black hair, and that was pretty much all that could be said about him that would differentiate him from the other campers. He was maybe one year younger than Kevin, which was visible from the fact that he had a baby-smooth face and mustache that was so sparse and thin that Kevin imagined staring at a kiwi.

Rob was holding his tray of food, and it was visible that he took a bite out of his chicken drum and the old bread. He stood up and passed the tray through the little opening in the middle of the door, staring at Kevin.

"What?" Kevin frowned, his mouth beginning to salivate again at the thought of eating. "No, I can't. You won't have anything to eat."

"Oh, don't you worry about me. There's a reason they call me Sneaky Rob. Remember how I told you that I snatched some food from the storage?" he winked.

"Wait. You have some in here?" Kevin asked as he tentatively grabbed the tray from his side.

"Yup. A couple cans for emergencies. So don't worry about me."

Kevin looked at the tray of food and then back at Rob. He was starting to feel like a burden for having others constantly give him food.

"Are you sure about this?" he asked with a furrow of his forehead.

Rob nodded, letting go of the tray.

"Alright, man. Thanks a bunch. I'll repay you somehow, I promise," Kevin said, immediately grabbing the chicken drum and taking a giant bite out of it, feeling his anger instantly subsiding.

The skin of the drum was coated in oil, but he didn't care. The meat was delicious. He clasped the spoon and took a bite out of the watery mashed potatoes, after which he bit down on the old bread. He never thought he would be able to enjoy this shitty food so much.

The last time he had food this bad was when he was in the hospital to have his appendix removed. He couldn't eat for three days straight and was only given glucose. When the doctor finally gave him the green light for some light food and the hospital staff brought him chewy mystery meat and bland rice, it was the best meal he'd ever had. Every subsequent meal in the hospital tasted progressively worse. The food from Camp Firwood heavily reminded him of the hospital meals.

He quickly finished the meal, even going as far as eating the old bread, before giving the tray back to Rob to avoid getting caught.

"Thank you. Really," Kevin stated with a slight bow of his head.

Rob dismissively waved.

"We gotta stick together. Especially in a place like this, you know?"

Kevin nodded as he used his forearm to wipe the oil off his mouth.

"Well, anyway, I gotta clean up the mess that asshole made," he said and went over to finish his job.

The sight of the mess reminded him of what the counselor did, and it caused his rage to reawaken. He managed to scoop up most of the mess from the food. However, before he could finish, the cellblock door clicked and swung open. Peter stood there with a satisfied look on his face and his hands on his hips.

"You still haven't cleaned this up? Do I have to give you an incentive to hurry up?" he asked with a grimace, which Kevin wanted to extinguish with his entire being.

"I'm working on it, but you made a huge mess," he instead replied while kneeling, using the sponge to pick up the remains of the food between the floor and wall and put them in his hand.

"You mean *you* made a huge mess, right?" Peter asked.

Kevin ignored him. He was determined to continue giving little bits of defiance to the counselor. The more he was in his presence, the less he was sure who he hated more—Dwight, Mr. Adams, or Peter.

If he wants to give me some extra chores to do, let him.

"Alright, hurry it up so I can put you back in your cell, will ya?" Peter finally said, his sarcastic smirk shifting into an irritated retort.

Once Kevin had finished cleaning up, and Peter made sure it was spotless, he took the bucket and other things from Kevin and locked him back up in cell number eight.

"That was only cell number one. Expect to clean the other ones later, too," Peter said and looked to his right where Rob was. "You'll be doing work too, camper, so don't get too cozy."

He winked and produced a clicking noise with his mouth before leaving the block. Kevin was starting to feel angry again, but he knew it would do him no good to let his emotions take control over him. So whenever he started getting angry, he reminded himself to calm down.

I'll get back at them later. Right now, I can't, but I will in the future. Just gotta be patient.

He sat down on his new bed and stared at the wall in front in silence. He had to start thinking of a way out. He could simply leave the camp under the cover of night, just go into the woods and disappear. It was that easy. But it wasn't that easy, was it? If what the campers told Kevin is true, then he wouldn't be able to just up and leave. He had to find another way.

What if he somehow managed to get his cellphone from the locker and climb up on the watchtower in the woods he saw? Maybe he could get a signal and call for help? No, that wouldn't be possible. He would need to charge his phone first since the battery was probably already dead. The problem was there were no outlets anywhere in the cabins, not from what he saw. He could go to the laundry and plug in his phone there, but it was a stretch. He would first need to get his phone back unnoticed, and he doubted that anyone besides Mr. Adams actually had access to the lockers. No, the cellphone was not an option. So, what then?

"Hell of a day, huh?" Rob interrupted Kevin's train of thoughts.

"Uh, yeah," Kevin absently said. "Is it like this every day?"

"No, not every day. Most of the other days, you do some other duties. Hell, sometimes when they have no work to give you, they'll just give you something to do, just because they want you occupied."

"Great," Kevin groaned.

Silence filled the air again momentarily before Kevin approached the adjacent wall and asked, "Hey, Rob. You mentioned something about a batch of campers arriving on a bus."

"Yeah, what about it?" Rob asked with a hint of curiosity in his tone.

"Tell me more about that. Where did the bus pick you up, and how many campers were brought like that?" Kevin asked, now perking up his ears to hear every detail Rob was about to convey.

"Exactly fifty campers. Ten for each cabin. My parents took me to a station in the middle of the woods, and that's where the other campers were, too. We were loaded up into the bus, and a few hours later, we were here. I don't think our parents knew what they were signing us up for."

"You said there were fifty?" Kevin asked in bafflement.

"Yep. Fifty."

"I guess the empty spots are from the ones who left the camp after being picked in The Choosing, right?"

There was silence for a moment.

"They didn't tell you, did they?" Rob asked somberly.

"Tell me what? About the Firwood Wraith? About the campers being sacrificed in the woods?"

Rob went silent.

"Don't tell me you believe that shit, man," Kevin scoffed.

"I don't believe in ghosts, no. But something strange *is* going on in Camp Firwood, and nobody can deny that."

"Like what?"

"Like, noises outside the cabins at night. A lot of campers confirmed that they heard something rustling out there. Some even think they saw something."

"An animal, probably."

"That's what most of us thought at first, too. But then things started getting stranger. We'd come back from training to see some items missing or lockers ransacked. It couldn't have been an animal because the doors were closed the entire time. And then, some campers started seeing something moving in the treeline. They could never tell who or what it was because it would disappear too quickly."

"Hm," Kevin said.

Rob sounded rational enough to discern the paranormal from the realistic, so if he was skeptical about the happenings in the camp, something was definitely wrong.

"But campers get picked to leave if they're well-behaved, right?" Kevin asked.

"Yeah, there's always two for the trial and one for what we call Departure, but it's strange. It's like... sometimes you'll swear that a camper is going to get picked for that because he's the best-behaved one, but then Mr. Adams chooses someone else."

"Maybe other things are taken into account."

"Like what?"

"Shit, I dunno. Like speed of doing things, participation in activities, that kind of thing."

"Maybe. Anyway, the camper whose place you took in cabin four was named Bill. We called him Caveman Bill."

"Why?"

Kevin chuckled at the absurdity of the name.

"Because he knew a lot about survival in the wilderness. If anyone was going to ace that survival trial, it's him," Rob said.

"Have the campers ever tried talking to the counselors about this wraith?"

"We have, many times. But they say it's just our imagination. Mr. Adams says being in the woods for too long can play tricks on the mind.

"And what do you think?"

Silence followed for a while. Kevin was about to open his mouth to ask Rob if he heard him when Rob said, "I think this is some kind of prison. Maybe a re-education camp or something of the like. No matter who I've spoken to, most of the campers can confirm one thing – they were all sent here for different reasons."

"I don't know what to think anymore. At first, I thought the other campers were playing a prank on me, but now…" Kevin sighed and shook his head as his thoughts trailed off.

He'd had enough. He wanted out. He wanted to get out of this camp and never step into the woods again. He wanted to go home and see his friends. He wanted to talk to Amy, just to see her face and hear her gentle and comforting voice. But instead, he was stuck in here with abusive counselors and far away from home.

"Well, what's your story, then?" Rob finally asked. "Why were you sent here?"

"I organized a party in my parents' private yacht. My friends got a little drunk and ransacked the place."

"Just for that, they sent you here?"

"No, not just for that. The yacht was only the final straw, I guess."

"I see."

More silence descended. Kevin listened to the steady dripping of the tap coming from one of the cells. A part of him still believed that the campers were playing a prank on him, so he asked, "Hey, Rob? If you believe that this place is dangerous, then why don't you get out?"

"Oh," Rob's voice came from the other side. "Oh! That's genius! Why didn't we think of that during the past few weeks that we've been here? We've been doing all these chores, getting bullied by counselors and stalked by the Firwood Wraith, when all we could've done was just get out of here!"

"No need for sarcasm," Kevin hissed.

"Some of us wanted to get out. We really did. But our phones were snatched right at the start, and there's no way to get them back. Mr. Adams has the keys, but that wouldn't matter anyway because there's no damn signal here."

"What about just walking out?" Kevin asked, mostly to confirm whether the other campers were telling the truth.

"No. Not a lot of campers would want to step into the woods. It's bad enough that many of them believe in the Firwood Wraith, but the counselors also said it's too dangerous. Wild animals, traps, that kind of thing."

"So no one's actually tried running away?" Kevin suspiciously raised his eyebrows.

"One camper apparently did last year. Counselors say he died in the woods."

"Motherfuckers. There's gotta be a way out. What if we try to overpower them?"

"Not gonna work."

"Why not?"

143

"We overpower them, and what then? We don't have any means of escaping. The only vehicles I've seen arrive are the bus, which brings the campers in, and the director's car."

Kevin groaned in frustration.

"And just walking through the woods is not a viable option? We could try to overtake the kitchen and stock up on food. If a dozen of us is willing to step into the woods, the others may follow our lead."

"Not gonna work," Rob briskly repeated.

"Okay, why not?" Kevin gritted his teeth.

"I'm assuming you haven't been on watchtower duty. When you climb the watchtower and look around, you're gonna see nothing but miles and miles of trees with nothing else in sight. And they probably stretch even farther than that. Caveman Bill estimated that it would take us at least two days to get past the strips of trees that we can see. And that's only what we *can see*, and provided we don't get lost along the way and can go in a straight line, which won't be possible in uninhabited woods like these.

Secondly, the food in the mess hall is mostly raw and easily spoiled. There are cans and MREs too, but just simply not enough of them. We wouldn't last a day in the woods. None of us have adequate skills to hunt and survive for long periods of time in the wilderness. And again, if we stepped into a bear trap and broke our legs, or worse, ran into bears..."

"Okay, I get it," Kevin interrupted him, feeling defeated.

He was starting to despair a little, but he wasn't ready to give up just yet. He'd find a way out.

"Listen, I know you're eager to get out," Rob said. "We all are. But rushing things will only get you in trouble. The best thing you can do is wait until we find a way to get out. A few of the campers are actively trying to look for a way to escape, but a lot of them don't believe that they are kept here as prisoners and are waiting for their parents to pick them up after it's over. So the number of people who actually wanna work together is pretty low. Not to mention there's a risk of being ratted out by other campers. It already happened before."

"The longer we wait, the more people will go missing. Just like Bill and the others from The Choosing."

"But if we try something suspicious, even more people will probably get in trouble."

"*If* they're in trouble in the first place. Which we don't know," Kevin frowned.

Rob sighed.

"Alright, look. Too many kids have been sent here by their parents. Someone is bound to figure out something fishy is going on sooner or later if something bad really is happening here. They may call the police and send them to investigate. A summer camp can't just hide or kill fifty kids."

"I guess you're right." That made sense to Kevin.

He started thinking about the whole thing, and it just seemed like something straight out of a movie. The parents sent their kids to a summer camp, but it was actually some organization using teens for sacrificial purposes? And what if they really were prisoners? The camp couldn't have been going through all this trouble just to keep the campers here as prisoners, right?

Maybe this is exactly what the parents wanted like Nerdy Van said? Sending kids for corrections. Mark said he was sent here for weight loss, and the way the camp was feeding them would definitely ensure the results. As for Kevin, did his parents really send him here to correct his rebellious personality? They told him the camp was more for some skill learning, although it didn't look like he would be learning anything in the camp. The more he thought about it, the more it made sense that it was more of a correctional camp. If that were really the case, then Kevin would only need to simply wait until summer camp was finished.

But what if he was wrong? What if it didn't end when it was supposed to? Some campers said they were already supposed to leave. But coming back to what Van said, maybe that was part of the correction, keeping them uninformed about their time of departure?

His head started to hurt from all the overthinking. He had to get some rest, and later, he would figure out if he would wait, just like Rob said, or actively try to find a way out. If this place really was just a correctional camp, then getting in trouble wasn't a big deal. But if he was wrong and this was some kind of illegal prison, then the consequences of his meddling could be much worse. He lay on his bed and closed his eyes. He thought to himself how there was no way he was ever going to get some shuteye on this piece of rock when he started falling asleep.

***

He was abruptly woken up by Jordan loudly slamming the bars with his baton some time later.

"Work time!" he shouted as he slid open the cell.

Both Kevin and Rob were let out of their cells and given tools for work. Kevin had to continue cleaning the remaining cells while Rob was escorted out to do something else with garden tools. For the next couple of hours, every thirty minutes or so, Peter would come inside to check how Kevin was doing, making sure to look for any blemishes that he may have missed along the way. Kevin ended up having to go back to some of the previous cells in order to fix what he missed, but hours later, he was finally done with all the cells on both sides of the block and the corridor connecting them. His hands, knees, and back were killing him by the time he was done with the eight-cell, and he thought there was no way he could take any more work.

But he wouldn't show it to the detention counselors. Luckily, Jordan returned with a fresh-looking Rob, who looked like he hadn't been working at all in the past two hours.

"Alright, back in your cells, campers," the counselor ordered.

They did as he commanded, and he locked them back up, leaving the block without a word.

"Fuck that guy," Rob said from his cell. "Made me cut the grass around the building."

"That doesn't sound too bad," Kevin said, feeling a little envious of Rob's job.

"With a pair of small scissors," Rob finished.

Of course, they had to complicate it, the bastards.

"What about you? Been busy keeping this place spotless, I see?" Rob said with a somewhat moping tone.

He didn't show it physically, but Kevin guessed he was tired after all.

"Yeah," Kevin turned the valve on the faucet and let the suspicious water run.

"You finished it awfully fast. You shouldn't rush like that," Rob reticently retorted.

Kevin finished taking a few big gulps of the metallic-tasting water before wiping his mouth with his forearm.

"What do you mean?" he asked.

"I mean, you don't need to do *everything* like they tell you to. They give us tasks, but they can't punish us for being slow as long as we're doing them. Hell, what I sometimes do when given a task like what you just had is rush for around twenty-thirty minutes, and then I lie down and take a break for ten minutes or so."

"Huh." Kevin turned off the faucet.

"Yeah, because that way, when the counselors come inside, you quickly get up and pretend you're working. They see that you're doing *something*, no matter how slow it is, and then they can't really punish you. And they give you timed work. So that means that you do what you do for the time they decided, and then, whether you finished it or not, you go back to your cell."

"I… didn't think of that," Kevin lay on his bed to give his aching body a break.

"Yeah. You gotta abuse the system a little bit, you know? Because they aren't gonna try and make it easy on you. Just don't let these assholes get to you, you know?"

147

Kevin felt slightly insulted by Rob's advice. He considered himself fairly good at abusing the system without getting into trouble, but Camp Firwood was a completely different world where you had to be more cunning.

A few minutes later, Peter came in with dinner platters. This time, he didn't drop the food and just gave it to the campers before leaving without a word. They had baked beans with a side of lettuce, both of which were, to Kevin's surprise, good. He would have loved to have a soft, fresh bread that he could dip into the beans, but he wasn't complaining about this. The time after dinner was uneventful, and pretty soon, the lights went out inside the block, leaving Kevin in complete darkness.

"It's 10 p.m.," Rob said. "Guess we should try to catch some z's. They may wake us up in the middle of the night to do some chores, so uh... yeah. Be ready for that."

Fucking great.

Despite taking a nap in the afternoon, Kevin had no difficulty falling asleep. Luckily though, no one came to wake Kevin up until the lights went on in the morning. Both Rob and Kevin were immediately given work. Kevin had to go outside and cut the grass around the building with tiny scissors, which were barely good enough for clipping nails. Rob, on the other hand, had to clean the interior.

It was still pretty early in the morning because the sky outside was orange when Kevin started his work. He couldn't tell how long he had to do it, but by the time the counselors brought them breakfast, the sun was already somewhat high up in the sky. They spent the majority of the morning working until Peter announced it was one o'clock. They were then put back into their cells and were given a moment of rest. About thirty minutes later, Jordan came and opened Rob's cell.

"You're free to go, camper. Move your ass."

As Rob walked past Kevin's cell, he glanced toward him and said, "Remember what I told you, alright? I'll see you back at the cabin. I'm in three."

Jordan nudged him, reminding him to move it. As the cellblock door closed, Kevin felt lonelier than he did in days. His thoughts raced to the other campers of cabin four, and he wondered what Mark was doing right now.

Peter soon brought him lunch, and after that, there was more work to be done. Kevin initially thought that there was no way he would always be given something to do around a small building like this one, but those hopes were flushed down the drain when he was given the task of cutting the grass. At that moment, he realized that the counselors would always find some work to give him. The day went by like yesterday, and by dinner time, Kevin started to see bruises on his body from the beating he took from the counselors. He was careful not to lay on those parts of the body. However, it didn't really matter because sleeping on the prison bed would leave him aching anyway.

He was woken up in the middle of the night by Peter and taken out of his cell. They took him to one isolated part of the detention house and gave him a bucket. There was a hole filled with water in front of him and an empty hole on the other side of the room. They ordered him to get all the water from one hole into the other. Kevin started doing the job, but after dozens of times of lugging the bucket and pouring the water inside the empty hole, he started to realize that the water level wasn't decreasing at all. Furthermore, the other hole didn't seem to be filling up.

You can pretend you're working when they walk in, Rob's words echoed in his head, and that's precisely what he did.

He placed the bucket down and sat in the corner of the room. He started to feel sleepy, but he knew he couldn't allow himself to fall asleep. Otherwise, he could get another beating. With his bruises, it would only be more painful. He waited for the time to pass, and after an hour or so, the door opened, and Kevin quickly clambered up to his feet, pretending to carry the bucket. Peter told him it was enough and brought him back to bed. Kevin had an oddly satisfying smirk on his face when he drifted back to sleep.

***

He woke up to the sound of the cellblock door opening and a cacophony of voices. It wasn't just Jordan and Peter talking – there was a third voice there, too—an awfully friendly, sickening voice that Kevin found all-too-familiar.

"Any problems with him?" Mr. Adams asked jovially.

"Not at all, Mr. Adams. He was a little slow when working, but other than that, nothing. He did everything he was told to do," one of the counselors responded.

Kevin sat on his bed and waited until Mr. Adams and the two counselors were in front of the cell door.

"Hello, camper." Mr. Adams smiled. "How's it going?"

Kevin looked in his direction but ignored him. Mr. Adams nodded, leaning on the wall next to the bars. He motioned something for Peter, and the detention counselor whipped out his jingling keys before unlocking the cell and sliding the door open.

"Come on, you're done with detention," Mr. Adams said.

He gestured with his head for Kevin to follow him. Kevin was more than happy to get out of here, but he didn't want to show them how eager he was. He lethargically got up and stepped outside. Peter closed the cell, and the four of them walked out into the main room of the detention house. Jordan filled out some papers there regarding Kevin's name, the reason for detention, and time spent in detention. Mr. Adams took a note of something too, and when all was said and done, he put a hand on Kevin's shoulder and said perkily, "Alright, let's get you to the infirmary first, camper."

7
Repentance

"Take off your shirt and pants," Nurse Mary fumbled to take the stethoscope from her desk as she barked the order at Kevin without even looking at him.

Kevin obliged and placed his clothes on top of the examining bed. He sat on it – much more gently this time, to avoid Mary's scolding. The nurse hung the stethoscope around her neck and approached Kevin. She grabbed him by the chin and slightly twisted his head left and then right, examining his bruised face.

She then checked the rest of the bruises on his body before putting the stethoscope earpieces in her ears and the cold chest piece on Kevin's chest. It wasn't until she started touching his body with her hands in various places that Kevin started to feel pain in the bruised spots.

"Breathe deeply," she said, seemingly staring at his chest.

Kevin inhaled and exhaled a few times before the nurse checked his breathing from the backside as well. She waltzed over to her desk and placed the stethoscope down before picking up a tongue depressor and heading back over to him.

"Open your mouth," she said and placed the stick on top of his tongue. "Say *ah*."

"Ahh," Kevin uttered, feeling uncomfortable with the stick in his mouth.

Mary took out the stick, much to Kevin's relief, and threw it inside the trash bin before walking over to the sink and washing her hands. When she was done, she called out.

"Mr. Adams, can you come in here for a moment?"

The door opened, and Mr. Adams' thin figure peeked inside, head first before he shyly stepped into the examination room.

"Hey, Mary. Everything okay?" he asked.

She looked somewhat angry, which completely contrasted her flirtatious behavior with Mr. Adams the first time Kevin was here.

"He is pretty banged up, but other than that, he's fine," she said.

"So, he can go back to camp activities?" Mr. Adams smiled.

Nurse Mary paused for a moment before saying, "Yes," she looked at Kevin.

It felt strange to have her gaze locked on him. It was so scarce that Kevin felt that each look was either meaningful, or it meant he was in trouble.

"Go wait outside. I need to talk to Mr. Adams," she said briskly.

"Yes, ma'am," Kevin said and put his clothes on.

He caught a hint of impatience on the nurse's side. Once Kevin was dressed, he walked out into the waiting room and closed the door behind him. But he wanted to hear what they had to say, so instead of heading to the seat, he stayed close to the door, carefully leaning with his ear toward it. At first, all he heard were muffled, incoherent voices of the nurse and the head counselor. And then he heard Mary say in a hushed but still somewhat audible voice, "Marvin, listen to me. I can't keep patching up the campers that get physically abused like this. I understand that they need to be disciplined, but this is too much."

"Mary. Mary," Mr. Adams spoke in a near whisper. "With all due respect, you don't know what it's like dealing with campers. It's *my* job to keep them in check, and sometimes, I have to get a little rough."

"A little rough? This kid has bruises all over his body!" Mary raised her voice a little, enough for Kevin to hear every word clearly.

"Quiet!" Mr. Adams reprimanded her with a hush.

Kevin held his breath in the uncomfortable silence, feeling his heart beating faster than usual.

"You have to tell the counselors to stop abusing the campers," Mary continued. "What if they see them all bruised up like that? How are you going to explain it to them?"

"They won't see it. Alright, listen. I'll talk to the counselors to be more careful. But I need you to stay calm. Just a little longer now, and then we're out of here, alright? Summer's almost over. Okay?"

Mary sighed loudly before saying, "Fine, whatever. I have to check up on the admitted campers, so if you don't mind…"

Mr. Adams suddenly started speaking in a normal tone.

"Oh, no. Not at all. Sorry to disturb you, Mary. You have a good one."

Kevin quickly tip-toed away from the door and slumped down on the bench in the waiting room, staring down at his feet. Not a second later, the door swung open, and Kevin looked up at Mr. Adams, whose usual grin was gone. He stared at Kevin with an expressionless face for a moment, and Kevin couldn't stand his penetrating gaze, so he looked away.

Oh no, does he know I eavesdropped?

A moment later, Mr. Adams gave Kevin a forced smile before saying, "Alright, camper. Follow me."

Breathing a silent sigh of relief, Kevin stood up and followed Mr. Adams out of the infirmary and toward the main lodge. On the way there, as Kevin walked behind Mr. Adams, he couldn't help but replay the conversation the counselor and Mary had in his head. Who are 'they'? The parents? Camp inspection? This confirmed that Camp Firwood was doing something illegal off the record, but was there anything besides the beating? What about the missing campers?

"Right this way, camper." Mr. Adams opened the main lodge door and held it open for Kevin to walk in first.

Kevin shot him a suspicious glance before stepping inside and waiting for the counselor's orders. Mr. Adams got past Kevin while whistling that same annoying tune that represented Camp Firwood. He walked down the hall, past two counselors who were talking to each other. Those were the same ones that chased Kevin away a few nights ago when he tried to enter the lodge.

They nodded in greetings to Mr. Adams and failed to even glance at Kevin. Kevin was sure that they probably didn't even remember who he was with all the punishing they did. Mr. Adams and Kevin turned right and stopped in front of a door on the left side. The door had a pane of thick, Flemish glass with the letters HEAD COUNSELOR on it. Mr. Adams whipped out his keys and unlocked the office, swinging the door open, all the while still whistling.

"Here we are," he stopped his humming to say.

The office didn't look ostentatious by any means, but it definitely contrasted the rest of the camp with its cleanliness and tidiness. There was a desk inside, two chairs, some drawers on the left side of the room, and a diploma hanging on the wall behind the desk. A door stood open in the back, leading to the right, to a room that Kevin couldn't see from where he stood. The office looked cluttered, even with the scarcity of the items in it, but it looked comfortable if nothing else. None of that mattered to Kevin, though, because his eyes fell on only one thing in the office.

A simple, white landline phone, sitting atop the desk.

This is it. I can use this to call for help.

Mr. Adams flipped a switch next to the door, instantly illuminating the office in a sickly, yellowish light. He sat behind the desk and motioned for Kevin with his hand to sit on the other chair. Knowing that Mr. Adams wouldn't cease bothering him until he did and said everything he commanded, Kevin sat on the chair and awaited the imminent lecture.

"Let's see here..." Mr. Adams opened a drawer and stared at the contents for a prolonged moment with a contemplating glance.

"Anyway, never mind," he said a moment later and slammed the drawer shut.

He turned to face Kevin and crossed his fingers, eagerly smiling.

"So..." he started, "Peter and Jordan weren't too rough, I hope?"

154

Kevin stared at him but said nothing. It was his way of telling him, 'You already know.' Mr. Adams nodded as he pursed his lips and stared down at his hands before looking back up at Kevin.

"I'll talk to them. Have them punished for being too rough. The campers' safety is my responsibility, and I should have made sure that they didn't go too far on a power trip. I apologize for that."

"When can I leave?" Kevin asked impatiently.

Mr. Adams scratched his cheek uncomfortably and then leaned back in his chair. He took a deep breath through his nose, giving Kevin a forlorn stare.

"See, here's the thing, Kevin. I haven't been fully honest with you. This isn't actually a summer camp."

He glared at Kevin in silence, as if expecting a response from him. Kevin continued staring, allowing the head counselor to continue.

"It's a correctional camp. Parents send their kids here when they deem it necessary for them to change. That change can range from fixing problems with a defiant kid to an overweight kid, to a lazy kid or whatever kid like that. But the problem is they can't just tell the kids they're sending them to a correctional camp. I mean, you can imagine how the kids would rebel then, right? It would make my job *really* difficult." Mr. Adams chuckled.

Kevin continued staring at him with a stare that clearly demanded more answers. Mr. Adams seemed to notice this, so he wiped the smile off his face and continued.

"Anyway, the correctional camp is usually eight weeks, but some campers stay less than that. However, some have to stay *longer*. Now, if I remember correctly, your parents sent you here because you were rebellious and lacking discipline. That was, at least, their description. But, since you were brought here much later than the other campers, you'll be leaving in just a few weeks. Isn't that great?" He smiled again, but again, Kevin refused to smile back.

"So, you're telling me that all this labor and abuse of the campers are part of the program?" Kevin asked skeptically.

"Yes," Mr. Adams nodded. "Unfortunately, some staff members here tend to go overboard with their authority, like Dwight, so we have to remind them often not to treat campers like inmates. But I can assure you all of this is part of the program."

"Even the part where campers go missing in the woods?" Kevin asked defiantly.

Mr. Adams' meager smile remained frozen on his face before widening into a grin.

"You're talking about The Choosing and The Trial. I see the other campers have already filled you in on the info. So, what was it they told you? The evil counselors send misbehaving campers into the woods to get killed by the Firwood Wraith? Or maybe that they are sent into the woods to fend for themselves and that the counselors don't care if the campers get lost and die of starvation or dehydration as punishment?" He laughed at his own joke.

Now that he said it that way, the missing campers case did seem far-fetched. Mr. Adams threw his hands in the air and said, "I can assure you those campers are a-okay. The ones who were picked for what we call Departure get to leave earlier due to good behavior. That means, if you behave well, you'd be out of here sooner than you think, too."

Kevin looked down at his lap, contemplating the whole situation. What if Mr. Adams was telling the truth? It wasn't like there would be an organization that could make so many kids disappear, all at the same time, right? Plus, the parents would come looking for the kids.

It all made sense, but Kevin still wasn't one hundred percent convinced. The camp may have been a correctional facility, but that didn't take away from the fact that they were incorporating illegal activities to keep the campers in check. He couldn't believe that his parents sent him to a place like this and even hid from him the actual purpose of the camp. But was that really so unbelievable? He was pretty rebellious, and he knew that they were getting fed up with him. It actually made total sense for them to send him here in hopes of having his behavior corrected.

That thought made him angry. He looked at the phone on the desk. His way out. He would not do as they wanted. No, he would still look for a way out of Camp Firwood even if the other campers wouldn't help him. Even if his parents would kick him out of his home. Hell, he hoped they would. But he couldn't tell Mr. Adams about it. He was already suspicious as it was and would probably have Keven monitored more closely. He would need to stay under the radar until the right moment.

"Alright, Mr. Adams," he said. "You may be right. Maybe I was just too paranoid about what happened to the missing campers. I watched a lot of thriller movies, and I just… well, you know."

Mr. Adams eyed Kevin for a moment before chuckling and saying, "Well, no hard feelings, camper. I can understand your skepticism. Trust me, I would like nothing more than for you to be released from this place as soon as possible. Unfortunately, I didn't make the rules, so both you and I have to abide by them. So, here's what I have in mind."

He leaned in closer, his expression contorting into a serious one as he interlocked his fingers. It took everything in Kevin not to look away under his intense stare.

"You do what the camp orders you to. Finish your duties and do your time, and I'll see if I can't put in a good word with the director. As I said, well-behaved campers are usually released early. But misbehaving campers, on the other hand… they can get an extended time. And not just for themselves but for their cabin mates, too. It would be a real shame if one of your friends… say, Mark… had only one week remaining, and then his time got extended because of something someone else did. You agree with me, right?"

He knows. He knows I became friends with Mark, and he's threatening me.

157

Kevin timidly nodded, feeling a mixture of anger and fear. Mr. Adams smiled and happily slammed his palm on the table.

"Good. So, we have a deal then," he stood up, his full height reaching toward the ceiling. "Alright, you head on to the mess hall. And after that, talk to Mr. Baldwin. I think he needs someone for watchtower duty."

"Yes, Mr. Adams." Kevin decided to play along as he mirrored the counselor's movement and stood up.

He threw a furtive glance at the phone on the desk one last time before turning around on his heel and exiting the office.

***

The other campers were already in front of the mess hall, lined up, waiting for their turn to grab some chow. Kevin inquisitively swiveled his head, looking for cabin four members. Barrel Mark saw him long before Kevin saw him, and a wide smile stretched across his face. Kevin smiled back and shrugged as if he hadn't just been through two days of hell. Once he located them, he rushed toward Steve and Michael.

"You guys mind making some room?" he asked with a conniving grin.

"Look who's back! And I can see they were pretty gentle with you," Steve called out with a pleasant smile while Michael just shot him a bemused glance.

Steve turned in front of him and nudged Slow Ethan, saying, "Move a little, will ya?"

Slow Ethan jerked around to see what was going on before inching a step closer to Mark.

"Thank you ever so much," Kevin ironically said, squeezing himself between Steve and a not-so-happy Michael.

He felt surprisingly good. For the first time since he arrived, he knew what he needed to do. He had a concrete plan.

"So, how was detention?" Steve turned around and grinned tantalizingly.

"Well, it's no five-star hotel, I'll tell you that." Kevin shook his head.

"That can't be," Steve said just in time for the line to move forward slightly. "Peter and Jordan give you trouble?"

"What do you think? They beat the crap out of me on the first day," Kevin pointed to the black eye, furrowing his nose at the memory of the searing pain in his body as he took the beating and being thrown in that cold, stinky cell.

He wanted to change the topic, so he asked Steve.

"Did you guys receive any punishment for my... insubordination?"

"Nah. I guess Mr. Adams wanted to punish only you. You know, you're fortunate to get out of detention so quickly. Mr. Adams does not take kindly to campers directly disobeying them. Or anyone else for that matter."

"Well, Mr. Adams can suck my balls," Kevin responded, much to Steve's snorted laughter.

The line moved pretty quickly from there on, up until it was Slow Ethan's turn to get the food. They had cereal for breakfast, and Kevin, for once, was looking forward to it. It had been days since he had any sugar at all, and he reckoned that he might have been getting moody because of it, on top of everything else that was going on.

When he grabbed his bowl and stepped out of the food line, he saw Mark loyally waiting for him with an eager expression.

"Come on, Cocky Kevin," he said. "There's room at this table."

Kevin couldn't help but smile. He had his doubts about ever keeping in touch with anybody from this camp once this was all over, but Mark's kind-hearted nature assured him that he definitely wanted to have someone like him in his life as a friend. They scurried over to one empty table and sat across from each other. Mark wasted no time digging into his cereals, making slurping noises each time he brought the overflowing spoon to his mouth.

159

Despite eating so voraciously, he remembered to stop after a few bites and look in Kevin's direction.

"So, what happened?" he asked.

Kevin took a spoonful of milk and cornflakes, feeling slightly disappointed at the soggy bread-like texture.

Better than the chewy ham from yesterday's breakfast, he thought to himself with self-assurance.

"You mean in the detention house?" Kevin swallowed and asked.

"No, I mean back home. Of course, I mean in the detention house."

Kevin laughed. Mark didn't look like the type capable of making sarcastic remarks, so this was a pleasant surprise.

"Well, have you ever been there?" Kevin asked, already knowing the answer.

"No. I'm a well-behaved camper," Mark said before putting two more full spoons of cereal in his mouth with an obnoxious slurp.

"Well, anyway," Kevin continued. "Not much happened. Some beatings, some useless chores, that kind of thing. I met a camper there. He said his name is Sneaky Rob."

"Oh yeah. Great guy, that one. He once stole spam and gave it to me because he doesn't like it."

"Why did he steal it if he doesn't like it?" Kevin confusedly frowned.

"He was supposedly in a hurry when the storage door was left open. He grabbed the first can he could find and wasn't looking at the label, I guess. Anyway, worked out well for me."

Kevin chuckled. He took another spoon of his food before turning serious. Mark had already finished most of his food and was now holding the bowl up to his lips with both hands, pouring the remaining contents into his mouth like it was a sewer drain.

"Hey, Mark. Let me ask you something," Kevin started.

Mark put the bowl down, his mouth messy from the milk. He wiped his mouth with his hand and asked, "Ask away."

160

"Does it make you angry that your parents sent you here for weight loss?" Kevin asked somberly, thinking back to his own parents and the bad relationship they have.

Mark shook his head confidently.

"No, not really. I already knew what they thought of me. I didn't expect them to do something like this, but I'm not surprised, either. I guess…" he looked left, outside one of the windows, toward the pine tree which delicately swung in the breeze. "I guess I don't know if I would have done the same with my kid. You know?"

"I know you wouldn't. You're not like your parents."

Mark shrugged disdainfully.

"Maybe they just didn't know how bad it really is here at the camp."

Kevin looked at his bowl of half-eaten cereals. The cornflakes were woefully floating on top of the milk.

"Yeah, maybe you're right," Kevin lied as he slid the bowl to Mark.

"You don't want it?" Mark asked, but the usual glare in his eye when seeing food was gone this time.

"Yeah. I'm not feeling hungry," Kevin truthfully said and waved his hand.

"Gee, thanks, Kev," Mark smiled, picking up his spoon again.

In a few minutes, one counselor stopped in the middle of the mess hall and shouted, "Campers! I want all of you to be on the Choosing grounds when you're done with breakfast! We've got Repentance! Got it?!"

Kevin looked at Mark, who looked like his face was drained of all color. He noticed just then that the other campers were suddenly looking worried as well as they exchanged anxious remarks with each other.

"Mark, what's going on?" Kevin asked.

"I… I dunno," Mark timorously said. "I guess we're having Repentance."

"What's that?"

"It's when someone does something really bad, and then the counselors need to choose one person who they send into the woods to survive for one week."

"What? That's absurd."

Mark looked at him but said nothing. The mood in the mess hall drastically changed from zero to one hundred in just a few seconds. Everyone went quiet, and once they were done with breakfast, they proceeded outside the mess hall. Although most of the campers were extremely distressed, some were behaving like nothing special was happening. A few of the campers asked Kevin about his experience in the detention house, but most of them, to his relief, didn't care enough to bother him with questions. He just finished listening to Tough Norton talking about wanting to beat the shit out of Jordan and Peter when he heard a voice behind him.

"Welcome back, Cocky Kevin," said the familiar voice.

Kevin smiled and, before even turning around, called out to the camper full of joy, "Sneaky Rob, you son of a bitch."

When he turned around, he saw Rob standing in front of him with a mischievous smile. He put his hand forward, and Kevin accepted it in a greeting. Despite being from different cabins, Kevin felt that he shared a special bond with Rob, having been a prisoner along with him for two whole days. Mark was still his favorite camper, but Rob's cheerful attitude didn't fall far behind.

"So, ready to start your life here, Camp Firwood style?" Rob asked.

"Not even a little. But I'll try to adapt," Kevin lied.

"If you don't get picked for Repentance, that is."

Kevin shook his head with a frown.

"Oh, speaking of which, I need to find Baldwin," he said.

"What for?" Rob frowned.

"Watchtower duty or something," Kevin absentmindedly said, looking around to see if the counselor's shiny head would be visible anywhere in the area.

"Lucky bastard," Rob replied. "Guess you'll have to do it after we're done with the Choosing. Anyway, try to stay out of trouble."

He patted Kevin on the shoulder and went back to his cabin mates. No counselors were anywhere outside, so Kevin assumed they'd be here a bit later before they took the campers to training. The campers' murmurs filled the air for a solid ten minutes or so until the shiny head of Mr. Baldwin appeared outside.

"Alright, campers, move it! I want all of you to be on the Choosing Grounds in five minutes!" he shouted.

The campers immediately began walking like they were being herded left of the mess hall, following a trail that wound between the main rows of buildings. The trail went straight between the rows of trees and then wound right.

"This is because of Cocky Kevin!" one camper shouted.

"Yeah, he's the only one who misbehaved recently!" another one said.

"Let's not jump the gun here, alright?" Steve said. "If it really was because of him, we can give him the blanket treatment later."

Kevin leaned closer to Mark and said, "Mark, what the hell is the blanket treatment?"

"It's when campers get around your bed while you're sleeping and tighten the blanket so you can't move, and then they beat you up with soaps in socks."

"Wow. Imagine if the campers put more effort into actually doing something useful," he hinted at escaping without actually saying it.

He didn't feel thrilled by the fact of possibly getting the blanket treatment, but if it came to it, he would take it like a man. He'd screwed up, but now he knew how to handle the camp's rules. The campers were mostly quiet all the way until the trail opened up to a vast meadow. Kevin squinted and saw what looked like a stage (which ominously reminded him of the gallows where they used to hang people in the old days) and, in front of the stage, rows and

163

rows of tree stumps placed like nature's seats. These were, without a doubt, the Choosing Grounds.

The campers quietly made their way to the stumps, and each took a random seat. According to Mark, it didn't matter where they sat as long as they just followed the basic rules – which included looking straight and not talking. Kevin took a seat next to Mark, somewhere in the middle, and patiently waited. The soft and now somewhat quieter murmurs of the campers filled the air as they speculated the reason for Repentance. A few contemptuous glances were cast in Kevin's direction, but he ignored them. He wanted to tell them to fuck off, but he knew that they were in the right, and he was in the wrong.

"Here they come. Everybody shut the fuck up," Steve said from behind Kevin.

Kevin glanced behind himself long enough to see Mr. Adams, Dwight, and a few other counselors walking down the trail toward the campers. A few minutes later, they arrived, and the campers had gone eerily silent by then, only the occasional chirping of a bird being heard. The counselors climbed on top of the wooden stage in front. Mr. Adams took up a spot right in front of the campers, looking even more like a grasshopper in an elevated position.

He was standing with his nose buried in his notepad as he annoyingly hummed the usual song. Moments later, he looked up and said, "Good morning again, campers!"

"Good morning, Mr. Adams," the campers roared, Kevin along with them.

He now knew the gist of what the camp was about. He would play along until it was time for his plan to come to fruition. Until then, order away Mr. Adams. Order away.

Mr. Adams smiled and said, "I know none of you want to be here. Trust me, I don't want to be here, either. However, recent actions of a certain camper have led to this, I'm afraid. You all know the rules, and yet someone decided that he was above them."

He placed both hands, along with the notepad, behind his back and scanned the campers with his gaze. When he found Kevin, he retained eye contact for a long moment, but Kevin refused to look away.

Look forward. Don't talk.

Mr. Adams continued glowering at the other campers before saying, "Cabin five, number six, stand up!"

Kevin pivoted his head to the left but then realized that all the other campers were still looking in front of themselves, so he quickly returned his gaze to the front.

"Cabin five, number six!" Mr. Adams repeated.

A low shuffling noise came from somewhere on Kevin's left.

"Step onto the stage, camper," Mr. Adams said.

There was a patter of soft footsteps upon the grass, and a camper whose name Kevin didn't know went between the rows of campers and timidly climbed onto the stage, stopping right in front of Mr. Adams, staring at him like a puppy. Mr. Adams continued staring at the seated campers before pointing the finger at the accused teen on the stage and said, "Upon searching the lockers this morning, we found that this camper has been stealing meds from the infirmary."

The camper looked terrified. His eyes widened, and he looked at the other teens before turning to Mr. Adams and shaking his head.

"Mr. Adams, I didn't-"

"You all know that we have rules that we can tolerate getting broken and rules that are not to be broken under any circumstances!" Mr. Adams started looking red in the face. "And equally to that, you know what the punishment is!"

He turned to the counselors standing on the stage behind him and said, "Counselors, escort this camper to the edge of the woods and send him on his way!" he then turned to the camper. "Camper, due to the nature of the punishment, you will be getting no supplies from the camp. But, you still have a chance to fix your wrongdoing.

Now, go into the woods, and think about your actions for seven days. After that, we'll see what to do with you."

"Mr. Adams, please!" The camper suddenly became hysterical.

Two of the counselors were already striding toward him, and he fell on his knees, pleading with the head counselor.

"Please, don't send me there!" He screamed as he was picked up and carried off stage. "The wraith is gonna kill me! I only took one box of pills, I swear! Please!"

Kevin watched in horror as the counselors carried the camper all the way to the edge of the woods on the other side of the Choosing grounds and shoved him forward. He continued pleading and refusing to go inside the woods until one of the counselors backhanded him, causing the camper to spin around and fall to the ground.

What the fuck.

The camper scurried off into the woods, disappearing in the trees.

8

Amy

The air fell silent once again. Mr. Adams subverted his glance down to his notepad, now completely calm and humming as if nothing had happened, carefully flipping through the pages. With his gaze transfixed on the papers, he mumbled, "Okay, we already had the roll call and routine before breakfast, let's see here..."

Kevin couldn't believe how indifferent he suddenly was.

"Oh, that's right. Dwight!" he called out, still focused on the papers.

"Yes, Mr. Adams?" Dwight, the ever-tough assistant counselor, immediately jerked his face in the head counselor's direction.

"Take... let's say... four campers and go to the main lodge. Get the tarps and hatchets."

Mr. Adams proceeded to explain something to the assistant counselor, but Kevin was transfixed on the treeline where the camper had disappeared. He couldn't help but wonder what the hell would happen to him, but at the same time, he suddenly felt much more afraid for his life. Whatever was happening here was *much worse* than he thought.

"Right away, Mr. Adams," Dwight energetically nodded multiple times before turning to the campers.

He pointed his finger randomly at four campers in the front row and said with much more authority this time, "You, you, you, and you. Come with me!"

The four unlucky campers were stupefied for a moment until Dwight's commanding shouts spurred them to move. They stood up from the tree stumps and followed him behind the rest of the seated campers. Mr. Adams looked at the remaining campers, who were still in a trance. The head counselor didn't seem to care about that, though, because he continued.

167

"Alright, campers, since most of you weren't satisfactory at tent-building, we're going to rehash today what we learned a while ago. We're going to be building basic shelter." He turned to Counselor Baldwin, who had returned to the stage by then. "Mr. Baldwin, when Dwight and the campers return with the hatchets, take them to the designated area."

"Yes, Mr. Adams," Mr. Baldwin nodded, the sun's reflection bouncing on and off his glistening top. "But before that, I still need someone for watchtower duty today."

Mr. Adams snapped his fingers.

"Oh, that's right, the other camper got sick today and is in the infirmary. There's one camper who just returned from detention. Where is he now…"

He glanced around the campers, searching for a familiar face, and Kevin just knew that this was a test. He knew damn well who and where he was.

Play along, Kevin. For now, a voice in his head told him.

Kevin raised his hand high up, still looking straight in front of him just like the other campers. Mr. Adams snapped his fingers again, meeting Kevin's gaze. He pointed at him and looked at Mr. Baldwin.

"That one there. He can replace the sick one."

"Camper, get over here!" Mr. Baldwin bellowed sternly while holding his hands behind his back, truly like a military type.

Kevin stood up and rushed between the campers and climbed up the stairs of the stage before stopping in front of Baldwin. They weren't looking directly at him, but Kevin felt the other campers' eyes on him.

"You're gonna do watchtower duty today!" Mr. Baldwin probed Kevin with a frown as if measuring if he was made of good material for this job.

"Yes, Mr. Baldwin," Kevin briskly responded.

"You got a watch?" Baldwin asked in what sounded like an accusatory tone.

Your boss took my fucking phone, he wanted to say but suppressed that thought and simply responded, "No, Mr. Baldwin."

Counselor Baldwin reached into his pocket with one hand and pulled out a tiny pocket watch. He stretched out the hand, holding the watch, and Kevin took that as a sign that he should get closer to take it.

"Keep this close. Don't lose it, or it'll come out of your pocket with some extra work. Understand?"

"Yes, Mr. Baldwin," Kevin gritted his teeth, feeling disgusted by his own obedience.

He took the pocket watch from the counselor and looked at it. It looked like it was at least ten years old, judging by the scratches on the glass and the worn-out colors on the case. It was fifteen minutes past eight when he looked at the time before he put the watch in his right-side pocket, which he promptly zipped up to ensure he didn't lose it.

"You know how the shifts for the watchtower work, don't you?" Mr. Baldwin speedily asked.

"No," Kevin shook his head.

"No, what?" the counselor asked him impatiently.

Mr. Adams was still flipping through the pages on his notepad while Mr. Baldwin stared at Kevin, leaning forward a little with both hands behind his back.

"No, Mr. Baldwin," he said.

Baldwin shook his head with a frown before sighing. By this time, Dwight and the four campers appeared in the distance again, carrying big, green bags and walking toward the group.

"Be at the watchtower at 10 a.m. You'll be there for one hour until the next camper relieves you. Then you have two hours off until your next shift. There are three campers, one on each shift, so you need to repeat this until 6 a.m. That means one hour on, two hours off. At 6 a.m. is when the next three campers take over. Got it?"

"Yes… Mr. Baldwin," he replied, realizing he'd come close to slipping again.

Addressing adults with respect didn't come naturally to Kevin. Addressing someone as rude as the counselors was even more demanding.

"Alright, get back in line. You're coming with the other campers until it's time for your shift," Mr. Baldwin ordered.

"Yes, Mr. Baldwin," Kevin pressed his lips tightly together and, relieved to finally be away from this asshole, turned around, making his way back to his spot.

The silence in the air, mixed with his muffled footsteps, made him feel uncomfortable. He wondered what the other campers were thinking of him now. He was so ballsy a few days ago, and now they had him castrated just like everyone else in the camp. He wouldn't be surprised if he didn't get to keep his nickname Cocky after this. Dwight and the other campers arrived moments later, and Dwight ordered them to place what looked like heavy bags on the ground and get back in line.

"There are forty-two hatchets, and forty-two tarps here, Mr. Adams," Dwight obediently stated.

"Good. Assign some campers to carry the bags, and then I have another job for you." Mr. Adams smiled under his thin mustache.

Dwight picked out six random campers, this time from the second row. Once each of them grabbed the bags, Mr. Adams looked at Baldwin and said, "All set? Alright, Mr. Baldwin, they're all yours!"

"Alright, follow me, campers!" Mr. Baldwin's voice boomed as he got off the stage and began strutting to the right toward the trees, his arms occupying a wide portion of the path due to his inability to put them down from his latissimus muscles.

The campers began walking like a herd again, silently following the counselor, making a huge arc around the stage—and Mr. Adams, who had his nose buried in his notes again. By then, the campers had formed a long line. Mark somehow sneakily appeared next to Kevin. Baldwin led the campers through the small thicket of the woods until they emerged on the left side of the meadow, near the groundskeeper's home. Kevin noticed the groundskeeper's figure returning just then from the woods. He was carrying a backpack over one shoulder before disappearing inside his cabin.

"What was he doing in the woods?" he asked.

Mark shrugged.

"Probably has some chores over there. Something groundskeepers need to do, no idea."

Kevin glanced at the wooden tower in the distance, swarmed by the sea of trees around it. It would be pretty easy to get lost in the woods there.

Or disappearing.

His thoughts suddenly returned again to the camper who was sent for Repentance. He wondered what he would do if he found himself in that situation – without any equipment, surrounded by thousands of acres of trees.

"You know how to reach the tower?" Mark asked, albeit somewhat quieter than usual, probably because of the proximity Baldwin was at.

Kevin looked in his direction before glancing back at the tower.

"I don't. But it's not that far, is it?" he asked.

"There's a path. Come here." He gestured with his hand.

Kevin followed him to the right, a little bit away from the other campers so that their view was clear.

"Look there," Mark pointed his index over yonder.

Kevin squinted, unable to see what Mark was pointing at. He darted his eyes around in futility until Mark said.

"Over there, where the path ends in the woods."

Kevin followed the small path with his gaze. Somewhere in the middle, it turned left and led to the groundskeeper's cabin, but it also led straight between the trees, disappearing in the shadows ahead.

"Okay, I see it," he said.

"Cool. So just follow that path, and you'll reach the tower in about five minutes. But make sure not to stray off the path."

171

"Why would I stray off the path? It's not like I'm trying to escape or anything." Kevin grinned connivingly.

Mark didn't return the gesture.

"If you wanna make it in time, you should ask Mr. Baldwin to leave at about ten minutes to ten," he coldly retorted.

"But what do I do up there?" Kevin scratched the back of his head.

"The camper who's up there will fill you in on the details. You just gotta make sure to show up on time."

Mr. Baldwin and the campers had turned slightly right and got off the trail, moving toward the treeline ahead. The concrete building, which was visible on his right, caught Kevin's eye before he looked back at Mark.

"Have you ever been on the watchtower?" he asked him, averting his gaze from the building.

"So far, only twice. It's actually one of the better duties. All you gotta do is sit there and keep a lookout for fires or anything like that," Mark shrugged.

Kevin looked to the left at one of the campers lugging the big bag over his shoulder. Beads of sweat were running down his forehead, and he was hunched over, wearing a grimace that looked like he was in a lot of pain. Kevin wanted to offer to help him, but another camper rushed before he could and took over the load from him, much to the troubled camper's relief. The group was led by Baldwin toward a small, barely visible trail that started at the foot of the treeline and disappeared inside the woods.

"Form up in a line! I don't want to see anyone going off trail!" Baldwin barked, the glistening on his bald head disappearing as soon as he entered the shade of the trees.

It took the campers a moment to reorganize their positions according to the cabins, and when they finally did, a few minutes had already gone by. It was considerably darker inside the forest, even so close to the open meadow. The firs were blocking a lot of the sunlight, and the somewhat quiet air from the outside now seemed to be riddled with sounds of various birds chirping. Kevin couldn't help but revel slightly in the situation.

It reminded him a lot of the trips to Tryon Creek State Park he had with Henry, Rick, and Luis. They used to go there on the weekends so they could sit, relax and smoke some weed. Kevin didn't smoke, and he didn't mind them smoking - he just enjoyed spending time with his friends in nature. He invited Amy to go there with him once, but she instead suggested they go to Barton Park. Just the two of them. Feeling intrigued by her description of the place, he went with her to the other park, and they ended up talking for hours while drinking beer. Now that he was in these woods, which seemed so familiar and yet so hostile, he couldn't help but vividly recall that day in his mind.

***

"Let's sit over there, huh?" Amy enthusiastically suggested, pointing to the shore near the river.

No one was sitting there since it wasn't exactly a spot designated for hikers or campers. A big bridge hung sturdily above the Clackamas River to their right, under the gleaming afternoon sun. The place Amy was pointing to was restricted by a sign warning hikers not to get on the shore due to the potential dangers of falling inside the river and drowning. Apparently, the current in Clackamas was so strong that one time, three swimmers drowned in just one day before lifeguards were placed on duty.

Before Kevin could protest anything, Amy rushed down the small hill leading and to the shore, unsteadily swaying her arms left and right, her oversized black t-shirt gyrating behind her from the gust. Kevin followed, stepping off the trail and gaining momentum down the hill but controlling it to prevent running straight into the river. Amy stopped on the bank, a few feet away from the water, and sat on the grass, her black hair fluttering in the wind. Kevin sat next to her, carefully placing the bottle of beer on the portion of the ground that wasn't steep. Amy stared at the river with what looked like delight on her face while Kevin stared at her. He enjoyed seeing the hair flutter against her face and her gently moving it behind her ear.

She didn't look like the type to enjoy the beauty of the great outdoors, but then again, Amy was surprising in her own ways. When Kevin first met her, he thought she was a typical goth girl who enjoyed drinking, listening to heavy metal, smoking weed, and performing satanic rituals in cemeteries in her free time. The fact that she only did the first two pleasantly surprised Kevin when he got to know her better.

They first met at Josh's party. Josh was a nerdy kid who wanted to fit in, so he threw a big party in his parents' place when they left on a business trip. Kevin arrived with his gang around the time when the illegal drinking was already at a full boom, with loud music blaring enough to alert any nearby neighbors. Kevin didn't even see Amy until she just suddenly appeared in front of him with a red paper cup. The first thing he couldn't help but notice was how cute she was. She said something he couldn't hear over the loud music and pointed down at his feet. He looked down and realized that his shoelaces were untied.

By the time Kevin realized what she was pointing to, she rolled her eyes, nudged the plastic cup to him, and bent down to tie his laces. When she stood up, she flashed him a toothy smile and made a goofy ta-da pose. Her friend Carla came to her by then and noticed that she was supposedly talking to Kevin. Kevin asked the two of them if they wanted to join him with his gang out front by the porch, to which they happily obliged. They spent the night hanging out with Kevin and Amy managing to sneak more private conversations with each other when they were left alone for the brief moments while a drunk Luis tried demonstrating his skateboarding tricks to the others. From there, they exchanged social media info and stayed in touch.

Although Henry found Carla hot and wanted to bang her, he ultimately gave up the idea when Rick told him *bros before hoes* and that 'banging bitches can ruin friendships.' Although the entire gang followed that code, it was pretty much an open secret that Amy and Kevin had a thing for each other. Henry would often try to find ways to get them alone to give Kevin a chance to hit on her. Kevin, unfortunately, was too much of a chickenshit to do anything drastic.

"So you've never been here?" Amy asked with a look of intrigue in her eye, her hair fluttering back into her face from the intermittent breeze.

"Never. The guys and I only went to Tryon," Kevin took a sip of his beer and looked at the raging river.

"Well, I showed you my favorite place, so you can show me yours next time," Amy smiled.

"Sounds like a deal," Kevin winked.

They talked about nonsensical things like school and their interests until the topic shifted into what they planned for the future. Amy liked Portland. She didn't know exactly what she wanted to do with her life after school, but she knew she wanted to stay in Oregon. When she asked Kevin about his own plans, he shrugged and said that he just wants to move out of his parents' place for now.

This prompted them to talk about their families. Amy told him about her extremely strict step-father, how he set up curfews for her - which she always ended up disobeying - ordering her around, which she ended up ignoring, and a half-dozen other things. Her mother mostly held her step-father's side, so she never stepped in to stop the abuse. Kevin told her about his own parents, about how they constantly put pressure on him regarding his behavior, how they wanted him to be more like his cousin Neil, that he would never make it far in life like this, and so on.

They commiserated together, and from there, they went on to talk about other topics. Night had already fallen, and Amy mentioned it was getting late and that they should be heading home soon. Kevin just then realized how hungry he was since he hadn't eaten in over five hours which he spent with Amy. Just as they were about to leave, a park ranger, who happened to be patrolling, called out to them, telling them that they weren't supposed to be there and that he would call the police on account of underage drinking, littering, and trespassing. Kevin told him to chill out, but the ranger stepped down the hill and moved their way.

Amy tugged Kevin's hand, and the two of them started running down the shore, ignoring the spiteful shouts of the ranger. Eventually, they managed to get in the cover of the trees and stopped to take a breather. They were both giggling and panting together but tried being quiet to avoid getting the ranger's attention. Amy went over to a tree and peeked around it while Kevin got behind her, looking over her shoulder.

"He's not there," she said and turned around, practically bumping into Kevin.

They stared into each other's eyes for a prolonged moment with nothing but the sound of crickets surrounding them. Kevin suddenly grew self-conscious about his breath. He wondered if Amy could smell it, or if her own breath was masking it. He felt his heart beating heavily, and it wasn't from the running. He raised a hand and gently moved the hair from her eye.

This is it. Kiss her! Now! he shouted at himself.

He leaned closer and then-

They heard the voice of the ranger in the distance once again, which caused them to snap their heads in the direction of the voice. As they snuck out of the park, Kevin felt, for the first time in a long time in his life, alive.

Remembering that day with Amy brought him some comfort. He spent many nights imagining what it would have been like if he'd actually kissed her then. Would they be a couple now?

He smiled at the thought before Mr. Baldwin's voice jolted him back to the morbid reality he was in.

9

Watchtower

"Alright, campers! Gather round!" Baldwin shouted from the front.

They reached a large open portion of the forest grounds where the trees mostly retreated to the back, in a way that essentially formed a circle in the area. It was evident from the unnaturally beaten ground that the camp used this area to host any number of forest activities. The campers formed a big circle around Mr. Baldwin, careful not to get too close to him. The ones carrying the bags put them down next to each other, close to Mr. Baldwin, with a grunt of relief.

"Alright, listen up!" he roared. "We'll be making tents today. I want every one of you to grab a hatchet and cut down three sticks like you've been shown before. Bring them here, each on your own pile, and then we'll get to work. Move it!"

Kevin didn't even need to look for Mark since the camper already had his hand on his shoulder to indicate that he should follow him.

"Come on, let's get our hatchets, and I'll show you what to do," Mark said, waiting for the group of campers around the big bags to clear out.

Once they dispersed, Kevin saw the bundle of small hatchets in the untied bags. Mark took two and handed one to Kevin. Kevin took it and felt its weight in his hand. He imagined it would be relatively easy to swing it. As he glanced at the majority of the campers who had the hatchets, he thought about how easy it would be to overtake the camp with the weapons in their hands. But to do that, they would need to be unified, which they weren't. Most of the campers were blindly obedient and would not even think about raising their hands on the counselors. Even Norton, whose nickname was Tough, was obedient to an extent - despite the heroic stories told about him - and just wanted to stay out of trouble, which was understandable.

The campers were already dispersing into the woods with their hatchets, and Mark led Kevin in a random direction through the foliage. Kevin was dying to tell Mark what Mr. Adams told him when he took him into the office, but he wasn't sure how he would react, so he ultimately decided against it. They walked in a straight line for about a minute, putting some distance between themselves and the other campers. They could still see some of them here and there and hear their voices, but it was much quieter now.

"We need to cut down three strong branches," Mark said.

"Alright. What kind?" Kevin inquisitively asked.

"Like this one," Mark pointed to one sturdy, fallen branch.

He approached it, eyeing it before gripping his hatchet firmly and kneeling down. He held the stick down with his left hand and started hitting it with the hatchet near one end.

"It needs to be around ten to twelve feet," Mark said as he chipped away at the stick, sending tiny pieces of wood sent flying in various directions with each hit.

"What can I do?" Kevin asked.

"Try to find another stick like this one. But make sure it has a wedge on one end. Or find four sticks of about four to five feet long. But make sure they're strong." Mark continued hitting the wood, beads of sweat already forming on his forehead.

"Alright, I can do that," Kevin swiveled around to see if he can find any potential stick candidates.

He walked around and found stacks of fallen branches; however, most of them proved to be too fragile. He ended up using his hatchet to chop up a sturdy bough, which fell with a whooshing and rustling sound. He stripped it of all the little twigs and greenery, using his eye to measure it. Once he was satisfied with the length, he went back to Mark. Mark was now somehow shaping the tip of the branch with the hatchet, and curious, Kevin asked him, "What are you doing?"

Mark glanced in his direction, red in the face from the heavy work, before looking back down at his stick and saying, "We need to shape the sticks to be pointy so that we can stick them in the ground more easily. Try doing it to the stick you just brought."

Kevin confusedly inspected both ends of the stick before figuring out which one was sharper. He opted for shaping that one, so he placed the stick on the ground, held it down like Mark, and used the hatchet to gently chip away at the wood. It was harder than it looked. Mark seemed so proficient at it, making neat-looking points that could even serve as spears, whereas his own ends of the stick were crudely shaped. Mark jumped in to help him, and in a matter of fifteen minutes, they had two big sticks with wedges and four smaller ones.

"Hurry it up, campers!" Mr. Baldwin's voice roared from somewhere in the distance, and Kevin knew it was time to get back to the impatient counselor.

He put all the sticks they had on one stack and picked them up, much to Mark's protests.

"You did all the heavy work. Let me at least do this," Kevin insisted.

They made their way between the trees, the sound of their shoes rustling in the grass and leaves with each step, while the birds chirped loudly from various directions.

"I never asked about you," Mark suddenly said.

"What?" Kevin asked in confusion, not sure what Mark was referring to.

"About what you're like back home. I never asked you. Like, I know a little bit about what you like to do in your free time, but that's about it. And I didn't want you to think I didn't care enough to ask because, I mean, I do. We just didn't have the time to talk about it."

Kevin chuckled heartily, feeling a sudden surge of even more respect for Mark.

"Well, what exactly do you want to know?" he enthusiastically asked him.

"I dunno. What bands do you listen to?"

"Good question," Kevin frowned, carefully staring at the ground to make sure he didn't step somewhere hazardous. "I guess I spend a lot of my time listening to Rise Against, System of a Down, and then some old ones like The Offspring, Blink 182... that kind of thing."

"Hm. So you probably like to party a lot, huh?"

"Sometimes."

There was a moment of silence before Mark asked, "Did you have anyone... special? Back home?"

Kevin exhaled. That question hit him like a knife in the heart, but at the same time, he felt a warm feeling that he couldn't explain. He nodded.

"Yeah, I guess I did. Her name's Amy. She and I are good friends, but, um..." he stopped to choose the right words.

"Is she taken or something?"

"No, nothing like that."

"She doesn't like you back?"

"No, no. I think she does, but-"

"She doesn't like boys?"

"No, what? No, that's not it. I just... I kinda chickened out whenever I had the chance to try something with her," he woefully replied, suddenly feeling sad at the thought.

"Hey, don't beat yourself up. You'll get a chance to ask her once you're out of here. I'm sure she's gonna be waiting for you." Mark smiled as he patted Kevin on the back.

For a moment, Kevin wondered if Mark could read his mind. He smiled at Mark's encouragement.

"Thanks, Mark," he said, feeling better already.

They continued walking, and then Mark asked, "So, what's she like?"

Kevin felt an inadvertent smile forming on his face.

"She's like a goth girl. Black hair, usually wears black clothes, too. But she's not troublesome like the chicks in the movies and TV shows. She's really smart, really good at knowing what to say and when to make people feel better. She's good at drawing. Creepy stuff, but still good."

"Is that why you like her?" Mark asked.

Kevin frowned. That was a valid question. He never thought about it actively, but now that Mark asked him, he could name a number of reasons why he liked her: the way she smiled, her green eyes, the jokes she made, the way she didn't have a care in the world…

"Yeah. That and many other things," Kevin said before quickly turning the tables. "What about you? Got someone special at home? I mean, special in a non-family kind of way?"

"No. But I do have a dog back home. His name is Ben. He's a dachshund. You know, one of those dogs that look like a sausage."

"That breed is great," Kevin laughed.

"Well, I often let him sleep with Sherry and me in the room during winter since he's a little old and can't stand the cold."

"Your parents give you shit for that?"

"No, I usually hide him under the bed. He sleeps a lot, so he doesn't flinch when they come in." Mark smiled.

"Good dog."

"Yeah. I kinda miss him. I hope Sherry's taking good care of him. And I hope he remembers me when I come back," Mark somberly said.

Shit, what do I say now?

Unlike Amy, Kevin was terrible at making people feel better.

"Hey, don't worry. Dogs don't forget. So when he sees you, you can probably expect him to jump on you out of happiness."

Mark smiled contentedly, which Kevin took as a sign that what he said was somewhat good.

When they made it back to the open area where Mr. Baldwin was, most of the campers had already returned. Each camper was standing in front of his own pile of sticks, and Mr. Baldwin ordered them to keep some space between each other for easier tent-setting. Mark and Kevin took up spots at the back of the circle, dividing the sticks between each other.

"Hurry up, hurry up!" Mr. Baldwin impatiently shouted at random campers. "My dead grandmother can move faster than you!"

In a matter of minutes, the commotion had died down, and everyone was back at the meeting place, each in his own spot. Mr. Baldwin made sure to count all the campers, and once everyone was accounted for, he put his hands behind his back and cleared his throat.

"Alright, listen up! Set up the skeleton of the shelter. For those of you who don't know how to do it, look at your fellow campers and copy them."

"Mr. Baldwin, how do we do it without the string?" one camper asked.

"Make do with what you can. Wedge those sticks real good. I don't wanna see any flimsy tents here! Get to it!"

The campers unanimously began bending down and picking up the largest sticks of their bunch. Kevin looked right in Mark's direction, and when he realized he was doing the same as the others, he mimicked their movement and lifted the big stick from the ground, too.

Mark looked at him and said, "Okay, listen. Here's what you do. Take the big stick and stab it into the ground like this as deeply as you can."

He proceeded to demonstrate the motion by raising the stick above his head and thrusting it into the ground at a forty-five-degree angle. He pulled the stick out of the ground, and measuring it with his eye, he thrust it forcefully into the ground again, making sure to bury it as deep as possible. Still holding the top of the stick with one hand, he picked up the smaller stick and placed one end of it on the wedge of the already buried stick. He proceeded to put the smaller stick in the ground as well before grabbing the third one and doing the same thing so that the three sticks formed a sort of pyramid, the two smaller ones forming the letter A, with the big stick's wedge at the top as support.

Mark made sure that each stick was in the ground and stable, after which he gave them a little shake. The sticks didn't rattle, which Kevin thought was a good sign. Breathing heavily, Mark turned to Kevin and said, "Okay, now let's do yours."

Kevin didn't think that making a shelter like this was overly hard, especially after seeing Mark's demonstration. However, he soon realized how wrong he was. Wedging the sticks together so that they supported each other was way more complicated than when he was just watching Mark do it, and he ended up riddling the ground around with multiple holes from stick thrusts. Eventually, with Mark's help, he managed to finish the skeleton of the shelter, making it look almost as good as Mark's. Most of the campers were already finished by then, which Baldwin seemed to notice, so he started shouting again.

"Alright, when you finish the base of your shelter, find four strong twigs, and return here!"

Kevin looked to Mark again, who was already standing in front of one of the trees near the edge of the big circle. He snapped an eight-inches long twig and turned around to show it to Kevin.

"Find four like these," he said, handing the one twig to Kevin as a courtesy.

"Roger that," Kevin responded.

A few minutes later, most of the campers found the twigs with the exception of Slow Ethan and a few others, and Mr. Baldwin roared once more, "Alright! If you found your twigs, grab a tarp and finish up your shelter. I'll be inspecting it as soon as you're done."

Mark rushed over to the center where Baldwin and the open bags were. He pulled out two neatly folded tarps from the bag and returned to his shelter. He handed one tarp to Kevin and said, "Okay, now watch."

He swung his tarp like a blanket, unfolding it with a crackling sound. He slid the tiny hole of the tarp over the top of one of the sticks that formed the A letter and covered the big stick with it like it was a blanket. He then picked up one of the twigs and stretched the tarp to the side along with the smaller stick, holding it firmly while sticking the twigs through the hole of the outstretched tarp and into the ground. He repeated this for all four holes, two sides on each until he had the tarp stretched across the sticks and held firmly upon the ground in an authentic, wedge-tent-like fashion. It looked a little small but large enough for one person to sleep in for the night.

"Wow," Kevin said in awe, amazed at Mark's skills.

"Now, you." Mark pointed to his shelter.

This one was easier than setting up the sticks. Kevin mimicked Mark's movement, stretching the tarp across the forty-five-degree stick and wedging the holes on both sides into the ground. Although he had help, he was proud of the shelter he made.

"Nice work," Mark said. "That's it."

"Hurry it up, you grannies!" Baldwin bellowed.

The campers frantically and hurriedly proceeded to set up their tents while their murmurs filled the air. Kevin heard a few of them arguing with each other about stupid things like encroaching on their space and swapping sticks when they weren't looking. Others who were done were testing out their shelters by squeezing inside them. In minutes, Baldwin looked at his watch and shouted.

"Time's up! Let's see what you miserable excuses for campers have got!"

The few remaining campers who didn't manage to finish it up quickly did what they could to make their shelter look presentable before Baldwin arrived. Baldwin started walking in circles, inspecting the closest shelters first. Each one he'd pass by, he would give a nudge to see how firm it was.

"A little loose, camper," he said when he rattled the sticks Ninja put together.

Kevin soon realized that if Baldwin didn't say anything, it meant they did a good job. Kevin reached into his pocket and pulled out the watch Baldwin had given him. It was 9:45, so he would need to go soon. The counselor continued his inspection, and when he finally reached Mark's shelter, he tried rattling it before giving it a mild kick.

"Not bad, camper," he said, moving on to Kevin's shelter.

He proceeded with the same rattling motion as the previous ones. He pursed his lips and nodded in what looked like surprise.

"Surprisingly good for your first time. I expect it to be better next time."

"Mr. Baldwin? I have to go to watchtower duty now," Kevin said nonchalantly.

Baldwin nodded, not even glancing in his direction before he turned to continue inspecting.

I guess that's a yes?

He thanked Mark for all the help and turned around to leave in the direction from which they had come from. The last decipherable thing he heard before he left the group was Baldwin shouting.

"Campers! If you have no twigs, you can substitute them by putting rocks on your tarp!"

***

Kevin was glad to be away from the shouting counselor. He made his way through the dense forest until he saw the beams of sunlight gleaming ahead more prominently. He stepped into the open field of the campgrounds and located the watchtower in the distance. Remembering what Mark told him, he followed the treeline with his gaze until he located the tiny path disappearing into the woods. Feeling reinvigorated, he jogged to the trail and, from there, proceeded with a quick-paced walk.

Within seconds the trees enveloped his viewpoint, blocking out a lot of the sunlight. The path wound slightly, which made it look like the trees were encroaching on the trail, but Kevin wasn't worried. As long as he stayed on the path, he wouldn't get lost. Although a part of him was hoping he *would* get lost. He wasn't even sure if he was going in the right direction anymore since the path wound so many times in the five minutes he spent walking. There was no way for him to see the tower or even the campgrounds from here.

Just when he started to wonder how long he had until he reached the watchtower, the path started ascending slightly with makeshift wooden steps consisting of half-rotted planks paving the way. Carefully, Kevin started climbing the steps, which slightly wound to the left, until he saw a big, wooden structure towering high up, right in front of him. He couldn't tell how tall it was, but when he looked up at the top, he saw that the tower platform easily stood above the fir trees surrounding it by at least a dozen feet. Symmetrical-looking steps ascended around the tower on all four sides like a python that wound around its prey, reaching all the way to the top.

I'm supposed to climb this thing?

Kevin approached the tower, admiring the massive logs that were put together to create this monstrosity. His heart sank a little when he saw how tall and narrow the steps were. They looked barely wide enough for him to wedge half of his foot on each step, and the steps he would need to take looked around the height of two normal steps.

Well, let's get going then.

He firmly held the wooden railing on both sides as he climbed the first step. Then came the second, and then every subsequent one came with a little more ease. He tried not to look down between the steps as the ground grew farther and farther away with each step he took. He usually felt dizzy when he was high up, but right now, he had no such feeling, although he did feel uneasy. By the time he climbed the second set of stairs winding around the tower, he was already sweating, panting, and his legs were burning. He stopped to catch his breath before continuing to climb up.

A few steps here and there made unsettling, creaking noises, as if the wood wasn't stable enough, so he made sure to avoid putting his entire weight on those planks. After what felt like ten minutes, even though it was around five, in reality, he saw the railing on the top platform above him and the roof of the platform on top of it just a dozen steps ahead. He used his remaining strength and chugged up the final steps, stepping with both feet on the top platform, still not daring to let go of the railing. The platform was no larger than maybe five square feet, and at the sudden realization that he was so high up on a structure that looked so flimsy at the top, his dizziness kicked in.

"Hey, you okay?" The camper who stood at the top of the platform as if he was just admiring the view from a building looked at Kevin with concern.

"Just great! Never better!" Kevin exclaimed, still firmly holding the railing and casting one daring glance down below.

That was a mistake. The ground was so far below that Kevin comically figured he'd have enough time to scream and catch his breath for another scream before hitting it.

"Don't worry, the watchtower is the safest place in the camp," the camper said confidently. "They make sure to inspect it every now and again."

Yeah, that doesn't instill any sense of security, Kevin thought but said nothing.

"Well, uh... I'm here to replace you," Kevin said, tentatively releasing one hand from the railing.

"Alright. You're the new guy, right? Cocky Kevin?"

Kevin nodded.

"I heard about you. People talk about how you made Dwight fume. I'm Larry," he outstretched his hand for a handshake.

Kevin took it, feeling Larry's firm grip compared to his wobbly shake.

"Alright, here's what you need to know," Larry started. "Just keep a lookout for any smoke, fires, anything rustling in the trees, or like, groups of birds suddenly dispersing from one spot. Also, listen to the noises. If the forest goes quiet, it usually means there's a predator nearby. Really, the only thing you need to worry about is the fire. If you see any signs of it, head back to the camp and report it to the counselors immediately."

"Alright. Anything else?" Kevin let go of the railing with his other hand and stood with way more balance than he expected on the platform.

"Yeah," Larry nodded. "Relax. This is the best job in the camp. You can just relax and maybe even take a short nap because the counselors are usually too lazy to come up here to check up on us."

"I doubt I'll be sleeping in a place like this, but I will try to relax. Thanks for the tip."

Larry nodded again.

"Alright, I'm heading back. Clean Ryan will be here to replace you in an hour. Then you get two hours off until your next shift."

"Got it."

Larry said his goodbye and began descending the stairs with the speed and confidence that stated he had already done this multiple times before. As soon as the creaking of the stairs stopped, Kevin was left alone with his thoughts and the sounds of the forest surrounding him. Only then did he take in the view around him and spend a long moment admiring it. As far as the eye could see, all around him were rows and rows of fir and pine trees, densely covering the entire area. There were behemoths of tree-covered mountains far ahead in the distance, stretching across the horizon.

The only area that differed from the towering trees was the campgrounds, which Kevin could see from the top of the tower. He could easily recognize most of the buildings from here, but it still took him a moment to orient himself so he could calculate where he came from and where each important landmark was. It was too far away for him to see any people clearly.

Any human movement he saw from the tower looked like ants to him, and he knew that they couldn't see him, either. Kevin glanced around in all directions one more time, slowly rotating from left to right until he came full circle. There was nothing man-made visible around besides the camp, and if there was, it was swallowed by the tall trees. As hopeless as Kevin felt being surrounded by nature in such an encroaching way, with no other civilization anywhere in sight, he couldn't help but also stare in awe at the vistas in front of him. He'd been camping before, but he never had the opportunity to witness such marvelous scenery. As if snapping out of his trance, he reprimanded himself for enjoying the view and reminded himself that he needed to look for a way out of this hellhole. He leaned on the railing overlooking Camp Firwood, feeling much more confident at the height now that he spent a few minutes up here.

Think, Kevin, think. How do you get into Mr. Adams' office and make the phone call to the police?

His thoughts suddenly rushed back to the conversation he'd had with Mr. Adams back in his office.

This is not really a summer camp. It's actually a correctional camp where parents send their children.

If that were the case, wouldn't that mean that the police would be powerless to do anything to help him? He could call Amy or Henry. They could look up online where Camp Firwood was located, and they could come there by car. Henry's older brother Quentin could drive, so they could arrive here in the middle of the night, and he could sneak out. Yeah, that would work. But that still begged the first question – how would he get inside the office unnoticed *and* make the phone call?

Maybe he could get someone to create a diversion. But who? Rob told him that most of the campers didn't believe that they were in any danger, which was probably true, especially after what Mr. Adams told him, but the place was still bad. If the others wanted to stay, they could do so, he didn't care. Maybe Ninja? According to the stories, he was an expert in sneaking and going undetected. But maybe that's why he should be the one to make a phone call to a friend to bust him out. No, that probably wouldn't work. Kevin memorized Amy's phone number, and if Ninja had no memorized contacts in his head, Kevin would have to be the one to make the call.

He shook his head dismissively, telling himself that it didn't make any sense thinking about it right now. When he's back in camp, he'll talk to Ninja. If Ninja wasn't on board, then someone else will be. At least, he hoped they would. The rest of his shift went by extremely slowly, and glancing at his watch every couple of minutes didn't help. He lay on the floor, grateful that the roof of the tower was blocking the sun. He couldn't imagine what hell it would be like roasting in such temperatures with no shield.

Around five minutes to eleven, he heard (and felt) heavy footsteps on the stairs close to the top of the platform. It was followed by a wimpy panting before Clean Ryan finally managed to step onto the platform. He made a disgusted grimace as he looked at his palm before wiping it on his shorts.

"Disgusting," he said pompously. "Do they ever even clean this place?"

"Probably not, but I'm sure they'd be happy to assign you to do it if you asked nicely." Kevin grinned.

"Well, I'm actually tempted to suggest it," Ryan said, still busy staring at his palm with a glare that said he wasn't convinced it was entirely clean.

"If you do that, then all of us will have to suffer the consequences. So uh… don't do it," Kevin somberly said.

"Relax, I'm just kidding. I am a germaphobe, but there's no way I would climb all the way up here with a bucket of water and detergent to clean this place."

He wiped his palm on his shorts once more before turning to Kevin and asking inquisitively, "Anything to report?"

"Well… there's a lot of trees. Other than that… no."

Ryan nodded with a serious expression on his face, and for a moment, Kevin thought that he took him seriously.

"Alright, well, you get yourself back to the camp. They are still doing shelter stuff, so you best head back there," Ryan said.

"Wait a second," Kevin raised one hand. "Baldwin said I get two hours off."

Ryan inhaled with a hiss before making a painful grimace and saying, "Yeah, um. About that. You get two hours *off watchtower duty*. But you still need to do the other stuff, you know?"

"Man, this is bullshit!" Kevin threw his hands up in the air.

How am I supposed to plan my escape if I can't get a moment to breathe? That's probably exactly what they want.

"Alright, well, thanks, Ryan. Good luck with your shift," he said before patting Ryan on the shoulder and making his way to the steps.

Descending was even more problematic than ascending as he carefully had to plunge with each step onto the plank below while holding the railings firmly. When he was done with the first side of the steps, his heart sank at the utter realization that he had to descend three more sides like that, which would effectively take him around five or so minutes.

Well, better than listening to that bald bastard. He shrugged, hoping he wouldn't be in too much trouble for being late.

***

By the time he made it back to the camp training area, around fifteen minutes later, all the shelters made by the campers had been disassembled, and the sticks were thrown onto one pile near the center. The tarps and hatchets had been returned to their respective bags, and the campers still formed a circle around Mr. Baldwin, sitting on the ground and attentively listening to his lecture.

Mr. Baldwin was kneeling next to a flawless-looking shelter he apparently made in the same fashion as the campers before him, and he was explaining something to them. Kevin silently made his way to the empty spot next to Mark, expecting Mr. Baldwin to start shouting at him for some reason any moment. When that didn't happen, he sat down and proceeded, listening to Baldwin's lecture. He was showing the campers ways of making the shelter stable with either rocks or sticks, after which he proceeded to tear down his shelter and create new, different-looking ones from various sticks in a pile.

He was doing it with such elegance that Kevin figured Baldwin must have done this millions of times before, maybe each year when he was working as a counselor. Each time he would finish explaining about the shelter and tearing it down, Kevin's hopes would surge that the lecture was over, but Mr. Baldwin would just proceed to make a new, different kind of shelter. This lasted for around an hour, and Kevin had to fight the urge to fall asleep multiple times. The only thing that kept him awake was the fact that Baldwin had his hawk eye on all the campers, somehow on all nine of them.

Multiple times, he would reprimand some campers for not paying attention, forcing Tough Norton and Javier to do pushups as punishment. Tough Norton had no trouble with it whatsoever, but Javier fell after ten or so repetitions. Baldwin gave the campers a short break at around noon and ordered all of them to be back in ten or so minutes. Otherwise, there'd be consequences.

Around this time, Dwight arrived with a handheld portable water tank in his hand and placed it at the edge of the circle. The campers were all parched by then and rushed to drink from the tank (with Baldwin's permission). Kevin himself was thirsty as heck after the climb up to the tower and couldn't wait for his turn at the tank. Drinking the water and letting it slide down his cheek messily never felt as good as in that moment. Once everyone was done drinking, Dwight picked up the half-empty tank and left without a word.

"So, how'd you like the tower?" Mark asked enthusiastically.

"It's a tough climb, but the view is pretty amazing, I gotta say," Kevin nodded.

"Sure is. A little claustrophobic though, being surrounded by all those trees with nothing else in sight, huh?"

"You said it."

The two of them made their way to the small group of campers, which formed a half-circle on the ground, a little distance away from Baldwin. They arrived at the group just in time for Steve to finish talking about something related to someone being given toilet duties. They glanced in Mark and Kevin's direction before continuing to chit-chat with each other, seemingly giving the two of them the green light to sit by them. Mark slumped on the ground and was immediately met with Steve's appraisal of shelter-making. Mark dismissively waved as if it were no big deal.

"Cocky Kevin, you wanna sit down or what?" Steve asked.

Kevin glanced at the group. There was Steve, Mark, Slow Ethan, and Nerdy Van.

"Hey, where did Ninja go?" he asked with a frown.

"He's got wood-chopping duty today, I think," Steve said.
Dammit.

"So I guess he'll be back in the evening, yeah?"

"Probably. Why do you need him?" Steve scratched his chin with no particular interest in the question.

"No reason," Kevin disappointedly said before sitting down and completing the circle.

He noticed Mark shooting him a contemptuous glance, but only for a moment before averting his gaze and seemingly staring at the ground. The campers talked amongst each other about unimportant things before Baldwin croaked for them to get back to the circle. Baldwin had the campers each take three sticks – like the

193

ones they brought – and made them remake their shelter once again. Once everything was done, with the tarp set in place and all, he ordered them to tear down the shelter and make it again. Each time they'd have to do it, Kevin groaned in frustration, but the other campers seemed untouched by Baldwin's orders.

They must be used to this every frigging day.

He was able to remake his shelter four times before excusing himself for watchtower duty again. Baldwin reminded him to get to the mess hall for lunch as soon as he was done and that if he happened to be late, he should tell the lunch lady that he was on watchtower duty since they save the food for the campers who would be late due to their jobs. Kevin muttered a self-nauseating *yes, Mr. Baldwin*, before turning around and heading in the direction of the campgrounds. He heard another shrieking order of the counselor telling the campers to build their shelter again.

By the time he replaced Larry on top of the tower, he was feeling tired, hungry, and fed up with the camp. This felt like slaving away. It wasn't fair. He allowed himself a moment to lie down on the tower floor, which Clean Ryan would call 'heaven for germ reproduction.' He stared at the ceiling and listened to the chirping of the birds and the blowing of the breeze. It was tranquil. But in that moment of silence, he found his thoughts wandering back home. Before he could give himself a chance to be sad, he kicked up his feet and stood up, instead deciding to focus on a plan B for escape, if possible.

If he couldn't get into Mr. Adams' office for a phone call, he would need to trudge through the woods for his escape. But what was the best way out of here? Where would he be traveling the least before running into another human being? He had no idea where he was right now and no idea which direction to go, but his assumption was that he should go down the road his parents took him. He doubted there were any other trails anywhere nearby, and the chances of him getting lost in a dense forest like this were extremely high while the chances of being found were abysmal.

194

The hour went by faster this time, and before he knew it, Clean Ryan was there to replace him. Kevin updated him on the eventful shift he'd had and headed back to the campgrounds. His stomach was rumbling by then, and he hurriedly entered the mess hall, in time to see the room full and campers chowing. He made his way to the food line, and the lunch lady splotched the ladle of mush that was served for lunch into his bowl. He didn't bother thanking her but instead just took two pieces of hard bread, just in case the mush proved to be insufficient. He searched the room frantically, trying to find Ninja, but he was nowhere in sight. He didn't want to look too suspicious, so he quickly took the closest seat at a table where only one other camper sat.

"Is it okay if I sit here?" he asked courteously.

The camper sitting across from him nodded with his mouth full of the food, not bothering to look up at Kevin, before slurping another spoonful. Kevin looked down at his bowl, too hungry to worry about Ninja right now. He couldn't tell what exactly this dish was, but he did recognize pale pieces of meat, which he assumed were chicken, and overcooked vegetables, which were literally falling apart in the soupy substance. It at least smelled good, and he was starving far too much to ask the generous lunch lady for another meal. He put a little bit of the food on the tip of his spoon and bit into the bread before dousing it in the mushy food in his mouth. It wasn't half as bad as he expected.

The meat and vegetables were tender, and the soup was just the right saltiness, despite being too thick and oily. He downed the entire bowl and ate both pieces of bread, feeling like he could go for seconds. The other camper in front of him was gone by this point, and Kevin spent the next ten minutes pretending to scrape his bowl while looking for Ninja.

I guess he'll get lunch later… or won't get lunch at all.

Once he made sure that Ninja still wasn't around, he proceeded to waddle to the window where the dirty dishes were disposed of and then proceeded outside. The campers who had finished lunch were outside and waiting for the annoying counselors to come and give them new orders. Kevin looked around, searching for familiar faces in the crowd.

Who would be willing to go with my plan to sneak into Mr. Adams' office?

His eyes fell on Tough Norton, and he reticently smiled, ready to isolate him from the crowd and propose his suggestion to him. He happened to glance inside the mess hall and saw Mark standing in front of Dwight, in the middle of the room. It looked like they were talking about something as Kevin saw not only Dwight's mouth opening to utter orders but Mark saying something back, too. A few moments later, Dwight dismissively waved him away and turned away from him. Mark came outside, his eyes immediately falling on Kevin. He joined him with a somber glance on his face.

"What was that about?" Kevin asked.

"Oh, you mean with Dwight? Uh, nothing. He's giving me some chores for later."

"What kind of chores?"

"Cleaning the resting room in the main lodge. Doesn't matter," his face turned stern. "I know what you're planning to do, Kevin. Don't."

Kevin yanked his hand away and frowned at Mark.

"What are you talking about? I'm not planning anything."

"Come on, Kevin. I know you got the nickname Cocky, but do you really want it to get changed to Stupid?"

Kevin stared at Mark in bafflement, pretending he didn't know what he was talking about and hoping that Mark was just taking a shot in the dark. He apparently noticed Kevin's fake-confused glare, so he pressed his lips together firmly before saying.

"You went to Mr. Adams' office this morning. He always takes campers there to strike a deal with them. He gives them some sweet talk, and they agree to his demands in hopes that they'd be released soon. But not you, Kevin. You're different."

Mark looked down at his feet, which Kevin took as a sign that he still wasn't finished speaking. He gave him a moment. Mark looked back up before saying.

"You want to use the phone, I know. Don't do it. It's too risky."

You smart son of a bitch.

Kevin chuckled, knowing he was caught red-handed. There was no use lying now, especially not to someone as clever as Mark. The question was – as much as he hated asking it of himself – would Mark be a threat to his escape? Would he potentially snitch on him to the counselors in order to potentially avoid getting into any trouble himself?

No, that's ridiculous. Mark wouldn't do that. He's a good friend, despite us knowing each other for only a few days.

"Well, you got me," Kevin said, guiltily shrugging and spreading his arms in an I-don't-know gesture.

Mark got closer to him and said in a more hushed tone this time, "Listen, you don't want to do this. If they catch you in his office, you have no idea what they'll do to you."

"And you do? That's why you're so afraid, right? Because you know exactly what happens to the campers here, right?" Kevin inadvertently raised his tone.

Mark was taken aback by this, which was visible from his shocked facial expression. He stepped back and said, "I know that nothing good can come out of it. It's not worth the risk."

"And waiting is? Our parents put us in here against our will, Mark!" Kevin snapped. "How can you just sit back and allow these assholes to bully you like that while your sister is at home probably going through hell?!"

Mark's face turned sour as if he just bit into a lemon. This stung Kevin's conscience, so he immediately got defused and said, "I'm sorry. But, I thought we were friends. I thought you hated it here. But if you're not willing to help me so we can both get out of this mess, then… then I guess I'll have to find someone who will," he threw his hands up and let them fall limply against his thighs.

197

"You'll do well to be really careful who you talk to around here about escaping," Mark calmly said.

"Yeah, well, we'll see about that."

Mark continued staring at him with a visibly disappointed facial expression, although Kevin wasn't sure where the disappointment was directed – at him or his intentions. He didn't care at that moment. He couldn't bear to be around Mark any longer. He turned around and made his way through the crowd, silently grateful that they were no longer looking at him, and to the other side of the group, as far away from Mark as he could be.

Mr. Adams came out of the mess hall in minutes, and after lining up the campers, he performed a roll call. Once everyone was accounted for, he started calling on campers and giving them duties in groups. Various jobs needed to be done around the camp, including chopping wood, transferring wood back to camp, cleaning the mess hall, helping out Nurse Mary, helping out Groundskeeper Andy, folding laundry, and many more. A lot of the jobs seemed to revolve around cleaning camp buildings, therefore, the majority of the campers were assigned to those duties. Kevin, Javier, and Tough Norton were assigned to go help Groundskeeper Andy with whatever job he gave them.

Although Javier and Norton weren't terribly pleased to be helping the old grunt, Kevin was ecstatic because he'd get a chance to talk to his fellow campers about his escape plan. If he could get Tough Norton in on it, he'd be set for sure.

"Dwight, you take the lead of the campers in charge of cleaning around the infirmary and mess hall, I'll take the ones for the main lodge. Alright, campers, get to it!" Mr. Adams ordered, and the campers immediately began dispersing in groups, each in his own direction.

"Can't believe that of all the people, I have to go help the groundskeeper," Javier exclaimed, as soon as the campers put some distance to the counselors.

198

"Well, better that than being in The Choosing, no?" Norton punched Javier in the shoulder mildly.

Javier winced and rubbed his arm before saying, "I guess you're right."

The groundskeeper's cabin stood dormant in the distance, near the edge of the woods, the groundskeeper himself nowhere in sight. Javier and Norton got suddenly quiet, and as tempted as Kevin was to talk to them about his escape plan, something told him that this was not the right moment. When they finally reached the cabin, they stopped in front of the door, dumbly staring at it in silence.

"Well, come on, go on, knock on the door," Norton urged Javier.

"No, you do it. You're the one they call Tough." Javier shook his head.

"Yeah, but Kevin has the name Cocky." They both turned their heads in Kevin's direction, and it was at that moment that he knew that he was outvoted.

"Fine, you pansies." He rolled his eyes and approached the steps in front of the door.

He raised one hand and gently knocked three times on the wooden surface. He turned around to look at Javier and Norton standing in place, not moving an inch. Kevin spread his hands in a gesture that said this wasn't a big deal when Javier's eyes widened. Kevin turned around and had to catch himself to keep from stumbling backward when he saw the groundskeeper's menacing figure towering above him where the door had been a second ago. Kevin stifled a scream and took a step back, trying to mutter a coherent phrase in his state of startling.

"Uh… Mr. Adams sent us… gave some duties here…"

The groundskeeper angrily stared at Kevin for a moment before slamming the door shut in his face with a loud bang.

"Well, great job, Cocky Kevin." Javier clapped silently.

"Shut up," Kevin retorted.

The cabin door swung open a moment later, and the groundskeeper stumbled outside and around the back of the cabin.

The sound of a creaking door opening rose from the back. The three campers stood silently while he rummaged through what Kevin assumed was his tool shed. A moment later, the creaking door slammed shut, and the groundskeeper emerged from around the corner, carrying three mops in a bucket.

He shoved the items to Kevin, who took them with a wobble, nearly losing balance in the process. Groundskeeper Andy started walking to the right, toward the old concrete building Kevin saw earlier on his way to the morning training. The three campers exchanged glances, and Norton silently gestured with his head for them to follow the groundskeeper. They had to jog to catch up with the groundskeeper, but after that, their pace was much slower than usual. After a few minutes of silence mixed with the shuffling of grass under their feet, they reached the old building. The groundskeeper led them around and opened the door on the side.

They entered what looked like a locker room with long benches on both sides. There was a door on the other side, and upon opening it, the groundskeeper revealed a huge shower room. There were no separating stalls or anything like that in the room, just shower heads hanging from the ceiling, dozens of them, pointing down at the numerous drainages on the concrete floor. The groundskeeper turned around and looked at the campers, which made them freeze.

"Clean the locker room and take out any garbage from the showers."

It can talk, Kevin comically thought to himself when he heard an actual relatively complex sentence come out of the groundskeeper's mouth.

With no other word, the old man left the showers and closed the main door behind him.

"Well, time to get to work. Dibs on the locker room," Javier said.

Kevin handed one mop to each of the campers and filled the bucket with water from the tap in the dressing room. He placed the bucket at the entrance between the showers and the dressing room.

200

Since Javier already decided to do the dressing room, Kevin took the showers with Norton, which worked out perfectly since he could talk to him. They soaked their mops and made their way to the other side of the showers, looking for any potential trash. Kevin didn't want to waste time, but he also didn't want to be too direct. He pretended to clean for a few minutes before he subtly got closer to Norton.

"So, it's like this every day?" Kevin asked.

"Pretty much. Working, learning, more working." Norton shrugged.

"Well, it's too abusive toward the campers. I don't think what they're doing here is legal."

"Yeah, no shit," Norton slightly chuckled.

"If anyone found out about what they do here, I reckon they would shut down the camp so hard that Mr. Adams' annoying smile would drop like an anchor."

Norton glanced at Kevin before silently continuing to mop.

I got him now. He's interested in what I'm saying.

"Sounds like you have something in mind," Norton said, moving into the corner of the shower room and beginning to mop from there.

"Maybe. If you're willing to listen."

"Go ahead," Norton said, mopping up a juice box and half-used soap onto a pile of already mopped-up trash.

"Have you ever tried escaping from this place?"

Norton stopped mopping momentarily and glanced in Kevin's direction with raised eyebrows. A second later, he continued mopping, staring at the trash, as he said, "I planned to. But I never found a way out."

Great, this is it.

"Well, what if I told you I found a way out?" Kevin leaned on his mop, giving Norton his full attention now.

This, in turn, seemed to intrigue Norton as he stopped mopping and turned to face Kevin with a curious expression on his face.

"I'm listening."

Kevin glanced at the dressing room. Javier was mopping the floor, facing away from them. Kevin got closer to Norton and said in a hushed tone.

"There's a phone in Mr. Adams' office. If we could sneak inside, we could call someone to pick-"

Before Kevin even finished the sentence, Norton was already shaking his head, the curious glance instantaneously gone from his face. He gripped his mop, ready to go back to work as he looked at Kevin disappointedly and said, "I'd hate to crush your hopes, Kev. But everybody knows about the phone. There's no way to get in there. The office is locked all the time. There's no way of getting in there."

"We can try, man," Kevin desperately tried convincing Norton. "I just need a minute on the phone, and I can get us someone for a rescue. I just need someone to distract Mr. Adams."

Norton shook his head again.

"Trust me, you don't wanna do it. The last person who tried breaking into the office and making a call – and no, you're not the first person with that idea – ended up getting sent in the woods for Repentance. He never came back."

Kevin was taken aback for a moment before regaining his defiant composure.

"So you're just gonna sit and do nothing? And hope they let you go when the time comes? Come on, Norton, don't be an idiot!"

Norton looked at him angrily, and Kevin thought for a moment that he was going to punch him.

"Yeah, that's exactly what I'm gonna do!" he furiously retorted. "I'm serving my sentence so I can leave when this is all done!"

"You said you were supposed to leave a few weeks ago."

"Mr. Adams told me recently that I only have three weeks left until I'm released, so stay away from me with that risky bullshit before you get the both of us in trouble! Now, if you'll excuse me, I have work to do!"

He turned around and furiously continued mopping. Kevin glanced in Javier's direction. Javier was staring at him, but he quickly looked down and continued doing his mopping upon locking eyes with Kevin. Feeling a little discouraged, Kevin proceeded with work in silence.

Some time later, the groundskeeper came by and told them to pick up their things and take them back to his shack. He ordered them to pick up the shears from the shed. However, it was time for Kevin to get back to his watchtower duty. He had almost forgotten about it until he accidentally felt the pocket watch in his pants.

He had only thirteen minutes to get to the tower, so he hurriedly ran to the groundskeeper and asked him to go. The groundskeeper shot him a bemused glance before turning away from him as if he was looking at something as unimportant as a worm in the mud. Kevin took that as a sign of approval, so he let Javier bring back the mops while he rushed to the tower. By the time he arrived, the sky was already turning orange, and it was much harder to see anything amongst the trees. He relieved Larry of his duty and sat on the floor of the tower, mentally scratching Norton off his list.

That just leaves Ninja and Sneaky Rob. If they don't wanna try my plan, I'll try to find someone else, no big deal.

He kept telling that to himself, despite a sense of dread gradually growing within him. A panicked thought kept emerging at the back of his mind. Something nagging that kept warning him that he might stay trapped here. And not just until the end of his sentence. He had to fight really hard to push it back this time. He was relieved to have Clean Ryan arrive five minutes earlier. After complaining about how unclean the tower was, he took over the shift, and Kevin was on his way out of there.

"Oh, before I forget!" Clean Ryan called out. "Don't forget you have lectures now. Get to the study hall, classroom four."

Fucking great.

When he arrived in the classroom, the counselor was already giving his lecture. He authoritatively gestured for Kevin to sit down before continuing with his presentation. Although Kevin was in the seat right in front of him, he paid no attention to the topic, despite Mark warning him about having to memorize the things they were being taught.

Once the lectures were done, the campers got a moment of reprieve. Kevin didn't have a lot of free time, though, because, at 7 p.m., he had to go back to the tower. He was starting to feel exhausted by this point, and with it, his motivation for escape was waning. He entertained the thought of trying to escape tomorrow when he had more available time but quickly dismissed it, scolding himself for even thinking that. After his shift on the watchtower, he went back to the camp and into the mess hall. He ate the porridge, which was much blander than the mush he had for lunch, and unsatisfied, he made his way back toward the cabins.

Ninja has got to be back by now, right?

When he entered the cabin, most of the campers were already in their pajamas, save for the ones who had duties later on like toilet cleaning and watchtower. To his delight, Ninja was finally there. He was lying on his back in the bed in his pajamas with one arm over his eyes to block the light. Kevin wasted no time approaching him.

"Hey, Ninja. You still awake?" he asked, kneeling next to his bed.

Ninja moved the arm that was covering his eyes and looked at Kevin in curiosity. He looked way more tired than Kevin had seen him in the past few days. Wood chopping duty must have really gotten to him.

"Hey, what's up, Kevin?" Ninja asked in a somewhat croaking voice, which indicated he was either woken up or on the verge of falling asleep.

Kevin looked around at the other campers. All of them were busy with their own things. He happened to glance at Mark, who was placing his hygiene items back inside his locker. A pang of guilt struck Kevin over the harsh conversation he'd had with him earlier. Since none of the campers seemed to be focused on him, he turned back to face Ninja and said in a whisper, "I intend to get out. And I have a plan. But I need your help."

Ninja blinked like a confused goat before licking his visibly dry lips and saying.

"Alright, that's great. But um, can we talk about that tomorrow? I'm literally dead tonight."

"Okay, yeah. Sure. No problem." Kevin nodded.

Ninja had already placed his arm back over his eyes and continued dozing off. As Kevin brushed his teeth and got ready for the roll call and his 10 p.m. shift on the watchtower, he could only ponder one thing.

It's going to be a long night.

10
Barrels

He wasn't sure what time it was when he heard it. He was on watchtower duty, and his eyelids were becoming progressively heavier. He had decided to sit down and prop his back against the wooden railing, hoping to maybe catch a few minutes of shuteye. Mr. Adams climbed the tower and stared at Kevin with the look of a disappointed parent. No, he wasn't really there. Kevin was in limbo, in that instance between dreaming and being awake, and he imagined seeing Mr. Adams there. He kept snapping his eyes open every few minutes like that even though it felt like he was napping for hours.

And then something shook him wide awake. What was it? He looked around but was alone on the watchtower. His heart was pounding, and his eyelids were no longer heavy, so what was it that snapped him awake? Feeling suddenly paranoid, he clambered up to his feet and leaned against the railing. He stared at the vast canopies of the trees stretching across the horizon and the stillness it imbued.

The stillness.

The forest was quiet. Too quiet. Up until now, it was brimming with all sorts of sounds – owls and other unidentified birds, crickets… now, a hush filled the air. Was the forest supposed to be quiet at night? That's not how Kevin remembered learning about it. He remembered that his teacher once said that most of the wildlife in the woods comes out at night and that the only time they go silent is when a predator is nearby. Kevin couldn't help but scan the canopies with more scrutiny now that he was aware that a dangerous animal might be nearby. It was impossible to tell if anyone was moving there, so he decided to rely on listening instead. Aside from the regular noises of the crickets and birds chirping here and there, he heard nothing unusual.

Snap.

Something broke somewhere in the distance. It sounded like a twig but maybe a big one because it also sounded like it was far away. And then... a whistle pierced the air, low, and then climbing up until it reached a crescendo. And then it stopped. Kevin held his breath as he listened. He tried telling himself that it was just a night animal, but his mind shouted at him over and over that it-

A scream suddenly pierced the air. Kevin noticed a flock of birds flying off a tree and upward as if startled by something. It was, by Kevin's estimation, around seven hundred feet away from the watchtower.

Something was going on there.

Was that scream just now his imagination? It sounded human. In fact, it sounded like the screaming of a scared boy. Another snap echoed, followed by a loud, long whistle. That was no animal, he was sure of it. At least, it sounded like human whistling. Kevin swallowed, his heart pumping violently as he stared at the trees, waiting to see any further signs of movement in the woods. Nothing. He waited for what felt like hours, constantly pivoting around to see if anyone would magically appear behind him. He checked the pocket watch and realized his shift would be ending soon. Just a little longer until Clean Ryan relieved him of his duty, and then he could get the hell out of this place.

He kept thinking about the sounds he heard. The scream might have belonged to the camper who got sent into the woods earlier that day. But the whistle... what could it be? It didn't sound like any animal. Even mountain lions produced specific sounds. This, however, sounded too long, too... rhythmic. One thought kept coming into his mind over and over.

The Firwood Wraith.

He tried dismissing that thought. There are no such things as ghosts. Still, he couldn't help but spend the remainder of his shift glancing at the stairs of the watchtower every couple of minutes, expecting to see some transparent ghost-like creature staring up at him with glowing eyes. Clean Ryan couldn't have arrived fast enough. Kevin didn't tell him anything about what he heard since Ryan was adamantly opposed to the belief in the Firwood Wraith, even though the distress was probably visible on Kevin.

***

He heard Camp Firwood's anthem in his dream and only woke up around ten seconds into it, realizing that it was early morning and that the anthem was blasting away in reality. Most of the campers were already up, scurrying around, getting ready to start their day. Kevin sat upright, blinking furiously and rubbing his eyes, trying to clear the blur away. Was it really time to get up? He felt like he had just slumped into bed five minutes ago. The sounds in the woods from last night were still embedded in his mind, but he decided not to entertain any morbid thoughts. Now that it was morning, he was able to think with more clarity.

Just animals, that's all it was.

When he returned from the watchtower duty last night (much faster than usual), he didn't even bother taking his uniform off since it would take him way too long to change into his pajamas, so he instead placed the blanket over his bed and slept in his uniform the way the campers did during the day. Now that morning came, he folded his blanket and straightened the wrinkles on his bedsheets, already a pro when it came to doing it effectively.

Thanks for showing me the ropes, Mark.

He inconspicuously tossed a glower in Mark's direction. Mark was stumbling with his toothbrush toward the toilet with his eyes half-closed, his slippers making loud shuffling noise in the process. Some time later, the campers assembled in front of the cabins for a roll call. Dwight arrived with his arrogant, punchable face and called out each camper. Once everyone was accounted for, he took them to the mess hall.

The line in front of the hall seemed to move much slower than usual, and Kevin had difficulty standing on his wobbly legs. He felt like he could fall asleep in that position, but that wasn't an option. Not in Camp Firwood. He was relieved momentarily to sit down with his scrambled eggs, but only seconds later, his head started slumping down. Each time, he'd close his eyes for longer than a second. He quickly ate his eggs, despite not having an appetite, and headed outside. A bunch of campers were already out, talking about their own things, their voices sounding much louder than usual. Kevin glanced around the campgrounds, desperately looking for a place where he could sit down and take a nap, just for a minute.

He spotted a big tree stump across from the mess hall just calling him to lean his back against it and close his eyes. His sleep-deprived mind realized only a second later that the stump was too close to the main lodge, which most of the counselors were coming out from every couple of minutes. He was sure they would not take kindly to him dosing off over there like a homeless guy. No matter, he would sleep tonight instead. He gently slapped himself a few times, hoping it would snap him out of his stupor.

I just need to start doing something, and I'll feel less sleepy, that's all, he thought to himself optimistically.

He decided that it was time to find Ninja and talk to him about the plan he had. Luck would have it that it wasn't his day because, as if on cue, counselor Torres sauntered out of the mess hall and roared.

"Lunch Lady Daisy needs extra help today. You three..." he pointed at Mark, Ryan, and Ethan, before looking in Kevin's direction.

Oh, crap, please don't choose me.

"You there, detention boy," Torres squealed, pointing his finger directly at Kevin.

Kevin spun around, hoping against hope that someone stood close to him and that Torres was pointing at them, but no. That, unfortunately, wasn't the case.

"The four of you go talk to Daisy," Torres roared.

The three campers who were initially chosen confusedly exchanged glances, not budging.

"Move, you snails!" Torres shrieked at them, and the campers immediately broke into a jog around the back of the mess hall.

"What are you waiting for?! Move your fucking ass!" It took Kevin a moment to realize that Torres was shouting directly at him.

Annoyed out of his mind, he followed Mark, Ethan, and Ryan with a half-sprint to avoid losing them.

"See, I told you it's a bad idea to go outside earlier!" Ryan scoldingly said to the other two.

"How were we supposed to know? Steve got picked for some other duty last time because he stayed inside for too long!" Slow Ethan angrily retorted.

Ethan and Ryan seemed to be equally frustrated as Kevin. But not Mark. He seemed to maintain his calm composure on the outside. Kevin wondered if he was actually calm and how long it would take until he snapped.

"Wait, where's Kevin? Oh, here he is," Mark spun around, visibly startled (or pleasantly surprised) to see Kevin right behind him.

"Worried you'll have more work to do if I don't show up?" Kevin ironically asked.

"No, it's not that. It's just that we'll all be in trouble if one of us goes missing or doesn't show up. Or if the work doesn't get finished," Mark said from the front, only just then realizing Kevin's obviously sardonic remark.

They went through the backdoor, which led them to a small corridor, which had doors on the left side. The first door led to the bathroom, but the campers went through the next door, which led into a small locker room. Three campers, whose name Kevin didn't know, were sitting on the benches. They weren't wearing their usual camp uniforms but the white clothes and caps that kitchen staff usually had to don. Instead of shoes, they had white, uncomfortable-looking clogs. Upon seeing them enter, one of the campers grinned and spread his arms welcomingly as he exclaimed poetically, "Barrel Mark, Clean Ryan, Cocky Kevin... and Slow Ethan," he said the last name with an audible drop in enthusiasm.

The other two campers burst into laughter before the one who called out the names said, "What are you guys doing here?"

"The kitchen hag needs some help, apparently," Ryan exclaimed as he opened one of the lockers.

Inside were white clothes like the ones the three campers were wearing. Mark and Ryan opened two other lockers, and all three started changing into the white clothes. Seeing that this was something mandatory, Kevin sighed and opened a locker of his own. Although white at first glance, the clothes in the locker seemed to be stained with yellowish and reddish faded splotches. Kevin was sure that the camp tried washing those but was unable to remove the stains and didn't want to recycle the clothes.

Reluctantly, he put on the pants, which happened to be short enough to reveal his ankles and a shirt that was missing two buttons – one at the top and one at the bottom. The clogs were as uncomfortable as they looked, but at least they were the right size. He would just need to be careful when walking not to twist his ankle.

"Don't forget your cap," Mark pointed to his own white cap on his head.

"Oh, right," Kevin glanced back at the locker and saw the netted cap on the top shelf.

He put it over his head, feeling the elastic part of it already beginning to make his head itchy. He was tempted to ask if the cap was even necessary, but he already knew the rules in the camp by now.

"Well, let's go see what the witch wants, then." Clean Ryan shrugged and went out through the door they came in.

Kevin followed their lead as Ryan was the first to step into a humongous area, which was brimming with loud machinery-like noises and filled with all sorts of big cauldron-like devices that he didn't recognize. There were machines for chopping vegetables and mincing meat, numerous ovens with comically large frying pans and pots, and on one of the walls hung a plethora of knives, ladles of various sizes, kitchen turners, and other utensils. Ryan made his way toward one corner of the big area where something that looked like a guardhouse was sitting. When they got closer, Kevin realized it was actually an office, and through the glass panel on the door, he saw the lunch lady's encroaching figure sitting inside, taking some notes on a paper with her stubby fingers.

Ryan was the one who gently knocked on the door. The lunch lady didn't acknowledge his presence, and he seemed hesitant to knock again. After ten seconds or so, he raised his hand again, but the lunch lady stood up and swung the door open.

"Where have you been this long? You're already late!" she screeched at them, flailing her massive arms about, her soft triceps shaking like pudding.

"We were just told a few minutes ago by Mr. Torres that-" Ryan started, but Daisy interrupted him with her powerful voice, which seemed to drown out the loud machines in the kitchen.

"I don't wanna hear excuses! You two"—she pointed at Ethan and Ryan—"go clean the storage room! And you two"—she pointed at Mark and Kevin—"follow me," she ordered.

She waddled like a duck through the loud kitchen, leading Mark and Kevin through the corridor and outside to the back of the mess hall. It was great to be away from all that noise in the kitchen. The lunch lady turned right and pointed behind two large trash containers and spoke with a voice equally loud as it was inside, this time with no machines around to somewhat muffle it.

"There are barrels around the corner. You have cleaning products there. I want you to clean the barrels until they are sparkling. Understood?" she put her hands on her hips and angrily stared at Mark.

"Yes, Ms. Daisy," Mark obediently said.

The lunch lady looked at Kevin, seemingly in anticipation, and he resisted the urge to roll his eyes, as he said, "Yes, Ms. Daisy."

She went back inside, leaving Mark and Kevin alone, surrounded by silence.

"Well, guess it's time to work, then," Mark shrugged.

Kevin nodded and took the lead toward the corner where Daisy had pointed. The smell of something rotten hit his nostrils, and he almost gagged. The smell reminded him a bit of Daisy's food, only it smelled like it had been left out in the heat for a while. When they rounded the corner, Kevin saw five large metal barrels, relatively light-blue in color. However, they had been rusted long since, the blue color only a remnant in the infestation of the rust. Next to the barrels were cleaning brushes in a bucket. Kevin approached the barrels and immediately stepped back when a gust of the odor hit him in the face. It smelled even worse than the trash containers, even though they were empty.

"Ah, geez. Was there a dead body in there?" he pinched his nose with his index finger and thumb.

Mark tentatively approached, glancing inside before furrowing his nose and waving his hand in front of his face to chase the smell away. He puffed up his cheeks and exhaled loudly before disappointedly approaching the bucket with brushes.

"Well, at least we won't have to do training for a while," he shrugged, but Kevin wasn't thrilled by that.

He wasn't sure yet if he would rather spend his morning cleaning rusted barrels or listening to Baldwin's annoying order-barking. In the end, he knew that the buckets needed to be cleaned, and there was no way around it. He took a brush from the bucket and approached one of the barrels.

The stench emanating from it was tear-inducing but less so than it was a moment ago when he first smelled it. He assumed that by

214

the time he was done, he would already get used to the smell. He grabbed the edge of the bucket and began scrubbing the inside of it. The substance that was stuck on it was stubborn, and barely any crumbs detached, like dandruff from a dirty head, even when Kevin used his full strength. The sound of scrubbing coming from their brushes was so loud that he and Mark probably wouldn't hear each other if they talked.

Okay, I just need to do this thing, and then I can talk to Ninja, and we can plan our escape, he tried telling himself to avoid that small shred of doubt taking over.

More and more, though, thoughts began seeping out and sowing despair and hopelessness in him like rot which gradually spread.

There's never time for that. Even if I talk to Ninja, when will we escape? We never have time to plan anything. And what are the chances of us even approaching the main lodge, let alone Mr. Adam's office? No, I'm going to be stuck here, probably for a long time. I won't get to see my friends, and by the time I come home, if I ever do, they will have already forgotten about me.

"I guess they just wanted to occupy us with something, didn't they?" Mark said.

"Uh-huh," Kevin absentmindedly replied.

At this point, he wasn't scrubbing anymore. He was leaning on the barrel's edge, staring down at it, the brush limply dangling from his fingers. The stench no longer bothered him. As he stood there, he felt something tight forming in his chest. He was broken, the camp finally managed to break his will, and just like that, his motivation for escaping was gone.

"This place is total bullshit," he muttered, on the verge of tears.

"Yeah, I know," Mark said.

He had stopped scrubbing and was staring at Kevin with concern. Kevin suddenly became aware of the silence, so he started scrubbing again with the same futility as moments ago.

"They treat us like shit. They're just using us for their own fucking chores," Kevin continued complaining.

215

"I know, Kev. But this will all be over soon. You just gotta hang in there for a bit, and we'll be out soon."

Kevin scrubbed harder, his vision getting blurry from the tears forming in his eyes. He blinked firmly, and a tear fell out of his eyes onto the bottom of the barrel with a metallic echo.

"And fuck these barrels and whoever gave us this duty! This shit can't be fucking cleaned!" he snapped and tossed the brush and barrel aside. The barrel loudly clattered sideways with a hollow, metallic sound and rolled for a bit before forlornly stopping. Kevin put his hands on his hips, facing the barrel, hiding his face from Mark. He wiped his tears with the sleeve of the white-yellowish shirt and sniffled, staring at the ground, while new tears already started forming in his eyes.

"I know how you feel, Kevin," Mark softly said. "But hey, this isn't as bad as it seems to us right now. One day, when we meet outside the camp, we'll be laughing at how we had to clean these barrels, you know?"

"I don't think we will be laughing at the barrels, Mark." Kevin shook his head with a disbelieving half-chuckle.

"Yes, we will. Because we're going to find a way to escape from here," Mark said with a tone of finality.

Kevin jerked his head in Mark's direction, not bothering to wipe the newly formed tears and well-aware that his friend could see them. Mark stood behind the barrel he was cleaning with a serious facial expression. But there was something else in his look, too. Determination. Did he just hear right what Mark said?

"You… you wanna escape?" Kevin asked, not recognizing his own trembling voice.

"Well, I like the food. But their services here are terrible. I'm thinking of leaving a one-star review once I'm out."

Kevin laughed. It was the best thing he'd heard in days.

"So, what do you say?" Mark asked. "We discuss our escape plan while cleaning the barrels?"

"Are you just bullshitting me now?"

Mark shook his head.

"I thought about it for a bit, and you're right. We shouldn't be here."

He detected no lies in Mark's tone. Kevin nodded. He felt reinvigorated like he could run for miles without stopping. He clambered up to his feet and approached the sad-looking turned-over barrel. Grabbing it by the rim with both hands, he carried it over next to Mark's barrel and bent down to pick up the brush that fell inside. The stench was more pungent down there, so he was glad to have his head out of there in mere seconds. He leaned on the barrel and used the sleeve of his shirt to wipe the remaining tears on his face.

"Alright, let's talk then," he said with newfound motivation and hope, the voice of doubt pushed back into no more than an inaudible whisper.

He told Mark about his plan to make a phone call from Mr. Adams' office to his friends. His friends would look up on the internet where the camp was. If the information wasn't online, they would get it from Kevin's parents. After that, they would drive to the vicinity of the camp with Henry's brother Quentin and wait until nightfall. At night, once the dust settled, he and Mark would sneak out of the camp and go out to the road leading to the camp, and once they were in the car, they'd be home free.

It sounded somewhat flawed when he spoke it out like that, but it was the best thing they had right now. Mark attentively listened to Kevin's detailed plan, the whole time continuing to gently scrub the barrels. He didn't complain once throughout the entire explanation, and once Kevin was done laying it out, he asked Mark, "So, what do you think?"

"Well, we're missing just one more detail then." Mark nodded as he looked somewhere ahead of himself.

Kevin followed his gaze and noticed that he was staring at Mr. Adams in the distance, who happened to be talking to another staff member in the middle of the road between the mess hall and the study hall. The counselor looked even thinner and taller from this far away, which creeped Kevin out.

"How to sneak into the office," Kevin completed Mark's sentence somberly.

"We need a diversion," Mark said as continued scrubbing the barrel, although by this point it was more pretend-scrubbing to avoid getting into trouble.

"Yeah. I haven't thought about that far enough," Kevin sighed.

"Well, I have an idea." Mark looked at Kevin.

Kevin glanced at his friend and smiled, pleasantly surprised by the rate at which he was getting into the swing of things. Mark leaned closer and said, "There's no way we can get close since we always have some duties and training. Not to mention that the building is crawling with counselors most of the time."

He tossed a skeptical glance in Mr. Adams' direction before turning back to Kevin.

"Except on the weekends."

"What happens on the weekends?" Kevin breathlessly asked, practically on the edge of his imaginary seat.

"First, we eat breakfast and then de-dust our blankets. That takes about ten minutes. And then we are given duties. Most counselors are spread out, leading small groups of campers to their respective jobs, but they don't monitor them too closely. Wherever we are, we can make up an excuse that we need to, I dunno, grab some tools, go to the infirmary, whatever."

"Okay, I see your point. We can move more freely during the weekend. But how does that give us access to Mr. Adams' office?" Kevin asked with a whiff of suspicion in his tone.

"The groundskeeper will help us."

Kevin stared silently at Mark for a moment, waiting for the punchline. When he noticed how serious Mark was, he burst out laughing.

"You must be out of your damn mind."

Mark shook his head.

"He won't help us willingly. He's just gonna provide the key."

"Mark, maybe you're the one who deserves the nickname Cocky, not me," Kevin chuckled.

"Here's what we do. When we find an excuse to leave wherever tomorrow, we can go to the groundskeeper's cabin. You hide somewhere in the trees, and I'll distract him, tell him that he's needed somewhere. He *never* locks his cabin, so you can go inside and look for the key. The one that goes to Mr. Adams' office is a small red one. You need to detach it from the keyring and get out. I'll keep the groundskeeper distracted for as long as I can."

"Wait, why don't I distract the groundskeeper? It sounds like you know your way around his cabin."

Mark shook his head.

"I'm better with words; you're faster. Once you have the key, we can go to Mr. Adams' office. You can go inside while I stand guard outside. If Mr. Adams is about to come, I'll knock, and you hide."

"But what if the groundskeeper brings the key with him?" Kevin frowned.

"He won't. He never brings it unless he needs it. And I'll try to rush him so he forgets it." Mark shrugged.

"Alright, deal." Kevin's heart began pumping a little faster.

He was excited but also scared. What if they were caught? Would they be thrown into the detention house? Or something worse? His thoughts were interrupted when the lunch lady's blaring voice came from around the corner.

"Are you two doing any work at all?! Or just talking?"

"We're trying to scrub the barrels, but it's too hard, Ms. Daisy," Mark timidly said, and Kevin began to suspect that Mark may have been faking that voice in front of the camp staff to look more innocent.

"*It's too hard.* Quit your whining, boy!" Daisy mimicked Mark with an ugly grimace on her face. "Alright, drop what you're doing there. I need you in the kitchen, now!"

Kevin almost regretted having to stop cleaning the barrels. He and Mark at least had some privacy here. In the kitchen, it would probably be more challenging to plan anything. It didn't matter, they already fleshed out the main plan, and it fueled Kevin to go through this hell of a day. Daisy gave Mark the task of counting all the food in the storage under her supervision (poor guy). Kevin, on the other hand, was sent to the kitchen's dishwasher room and told to assist Michael in washing the plates. Obviously, neither Michael nor Kevin were thrilled to see each other, but a job was a job.

Upon seeing him, Michael turned away from him and sunk his gloves into the sink water, which had a myriad of bubbles playfully floating around. He continued washing the plates inside the sink, putting the newly cleaned ones on top of the pristine pile on his left. The sink to his right was vacant - saved for Kevin. Kevin glanced at the window across the room. Faint light fell through it, and as Kevin saw some people moving on the other side from time to time, he realized that the mess hall was on the other side of that wall, and the window was the place where the campers would leave their dirty dishes. Under the window was a big bucket, which was used for emptying the plates of the uneaten food.

Kevin reluctantly put on the pair of already soaked latex gloves and stopped right next to Michael, beginning to wash his own pile. The sound of ceramics and plastics and silverware clattered throughout the room as each new item was added on top of the clean stack. When the pile of plates started looking unstable like a Jenga tower, Michael took it over to a cloth-covered table and arranged the plates, one by one, so they leaned against the wall and one another like dominoes, for easier drying.

Kevin didn't need to ask him what to do since he saw what Michael was doing, so he simply copied him by washing the plates and arranging them like the other kid did. It was awkwardly quiet between the two of them, so Kevin was grateful for the loud clattering which filled the room. He deliberately tried to avoid looking in Michael's direction, in case they uncomfortably locked eyes. He had just finished piling the plates on the table for drying when Michael came by with his own stack. He looked at Kevin's carefully domino-ed plates before he uttered the first word since they started working together.

"You're not stacking them properly." Kevin hadn't even realized that this was the first time he'd heard Michael speak.

His voice was stern and confident, which made Kevin think that he was either used to being direct with other people, or he rehearsed that line in his mind multiple times. Kevin glanced in his direction and saw his co-washer standing with the stack of plates in his hands, holding them against his chest as he stared at Kevin in anticipation.

"Well, what am I doing wrong?" he asked.

"They're not arranged well," Michael retorted briskly before setting down his own stack and beginning to place them in position, one by one.

Kevin glanced at his row of plates and then at Michael's, metaphorically scratching his head.

"They look okay to me." Kevin shrugged.

"How long have you been in the camp?" Michael turned his head in Kevin's direction.

"About a week," Kevin frowned, suspecting that he was falling into some verbal trap that his fellow camper was preparing.

"Well, I've been here for eight weeks. So instead of being a smartass, maybe you should try to learn something."

Kevin naturally had a short temper, and the circumstances in the camp probably made it worse, so when Michael uttered that sentence, Kevin immediately blew a fuse. He loudly slammed the plate he was holding on the table. It clattered momentarily, obnoxiously loud, which made Michael jerk his head in the direction of the sound. Kevin took a menacing step toward him and, doing his best not to outright punch the guy right there, he said, "What is your fucking problem with me?"

221

Michael turned to face him, still with the same stern look in his eye. He was a little taller than Kevin, but their build seemed to be similar. Kevin reckoned he might have a chance at taking him down. They stared each other down for a long moment before Kevin spoke again.

"Ever since day one, you've been giving me that same look. What the fuck do you want?"

Michael pressed his lips together before opening his mouth.

"I want my friend back."

Kevin frowned curiously, and all of a sudden, he felt his anger slowly being replaced by intense curiosity.

"Your friend?"

Michael's eyes widened for a moment before they returned to their usual size. The Adam's apple on his throat visibly moved when he swallowed.

"You arrived the same day Bill was sent into the woods."

"Wait, you think I had something to do with the disappearance of your friend?" Kevin pointed the finger at his chest, chuckling at his own question. "Do you realize how ridiculous that sounds? I'm just as much a prisoner here as you are!"

Michael stood still with the same stern expression. His calm attitude contrasted with Kevin's erratic behavior.

"I don't know that. You show up when Bill gets sent away, and you start causing trouble – *and* getting away with it time and time again. I don't trust you. In fact, I think you're in league with the camp counselors."

Kevin laughed out loud. That statement was so absurd, and yet, at the same time, he saw on Michael's serious face how much he actually believed his own words. There was no way Kevin would be able to convince him that he had nothing to do with Bill's disappearance. It suddenly reminded him of the time when he was twelve years old and he was walking down the street next to a parked truck.

He happened to stop right next to the truck to tie his shoelaces, and before he knew it, someone started shouting and running toward him. A scary-looking, overweight person whose breath reeked of alcohol grabbed him by his wrist and started accusing him of doing something to the truck. Kevin confusedly shook his head, saying he wasn't doing anything, to which the trucker only screamed louder at him, demanding that Kevin show him the concealed tool he planned on using to damage the truck. Kevin overturned his pockets to prove to the man that he had nothing on him, feeling frightened for his life by this point. The man pushed Kevin in the opposite direction and told him to get out of there. Kevin started walking away when the trucker ordered him to run instead. He ran and, for close to a year after that, avoided walking through that street.

As he stared at Michael, who had a similar look of confidence in his own words, he knew that arguing with him would be futile. He shook his head in disappointment and took a step back as he threw his hands up in the air and said, "You know what? You believe what you want. I don't give a shit."

He went back to his own work, ignoring what Michael had told him earlier about the plates not being placed properly. After an hour or so, Mark waltzed inside the washing room and tapped Kevin on the shoulder. He said, "Hey, we're not needed here anymore. Let's change and get back to training."

Kevin was more than happy to be out of the kitchen. What he had to do today with the barrels and the plates was only an emergency thing, but generally, when someone was given kitchen duty, they would need to wake up at 3 a.m. to go to the mess hall and stay there all day until 10 p.m., after which their duty was officially done. He dreaded being chosen for that job in the future.

The day went by much too slowly as Kevin, Mark, Ethan, and Ryan went to join the training session held by Counselor Torres. In today's lesson, they learned about orienting themselves with the compass and then with the tools that nature would provide them.

223

Things especially went by slowly because they didn't actually have to do anything except listen to Torres croaking the whole time while occasionally reprimanding a camper or two for not paying attention. Once training was done, they made their way to the mess hall, where a pleasant smell of something being made for lunch floated through the air. Mark's eyes widened when he realized what it was.

"Burgers! Kevin, do you see this? Burgers!" he glanced back at his friend with a wide grin on his face.

Kevin had never seen him this happy, save for the time when he was *talking* about burgers. He gave him a silent thumbs-up, feeling a little excited himself. He glanced to the left where some campers were already taking seats and voraciously chomping their burgers. They didn't only look appetizing but were humongous as well. And on top of that, the campers also got a portion of French fries along with the burger. Mark could hardly contain his excitement when one of the campers they saw earlier in the locker room placed the biggest burger he could find on his plate and handed it to Mark.

"Here you go, Barrel Mark. I saved this big boy just for you!" he said with a satisfied smile.

"Oh, boy, thanks a lot!" Mark exclaimed, strutting to the nearest table.

As soon as Kevin got his burger, he joined Mark at the table.

"Thinking of staying now?" Kevin jokingly asked.

Mark looked up at him with his mouth full of the food, ketchup smeared around his lips. He swallowed and said, "The burger is great. Not as great as the ones back home, but still great. But no, they would need to throw in something extra if they wanted me to stay here."

"Excuse me, can I sit here?" a voice came from Kevin's left.

He looked up to find George, the camper Kevin saw in the laundromat on his first day. He was holding the platter with his food carefully, his shoulders tense as he intermittently looked at Kevin and Mark. Mark seemed to be too busy devouring his food, so Kevin waved George over and said, "Sure thing, man. We don't own this place, anyway."

George briskly smiled and placed his platter on the table, sitting next to Kevin. Two other campers from cabin one joined them soon, around the time when Mark was already done with his gigantic burger. Lunch was great, but it was too much for Kevin. He had eaten around half of the burger when he felt that he couldn't take another bite. Maybe it was the stress. He slid his platter to Mark, whose eyes lit up immediately.

"Wait, you don't want it?" he asked with hopefulness.

"No, it's too much for me. You go on ahead." Kevin was more than happy to share it with his friend.

"Thanks, Kev. Hey, I'll share some of my food with you next time."

"Don't worry about it, Mark." Kevin waved dismissively with a smile.

They didn't have much time to rest after lunch since they were given duties before their afternoon studies. Kevin and a few other campers were assigned to log duty, which was located on the side far opposite of the groundskeeper's cabin, through a trail that led into a connected mini-meadow. The duty essentially consisted of campers carrying chopped logs and stacking them on a pile inside a frame of some sort. Near the edge of the forest were already cut-down trees and woeful stumps nearby, which served as a testament to their once strong roots. There was a small shack nearby too, which contained various tools for cutting down said trees.

Today, however, there was no one assigned to log-chopping duty, and only the handful of campers who were sent there were assigned to carry all the logs into the frame. There were at least a dozen of the cut trees, and carrying them was no easy task. Although they have been cut into smaller logs, Kevin still had trouble carrying them with Norton. Norton, on the other hand, practically levitated the logs high above Kevin's level, his forearms' veins bulging with intensity.

By the time they were done, Kevin's biceps and back were aching like crazy, and he was winded. His hands had a couple of spots where splinters had annoyingly lodged themselves and were too deep to be pulled out with his fingers. When he got back to his cabin, he immediately looked for Clean Ryan and asked him to remedy his ailment. Ryan being Ryan had a pair of tweezers, which he promptly handed to Kevin. Kevin pulled out the splinters while wincing, after which Ryan gave him an alcohol gauze.

"Where do you get all these things?" Kevin asked, laughing at the absurd richness of the cleaning items Ryan had in his locker.

"I usually talk with the guys in the infirmary." Ryan shrugged.

Kevin thanked him. He got ready to jump into his bed until Norton held him back, waving his index finger and shaking his head.

"Your uniform is full of splinters and other stuff. You don't wanna dirty your sheets, trust me," he said.

"Fine," Kevin rolled his eyes and gently spread the blanket over the bed before jumping in.

The bed squeaked warningly in response. As soon as his head hit the pillow, he felt his eyes beginning to shut. He gave in to the sweet embrace of sleep, not caring if Mr. Adams himself would come in to shake him awake. He woke after what felt like minutes but was, according to Ninja, around an hour later. They had to go to lectures, and Kevin grumpily got up, remaking his bed.

The rest of the day was a breeze. Kevin absentmindedly attended the lectures and dinner, after which he got ready for bed. He and Mark spent some time talking in the foyer, going over their plan one more time. Once everything was set, they got ready for the roll call and lights out.

As he lay in bed, he listened to the dreadful anthem of Camp Firwood. He closed his eyes and thought to himself firmly,
Tomorrow will be the last time I listen to that shitty music.

11
The Call

When the anthem began blaring in the morning, Kevin opened his eyes wide. He was ready. He was the first one to jump out of bed and the only one to do it with such alacrity. The other campers sluggishly rubbed their eyes and dragged themselves to their lockers.

Kevin and Mark exchanged looks of determination before nodding at each other. After their morning routines of brushing their teeth, donning their uniforms, and making their beds, the campers began making their way out, one by one. Kevin overheard one of the campers saying they still had time since it was only a little after eight, which had him realizing why he was feeling so rested. Mark later confirmed to him that the campers woke up a little later on the weekends. Kevin was excited and nervous. Today was the day. If everything went according to plan, he would be out of here tonight. His mind raced back to the first day when he arrived, six days ago. Everything about that day – getting the uniform, being given a number in his cabin, seeing the campers' confused glares for the first time when he arrived; all of it seemed like just a distant memory. He felt like that day happened months ago.

What should have been only one day in his hellhole of a camp turned into an entire week, but he would stay no longer. He refused to be kept here as their prisoner and their slave. He was happy to have Mark on his side through this endeavor. He had already started imagining their ride back home. Henry would laugh at Kevin for being in the detention house and would mention how he would have loved to give a bitch slap to Dwight and the detention counselors. Quentin would be quiet for the most part while driving.

He was scary when Kevin first met him, but he soon realized that Quentin was just the strong silent type.

Amy would attentively listen to every detail Kevin shared, relieved to see him safe. Would she come with Henry? Would she even be worried about him? And what would they do when they got back? They couldn't just leave the others in the camp. Not to mention they would probably be punished once the counselors discovered that Kevin and Mark were missing. Kevin vowed to come back to rescue them, but a doubtful thought gnawed at his mind – would they even want to escape?

A few minutes after all the campers had come out of their cabins, two figures appeared in the distance, coming in the direction of the campers. The slim and tall figure was unmistakably Mr. Adams, whereas the somewhat shorter and much bulkier one was Zit-faced Dwight.

"Huh, that's weird. Mr. Adams never comes to pick us up here on the weekends," Mark muttered.

It sounded like he was talking to himself, but since Kevin heard him, he asked, "What do you mean?"

Mark jerked his head in Kevin's direction as if he was surprised that he was heard. He looked back in the counselors' direction and said, "I mean, when Mr. Adams comes to pick us up in front of the cabins on the weekend, it's either when he wants to announce The Choosing or take us there."

"Are you sure that's always the case?"

"I... don't know." Mark looked back at Kevin wide-eyed, visibly distressed.

This effect seemed to take place with other campers as well since the cabin area suddenly fell deafly silent, the only thing heard being the chirping of the birds. Now that he thought about it, Kevin noticed how much the campers' mood contrasted that of the rest of the days. A few silent murmurs surged from other campers in the distance, but only briefly. Everyone had their eyes fixated on the counselors, whose approach couldn't come fast enough and end the anticipation that everyone was in.

The shuffling of grass coming from the counselors' feet grew audible and became louder by the second. Once they were in the cabins' proximity, it became apparent that Mr. Adams was explaining something to Dwight while walking. Dwight stared at Mr. Adams with undivided, ass-licking attention. The two of them stopped, and Mr. Adams turned his head in the direction of the campers. He took a deep breath, his chest heaving as he shouted, "Form up, campers!"

The campers were slower today. It was as if it took them a moment to register what Mr. Adams was ordering them to do. As soon as the first camper clambered up to his feet and began rushing into his position, the other campers seemed to be affected by this like a domino effect, and they too began rushing to form up. As Kevin got up, he noticed that Mark still seemed to be in a somewhat stupefied stance, so he tapped him on the shoulder. This broke him out of his trance, and he immediately got up, rushing to his own spot. During this whole commotion, Mr. Adams was facing Dwight and talking to him about something, which was evident from the way he was gesturing around with his notepad; however, it wasn't audible due to the stomping of other campers.

"…so you can still use it even after its expiration date," Mr. Adams finished telling Dwight before he turned back to face the now-formed campers.

He smiled widely with his usual courteous grin.

"Good morning, campers!" he exclaimed.

"Good morning, Mr. Adams," the campers replied but with much less fake enthusiasm than usual.

Mr. Adams seemed to notice this as he put his hands on his hips and shook his head, the smile still plastered across his face.

"What, did you guys not get enough sleep or something? I can't hear you!"

"Good morning, Mr. Adams!" the campers roared much louder this time.

This seemed to satisfy Mr. Adams as he chuckled with a nod. He raised the hand holding the notepad and pulled out the pen from his front pocket. He clicked it multiple times before beginning to go through his notes while humming the annoying Camp Firwood song. He flipped a page, put his pen to the paper, and went silent. He then began calling campers' names out one by one, scribbling something that Kevin imagined would be a checkmark every time the camper who was called out responded. A couple of minutes later, when that was finished, Mr. Adams continued staring at his notes silently. All eyes were fixed on him, including Dwight's, but the head counselor didn't seem to be aware or simply didn't care enough to acknowledge that. When he finally decided it was time to give the nerve-wracked campers his attention, he clicked and placed his pen back into his front pocket and looked up at them.

"Alright, campers. I have some news for you," he said.

Oh, no. Mark was right. Something is about to happen.

"Today is not an ordinary day. We'll have the director of the camp coming in for a visit sometime during the day."

Loud gasps escaped the mouths of a few campers. Mr. Adams obviously heard their dismay, despite not visually showing it, when he continued.

"Now, now. There's nothing to worry about. The director is only coming to see if everything is okay with the camp, so all you need to do is go on with your duties. And, of course, stay out of trouble. The last thing we want is for the director to witness an incident similar to what we've seen the past week." he briskly glanced in Kevin's direction. "Now, you'll all be given jobs today, just like any other weekend, and in the afternoon when the director comes, just do what you were taught so far, and you'll be okay. How does that sound to you guys?"

Mr. Adams's grin was creepily wide as he swiveled his head from left to right, glancing at the rows of campers. Then one voice briefly responded with a meager, "Yes, Mr. Adams," and again, the domino effect followed as all the other campers responded with the same acknowledgment.

"That's great." Mr. Adams nodded in approval. "Now, go get breakfast, and then Dwight will assign you to your duties."

The campers quickly began moving, circling around Mr. Adams and Dwight like a school of fish, making sure not to get too close to the evil counselors. Everybody seemed to be somewhat at ease now that they knew what the big announcement from Mr. Adams was. Some skeptics, however, were still just as on edge as before.

"Ay, Dios mio. This isn't good news at all, guys," Javier said. "The director only comes when there's a Choosing going on. Why would he drive all the way out here just for a simple inspection?"

"Don't be stupid, Javier." Norton smacked him over the back of his head. "It's what all directors do. Nothing to be worried about."

Javier rubbed the back of his head in pain.

"Javier is right," Steve said.

His authoritative voice resounded among the campers, and the ones who had been murmuring thus far had suddenly gone silent. It was clear to Kevin from day one that Steve had a trait of leadership in him, and the way the campers listened to him only strengthened that belief. Steve continued, "Something always goes wrong whenever the director comes. Something is up, I'm sure of it."

"What could possibly be up?" one camper from another cabin asked. "They always announce The Choosing, and it's every two weeks, so I don't think we need to worry about that."

"Yeah, well, maybe they have some urgency and need to feed us to the Firwood Wraith faster," Steve finished.

They were silent on their way to the mess hall.

After breakfast, the campers lined up in front of the mess hall for Dwight to give them their roles. It was weird having only Dwight giving them orders, but Kevin assumed that all the other counselors were taking it easy on the weekend.

231

Good for them.

One by one, he picked out campers for various duties in groups of four to five. Kevin dreaded that he and Mark would be separated during the job delegation, which was exactly what happened. Mark was given a job with five other campers to clean around the main lodge while Kevin, Steve, and Michael were supposed to clean around the study hall. Once the campers began dispersing, Mark ran up to Steve and asked, "Hey, Steve? Would you mind if we swap roles?"

"Sure, man, whatever." Steve shrugged.

He patted Mark on the shoulder and began walking toward the study hall. Kevin looked at Mark, full of enthusiasm, and asked, "Wait, you can do that?"

"Only on the weekends. Dwight doesn't know what he gave to who, so as long as the job is done..." Mark shrugged.

Kevin laughed out loud.

"Mark, you conniving son of a bitch. You're even more clever than you look."

Mark returned the smile. He glanced to the left at Michael, who was distanced from the two of them.

"Hey, Michael?" Mark called out.

Michael lethargically glanced in his direction but said nothing.

"Would you mind getting the brooms? Kevin and I have something the groundskeeper wanted us to do."

Michael nodded disinterestedly before heading off in the direction of the main lodge.

"Okay, now listen," Mark whispered to Kevin once they were away from the crowd. "We do what we talked about. I'll distract the groundskeeper, and you look for the key. It's a red one; you can't miss it."

"Do you think he'll notice that the key was missing?" Kevin asked with skepticism in his voice.

"Sooner or later, he probably will. That's why we need to be quick about it. And make sure to keep the key in your socks or something. If they find out the key has gone missing, they will probably frisk us to see who has it."

"Well, let's try to bring the key back before the groundskeeper notices, then," Kevin said.

They moved behind the row of buildings and onto the meadow overlooking the mysterious building and the groundskeeper's cabin. A soft, pleasant breeze was blowing, but grey clouds hung ominously in the sky above the cabin as if marking it as a cursed object. It would probably start raining soon.

"Alright, you head into the tree line and get behind the groundskeeper's cabin." Mark pointed in the direction of the trees.

"Roger that," Kevin nodded and began striding across the well-trimmed grass.

It occurred to him that someone must have been maintaining the campgrounds to have them so aesthetically pleasing.

The groundskeeper must have a lot of work mowing the lawn here. He then frowned when another thought rushed into his mind.

Not the groundskeeper. The campers probably do that work. He glanced to the left where Mark was standing in the distance. He was walking along the path, straight toward the groundskeeper's cabin. He locked eyes with Kevin for a moment before focusing back in front of him. Kevin broke into a light jog to catch up with Mark. When he got to the tree line, he carefully stepped over the foliage and turned back to see if anyone had been following him. No one besides Mark was visible. He took another step into the forest and shrouded himself in the shade of the towering trees. He felt safe here, concealed from the evil counselors' eyes that penetrated every corner of the camp.

With this sense of security, he felt like he could move more freely without worrying about being noticed. He knew that for someone to see him now, they would need to be really looking diligently in his direction and squint to make out what the movement was. Still, he didn't want to screw this up, so he took another step deeper into the woods and then turned left. He began walking along the edge of the forest, carefully stepping over branches, rocks, and other obstacles that practically begged him to step on them so he could twist his ankle. They would find he was not such easy prey, however. He had run across much worse terrain avoiding authoritative assholes while trespassing on private property past allowed hours, so walking on mildly inconvenient terrain like this one was like low level for him.

He occasionally glanced to the left, toward the campgrounds, which were obscured by the branches and trees that kept blocking the view. At one moment, he saw Mark step directly in front of the groundskeeper's cabin, drastically slowing down his steps in order to buy Kevin some time to catch up, presumably. Kevin broke into a jog again, evading and hopping over any obstacles, until he finally made it. He looked to the left and spotted the back of the cabin ahead of him. He couldn't see Mark from here. He remembered that the cabin had only one window, which was on the front side, so he didn't need to worry about Groundskeeper Andy seeing him while he was here.

He took a moment to steady his breathing before taking slow steps toward the edge, careful to avoid any fallen branches that might crack loudly under his shoe. He stopped behind a thick tree and leaned on it with his hands, peeking behind it but still not seeing anything. He realized that there was no way he would see Mark or the groundskeeper leaving unless they were closer to the mess hall, so he took a few more steps to the left, just enough to see the path ending at the cabin. Three muffled knocks sounded on the cabin door from the front.

Kevin slowly got down on the grassy ground, ignoring the fact that some insects might be there. He once years ago had a bunch of ants crawl up his shirt and pants like that when he was playing hide and seek, but right now, he didn't care about that. He heard the door swinging open loudly, and after a moment of silence, Mark spoke up. Kevin couldn't tell what he was saying, but what he was sure of was the fact that the groundskeeper kept silent for the duration of the conversation. Mark briefly explained something, after which a long moment of silence proceeded.

Kevin started to worry until, a moment later, he heard the loud bang of the door slamming shut. And then, he saw the groundskeeper's gaunt, hunched-over figure walking down the path and toward the main camp area. Mark lagged behind him and, briefly, dared to turn around and look at the woods. He raised his hand in a thumbs-up and turned around to continue following the groundskeeper.

This is it. Gotta find that key.

Kevin waited for a bit until the groundskeeper and Mark were some distance away. He then emerged from the forest and snuck to the back of the cabin. He went around it to the right, and when he got to the edge of the right side, he peeked behind the corner at the path. Mark and the groundskeeper were maybe a hundred feet away and had a few more hundred to go before they were out of sight, but there was no time to waste. He slightly crouched and glanced around one more time to see if anyone was looking. The coast was clear.

It's now or never.

He rushed around the corner and hurriedly climbed the steps of the cabin. He grabbed the knob of the door and turned it, his heart skipping a beat as he pushed the door. It opened.

Oh, thank god, it's open.

He quickly stepped inside like a thief and closed the door behind him as quietly as he could, instantly dimming the room, the only light being the one glaring in through the window. He felt his heart beating rapidly as he glanced through the window and realized that the groundskeeper and Mark were still walking away. He hadn't been seen yet. He frantically fumbled around the wall next to the door, searching for the light switch. He felt it on his fingertips and pressed it. Weak, orange light coming from a miserly light bulb in the center of the ceiling illuminated the room dimly. The cabin looked small on the outside as it was, but now that he was inside,

Kevin couldn't even begin to describe how claustrophobic the interior was.

On the left side of the entrance was a small kitchen, which blended with the main room. Shelves above the kitchen were cluttered with various items, including dust-covered spices and bottles. Opposite the entrance was the door to the bathroom. Kevin assumed it must have been a comically small bathroom. Right next to the door was a bed that seemed to be on its last legs, with the mattress dangerously sunken down at the center. A table occupied the middle of the room with equally splayed items atop it.

As he frantically swiveled his head around the room, a thought crossed Kevin's mind that the groundskeeper's cabin reflected his personality, and he wondered if the cabin made him grumpy or the cabin was in this state because he was a slob.

Key, where's the damn key?

He went over to the table and looked at the items splayed on it. A plate of half-eaten eggs, a glass of some dark liquid (probably alcoholic), a tool belt with various tools inside, some dirty, rusted pots... No key. Kevin looked around the room, now starting to feel a surge of panic taking over. He ran over to the night table next to the bed and pulled out the drawer. A bunch of papers sat inside along with a picture resting on top of it. It was a picture of a young boy, maybe a couple of years younger than Kevin, smiling innocently. He barely registered that it may have been either the groundskeeper's son or a person of perverse obsession before he began rummaging through the items in the drawer. Nothing. He closed the drawer and turned around, now sweating bullets.

Dammit, where is it?

His eyes widened as they fell on the entrance door. How did he miss it? On the right side of the door, hanging on the nail in the wall, was a keyring. His heart jumped into his throat as he sprinted across the room, almost knocking the plate off the table. He took the keyring off the nail, which jingled loudly in response. He held out his palm and placed the ring on it with the other hand, turning

236

around to face the light for better observation. Panting, he remembered that he didn't have infinite time, so he looked through the window. No one was coming yet. Good.

He focused back on the keys and looked over them one by one. A lot of them varied, some of them big and bulky, others small and thin, so it was easy to differentiate which one was for which; however, some keys seemed to be entirely similar with some of their counterparts, and considering the fact that there were over a dozen of them, Kevin wondered how the groundskeeper got around to using them.

Red key, red key…

There it was. A small key with a red plastic covering the head of it. The key that would be his ticket out of this hellhole.

"Got you," he said aloud as he pinched it between his index finger and thumb, lifting it up.

The keyring jingled as if protesting his intentions. He slid the red key across the keyring until he found the edge of it. He detached it from the rest of them, taking a moment to observe it with a scrutinous glance. He bent down and placed the key inside his right sock, pushing it down next to his ankle. The socks were pressed tightly against his ankles, so the key would not be going anywhere. Kevin took another glance at the keyring just to make sure he got the right key. Once he was sure, he placed it gently back where he found it before taking another glimpse through the window. To his horror, he saw the groundskeeper and Mark coming down the trail toward the cabin.

Oh, shit.

He stared in futility, knowing full well there was no way he would be able to slip out of the cabin without the groundskeeper noticing him. He glanced around in desperation for a way out. He would need to burst out now, even if it meant being seen. There was no other way. The groundskeeper didn't seem like he was looking straight at the cabin, so maybe he could go unnoticed. He was getting closer by the second, each passing moment lowering Kevin's chances of going undetected.

Suddenly, the groundskeeper stopped. He turned around to face Mark, who was gesturing something back at the grounds.

Now!

Kevin got out and closed the door behind him, rushing behind the cabin with a quickened heartbeat, not daring to look back. He practically jumped around the corner to the back of the cabin, and once he was in the safety of the edge of the forest, he looked toward the groundskeeper. He was still staring at Mark but, only a second later, turned around bemusedly and continued walking down the path to the cabin while Mark turned around to return to the main campgrounds. Before disappearing, he glanced behind him at the tree line a couple of times.

Kevin breathed a sigh of relief, chuckling in the process, only just then realizing that Mark must have been trying to distract the groundskeeper. He did it. Kevin bent down and touched his right ankle. He felt the shape of the key, and relief washed over him. He was in the clear for now. He knew that his disappearance wouldn't go unnoticed for a long time, so as soon as the groundskeeper was back inside his cabin, he followed the forest edge back where he came from, attempting to reunite with his fellow campers before they got suspicious of him. He emerged from the woods and tried to keep his eyes in front of him while walking back.

When Kevin returned to the main grounds, Michael and Mark were in front of the study hall. Michael was silently sweeping the concreted area in front. Mark was standing with a broom, eagerly glancing in Kevin's direction. When he saw him approaching, he began sweeping, seemingly relieved. Kevin grabbed the broom that had been left leaning on the wall of the study hall, and he began sweeping the area next to Mark. He felt Mark's incessant gaze on him. He indulged his gaze and smiled.

Mark raised his eyebrows quizzically with clear intentions of asking if the mission was successful. Kevin smiled and nodded with a mischievous wink. Mark exhaled in relief, wiping the sweat off his forehead. They continued sweeping the area for a while in silence. Dwight came to check up on them around thirty minutes later and barked an order at them to hurry it up. He didn't seem to notice that Mark had somehow snuck into the study hall sweeping duty as he left after giving the lazy order. After they were done sweeping the area outside, they had to go inside and clean the interior. There wasn't as much work in there, luckily, but more importantly, Kevin and Mark had more privacy to talk.

"So you really got it?" Mark asked as he lifted one of the chairs in the classroom and placed them upside down on top of the desk.

"You think I'd lie to you?" Kevin chuckled.

Mark stepped closer to him and said with a seriousness in his tone, "Show me."

Kevin glanced behind himself at the entrance door. There was no one in the building besides the two of them and Michael, and he was in the classroom across the hall. Kevin bent down and reached into his sock. When he straightened his back, he presented the little red key in his palm to Mark. Mark's eyes lit up as a smile stretched across his face.

"You did it. I can't believe you actually did it."

Kevin put his index finger on his mouth to shush him since he raised his tone a little.

"I'm actually impressed at what *you* managed to do," Kevin said. "I mean, how did you even get the groundskeeper to leave the cabin?"

Mark shrugged.

"Just told him that there was a problem with the lights in our cabin."

"And he believed you?" Kevin snorted.

"Well, he unscrewed and checked the bulb and said everything was fine with it. I said that the light was flickering a lot, and he offered to give me a new one. And then on the way back, I told him that I don't have the time to pick up the new bulb and bring it back since I got duties, so he said that if we continue to have problems, we should call him to swap the bulbs."

"That's genius. You saved my ass. I don't think I would have thought of that myself," Kevin said.

"Thought of what?" a voice came from the doorway.

Both Kevin and Mark jerked their heads in the direction of the voice. Dwight was standing in the doorway with a stern expression on his face. Kevin felt something get stuck in his throat. The key was still in his hand, and he clutched it firmly.

"We were just exchanging how to hold the broom to sweep faster," Mark rapidly interjected with a slight tremble in his voice, which Kevin hoped Dwight wouldn't notice.

The assistant counselor stared at Mark for a prolonged moment and then turned to Kevin. He looked down at Kevin's firmly closed fist before glancing up at Kevin.

"Well, less talking and more sweeping. The director will be here within an hour, and I want this place cleaned by then. Mr. Adams is busy making detailed inspections in the mess hall, and when he comes here, this place better be spotless." With that, he turned on his heel and left the study hall.

Kevin bent down faster than lightning and stuck the key back inside his sock. He breathed a sigh of relief over what could have been a stupidly ruined plan. He turned to Mark, grabbing his shoulder.

"Hey, did you hear what he said?" he asked, full of enthusiasm.

"That the director will be here soon?" Mark asked with a slight delay.

"No, not that. Mr. Adams is in the mess hall. This is our chance." His heart racing from before hadn't abated, and the thought of actually breaking into the head counselor's office only made it speed up more so.

"Right now?" Mark asked with skepticism in his tone.

"Yeah, we gotta do it before they arrive and while we still have a chance. Come on, are we doing this?" Kevin heard his own voice slightly tremble.

Mark looked down for a moment as if hesitating. He looked back up at Kevin and frowned as he nodded.

"Hell yeah. Let's go."

"Fuck yeah," Kevin said as he leaned the broom on one of the desks.

They quietly made their way out of the study hall as Michael's distant sweeping noise repeatedly filled the air from one of the classrooms. Kevin hoped that he wouldn't notice they were gone and that he wouldn't rat them out if he did.

"Just act natural," Kevin said, once they were outside and he saw Mark glancing around wide-eyed.

"I am acting natural," Mark responded.

"You're not. Your face would give you away from a helicopter. Just calm down and follow me." Kevin put his hand on Mark's shoulder reassuringly.

Mark nodded. He was visibly scared, but he was doing this nonetheless. Kevin couldn't help but admire his courage. Once they were near the back entrance of the main lodge, Kevin said, "I'll go inside, and you wait outside the office. If anyone starts coming our way, knock once. If it's safe, knock twice. If Mr. Adams is coming, knock three times. Alright?"

"Once for danger, twice for safety, three times for huge danger. Got it," Mark recited obediently.

Kevin nodded. With a deep breath, he pushed the doors of the lodge open. The murmurs and shouts of staff members immediately began imbuing the air, increasing Kevin's anxiety tenfold. He could see that the effect was the same on Mark, too, since his mouth hung open and his breathing was a little shallower than usual. A few counselors walked in and out of the rooms and through the hall with hurried steps. For a moment, Kevin thought that their eyes would fall upon the intrusive campers and order them to get out, but they seemed oblivious to their presence.

"They must be really stressed that the director is coming," Kevin quietly muttered, to which Mark nodded. "Come on, let's get our asses to the office before we're too late."

They proceeded down the hall, but not with hurried steps so as to avoid arousing suspicion. Kevin felt like walking on needles each time he'd pass by a counselor, expecting any of them to just stop them and ruin their plan. They turned where Mr. Adams' office was located and continued walking straight. The office was so close. Just a few dozen feet and they'd-

"What are you two doing here?" a voice shouted from behind authoritatively.

Mark and Kevin stopped dead in their tracks. Kevin's heart was now effectively beating against his chest like crazy as he slowly turned around to face the person shouting.

"We're on laundry duty, sir," the voice of a young teenage boy replied.

When Kevin looked in the direction of the voices, he saw a counselor standing at the end of the hall, facing two other campers, who stood in front of him with timid postures.

"Well, laundry duty is over for now, campers. The director will be here any minute. Get back to your cabins," the counselor ordered and motioned for them dismissively to leave.

The two campers turned on their heels and left at a flashing speed. Another counselor came up behind the one who gave the order and tapped him on the shoulder, as he said, "Come on, Adrian, Mr. Adams wants us in front of the entrance," he said as the two of them rushed behind the corner and out of sight.

Kevin wiped the bullets of sweat that formed on his forehead and breathed a sigh of relief. When he looked in Mark's direction, he realized that his face was drained of all color.

"Mark. Hey. You still with me?" Kevin forcefully put his hand on Mark's shoulder.

This, in turn, seemed to snap him out of his trance as he frenetically nodded and muttered a meager 'let's go.' They stopped in front of the head counselor's office and looked around. The coast was clear and the voices much less prevalent than they were a minute ago. The building was emptying, which meant that they didn't have much time until the counselors inevitably made their way back here. Kevin leaned toward the office door and squinted through the pane of glass. It looked dark inside, and although it wasn't clear, he detected no movement. Just to be on the safe side, he knocked on the door three times.

"Hello? Mr. Adams?" he tried to announce himself as loudly as possible and held his breath.

He felt his heartbeat all the way up to his throat as he listened to the silence invading the air. No response.

"Alright, I'm going in," he said to Mark. "Remember. Knock once if someone is coming, twice if they are gone, and three times if Mr. Adams shows up."

"You can count on me," Mark nodded and stepped in front of Kevin to block him out of view as he faced down the hall.

Kevin bent down and pulled the key out of his sock with trembling hands, nearly dropping it in the process. As he slid it inside the keyhole, he silently prayed that Mark wasn't wrong and that the key was indeed the right one. He turned it, and the door clicked. His heart skipped a beat as he pulled the key out and turned the knob. The door opened. Feeling adrenaline rushing through his entire body, he cracked the door ajar just enough to slide inside and slipped into the office like a thief in the night. He locked the door behind him and placed the key back in his sock.

His eyes immediately fell on the phone located on the table. His salvation. His way out of this place. He got around the desk and, breathing heavily, picked up the receiver, placing it up to his ear. There was a low, staticky noise coming from it. That's not good, isn't there supposed to be a steady, beeping sound? He hovered his other hand above the dial, hoping that he didn't need to dial a certain redirecting number before actually calling who he wanted.

He had Amy's number memorized by heart, and so he began dialing it, slowly pressing each digit, one by one, to avoid making a mistake. The entire time, he kept glancing at the door, expecting Mark to knock any second. He looked behind himself at the doorway leading to the backroom. He hoped that there was a place where he could hide, in case it became necessary. He finished dialing the number, but the low humming never ceased.

"What the hell?" he removed the receiver from his ear and looked at it instinctively as if he would be able to see what the problem was.

He tried placing the receiver down and picking it back up, but the phone still didn't work. His frustration began building up immensely, knowing that he didn't have a lot of time. He glanced at the cable connected to the phone and followed it to the nearby wall where it ended. It was connected, so why wasn't it working, dammit? He picked up the phone and turned it over to see if there was anything faulty on it, despite not knowing shit about fixing phones. There was a white label plastered on the bottom and tiny black letters printed on it. Kevin squinted at the letters.

Phone for receiving calls only.

"No, no, no, no. That's gotta be wrong, dammit." Kevin sighed in disappointment and despair.

He was just about ready to give up right then and there. And then something broke him out of his wallow of misery.

Knock.

A single knock on the door. Kevin jerked his head in the direction of the entrance and placed the phone down gently. He got ready to run into the back room and-

Knock.

Another one came at the door. He stared at the door in anticipation as he held his trembling breath, praying to god it would stay silent.

244

Knock.

Kevin's eyes widened at the third knock.

Shit, it's Mr. Adams!

A group of muffled voices began echoing outside the office in the distance, incoherent for Kevin to make out. He jerked his head toward the door. And then the familiar voice of Mr. Adams shouted, "Camper! What are you doing here?!" he sounded frustrated.

"Mr. Adams, I was actually waiting to speak to you," Mark exclaimed, and even from here, Kevin could hear how frightened he was.

"Well, can't you see I'm busy right now? The director and I have some things to discuss. Go on, join the other campers!" Mr. Adams retorted.

"Yes, Mr. Adams!" Mark shouted, and a shuffle of footsteps sounded before gradually fading away in the distance.

"Goddamn fatso. I'm sorry about that, Mr. Director," Mr. Adams said, followed by a familiar, loud jingle of his keys.

Kevin saw silhouettes appearing through the glass pane.

Oh no, he's entering the office.

Kevin turned on his heel and bolted for the backroom. Through the darkness, he saw something that looked like a wardrobe. Not thinking twice, he opened it and jumped inside among the clothes he couldn't see, making sure to gently close the door behind him.

The entrance lock clicked, and the door creaked open.

12
The Director

"Right this way, Mr. Director," Mr. Adams said from the main room.

It was much darker than it had been a moment ago now that the wardrobe was closed, and Kevin heard his trembling breathing more prominently in the enclosed space. His heart was beating fast, and he hoped to god that Mr. Adams wouldn't need to retrieve anything from the wardrobe.

"Go on ahead, take a seat, Mr. Director," Mr. Adams said from the other room.

The sound of chairs being pulled was followed by a moment of silence. Then, Mr. Adams continued, "Mary, I'm sorry, I don't have any extra chairs in here."

"That's alright, Mr. Adams," the nurse's distinct voice came from the same room.

She's with them, too?

Mr. Adams cleared his throat.

"So, I hope the camp is up to standards this time, Mr. Director? We've had to make a few changes since your last visit here."

"It's… better," the director spoke with a deep and calm voice. "Not ideal but better."

Kevin heard Mr. Adams clearing his throat before he said with an audible awkwardness in his voice.

"So, I assume you didn't come all the way out here just for an inspection, right? Is there anything I can do for you, sir?"

"As a matter of fact, you can," the director's confident voice claimed.

The sound of a chair creaking was heard momentarily before the director continued.

"I need you to organize another Choosing."

Silence fell on the room for a moment before Mr. Adams spoke up.

"Well, I guess we could host one by the end of the week and-"

"I need it done *today*," the director sternly said.

"I see. Well, usually, when we host The Choosing, we pick the camper you specifically chose for Departure and two for The Trial, which we randomly choose. So, let me just see here..."

The silence that followed was so deafening that Kevin heard his own heart thudding rapidly against his chest, so loudly that he half-expected the counselor and the director to hear him, even from that far away. The sound of a drawer opening preceded Mr. Adams saying, "Here's the list of campers for you, sir."

"Thank you," the director responded.

The silence lasted much longer this time. Kevin turned his head sideways to listen more carefully, but he couldn't hear anything. Just as he swallowed through his dry throat, the director finally spoke up.

"Alright, I've marked the camper that I need."

"Mhm," Mr. Adams said with a hint of curiosity in his voice. "I don't want to get in your business, Mr. Director, but I really think you should reconsider and choose a different camper."

"Does it really matter who I chose?" the director asked.

"With all due respect, this camper should wait a little longer. He still needs a lot of work. Plus, he's been *very* problematic lately, so we need a little more time to bring him in order."

"Alright, fine. So, who do you recommend then?"

"Let's see," Mr. Adams said. "Alright, you can go for four dash three. He's proven to have extremely high intelligence and ability to adapt to volatile situations."

"Hm," the director said as the sound of chair creaking reached Kevin again. "Alright, fine. Then the one I chose initially - put him for the trial. There's a lot of money at stake here, and they don't like to be disappointed."

"Understood, Mr. Director," Mr. Adams said with more calmness in his voice.

"There's... one more thing I need to mention," the director said with audible hesitation.

There was a prolonged moment of silence before he continued.

"The clients were *extremely* satisfied with the success of the camp's business so far. You know what that means."

A disappointed grunt came from the nurse, but the director ignored it and finished speaking. "We will have another batch of campers on the way soon."

"Are you joking?" Mary raised her voice.

She sounded like she was on the verge of tears. Mr. Adams raised his own voice to match hers as he said, "Now, Mary. I know that this hasn't been-"

"I can't do this anymore, Marvin! You said that this was the last batch, for the last three batches! How much longer are we gonna have to stay here?!"

Kevin didn't even need to perk up his ears anymore since the voices came through so loudly and clearly.

"Mary, please calm down," the director said with his usual tone as if he wasn't talking to an upset woman. "I promise you after this one is done-"

Before he could finish his sentence, an angry stomping of footsteps rumbled across the floor before the sound of the door opening and slamming shut, leaving the entire room in utter silence. This lasted for a moment before someone in the room sighed, and Mr. Adams said, "I apologize for that, Mr. Director. Mary has been under a lot of stress lately."

"Yes, I understand. As long as she doesn't jeopardize the camp. I take it you'll keep a close eye on her?"

"You can count on it, sir. Now, let's celebrate another successful batch, shall we?"

A chair scraped against the floor before Mr. Adams said, "Let me just retrieve one thing."

Footsteps began moving toward Kevin, and he held his breath. He heard Mr. Adams rummaging in the room somewhere close to the wardrobe. It sounded like he was opening and closing something, followed by the distinctive sound of glasses clinking against each other. He saw his silhouette moving past the crack of the wardrobe to the left and then rummaging some more before moving back in the opposite direction. The footsteps faded into the other room, and Kevin was able to breathe a momentary sigh.

"I always save the best drink for when you come, Mr. Director. I know that this one is your favorite," Mr. Adams said victoriously as the sound of liquid being poured reverberated in the main room.

There was a clink of glasses clashing together and then silence for a prolonged moment.

"Good. Really good," the director said. "Now, I can't stay for much longer, so I trust you'll do all the preparations for the transportation of the camper?"

"Of course. He can be ready to leave as soon as we finish The Choosing, Mr. Director," Mr. Adams politely said with a chuckle.

"Good," the director loudly exhaled after the sip he took of whatever the strong alcoholic beverage was.

Kevin heard the sound of chairs sliding once more, and the director said in the midst of it, "I will join you shortly. There's a call I need to make."

"Understood, sir. I need to assemble the campers, anyway." Mr. Adams had apparently shot up from his own chair.

A jingle of keys mixed in with the loud lumbering of footsteps. The door swung open, and Kevin heard Mr. Adams talking to the director about something that he couldn't make out before the doors shut behind them and the lock clicked. Kevin remained inside the wardrobe for a solid ten more seconds before daring to open the door just a crack. The coast seemed clear. He stepped out, tentatively glancing at the entrance to the main room. His heart was racing so fast that he thought it was going to just stop suddenly. He peeked into the main room and realized it was empty. Two half-empty glasses and a glass pitcher full of brown liquor stood still on the desk.

Pulling the key from its concealed spot in his sock, Kevin tip-toed to the door and placed the key inside the lock. Steadying his hands as much as he could, he turned the key. The lock resounded much louder than he hoped it would, and he could only hope that no one stood right in front of the door. He gently turned the knob and opened the door slightly ajar, enough to peek outside. He glanced left and right. The hall was empty, but he heard some voices in the distance. And then a loud whistling noise echoed through the entire main lodge, startling Kevin.

They must be gathering the campers for the Choosing.

Kevin pulled the key out of the keyhole, hesitantly stepped outside, and shut the door gently. He locked it behind himself, feeling overwhelmed by an inexplicable sense of dread. He hastily tucked the key back into his sock and looked left and right. Still no one around. The whistling came again, followed by a loud, masculine shout, "Come on, campers! Line up! Everyone to the Choosing Grounds! Now!"

All Kevin could think at that moment was that he had to get back with the others before someone noticed him. He proceeded down the hall and turned left. He saw a commotion of campers making their way around the few counselors and merging into a big group outside the main lodge. He kept his head down as he tried to blend with the meager crowd of campers in front. He glanced to the right at Mark, and the two of them exchanged worried looks with each other before another shout interrupted them.

"Hurry up, slowpokes! Hurry the hell up!" It was Baldwin.

The whistling was now much more frequent and louder, and it seemed to echo from throughout the campgrounds, close and far, sometimes overlapping with other whistles. Campers from all directions were converging toward the trail leading to the Choosing Grounds, all of them looking equally worried.

"Did he see you?" he heard Mark's voice say to his side, mixed in with the cacophony of hushed murmurs and footsteps on the soft ground.

"No," Kevin briskly said.

"You're so lucky," Mark shook his head.

"You have no idea," Kevin frustratedly retorted, staring in front of him, at Steve's back.

The group was awfully quiet, although some worried murmurs rose here and there. The murmurs soon got much more confident until they turned into audible, decipherable sentences. Even then, most of the conversations revolved around speculations as to why another Choosing was called.

"So, what happened?" Mark asked.

"I couldn't make the call. It's a receive-only phone."

"Oh, darn it!" Mark gasped, his face visibly contorting into visible disappointment.

"We'll just have to find another way out," Kevin said, determined to not give up.

After around five minutes, the incessant whistling and shouting seemed to fade away and then completely stop. The campers themselves got quieter, probably at the sight of the Choosing Grounds in front of them. Even Kevin himself felt uneasy now that they were getting closer. Seeing the Choosing stage made it real and scary. He suddenly remembered the camper who pleaded with the counselors not to send him away. And then the scream he heard in the middle of the night. He wondered if the camper was still okay. The campers began taking up seats in front of the Choosing stage, most of them looking even paler than they were a few minutes ago. In a matter of minutes, the commotion died down, and everyone seemed to be accounted for.

"Ay, someone's gonna get chosen for The Trial! Mierda, I knew this would happen, they need to feed the Firwood Wraith more often, Dios mio!" Javier's voice came from one of the seats.

Kevin glanced at him to see him with his hands clasped together in prayer.

"There's no such thing as ghosts!" Clean Ryan retorted. "You're being stupid!"

"Shut up! Here they come!" Steve retorted.

Everyone went silent with all the heads turning to look behind themselves. The counselors were approaching the Choosing Grounds like a herd, striding with long steps toward the campers. They proceeded to climb on top of the stage, taking positions at the far back.

"Dwight, you have Mr. Adams' notepad?" Baldwin barked.

"Yes, Mr. Baldwin," Dwight obediently said, raising the notepad above his head.

Just then, Kevin noticed that he also had two backpacks that he was carrying over one shoulder.

"Good. Do a roll call," Baldwin ordered.

Dwight stepped forward and began calling out campers' names with much more authority in his voice than he ever displayed talking to any of the counselors. Once everyone was checked as present, Dwight stepped back in line next to the other counselors. As soon as his pounding footsteps faded, unnerving silence filled the air with nothing but the sound of the soft breeze blowing between the branches. Even the counselors were utterly quiet, staring blankly in front of themselves as if they were part of the campers' ranks. They would usually talk to each other, share jokes, or whatever. This time, they seemed just as distressed as the campers.

Kevin wasn't sure if the director's presence simply put them at unease or if they expected to be in some sort of trouble, but he didn't care. His thoughts were on the escape plan. Although he was devastated at not being able to make the call, he was glad he managed to get out before anyone could spot him.

"Eyes up front, camper!" Mr. Baldwin broke the unpleasant silence when one of the campers looked somewhere to the left.

His piercing voice was so commanding that the camper immediately jerked his head back in front and sat even more still than he did up until that point. This effect seemed to transfer to the other campers as well as they stood still like statues. Although he couldn't move, Kevin darted his eyes around, glancing at the worried counselors' faces. They were pivoting their heads and shifting the weights from one leg to the other but were so still that they could have easily blended in with the campers.

Incoherent murmurs started filling the air from somewhere behind the Choosing stage. Within seconds, Kevin recognized the voice as one belonging to Mr. Adams. Sure enough, Mr. Adams and an older man appeared on the right, slowly making their way toward the stage. Kevin stared at the old man with his peripheral vision. He had slick white hair and flawless facial features despite his age, which made Kevin think he took really good care of himself with skincare products (or Botox injections). His suit was perfectly tailored for him and looked out of place in the summer camp environment, which threatened to put a stain on it with every breeze that blew. His shoes were so shiny that they looked like he had just polished them, despite walking on the grass and dirt of the campgrounds.

So you're the director.

That pretentious smile, that expression radiating self-importance, that expensive suit – all of it cried out *malice* so obviously that he could play a villain in any action movie. Mr. Adams was talking about something to the director, scrupulously staring down at his higher-up from his height. The director calmly walked beside Mr. Adams, staring in front of himself, not giving any indication that he was listening to the head counselor. When they finally climbed the stage and stopped in front of the campers, Mr. Adams finished explaining whatever he was so quietly talking about.

The director nodded bemusedly, not dignifying the counselor with even a glance. Dwight rushed to give Mr. Adams his notepad where the head counselor wrote something down and clicked his pen multiple times, vigilantly returning it to his front pocket. The director observed the campers with scrutiny. Kevin felt the campers wanting to move their glance away but were unable to due to strict orders. Two bulky men appeared on the right side of the campers, striding in unison toward the director. Immediately, Kevin realized that the two men wore black uniforms with the name *SECURITY* on the sleeves. His eyes fell on their sidearms. Kevin's thoughts raced back to the first day when he arrived in Camp Firwood. He remembered seeing those two armed security guards escorting a camper somewhere through the main lodge. He felt a knot forming in his stomach.

Oh, this place is bad. Something really bad is going on here.

As if on cue, Mr. Adams placed his notepad behind his back and shouted, "Campers! Please welcome our director!"

"Good afternoon, Mr. Director!" the campers chanted in unison.

Kevin wasn't quick enough to react to this, so he simply hoped that no one would notice his lack of synchronicity. Mr. Adams brought his notepad forward and squinted at it before saying, "Campers, recite!"

The campers recited in unison the Camp Firwood core values. Kevin still couldn't follow through, but he tried mouthing the words, only managing to throw the word 'discipline' here and there. Once they were done, Mr. Adams looked at the director as if looking for confirmation or appraisal like a dog. The director continued staring at the campers, still not giving any indication that he was aware of Mr. Adams' gaze. Mr. Adams faced the campers and said, "Campers, it's your lucky day. We get to have another Choosing. What that means is that some of you get to go home earlier. Just like usual, we'll choose a well-behaved camper to go home and two random campers for The Trial."

He stopped for a moment, scanning the campers with his surveillance camera-like gaze, before saying.

"Alright, the honorary camper for Departure today... is..." he stared for a long moment, seemingly keeping the campers on the edge of their seat.

Everyone held their breaths in anticipation of what was to come.

"Camper Van, cabin four!" Mr. Adams exclaimed.

A few disappointed grunts escaped the mouths of some campers, swiveling their heads in search of Van. Nerdy Van stood up from his tree stump and, as if in a trance, made his way through the ranks of the campers and all the way up on the stage, next to Mr. Adams. Mr. Adams smiled at Van and said, "Congratulations, Van. You were a great camper. Did you want to say goodbye to your friends before leaving?"

Van looked at the penetrating gazes of the seated campers and opened his mouth momentarily. He then closed it and looked at Mr. Adams.

"Um, no. I just want to leave, please."

"Very well." Mr. Adams grinned before motioning the director toward the camper. "Mr. Director, he's all yours."

Van's confused expression changed into one of fright as he stared at the director approaching him with a friendly smile.

"Right this way, camper," the director said just in time for the two security guards to stride behind and follow him.

Van cast a glance at the seated campers, and Kevin wasn't sure if he saw in his eyes shock over getting picked for Departure or fear over not knowing what was in store for him. The director, the guards, and the chosen camper were soon out of sight, and Mr. Adams had to remind the campers to stare in front of themselves. He smiled a PR grin and said, "Now, as usual, I'm going to start with the same question. Any volunteers?"

Silence fell on the camp, so deafening that Kevin heard his own spit sliding down his throat when he swallowed. Mr. Adams pivoted his head left and right, zealously staring at the campers.

"Me!" one voice pierced through the air to Kevin's far-right.

All the heads turned in the direction of the voice, seemingly not caring about the stare-forward rule. Ninja stood up and, with the wave of his hand, started making his way through the ranks of the campers.

"I'm gonna put these Firwood Wraith rumors to rest once and for all," he said confidently as he climbed onto the stage.

"Atta boy, camper. That's the Camp Firwood spirit that we've been trying to encourage since the start," Mr. Adams said in his patronizing tone. "What's your cabin and number, camper?"

"Cabin four, number two, Mr. Adams," Ninja clearly enunciated.

Mr. Adams looked down, scribbled something in his notepad, and said, "Okay, you have four days of survival, camper. Now, we still need one more, so let's see here…"

"I'd also like to volunteer!" Tough Norton's voice came through.

"Sorry, camper. We only take one volunteer per Choosing. But I'd be happy to mark you down for next time if you like." Mr. Adams grinned at Norton.

Norton put his head down, and the way Mr. Adams turned back to his notepad indicated he was expecting that answer from the camper.

"Okay, so… the second camper for The Trial is…"

He looked up from his notebook, darting his eyes around the campers. Kevin felt his heart thumping violently, even worse than it did back when he was in the office wardrobe. Cold sweat started to envelop him, and he rubbed his sweaty palms against his pants.

Mr. Adams continued staring at the campers with a half-smirk on his face. He was enjoying torturing them like this.

"Camper Kevin, cabin four!" the head counselor finally exclaimed, and his voice penetrated through every other sound in the area.

Kevin felt like he had heard Mr. Adams from a tunnel, and yet his brain didn't register that it was his name that was being called out. Even when the heads of the other campers started turning toward him, he refused to believe that it was happening. It couldn't have been happening. There were so many campers. Why did they choose him?

"Camper Kevin!" Mr. Adams called out again, but Kevin refused to budge.

"Kevin!" the other campers began calling out his name, and like a brick to the face, he finally understood the predicament he was in.

Kevin stood up and shook his head.

"No, this must be a mistake!" Kevin shouted, staring at Mr. Adams up on the stage. "I just arrived this week! I don't know anything about survival!"

"That's why you have your fellow camper here with you. Now, come on up on the stage."

Kevin remained entrenched in his spot. Mr. Adams' grin furrowed into an angry expression, and Counselor Baldwin began taking steps toward the stage stairs, locking eyes with Kevin.

"Camper. Now. Before I add another day to your trial," Mr. Adams said with a stern tone, and Kevin knew that he had no choice but to obey.

He shot Mark one glance, who stared back with worry in his eye, pale-faced. Kevin then proceeded to make his way between the seated campers and climbed on top of the stage, stepping past an angry-looking Baldwin and stopping next to Ninja. Even as he stood on the stage, staring down at the frazzled and now more visibly relieved campers, he still couldn't believe this was happening.

"Camper Kevin, you have three days in The Trial. Two as default and one negative point," Mr. Adams said and motioned Dwight to come closer.

Dwight rushed over with the backpacks in his hands and shoved one into Ninja's hand before proceeding to violently slam the other onto Kevin's chest. He leaned in closer and said, "Have fun out there at night with the wraith, loser," he then returned to his position next to the other counselors.

"Inspect your backpacks, campers. Make sure everything is there," Mr. Adams said. "You should have three MREs, a flask of water, knife, battery flashlight, lighter, first aid kit, antibiotics, water purification pills, a hatchet, a rope, and some other minor things."

Kevin dug into his backpack, his hands violently shaking. He pulled out what looked like an MRE. He observed the contents, seeing that it was a transparent airtight package that consisted of multiple compartments. From what he could tell, there was a compartment with meat swimming in some kind of red, oily substance, one compartment for rice, one for a mixture of vegetables that looked like someone's vomit, and at the bottom, a power bar. The other two MREs looked even less pleasing, one being a packaged mac and cheese and the other being a can of something. After rummaging through the rest of the things, he realized that he had everything that Mr. Adams mentioned should be inside.

That's a start, but what the fuck? How do I survive in the woods?

He looked in Ninja's direction, seeking some kind of solace. Ninja had just zipped up his backpack and put it over his shoulders, staring at Mr. Adams for further instructions. Kevin mimicked his movement and looked up at the head counselor.

"Campers," Mr. Adams said loudly. "This is a great honor in Camp Firwood. If you pass The Trial, you get to go home earlier. If not, you come back here, and we extend your time. Find shelter before dark, and make sure not to eat your MREs until you really need them."

He looked at Counselor Baldwin, who looked like he was itching to toss someone off the stage, with his veiny forearms' muscles dancing with each clench of his fist.

"Mr. Baldwin, escort the campers," Mr. Adams said politely.

Baldwin wasted no time turning Kevin and Ninja around forcefully and shoving them in the direction of the stairs. Kevin almost tripped but managed to regain his balance. He followed

Ninja, who seemed to know exactly where they were supposed to go. He went toward the thick tree line at the far back of the Choosing Grounds. The forest edge looked darker than usual to Kevin, and he couldn't help but imagine monstrosities lurking in the shadows beyond what his eye could see. It felt strangely like walking into the embrace of the Firwood Wraith.

Ninja seemed unaffected by any of this because his walk was confident and full of life, massively contrasting Kevin's timid steps. A few times, Baldwin had to shove Kevin and mutter a 'move it' in order to prevent him from slowing down. Once Ninja was right in front of the first fir, he turned around. Kevin got next to him and did the same. Baldwin put his hands on his hips and said, "Well, what are you waiting for? Get going!"

Kevin refused to budge, wanting to offer one final act of defiance before he was sent off. But not only that. He wanted to glance at Mark one more time. It was impossible to tell at this distance if Mark was staring at him or something else.

Sorry Mark, but you'll have to plan an escape on your own.

A moment later, he complied and followed Ninja, stepping off the campgrounds and into the dark unknown of the forest.

13

The forest

As soon as they stepped amongst the trees and were on the uneven terrain of the forest, the visibility got much lower. Kevin and Ninja put some distance between themselves and Baldwin, who eagerly stood at the forest edge, probably to make sure they left. The rays of grey light gleaming between the tree branches and canopies were sparse – and it was getting darker by the minute. The sounds of forest life grew much louder here, the chirping of the birds saturated the air from all directions and echoing throughout. An occasional unfamiliar sound pierced the air somewhere in the distance, but it sounded like a harmless bird rather than a dangerous predator.

The lush green thickets of fallen trees and bushes and moss-covered ground made the area difficult to traverse, but it wasn't like they had to reach a destination. Or was it? Maybe this was a blessing in disguise. Maybe they could find their way out of the camp and back to civilization in three or so days? No, that couldn't be the case. From what Kevin saw from the watchtower, there was no way they would be able to navigate their way through the woods to the other side. Not to mention, they had no idea what was on the other side. For all they knew, it could be just more trees.

Kevin still couldn't believe what just happened. He was picked in The Choosing, and now he had to spend three nights in the woods. But what would happen after that? How would he know when The Trial was over? He wanted to ask Ninja about the details, but he figured they had more than enough time to talk in the next few days – provided that the Firwood Wraith didn't get to them first.

Ninja took point through the woods, and since Kevin was sure that he had way more experience, he simply followed him. Once they were far away enough so that the green pasture of the Choosing Grounds was no longer visible, Kevin started to understand just how disorienting the woods can be. He looked back and had no idea which direction he should go to get back to the camp. How was any of this part of the summer camp activities? What if the campers got lost? That thought was extinguished when he realized that the counselors probably didn't want the campers to come back alive.

They're sacrificing us to the Firwood Wraith.

His thoughts raced a million miles a minute. The conversation Mr. Adams and the director had, now The Choosing. He didn't even have enough time to warn the others. Ninja pulled a tiny compass out of his pocket and glanced down at it, stopping in his tracks. Kevin stopped next to him, looking down at the object's needle. It pointed between North and North-West. Ninja looked up over yonder, squinting as if he was measuring something.

"Okay, so we should remember that the camp is around South, South-East, in case we get lost. We should continue going for a little bit and then set up camp when it gets dark."

"Why? Can't we just stay here for three days?" Kevin asked.

"No. They apparently send the guards patrolling at night to see how far we've come. If we're too close to the camp, they wake us up and force us to move farther in the middle of the night," Ninja retorted.

"How do you know that if you've never been in the trial?"

"The counselors told us that. There was a camper who returned to the camp in the middle of the day once, and they added two extra days to his trial before sending him off."

"What a bunch of bullshit. So what the hell are we supposed to do?"

Ninja scratched his chin before continuing to walk in the direction his compass was pointing.

"We find a campsite, make camp, set up some snares, and if possible, find some food. Then, we start looking for a source of water in the morning. There's apparently a lot of creeks around here, so we should be able to find something before we get parched."

"And then what?"

Ninja shrugged.

"I dunno. Wait, I guess. We survive for the allotted number of days, and they should let us leave, I hope."

Kevin refrained from mentioning anything about the Firwood Wraith. He didn't exactly believe it was the wraith that stalked the woods, but the thought of having a pack of wolves or a bear around didn't exactly make him feel safe, either. They walked in silence for a few minutes, the sounds of the woods surrounding them. Kevin appreciated the silence, but he figured he'd only be able to go for so long before the forest sounds began driving him crazy. He decided to make some small talk with Ninja.

"Hey, where'd you get the compass?"

"Rob swiped it off Torres when we had compass training."

"Wait, Sneaky Rob? He *swiped* the thing off Torres? How?" he asked.

"He literally just snuck up behind him while we were walking back, and he somehow managed to pickpocket him," Ninja shrugged like it was an everyday occurrence, not bothering to look back at Kevin.

Kevin never really spoke to Ninja alone or in detail, so he wondered if this nonchalant behavior of his was his personality or if he was simply trying not to show his nervousness.

"So, you and Rob have been planning an escape?" he asked.

"Yeah," Ninja said, a bit louder this time since he was a dozen yards away and the rustling of leaves under his feet drowned out his voice.

Kevin began feeling irritated with Ninja's brisk answers. He gritted his teeth and asked, "Well, how many campers are actually planning to escape?"

"A lot," Ninja said.

Kevin opened his mouth to ask for additional information, but Ninja interjected before he could say anything.

"There has been a group of us planning an escape for weeks now, ever since the second Choosing took place. More and more campers were going missing, and we knew we couldn't just sit idly."

"So, what have you guys tried so far?" Kevin asked as he ducked under a branch Ninja had brushed again, which swung back and almost whipped him in the face.

"Lots of things. Getting our cellphones back was the first thing we wanted to do, but that proved to be impossible. The storage is always locked tightly. The next thing we wanted to do was send a small group out into the woods, but most of the campers wouldn't even wanna hear about it. Plus, this is probably hundreds of miles of wilderness we're talking about. No way they'd make it anywhere, even with Caveman Bill. And Bill is no longer with us."

"Huh," Kevin simply said, more perplexed by the length of Ninja's answer rather than the answer itself.

"The next thing we wanted to do was highjack the director's car, but we didn't want to get into any legal trouble on top of everything. And that was the best-case scenario. The worst case would be we get shot up like Swiss cheese by the guards."

"Yeah, I get it. Well, if we survive The Trial, what then? We just get to go home?"

"That's what the counselors claim. But I've never seen anyone come back from The Trial."

Kevin scratched his head for a moment, observing Ninja's nimble movement through the inhospitable terrain.

"So, why'd you volunteer?" he asked.

"What do you think? I wanna go home."

"And you're not afraid of… the woods?"

"You mean the *wraith* in the woods, right?" Ninja briefly looked at Kevin with a conniving rictus. "Nah. I don't believe in that shit. A forest is a strange place, and all sorts of animals can make strange noises in the night, but I don't think that's anything supernatural."

"What about the campers who said they saw something outside the windows?"

"Imagination. I've snuck out at night multiple times and wandered the campgrounds and never once saw anything strange."

They had just made it to a more open area where firs were sparser, leaving more of a walkable terrain between them. The trees stretched far up in the sky, their canopies blocking out most of the sunlight, reminding Kevin of the gigantic Elven treehouses he saw in *The Lord of the Rings* movie. It felt tranquil, walking under such behemoths and having so much more visibility throughout the forest.

"So you've been sneaking out at night to find a way out, huh?" he asked Ninja.

"Yeah. But made no progress," Ninja forlornly responded.

Kevin gave him a moment to add information to that, but none came, so he asked, "Anything you *did* manage to find while out there?"

"No," Ninja said.

"Why are you being so weird? You're freaking me out," Kevin blew a fuse.

"Let's just focus on finding a good campsite," Ninja said with the same tone.

This made Kevin even more irritated, but he sighed and silently thought to himself.

Alright, screw it. Just focus on The Trial; that's the most important thing right now.

Ninja refused to say a word throughout their trek through the woods. He occasionally stopped long enough to glance at his compass, mostly when they needed to go around a thicket, a fallen log, or a slope. They appeared to be on the right route (the right route being the direction opposite the camp as much as possible), despite Ninja having to redirect them a couple of times. Daylight was fading too quickly for Kevin until he realized that black clouds above their heads were blocking any meager sunlight from penetrating the woods. Pretty soon, he felt the first droplet of rain on his face. From there, the rain intensified until Kevin heard the droplets hitting the soft ground and above in the branches. It wasn't anything serious that would force them to stop immediately, just light droplets that were cold on Kevin's face and exposed arms and legs.

The sound of rain drumming against the ground and fallen leaves soon increased in intensity but remained constant after that. The rain wasn't enough to even soak the soil or make any mud, so traveling through the forest wasn't any more grueling than before the rain started.

"Shouldn't we collect this rainwater somehow?" Kevin asked.

"Nah, no need. Like I said, there are some sources of water probably nearby."

"The counselors said that there are bear traps around here. Is that true?"

Ninja shook his head.

"No. Or if there are, they are so scarce that you'd have to have extremely bad luck to step into them. So I think the counselors lied. If they wanted to place bear traps, they would need to tend to the traps daily. Plus, you can't set bear traps wherever you want just like that. You need a permit and stuff. In short, the counselors were probably bullshitting us to prevent us from running away."

"And do you think there may be some traps that people abandoned? Like, in the middle of the woods here?" Kevin asked, his curiosity piqued.

"Don't think so. Traps are set with a specific purpose and precision. I don't see the point of setting a trap in the middle of a forest, especially if it's not bear territory," Ninja said.

Throughout their entire interaction, he hadn't made eye contact with Kevin but rather focused on the path ahead.

"How do you know all of this?"

"I used to go camping with my old man. He made sure to teach me everything about surviving in the wilderness."

Kevin raised an eyebrow, intrigued that Ninja was willing to open up to him.

"Why?" Kevin asked.

Ninja chuckled and shook his head. The sound was surprising but not unpleasant.

"Well..." he started. "He has a certain... belief."

"Uh-huh?" Kevin said.

This time, he patiently waited for Ninja to continue, which he did a moment later.

"He's a very firm believer that we may or may not experience the apocalypse in our lifetime, one way or another. He thinks that it's essential to know how to survive in the woods because we may not be able to survive in the city with all the people fighting over supplies. So he often took me out camping."

"Doesn't sound like the type of camping one would enjoy, though," Kevin said.

"Nope. It was hell. He refused to bring any rations and forced me to identify and survive off edible berries and mushrooms. He'd often make me sleep out in the cold if I didn't make my shelter right. He also taught me how to make bird and rabbit snares and how to hunt other wild animals like deer, foxes, and squirrels."

"Jesus. That sounds horrible." Kevin listened to Ninja's story, enthralled but irked by his father's cruelty. "So why'd he send you to camp?"

"Because I refused to shoot an elk. He thinks I'm too soft and wanted me to become more hardened. He says he would have forced me to shoot a *human* if it were legal just so I could get practice for doomsday."

267

"What a dad," Kevin somberly said, suddenly feeling a little more grateful for his own parents, despite them putting him into this hellhole.

They walked in silence for a minute or so before Kevin mustered the courage to say, "Hey, if you don't mind me asking, how exactly does your dad think the world will end?"

Ninja shrugged. "I dunno. I don't think even he knows. He often raves on about nuclear wars, bioweapons, and deadly viruses, that kind of thing. Says it's gonna be survival of the fittest," he made quotation marks with his fingers.

"Huh. Alright..." Kevin frowned.

What he really wanted to say was that his dad was a nutcase, but he kept that to himself since he wasn't sure how much Ninja actually respected his dad. He sensed no hate or a change in his tone when he spoke about his dad, but then again, maybe he was just naturally bad at having an intonation. He wanted to ask about his mother too but decided that it would be best not to prod and instead share a little bit about himself.

"Hey, you know, my own parents are unbearable to live with. That's why I was always out with my friends Amy, Henry, Rick, and Luis. My parents didn't like me hanging out with them and constantly complained about what a troublemaker I am. Eventually, they ended up signing me up for camp."

"That's rough. I'm sorry to hear that," Ninja said.

It sounded like patronizing until he added.

"Why exactly did they send you to camp?"

Kevin shrugged.

"Well, I organized a party on their private yacht, and my friends drank a little too much... we ended up crashing the yacht... and sinking it."

"Seriously? Did anyone get hurt?"

"Nah. It was right next to the coast, we crashed into some stray rock. But my parents were pissed."

Ninja produced a 'hm' sound before saying, "So you're a rich kid?"

"I guess so. Even though I don't really get to share in their riches."

"So, not the spoiled rich type, huh?"

"I'd like to think so."

They walked on for a few more minutes before Ninja asked, "Where are you gonna go after we're out of here?"

Kevin lowered his head down. He actually didn't know the answer to that question. He hadn't even thought about it during this whole time. The first person that popped into his mind was Amy. He wanted nothing more than to see her right now and tell her how much he missed hearing her laughter and seeing her smile. But he didn't want to sound soft in front of Ninja, so he said, "I still haven't thought about it, actually."

He noticed Ninja glancing over at him, so in order to get the heat off him, he asked, "What about you? Where will you go?"

"Back to my mom's place. She and my dad don't live together. It's probably something I should have done a long time ago."

There's the missing detail.

"Your mom's not a doomsday prepper?"

"No, she left my dad because of that... among other things. I decided to live with my dad because I felt sorry for him, thought he was gonna be lonely and needed help coping. Turns out it came right back around to bite me in the ass. How about that, huh?"

"Yeah, that's irony for you," Kevin scoffed.

The light drizzle had already dissipated by then, leaving behind it the smell which Kevin could only describe as forest scent – a mixture of grass, trees, and something he couldn't recognize.

"So, what do you think about the Firwood Wraith rumors?" Ninja asked.

Kevin looked at him to see if he was making fun of him or being serious. He had a stern look on his face, which Kevin took as a sign that he wasn't joking.

269

"Well, I'm not entirely sure, to tell you the truth. I don't believe in ghosts. But I did hear someone scream the night I had watchtower duty."

"Someone scream? You sure it wasn't an animal?"

"No, this scream was definitely human. But I also heard some kind of whistling. Something I didn't recognize."

"Hm..." Ninja said. "I guess camper Carlos may have seen something out there."

Kevin considered Ninja's indifferent statement.

"Carlos? Was that his name?"

"Yeah. I never spoke to him personally, but he seemed like a good guy."

"Well, I hope he made it," Kevin said, despite not believing that the camper was still okay.

He gritted his teeth. He wondered if revealing to Ninja what he heard the other night was a smart idea. Based on his responses, Ninja firmly believed that whatever was stalking the woods was an animal, but he himself had no idea what kind of an animal it could be.

"How much longer do you think we have until we reach a good camping spot?" he asked.

"Not too long, I think."

They had been walking for what Kevin thought had to be close to two hours now, and he was starting to get tired. Ninja, on the other hand, looked like he was ready to go for two more hours. He could probably run a marathon and leave Kevin miles behind. At some point, Ninja began paying attention to the ground for any potentially harmful objects or animals. Kevin joined him in action, asking what would happen if they stepped on a trap that happened to be covered by leaves that were blown on top of it, but Ninja assured him that they were in no immediate danger.

As they got further into the forest, Ninja got more talkative, which was quite unnatural for him. He gossiped about the counselors in Camp Firwood, especially focusing on Dwight, stating how he was an asshole and needed a punch to the throat. He proceeded to loudly elaborate about the way Dwight had once given him the chore of cleaning a septic tank in the kitchen. It was apparently so smelly and dirty in there that he ended up putting on a gas mask when being lowered via the rope. According to him, he couldn't get rid of the smell of stale water on himself for over a week, much to the complaints of the other campers sharing the cabin with him.

By this point, Ninja was speaking awfully loudly and emotionally, his tone reaching a crescendo, and Kevin was afraid someone unfriendly might hear them. Ninja's tone continued to increase until it sounded like he was an actor in the theatre, trying to speak loudly and coherently enough for the people in the back to hear him clearly. Kevin was so taken aback by the camper's sudden talkative mood that he asked him what had gotten into him. His shock was short-lived when Ninja told him, equally loudly, that they needed to talk so they could warn the potential bears who might be nearby.

"What? How is that gonna help?" Kevin asked.

Ninja clasped his hands around his mouth and shouted in a random direction.

"Glad you asked, Cocky Kevin!" His voice echoed throughout the woods.

He put his hands down and continued speaking in a normal tone.

"The bear actually doesn't want to run into us any more than we want to run into it. So by shouting, we are giving it a warning that we are here and that he should stay away."

"Hypothetically speaking, if we *do* happen to have rotten enough luck to run into one, what is the best option to fight them?"

"Well, depends on what kind of bear you run into," Ninja scratched his cheek. "Let me remember, just a second… If it's a black bear, then lie down. If it's a grizzly, then pretend you're dead. No, wait, was it the other way around?"

He said the last sentence to himself curiously, placing one hand on his chin.

"You don't know?" Kevin said, not so much because he was terrified but out of surprise that Ninja would know all the things he knew about surviving but forget something as important as how to survive a bear attack.

"No, no, I do. Gimme a sec," he said and raised his hand toward Kevin in a stop sign.

He stared at his feet and mumbled, "If it's black, fight back..."

"What?" Kevin asked, not realizing that Ninja was still half-talking to himself.

Ninja snapped his fingers in a eureka moment and said enthusiastically, "Right! Now I remember! If it's an American black bear, you fight it back. Make loud noises, shout, flail your arms, that kind of thing. Eventually, the bear will hopefully get scared and run away."

"Bears are such pussies," Kevin huffed and shook his head, laughing at his own statement.

"Now, if it's a brown bear or a grizzly bear, then you lie down and pretend you're dead. He's gonna toss you around a little bit and leave when he gets bored. It's recommended to stay on the ground for at least twenty minutes to make sure the grizzly is gone."

"What about just climbing a tree or something?"

"No, are you crazy?!" Ninja looked offended. "You don't even wanna *think* about that option!"

He said it so dramatically that Kevin couldn't help but assume that he was simply doing it to scare away the potential bears. He imagined them discussing this topic in a normal situation back at camp.

How do you survive a bear attack? Kevin would ask. *Lie down and pretend you're dead,* Ninja would say with his robotic tone. Kevin couldn't help but chuckle slightly at this thought. Ninja ignored this quirk and continued.

"Bears are excellent climbers. First of all, you never even want to run because that makes the bear wanna chase you even more. They will only attack if they feel threatened or you walk right into their territory. And if they have cubs."

"Right. Well, that reminds me of a fable I read as a kid," Kevin said.

"Which one?" Ninja asked.

Kevin cleared his throat and began.

"It was about these two guys walking through the woods. They suddenly ran into a bear and panicked. One guy climbed a tree while the other dropped on the ground and pretended to be dead."

"Oh?" Ninja's intonation returned to its usual robotic self, but he seemed intrigued nonetheless as he glanced in Kevin's direction every couple of seconds.

"Yeah. So the bear came along and approached the guy on the ground. It got close to his ear and stayed like that for a bit before just walking away. Once the bear was gone, the guy on the tree climbed down and regrouped with his friend, happy that they both made it. He said to his friend who was on the ground that it looked like the bear was whispering to him when it was next to his ear."

He cleared his throat again and looked left and right, between the rows of trees, suddenly feeling a little paranoid.

"So the friend told him the bear *did* say something to him. The guy asked him what, and the other guy said, 'That's some friend you got there, to leave you for dead while he scrambles up the tree to save his own life.'"

Ninja looked at Kevin again, now wearing an expression like he was hanging on every word.

"Okay. Then what happened?" he asked.

"That's... that's it. That's the ending," Kevin said awkwardly, feeling like he had just told a joke without a punchline.

"Hm. Interesting," Ninja simply retorted in a way that sounded like it wasn't interesting at all.

They continued walking in awkward silence for a minute. Ninja glanced at the compass before saying.

"Well, anyway, if you ever forget how to deal with bears, there's a simple way to remember it."

"Alright, what's that?"

Ninja raised an index finger and theatrically proclaimed.

"If it's black, fight back. If it's brown, lie down. If it's white, good night."

"What?" Kevin let out a hysterical chuckle.

"Yeah. Black bears need to be fought back. With brown bears, you need to pretend you're dead. With polar bears, well... you're dead if you run into them."

"There's no failsafe technique against them?"

"Nope. The best way to survive a polar bear is to avoid running into one in the first place."

Kevin laughed at Ninja's statement. Ninja looked at him seriously, which made his obliviousness even funnier to Kevin. It must have been because he was away from the camp, but he felt more free, and as a result, he was probably able to laugh more at dumb jokes and situations. He had stopped thinking about what he experienced today back in Mr. Adams' office and was more relaxed now that he had spent some time in the woods.

Ninja patiently walked in silence while his partner laughed his ass off. It felt good having a conversation with Ninja. He couldn't imagine being alone in the woods, especially at night. He felt much safer with someone as experienced in camping as Ninja. They made it past a tiny creek flowing downhill and winding in various directions, disappearing under two moss-covered rocks, and emerged in a much more open area with sparse trees.

Ninja stopped and said, "Okay, I think this is a good camping spot."

"Finally." Kevin sighed in relief.

The grey light had transformed into dark orange, and even though it was only around 7 p.m., it was seriously dark in the woods. Kevin hadn't considered that before they set out, although he was sure that Ninja knew it all too well and knew how much time they had before it got completely dark. Kevin's feet were killing him, and he immediately dropped his backpack on the ground and slumped to the nearby root of a tree. He was overcome with immense relief to finally sit. Ninja, on the other hand, placed his hands on his hips and glanced around, looking like he was searching for something.

"Aren't you tired?" he asked Ninja.

"A little. Let's take a short break, and then we can set up camp," he said.

***

About an hour later, Ninja and Kevin were huddled outside of their shelters, sitting around the circle of rocks they made, which would serve as their campfire. Dry branches were messily stacked inside the rock circle, but the fire was not yet lit. The shelters they made were similar to the ones they had to make a few days ago during training – they found a few bigger branches they used as the foundation to form the pyramid, and then they used thinner, longer branches to line up along the bough, serving as the rooftop. Kevin's shelter was barely big enough for him to fit inside, and he hoped he wouldn't knock anything out of place during the night since he assumed sleeping on the pile of leaves he brought inside the shelter to serve as a mattress would be uncomfortable enough for him to toss and turn.

Ninja was working on setting up some snares, all the while explaining to Kevin how to make them himself. Kevin was having a difficult time carving the twigs as proficiently as Ninja, especially since he had no idea how they worked. But since Ninja had already made a few, it didn't matter.

"We just need to catch one rabbit and we're set for a little bit," he said.

"Unless the rabbit is really small," Kevin said, to which Ninja shrugged.

The forest was much darker than thirty minutes ago and was getting darker still by the second. The dim shades of orange were quickly replaced by marine and eventually black while the crickets started their shift in the woods. When Kevin asked him about the time, Ninja glanced at his watch and said it was only a little past eight. Kevin wondered what the other campers were doing around this time. Right now, they were pretty much finishing dinner and were getting ready to go to bed.

For the first time since he arrived at the camp, he envied them.

He and Ninja went to place the snares around the camp – in other words, Ninja did all the work. He set up the snares by burying one small stick in the ground and attaching another one to a nearby sapling with a tiny string of rope. He then wedged the two sticks together into the pre-carved crags so that the one on the sapling worked like a sling. He finally attached a small piece of wire he had in his backpack to the sling-stick in order to make the actual snare.

"So, the rabbit hopefully goes through here, and then it triggers the trap and gets caught."

"Now I get it," Kevin snapped his fingers at the metaphorical lightbulb clicking above his head.

With that, he helped Ninja set up the remaining snares. It was just about completely dark by the time they were done, so they lit up the campfire and sat around it on the ground, listening to the crackling of the wood and embers. The warmth and the light of the fire were comforting, especially now that the woods were engulfed in darkness. Kevin couldn't see past the shelters he and Ninja set up opposite of each other, and it terrified him. The longer he stared, the more he started to imagine pairs of eyes staring back at him. He averted his gaze and focused on the fire instead, tossing in two pieces of firewood that he and Ninja chopped up earlier with the hatchets.

The flame gyrated violently for a moment, the crackling intensifying before it stabilized. Ninja unzipped his backpack and rummaged through it until he pulled out the airtight MRE. He took out the knife, ready to start opening the packaging.

"Dinner time, I guess," he said with a shrug.

Kevin decided to dig into the mac and cheese instead since it looked like a smaller meal, and he didn't feel too hungry. He would have skipped dinner altogether had he not heard the rumbling of his stomach. The mac and cheese were surprisingly good, despite being a little soggy. He couldn't help but think about how Mark would have loved the meal. He hoped to be able to save at least one MRE for him when he saw him again. He wondered if he ever was going to see Mark again. If he passed The Trial, would he be sent home right away without saying a proper goodbye to the other campers? But then another thought crept into his mind.

What if we don't survive?

He cast a suspicious glance at the dark behind Ninja, staring at it for a prolonged moment before averting his gaze. He had finished his mac and cheese and tossed the packaging on the side when Ninja raised his hand and said with a full mouth of meat and vegetables, "Whoa, whoa." He swallowed with effort and said, "We don't wanna toss it around; it can attract animals. We'll throw them somewhere far away later on."

"Sure," Kevin said.

Once Ninja was done with his meal, he wiped his mouth and said, "You want me to throw the stuff, or will you do it?"

Kevin really didn't want to go into the darkness of the woods, away from the comfort of the fire, but he also didn't want to be dead weight. He deduced that it would be good training for him to get into the dark and see that there was nothing there that can hurt him.

"Sure, I'll do it. Just tell me where and how."

"Just go some ways in whichever direction, a hundred feet or whatever, and toss the packaging there," Ninja said as he burped.

"Got it."

Kevin picked up the mac and cheese packaging and Ninja's messily sliced-up packaging and pulled the flashlight from his backpack. He flicked it on and began walking in one direction.

"And be careful not to step in the snares," Ninja said.

"Yep."

Kevin illuminated the ground with the flashlight as he walked, careful not to step somewhere where he could twist his ankle. He barely missed stepping into one of the snares, managing to see it in time before pivoting around it. Once he was some distance away, he looked back toward the campfire. It looked small but still comforting, even from this distance. He suddenly realized that he was surrounded by pitch black, save for the beam of his flashlight, and it sent chills running down his spine. He scanned the area around him just to make sure nothing was there and tossed the empty MREs on the ground.

Snap.

Kevin instantly jerked his head in the direction of the sound, pointing his flashlight at the source. He saw a figure, a thin, pale figure staring right back at him.

No, not a figure. Just a goddamn tree. He exhaled in immense relief, feeling his heart beating heavily. He scanned the area a few more times with his flashlight to make sure nothing was there, and once he felt like nothing would jump on him from behind, he made his way back to the campfire with hurried steps.

"Well, I think I'm gonna get some shuteye," he said as soon as he returned.

"Already?" Ninja asked.

"Yeah, I haven't been getting enough sleep since I arrived at camp."

Ninja chuckled and said, "Well, maybe we can finally get some more sleep out here."

"I doubt I'll be able to sleep too much in a place like this, but I'll certainly try," Kevin scoffed.

He carefully slid into his makeshift shelter. Ninja tossed a few more firewood pieces into the fire – causing it to crackle - and got into his own shelter. Kevin made sure that his backpack was right next to him and firmly held onto his flashlight as he lay on his side. He couldn't help but feel like he did, back when he was a little kid, afraid that if he left one part of his body uncovered, the Boogeyman would come and grab him. Now that he was fully exposed, he felt entirely naked.

"Well…" Ninja said as he yawned. "At least, we won't need to worry about anyone waking us up in the early morning."

Kevin wasn't sure if he was right.

14
The Firwood Wraith

Kevin shot his eyes open and was instantly wide awake. A whistling of some sort caught his attention, too close by for comfort. Or was it just his dream? It was still dark, and the campfire had long since died, leaving only traces of embers, ashes, soot, and charred wood. Kevin raised his head and looked toward Ninja's shelter. Ninja was awake, too. Kevin could see his silhouette propped up on his elbow, his shoulders visibly tense. Kevin dared to crawl forward ever so slightly to get a better view of the area, but it was too dark. He wanted to turn on his flashlight, but he wasn't sure if it was smart. He was waiting on Ninja to give him a signal of some sort.

His silent prayers were answered a moment later when he saw the beam of Ninja's flashlight come to life. Ninja crawled out of his shelter and pivoted the flashlight in various directions while holding his hatchet. Kevin turned on his own flashlight and crawled out to join him, swiveling the beam frantically, scanning the trees. A few times, he thought he saw something that looked like a figure but then realized it was just the shape of a tree or bough and his mind playing tricks on him.

"You heard that, too, right?" Kevin asked, not looking at Ninja.

"The whistling? Yeah, I did."

"Was it an animal?"

"No, I don't think so. At least, I've never heard an animal that sounds like that. It was too… rhythmical, too musical. Made by a human."

That sentence sent shivers down Kevin's spine. If Ninja said it, then it must have been true. Whatever was out there was no animal. They continued scanning the horizon in silence, the beams of their flashlights dancing in various directions, illuminating only small portions of the woods.

Snap.

Kevin and Ninja jerked in the direction of the echoing sound but saw nothing. Their flashlight beams were now trembling and swaying, sending the shadows of the nearby branches and saplings dancing ominously against the background.

"That's... not good," Ninja reticently said.

For the first time, Kevin sensed some sort of apprehension in his voice. He looked entirely cool and collected up until then, but now his voice seemed to quiver slightly. Kevin looked at him and, in the dark, saw his face staring wide-eyed in one spot, his mouth agape. He followed his gaze but still found nothing moving around.

"Why is it not good?" Kevin asked.

Ninja's delayed answer came a few seconds later.

"Because branches only snap when something heavy steps on them."

As if remembering just then, Kevin ducked into his shelter to retrieve the hatchet. He flipped the flashlight into his left hand so that he could handle the hatchet with the dominant hand as he impatiently continued scanning the woods for any activity. A rustling noise came from the opposite side. Both Kevin and Ninja followed the source of the sound with their flashlights.

Nothing.

Snap.

Kevin was quick this time. He jerked the beam of the flashlight to the right, in the direction of the sound. He thought he saw something retreating behind a tree trunk uphill. He froze, keeping his beam trained on the tree. Did he imagine that just now? No, there was something there. He saw the leaves at the foot of the tree trunk shuffling momentarily, and at the edge, just barely visible was a part of something. Maybe a shoe?

Another whistle came through, much louder and closer this time, but it wasn't from the tree trunk. It was in the opposite direction. Kevin gasped and shot around but saw nothing. He quickly turned back to look at the tree where he just saw movement a second ago, but whoever was there was gone.

"Ninja?" Kevin asked, feeling panic welling up inside him and threatening to take over.

"Keep your hatchet close," Ninja said.

The two of them were practically back to back with each other, the beams of their flashlights fervently scanning the area, but to no avail. A lonesome pebble skittered somewhere in the distance, uphill from where Kevin had just seen the movement. It rolled down the leaf-covered hill and came to a halt right in front of Kevin's feet. Kevin shone the flashlight down on it and then traced the source of where it might have rolled down from. A figure peeked from behind the same tree trunk, not bothering to hide from the light pointed directly at it this time.

Kevin saw a pale, mouthless face with black orbs for eyes staring back at him. He froze in place, unable to budge. It felt like he was locked in a staring contest with the creature for an eternity. And then-

The creature jumped in front of the tree and screamed a muffled scream with its non-existent mouth, the skin stretching across the gap where the mouth should be, rushing toward Kevin with a hand raised above its head. Kevin couldn't see what the creature was holding, and he had no intention of waiting to find out.

"Oh, fuck! Ninja, run!" he barely had enough time to tap Ninja on the shoulder before he started running in the opposite direction.

He heard Ninja's stifled scream, followed by the avalanche of footsteps. The muffled screams of the creature behind them reverberated in the air, stopping every few seconds to inhale and then continue screaming the same psychopathic scream. Kevin jumped over a root blocking his path and continued running as fast as his legs would carry him. The adrenaline didn't even allow him to look at the ground for potential threats of traps, roots, rocks, or anything else. His and Ninja's panting filled the air as the beams of their flashlights violently bobbed up and down in the night, intermittently illuminating portions of the woods before engulfing them back in darkness.

The screams of the faceless creature behind them seemed to fade away, but only slightly. The campers had managed to scramble up a hill and continued running for a while when Kevin realized that the screams were no longer following them. Feeling a sudden burn in his lungs and legs, he stopped and turned around to see Ninja catching up with him. He scanned the hill with his flashlight, asking between breaths, "Is... is it gone?"

"Kill the light," Ninja said as he flicked his own flashlight off.

Kevin immediately did that, just then realizing how stupid it was to broadcast their position to the entire forest. As soon as his light was off, too, complete and utter darkness enveloped him. For a few seconds, he couldn't see a finger in front of his nose. But then, his eyes started to adjust, and he could make out some details that he was staring at just before the lights went out – trees here, branches there, a rock on the side...

"Okay, listen," Ninja whispered while panting. "We need to-"

A whistle pierced the air. Kevin couldn't tell the distance, maybe a few hundred feet away. Too close for comfort.

"Run," he said to Ninja, and the two of them turned around and began running again.

The whistling now came intermittently with brief pauses in between, and it always seemed to be equally distanced, despite the fact that they ran from it. They had made it to a part of the hill where it descended steeply into a ravine below on the left side while a cliff face sat on their right, leaving them with only a narrow passage in between. They carefully had to sidle on the path while hugging the cliff face to avoid falling into the ravine. Ninja went first, walking with his back against the wall, and Kevin followed him closely behind. They didn't have too far to go like that, maybe a few dozen feet by Kevin's estimation, but looking down into what looked like an endless abyss made that distance feel much greater than it actually was.

A minute or so passed since they last heard the whistling. And then it came again on Kevin's left. He couldn't see the Firwood Wraith in the darkness, but he knew it was there – and he knew it could see him. He hurried his steps up, panic overwhelming him. The whistling was getting closer by the second, and at this rate, it would catch up with him any moment now. He expected to see the faceless creature pop in front of him and pull him into the darkness of the woods while he thrashed and screamed. He expected to feel cold fingers wrap around his wrist and yank him like he was nothing more than a plaything. The thought of it made him shimmy to the side even faster.

This was a mistake because, in the next moment, he felt himself stepping on Ninja's shoe and losing balance. His foot slipped forward. He tried holding himself with the weight of his other foot, but it slipped under him, and the next thing he knew, he was sent tumbling down the hill.

"Kevin!" he heard Ninja's voice from above as he futilely tried clawing at something to grab onto.

At first, he simply slid against the moss, and then his side bumped into something, exploding with pain, and he was sent rolling down the hill, overcome with a sense of vertigo. Just as quickly as the rolling started, it stopped, and he was on the ground, no longer tumbling. His side hurt like a bitch, and he wondered how much damage he had sustained. The whistling from above continued, but instead of following him down, it proceeded in the direction where Ninja was moving. In seconds, the sounds began fading away and, within a minute, were completely gone.

Kevin was left with utter silence and an aching body. At first, he refused to move. He wasn't sure if moving was what would catch the wraith's attention, and he didn't want to test that theory. After what felt like minutes, he decided that he had to move before the ghost returned to finish him off. He slowly stood up, not wanting to put too much weight on his hands and legs, unsure if he had broken something. When he was sure that there was no pain in his limbs, he touched his side. He winced at the pain, but whatever the injury was, it wasn't bad enough to immobilize him... yet.

He rubbed his index and thumb together to feel if any blood came from the touch but luckily felt nothing wet. Probably just bruised up real good. He had no idea which direction to move in, but he reckoned that it didn't matter. The priority right now was finding a safe place. He still had his flashlight with him but refused to flick it on. The hatchet he dropped on his way down the hill and there was no way he'd find it in the dark.

With no way to determine which way to go, he decided to go for the most logical solution – putting as much distance as possible between himself and whatever the fuck that thing was. He hoped that Ninja managed to escape it. He was agile and fast, so he should be able to outrun it. But then another terrifying thought came to Kevin's mind. What if the Firwood Wraith was actually much faster than it let the campers believe? Maybe it could move with lightning speed but was just messing with them, building up their fear? That would explain why they heard whistling coming from various directions back at the camp.

Kevin couldn't get the wraith's face out of his mind. Pale, stretched against the skull-like features, with no mouth. Even though Kevin swore he could see the jaw moving, as if to open the mouth, the skin against the mouth tightened with its muffled scream. He shuddered at that. He kept glancing over his shoulder, paranoid that he'd see that face staring back at him from behind a tree trunk. He was tempted to turn on his flashlight, but he knew that the risk outweighed the reward in this case. He imagined himself being in the wraith's position, scanning the woods for Kevin and seeing a flashlight flicker to life somewhere in the distance before dashing like a bloodthirsty animal toward its seemingly unsuspecting prey.

I gotta find some shelter ASAP.

He had made it through the thicket of bushes that scratched his legs. He tried to be as quiet as he could, but the rustling and snapping were probably heard loudly. For the first time since he arrived in the woods, he was grateful for the loud wildlife that surrounded him. It made him feel less lonely, less exposed. If he was going to die here, at least, he knew it wouldn't be entirely alone, surrounded by nothing but trees, even though he doubted the animals would come to his aid like in some sort of Disney movie. The exhaustion was starting to get to him now. Although he was no longer winded, his legs were wobbly from the intense running. He was sure that if he survived, he'd have sore quads in a day or two.

As long as I survive, I'm not complaining. I'm never complaining about anything ever again.

His thoughts raced back to the campers, who were probably sleeping peacefully in their cabins. He imagined Mark snoring at this very moment, feeling momentarily angry at their obliviousness before realizing he was overreacting. It wasn't their fault. He had been walking for around thirty minutes by his estimation when he decided to sit on a nearby collapsed tree trunk. The adrenaline had completely subsided since the chase, and the fear of the Firwood Wraith somewhat, so he figured that taking five minutes for a break would be a smart thing to do. He was no good running if the wraith caught him in a tired condition like this one.

He exhaled deeply but tried not to produce a lot of noise in the process. He swallowed through his sand-dry throat and just then realized how thirsty he was. He had left his backpack back at the camp and, with it, all the relevant supplies, including food and water. Now, he had no idea where he was or which direction he should go in. He couldn't even remember what Ninja told him, which direction the camp was in, and even if he did, he didn't possess the knowledge to orient himself without a compass.

He had no idea what time it was, either. Was dawn coming any time soon? He couldn't stand being in such thick darkness. As tranquil as the woods were at day, they were tenfold scarier at night. What was going to happen to him? Would he die in the woods of starvation or dehydration? Or maybe he'd eat some berries and get poisoned along the way, vomiting and shitting until he had no more strength and died? Or maybe he'd get torn into bits by the wraith.

They're sacrificing us to the Firwood Wraith. The campers were right all along. I can't fucking believe it.

The panic subsided slightly, and desperation started to overtake him as he began hyperventilating. How the hell did he get into this situation? He wasn't supposed to be here. He was supposed to be back home. He was supposed to be spending time with his friends. He was supposed to be out on a date with Amy.

Tears filled his eyes at the thought that he may die here and that he would never get the chance to tell Amy he had feelings for her. She would move on with her life, maybe feel somewhat sad over the loss of her crush (if that was even what he was), but eventually, she would move into college, find a boyfriend there, get married after graduating, have kids, and so on. The same would be for Rick, Henry, and Luis. They would continue hanging out, and Kevin would be just a friend who tragically died in a summer camp back when they were teens, who they'd occasionally mention in passing. Kevin's tears flowed freely, dropping onto the ground below him. He suppressed his sobs as much as he could, which resulted in uncontrolled gasps for air.

A whistling noise broke him out of his self-pity. Kevin raised his head, perking up his ears. He wiped the tears from his face and stood up from the trunk. The whistle was close by, but he couldn't tell where exactly it had come from.

How is it here already?

The whistle came again, playful this time, like an owner calling his dog to come to him. It was closer this time. Was it even worth running? Would running give away his location? The forest had gone somewhat silent, and with no other plan in mind, Kevin decided to hide. The collapsed tree trunk was leaning against a part of the ground with a ditch near the middle, perfect for hiding.

Kevin climbed over the tree trunk and crawled under it into the ditch, using the tiny gap between the trunk and the ground as a peephole. He could see the area well from here, and he was sure that there was no way that the wraith could see him unless it came from the other side. The good thing about the hiding spot, though, was the fact that the side Kevin was hiding on was riddled with a rocky, uneven gradient, which no one would want to traverse in their healthy state of mind, so there was no way he could be ambushed from behind.

Not by a human, anyway.

The whistle sounded again, much closer, a few dozen feet in front of Kevin. Kevin squinted in the dark and darted his eyes all around the area in front. At first, he saw nothing. Another whistle, followed by the sounds of steady and heavy footsteps. They were coming from somewhere on the left side, but Kevin couldn't see anything there. The footsteps were getting closer and closer as if the person walking was not maliciously hunting someone but taking a casual stroll. They sounded like they were right in front of the trunk, and sure enough, in a moment, Kevin saw the tip of a boot stopping in front of him.

He clasped a hand over his mouth, doing his best not to breathe loudly. The boots shuffled in place before taking a step forward. The person wearing the boots seemed to be shifting weight from one leg to another, occasionally pivoting around, seemingly inspecting the area. Then, two taps came on the trunk above Kevin. Kevin felt the vibration of the knocks, and his heart leaped into his throat, but he refused to move. If the wraith really found him, he stood no chance of crawling out of the ditch in time to start running. If it didn't see him yet, then he couldn't risk exposing his position.

A moment of petrified silence filled the air as Kevin waited in anticipation of what was to come. He expected to feel sharp nails digging into his back any moment now or being snatched by the ankle and pulled out to be mauled to death. The boots proceeded to move out of sight to the right. Kevin closed his eyes and silently exhaled into his hand with a quivering breath.

When he opened his eyes, an eye was staring back at him through the gap.

Kevin screamed, backing away as much as he could from the face. It was the same face from before, the pale, mouthless face with black eyes. He managed to crawl out of the ditch much faster than he ever thought he'd be able to and turned around to run up the inhospitable rocky terrain. He felt something grab his shirt from behind, which gave him a sudden burst of energy. He flailed and twisted his body, feeling like his shirt was going to rip any moment, but the grip suddenly loosened, and Kevin was propelled forward, climbing up the gradient with an agility that would make Ninja jealous.

He felt a hand wrap around his ankle and momentarily lost his balance, catching himself before he could stumble back down the hill. He held himself firmly with his hands against deeply embedded rocks and used his other foot to kick the hand holding him. He couldn't even see who or what was holding him. He saw nothing except that pale face looking up at him with the same, expressionless look. He felt the grip around his ankle loosening, and he wasted no time continuing the climb, stumbling and slipping along the way.

He heard a frustrated grunt behind him, sounding muffled like before. He was sure that the wraith was furious now and was done playing around. It was going to hunt him down and kill him just like it probably killed Ninja. By the time Kevin had climbed the elevation, his entire body was screaming at him to stop and take a break while his brain told him to keep going. He panted along the way, unable to take in a proper breath.

He got up from all fours and began running, tripping and falling along the way. The whistle was right at his heels, and it urged him to stand up and keep going. He was a second too late because just as he was about to stand up, he felt a weight on his back, pushing him to the ground. He slammed with his chin on the ground but ignored the pain. He felt some of the dirt getting into his mouth, but that was of no concern to him at the moment. He had to get away.

He tried pushing himself up, but as soon as he lifted his body mere inches off the ground, he was pushed down again. He felt a hand grasp his shoulder with a vice-like grip and spin him around onto his back. He saw the Firwood Wraith standing above him in its full glory. Its black eyes stared down at Kevin, and even though it had no pupils, Kevin knew that the wraith was staring directly at him. He felt cold fingers wrap around his neck and squeeze hard, even though he saw no limbs or torso. The blank piece of skin where the mouth was supposed to be stretched slightly, and a muffled voice left its mouth.

"I got you now, kid!" the voice surprisingly sounded like it belonged to an average adult male rather than a ghost.

Kevin couldn't breathe. He repeatedly tried detaching the fingers from his neck, but they were pressed against it too firmly. He began hitting the ghost's invisible arms, trying to focus on the elbows to get the grip to loosen, but it wasn't working. His vision was getting progressively darker, and even the meager details that he was able to discern thus far were beginning to fade into nothingness. The strength of his arms was waning, and he wasn't even sure if he was hitting anymore.

Amy, I'm sorry, he thought to himself as the sounds around him began fading away.

And then, the grip on his neck loosened, just like that. He heard a grunt, and with his slowly regaining vision, he saw the wraith falling to the side with a smaller figure on top of it. Kevin coughed violently, trying to take in desperate breaths of air. He saw the wraith and the other figure wrestling on the ground. The wraith threw a punch at the figure, causing it to topple over. The wraith then withdrew something from its back and jumped on top of the figure. Kevin saw a glint in the wraith's hand as it tried bringing it down on the figure.

A knife.

Kevin had to help the figure, whoever it was. He didn't think. He didn't know if the figure was his friend or something else, but he knew for sure that the wraith wasn't on his side. He looked for anything nearby that he could use. His eyes fell on an object on the ground that oddly resembled his hatchet. He scrambled for it and, upon grabbing it, stood up and looked at the two figures wrestling. The wraith was turned with its back toward him. Without thinking, Kevin charged it, raised his hatchet above, and brought it down on the pale head of the Firwood Wraith.

All struggling instantly stopped, and the wraith fell sideways without a sound with the hatchet embedded in its head. The figure pushed the wraith and scooted away from it. Kevin was focused on the body of the wraith. A million thoughts were racing through his head. Had he just killed someone? What the hell is that creature? But as he stared at it, he realized that it couldn't have been a ghost and never was.

The mask with the pale face slightly slid up, revealing not a ghost but a human face, a mouth frozen in a half-agape grimace. The person was wearing something that looked like a black sweater and black pants with black gloves.

"What in the hell?" Kevin confusedly asked.

He approached the figure and tentatively knelt next to it. The mask was stained with dark red on top where the hatchet was still embedded. Using two fingers, Kevin pulled the mask gently up, revealing the full face of the man that tried killing him. He couldn't have been more than thirty. His open eyes vacantly stared at nothingness, and the realization that he just killed a human being made Kevin sick. He turned to the other side and emptied the contents of his stomach onto the ground.

"Oh god…" he mumbled with shaky legs.

He felt like he was going to faint.

"You had to do it. Otherwise, he would have killed you," the voice of the figure came from behind him.

Kevin had all but forgotten about the person until he spoke. He quickly shot around and faced him. It was a boy around his age. At first, Kevin was baffled as to why a teenager would even be in the woods at this time. But then he saw his shirt. It was dirty, and the logo, although somewhat faded, was still discernible. The circle wasn't full anymore, and one of the trees was missing inside it, but there was no mistaking it. It was the uniform of Camp Firwood.

The person who just saved Kevin's life exhaled and said, "My name's Bill."

15
The Cave

"Bill? The missing camper, Caveman Bill?" Kevin asked.

His head was spinning, and his brain had trouble processing what just happened. The campers were being sent into the woods to die. But it wasn't the Firwood Wraith killing them – it was a person. But who was he? And why was he hunting the campers?

Bill nodded.

"And who are you? I haven't seen you around the camp."

"My name's Kevin. They call me Cocky Kevin. I just arrived this week."

Bill frowned. He put his hands on his hips and asked, "How many campers did they bring along with you?"

"Just me. I was brought by my parents," Kevin said.

"Huh," Bill said with a timbre of bafflement and looked down.

Silence ensued for a moment. Kevin couldn't help but glance at the dead body of the attacker. His vacant eyes were staring directly at Kevin, making him uncomfortable. He averted his gaze and locked his eyes with Bill again.

"There's no time for talking now. We need to get to safety," Bill said as he glanced at the dead body with a furrowed nose.

He knelt next to the head and, with a groan of disgust, grabbed the hatchet handle with both hands. He tried pulling it out of the skull of the attacker but instead, ended up moving the head along with it, unable to pull out the blade. He groaned louder and stood up, putting one foot against the dead person's head and using both hands to yank the hatchet out. It came loose with a sickening, wet sound of what Kevin imagined was being produced by the skull and its contents. He still couldn't believe he just killed a person.

The gravity of that hadn't hit him fully yet, and he wasn't sure if it was going to at all, but he had no regrets – it was him or the attacker. And the attacker didn't look like he was about to show any mercy. Bill stared at the bloodstained blade of the hatchet for a moment before going to a nearby bush to wipe it on the leaves. Once he stood up and turned to look at Kevin, he said, "Come on, we need to move."

Kevin blinked a few times in perplexity. Move where? Did Bill have a hiding spot this whole time? How the hell did he survive for a whole week in the woods with this person prowling around?

"Wait, go where?" Kevin asked with a shake of his head.

"There's a hidden cave nearby. Come on, the others may come back soon."

"The others?" Kevin didn't think he could be even more confused than he was now.

Before he had time to contemplate what he was just told, Bill had already turned around and began walking down the rocky hill where Kevin had just been chased.

"No time, come on," he said, motioning Kevin with the wave of his hand to follow him.

Kevin happened to see the outline of his flashlight a few feet away from him, which was really lucky. He didn't even realize he had dropped the flashlight while running away from the fake wraith. He grabbed it and ran a few steps to catch up to Bill before saying, "Wait a second, another camper was being chased! We have to find him!"

Bill turned to face Kevin with a forlorn look in his eye.

"Listen, we'll look for your friend, but not right now. It's too dangerous. We'll wait until morning and then look for him."

He turned around, but Kevin spoke up again. "By morning, he could already be dead."

The camper turned around once again and said, this time with a hint of frustration in his voice.

"If we stay here, we're as good as dead ourselves. We're of no help to the camper if we look for him now. We'll wait until morning when we have more visibility, alright?"

He waited to see what Kevin would say. He swayed the hatchet back and forth in his hand impatiently, making Kevin feel like he expected an answer right there and then.

"Okay, fine," he said to Bill.

He knew that he was right. Looking for Ninja right now in pitch dark would get them nowhere. And going around the woods shouting his name and hoping he'd respond didn't seem like the best option, either. They needed to get their bearings and then look for Ninja.

Bill seemed satisfied with his answer, so he nodded and turned around. He prudently began stepping down the hill, using his free hand to hold onto the embedded rocks and crags in order to avoid tumbling down. Kevin joined him, careful with each step. Descending was much slower than climbing up, but then again, there wasn't a killer with a creepy faceless mask chasing after him. Kevin had a million questions, which he was sure Bill had the answers to, but now was not the time for talking. He would wait at least until they were on flat ground.

Every minute or so, Bill turned around to see if Kevin was still there. He seemed quite good at navigating the rocky hill, which made Kevin assume that he was either an athlete or an expert survivor in the woods. He then remembered that Rob told him Bill was called Caveman Bill due to his amazing survival skills in the wilderness. He couldn't help but consider how lucky he was – first, he was stuck with Ninja, whose knowledge about the woods was already exponential, and now Bill, who was even more skilled.

"Hey, thanks for saving me back there," Kevin said, once he hopped off the final rock and onto the moss-covered ground.

"Well, you saved me too. That guy was gonna stab me," Bill said.

"Who was that guy, anyway? And what did you mean when you said the others might come back?" Kevin impatiently asked.

"No idea. All I know is there's more of them," Bill said. "I don't know if they're living in the woods or whatever, but they hunt the campers who get sent for The Trial."

He paused for a moment while he jumped over the log where Kevin had hidden just before the attacker found him. Then, he continued.

"The camper I was with... camper Victor. He got killed right in front of me. I had to run away before they could see me."

"Jesus."

They walked in silence for a little bit while Kevin processed what Bill had told him.

"Why do you think they're hunting campers?" he asked.

"No idea. For fun? For meat? Doesn't matter."

"For meat?" Kevin was about to hysterically chuckle, more out of relief than anything else.

He first thought that Bill was sarcastic but then realized that having meat-eating killers hunting campers wouldn't be an impossibility. Nothing was a surprise anymore.

"I don't know," Bill said. "Maybe they're some kind of sick fucking cannibals or something. Maybe they're some kind of deranged freaks like those creatures in *Wrong Turn*."

"Wrong Turn?"

"You know, the horror movie?"

Kevin scratched his head. Bill realized that Kevin didn't get the reference, so he sighed and said, "Never mind. Either way, we're not safe. The counselors were sending us to die, and they knew it, I'm sure. If they didn't, they would have sent someone to pick us up by now."

"Why would they send us to die?"

"I don't know. Money? Although if these are some hillbillies living in the woods, I doubt they'd be able to pay them. Gotta be something else. Maybe a pact with them to stay in the woods or something."

Kevin grunted.

"How did you manage to survive for so long?"

"Holed up in that cave I mentioned. And had a little bit of help."

"From who?"

"I'll introduce you later."

They had walked past a wide creek, and Kevin asked Bill if it was safe to drink the water, to which Bill told him that it was risky without water purifiers. He said that he had water stowed away in his cave, so he just needed to hold on a little longer. Kevin didn't even realize how parched he was until that moment. His throat had been dry ever since he'd woken up in the middle of the night; however, he failed to think about it up until then due to the adrenaline. The temptation to drink from the creek was insurmountable, but he really didn't want to contract a disease that would leave him in pain or dying. He got food poisoning last year when he ate undercooked chicken, and it wasn't pleasant.

His parents had gone on a trip to the Bahamas, leaving him home alone for an entire week. He hadn't insisted on going with them, and they hadn't invited him, so the alone time came at a great time. His parents were thoughtful enough to supply him with all sorts of food that would last him for the week, including canned goods, frozen pizzas, and some other stuff. But there was also meat in the freezer. When Kevin got sick of eating frozen pizza for three nights in a row, he decided to fry some chicken breast and cook potatoes on the side. He had followed the recipe guide he found online to the extent he thought was important, and when he cut into the semi-cooked chicken, he ignored the raw middle, shrugging it off as unharmful.

The taste wasn't too bad, considering that he himself cooked it, and he was fine until the following afternoon. He then began experiencing severe stomach cramps, followed by diarrhea, nausea, and vomiting. He got so sick that he couldn't even drink water without vomiting it, but at the time, he didn't even think that it might be food poisoning. His Aunt Kelly, who had been calling him every day to make sure he was okay, got a little worried, but he assured her that it was probably just a virus. The following day, when he came down with a fever and the other symptoms didn't subside, Aunt Kelly insisted on taking him to the hospital.

He was severely dehydrated by then, and the doctors said that had he not come to the hospital, he would have suffered sepsis. He was put on IVs and given strong antibiotics and had to spend five days in the hospital. Kelly informed his parents right away, but Kevin's parents decided not to cut their vacation short, deeming his condition stable enough. When they returned a few days later, one day before he was released from the hospital, they made sure to scold him for worrying them so much and making them call off their cruise. They made sure to remind him of his accident with every chance they got, and it didn't take Kevin long to take the hint that they were pissed – not because he got poisoned but because he ruined their vacation.

"So, who's the other camper who was sent on The Trial with you?" Bill asked.

"Ninja."

"Fuck, man," Bill cursed aloud. "They chose Ninja?"

"Not exactly. He volunteered."

Bill chuckled before returning to his serious demeanor.

"Well, he always was brave. A lot of the folk at the camp thought he was just an excellent liar, but he's no bullshitter. Did you know he snuck out of the cabin on the first night and went around the camp, avoiding the patrolling counselors?"

"Yeah, I heard about that. I guess he and Tough Norton are the biggest legends around the camp, huh."

The dark was finally beginning to clear away, and the sky was transforming into gray, with the first clouds in the sky starting to become visible.

Dawn. Thank god, dawn.

Kevin didn't care even if someone attacked them now. Daylight was approaching, and with it came immense comfort. With the dispersal of the night, nothing could hurt him. Not for a solid eighteen more hours or so until the next nightfall. He dreaded the thought of staying another night in the woods but chased it away for the moment. He wanted to cherish the daylight.

"We're almost there," Bill said as he ducked under a branch and disappeared behind a tree, a rustling noise reverberating along with him.

Kevin followed him through the thicket of densely packed trees. At some points, he had to walk sideways to pass through the narrow pathway between the trees. Visibility was getting better by the second from the ever-increasing sunlight, and Kevin saw more details on Bill. He had unkempt, chestnut hair, which he assumed may actually be blonde when clean. His uniform was exactly the same as his own; however, Kevin saw how it was worn out, probably from the time spent in the woods. Most of his uniform was caked with either dried mud or dirt, giving him a sort of a camouflaged soldier-like look.

Whenever Bill put some distance between him and Kevin, he was more camouflaged in the environment, so the muddy stains on his uniform actually served him well. Kevin also noticed bloodied scratches around Bill's elbows, forearms and legs, indicating that the forest was not gentle to him. He couldn't help but be impressed by Bill and his ability to survive not just the woods themselves but the deadly killers who were after campers.

"This way," Bill jutted his head forward.

The sun had already begun rising by this point, and orange gleams of the light fell through the branches, illuminating portions of the woods, allowing for clear visibility of the surrounding. Kevin looked in the direction Bill was pointing toward the side of a cliff that blocked their path. The cliff stretched a few dozen feet upward, and it didn't look like there was a nearby way around. Kevin opened his mouth to ask Bill if he was sure he knew where he was going when he saw his companion heading toward what looked like a vertical crack on the cliff face.

That must be the cave.

The crack looked too thin for anyone to squeeze through, but when they got close enough, he realized that it was actually much wider than it looked. Bill went in first, sidling sideways to squeeze inside. He disappeared in the pitch black of the cave entrance, leaving Kevin momentarily exposed out in the woods all alone. He quickly squeezed inside the cave, getting enveloped in complete darkness. It took his eyes only a few seconds to adjust before he started seeing outlines of naturally-formed cave walls, floor, and ceiling. The narrow passage they had gone through suddenly swerved to the left and then widened, opening into a large area, big enough to be called a room. Kevin expected the room to be engulfed in darkness; however, some of the light from outside seeped inside the cavern, illuminating portions of it. He clicked his flashlight, instantly illuminating the area with his beam.

The cavern looked crudely roundish with a ceiling tall enough even for someone like Mr. Adams to stretch inside it without banging his head. Kevin noticed a sleeping bag on the left side of the room and, next to it, cans of food and bottles of water.

Bill shielded his eyes from the beam when Kevin inadvertently pointed it at him. He reached down for one of the full bottles and tossed it to Kevin. Kevin fumbled, nearly dropping both the bottle and the flashlight before clumsily managing to catch it. He couldn't remove the cap fast enough, and when he began drinking, he was doing it so fast that his throat started to hurt. The water was cold, and letting it slide down his throat was the best feeling in the world at that moment. When he removed the not quite empty bottle from his mouth, he took a few deep breaths.

"Thank you," he said.

Bill stared at him this whole time with an indifferent look in his eyes before pointing to the cans on the floor.

"You got food here if you're hungry. Sorry about the mess, by the way. I wasn't expecting guests."

Kevin pivoted the flashlight in various corners of the room. He noticed that there were a bunch of empty, opened cans of food strewn about the cave floor, looking like a squatter's den. Based on the number of cans, it looked like Bill had been here for a while – probably about as long as Kevin had been in the camp.

"I'm not hungry right now," he said. "I really just need a moment to take a break."

"Yeah, you do that. You can sleep in this sleeping bag. And don't worry about snoring or anything because this place is pretty well isolated from the usual danger zones. Plus, they only seem to come out at night."

"I still don't know who exactly *they* are."

"Neither do I, buddy," Bill shrugged.

Kevin slumped down on the sleeping bag with his ass, feeling immense relief. It wasn't until then that he started to realize just how exhausted and beaten up he was. His neck was painful, his hands and knees were all scratched up, and his side still hurt – albeit much less than it did back when he hit it. He lifted his shirt and pointed the flashlight to the hurt spot but saw nothing major except a big red scratch across his side. It wasn't bleeding, though, and the pain wasn't serious, so he hoped that it wasn't so severe that he would feel it in a day or two.

"Okay, listen," Kevin said. "I'm gonna take a break for ten minutes, and then we can start looking for Ninja, alright?"

"Sure. Try to get at least a little shuteye, though. You're no good to me if you're unfocused."

"You got it." Kevin gave him a thumbs up, slumping onto his back.

He groaned when his side warned him with a pang of pain not to do anything like that again.

"Okay, I'm going to head on out," Bill said.

"Wait, where are you going?" Kevin suddenly got skeptical.

What if this was all a ploy to get him trapped inside the cave so they could finish the job? No, that didn't make any sense. Why would Bill save him then in the first place?

"I'm gonna try to see if I can find Ninja's tracks out there. Do you happen to know which way he went before you guys separated?"

"Bro, if you asked me to show you the spot where you and I were just five minutes ago, there's no way I'd be able to take you back there," Kevin chuckled.

Bill nodded but showed no signs of disappointment before saying.

"Alright. Well, you get some sleep. I'm gonna take my hatchet with me."

"Why, don't you trust me?" Kevin asked, feeling a little paranoid again.

"It's not that. It's just that I need something to defend myself in case they're still out there. And I don't want you getting all jumpy when I come back."

"Fuck it, fair enough," Kevin said, turning his head toward the ceiling.

He expected specks of dust to fall into his eyes from the ceiling, but it didn't happen. Bill stopped at the cave exit and said, "Alright, sleep well, buddy."

"Yeah. I'll join you in a bit."

Bill turned and silently left the cave. Kevin felt his eyelids getting extremely heavy all of a sudden. He allowed his eyes to close, ignoring the burning sensation in his scraped knees and hands.

Bill is right. I need to get some shuteye, was his last thought before he passed out.

***

He woke up to the sound of footsteps echoing right next to his head. At some point during his sleep, he must have turned onto his uninjured side. He opened his eyes and, through his blurry vision, saw a large figure kneeling next to him. Although he couldn't see clearly who it was, Kevin was sure of one thing – it wasn't Bill. He jerked his head up and began scooting backward, his vision clearing up. The person in front of him was a calm, bearded man with messy, unkempt hair and dirty overalls.

"Groundskeeper Andy?" Kevin asked.

The groundskeeper was fixated on something on the ground in front of him, not glancing at Kevin even for a moment. Kevin looked at the ground and saw an open first aid kit on the ground, the contents neatly placed inside.

"You get any injuries?" the groundskeeper's rough voice came through, reverberating through the cavern chamber.

"No, I'm fine," Kevin retorted, still skeptically staring at the groundskeeper.

"I can already see from here that you're lying to me, boy." The groundskeeper finally looked up at Kevin, his glare shooting daggers in the camper's direction.

"Where's Bill?" Kevin asked.

Andy looked down at the first aid kit again and took out the alcohol.

"He'll be back soon. Come on, let me patch you up."

He removed the gauze and bandages and stood up. Kevin stared up at the man as he took one step toward the camper before he stopped. He seemed to notice the suspicion on Kevin's face, so he sighed and said, "I ain't gonna hurt you, alright? If I wanted to kill you or bring you back to the camp, I could have done so already. Now, come on."

What he said made sense. With that, he reluctantly allowed the groundskeeper to get closer to him and begin tending to his wounds. He winced every time the alcohol touched the parts of his body where the skin had been scraped, but the groundskeeper assured him that it was necessary in order to avoid an infection. Upon cleaning the wounds, it was determined that there was no need for gauze and bandages, only band-aids for his knees. Kevin already started to feel his scraped knees burning whenever he would contract or extend his legs, and from experience, he knew that it would take a few days for the scab to appear and then fall out.

"Make sure not to pick at that wound, alright?" Andy said. "And try to stay out of trouble while I'm gone. In fact, try not to go out at all unless Bill is with you."

He stood up and returned the remaining items into the first aid kit before closing it shut.

"You eat anything yet?"

"Not since last night. What time is it, anyway?" Kevin asked.

"Almost noon. Bill came by my cabin to tell me he managed to find a camper, so I immediately came out here to see what condition you're in."

"*You're* the person who helped Bill this whole time?" Kevin raised his eyebrows.

The groundskeeper didn't respond.

"Why? Why are you helping the campers?"

"I got my reasons," Andy sternly said. "And that reminds me. I'm gonna need my key back."

Kevin's heart jumped into his throat. His and the groundskeeper's eyes were locked in a staring contest, but he couldn't will himself to look away. The groundskeeper apparently noticed this, so he sighed and looked down at the ground, shaking his head.

"Sneaking into the head counselor's office was reckless and stupid. What if they caught you?"

"But they didn't," Kevin defiantly said.

"I caught you, didn't I? What do you think *they* would do if they did?"

"Throw me in the woods with some murdering psychopath?" Kevin was calm enough now to start making sardonic remarks.

The groundskeeper shook his head like a disappointed parent. This prompted Kevin to look down at his lap in embarrassment. He was right. Sneaking into the office was risky, but it was the only choice he had. Silence hung in the air for a prolonged moment.

"So, about that key..." the groundskeeper said.

Kevin hadn't even remembered that he had the key tucked away in his sock until the groundskeeper mentioned it. He refused to show it to him yet, though. Not until he got some answers.

"I'll give it to you. If you tell me who you really are and why you're helping us," he said as confidently as he could with a poker face.

Andy looked away for a moment before facing Kevin's direction with a glint of compassion in his eye.

"My name is not really Andy. That's an alias I assumed before I joined the camp. I suppose you wanna know what exactly I'm doing here. Well, might as well tell you. Not like I'd get in more trouble than I already am for helping you. Besides, I already told Bill, anyway."

He straightened his back and reached inside his overalls, into the front pocket of his shirt. A moment later, he brought out a photograph, staring at it with a look in his eye that seemed like he was reminiscing. Kevin noted a profound sadness in his eyes. Andy grasped the picture gently with both hands between his thumbs and forefinger. He outstretched the photograph in his hand toward Kevin, giving it to him. Kevin tentatively took the picture and looked at it.

He had seen this before. It was the photo he found in Andy's cabin back when he rummaged through it, looking for the key. The boy in the photo smiled innocently at the camera.

"That was my son, Owen."

Was?

Kevin stared at the photograph for a moment before returning it to the groundskeeper. The groundskeeper pulled the picture closer to himself and held it in his hands in front of himself, staring at it. He bit his lip painfully, slightly nodding at it.

"He would have been fourteen today. His birthday would have been a few weeks ago," he said, not taking his eyes off the picture.

"What... happened to him?" Kevin tentatively asked in a low tone, afraid to offend the groundskeeper.

Andy cleared his throat and stood up, walking to the back of the cave where another sleeping bag had been placed on the ground. He must have brought it with him.

"He went missing in Camp Firwood last year," he said, facing away from Kevin.

He sniffled, and Kevin saw him wiping his face with his knuckles, probably trying to remove the formed tears. He cleared his throat again and placed the photo back in his chest pocket. He then turned around and made his way back to the first aid kit. He was visibly redder in the face but was trying to hide it by not looking directly at the camper.

"He went missing? Here?"

"Yeah," Andy said. "Owen was living with my ex-wife Angela – his mom – at the time. We thought that it would be good for our son to take some extracurricular activities during summer, so we signed him up for the summer camp. Owen was ecstatic. He was really looking forward to some activities where he could potentially improve his painting and get to play more sports."

He took a moment of pause, staring at the passage leading outside the cave. The now slightly stronger light coming from outside illuminated half of the groundskeeper's face.

"Just two weeks in, Angela called me. Said that the camp called in and said Owen ran away and went missing. They said he got bullied by the other kids and that that's why he ran away. Now, that didn't sound like my son. Not one bit. Everyone liked him. He was a natural leader and a role model for the other kids. He wouldn't ever run away like that. I knew something else must have happened and that the camp was hiding it."

Kevin stared intently at the groundskeeper, practically on the edge of his metaphorical chair. He hadn't even realized that he leaned forward and had his mouth agape. Andy continued.

"I still worked as a police officer back then. A search party was organized to look for him in these woods, but I personally wasn't allowed anywhere near the place. My superiors said my emotions would impact the case. So I stepped back and let them do their job because I trusted they would do everything in their power to find my boy."

He sighed deeply and shook his head as if remembering something bitter.

"Anyway. They never found any traces of him. The case is still open as far as I was told, but that's just about all I know."

"So, what do you think happened to him?" Kevin interjected.

"That's where the whole story gets interesting, son," the groundskeeper smiled woefully. "A few months after Owen's disappearance, after the funeral with the empty casket and everything, I started to hear some murmurings about other kids disappearing in the summer camp called Camp Firwood. I went to investigate but could never find any official information. I went to talk to the parents of the missing kids, but they'd always deny their kid going missing. One of them even said they never had a kid, to begin with. But, it was suspicious because they all said pretty much the same things. It was like they rehearsed their story beforehand. Not only that, but as soon as I told them I'm a cop, they seemed to get frightened for their lives, despite smiling the whole time. It may have been that whoever operates this camp – probably the director – threatened them to keep them quiet."

He shook his head once more, wrinkling his nose in disgust.

"And that's when I got suspended and eventually fired from work, for snooping around too much. Too many things lined up, and I knew I was onto something. I continued investigating for a while and found the right people who would help me get a job as a groundskeeper in Camp Firwood. I changed my identity because they probably knew who I was by then and were tracking me. Once I had a fake new name, I applied for the job."

The groundskeeper said it matter-of-factly as if working for a secret criminal organization that kidnapped children was no big deal. He continued.

"They didn't run any special background checks or whatever. Just warned me not to ask any questions and pretend I don't know anything if anyone came knocking. I've been observing the camp ever since."

He looked at Kevin for a prolonged moment before turning his attention to the first aid kit on the ground again.

"How long have you been here?" Kevin asked.

Andy, or whatever his name was, snapped his head back in Kevin's direction and said, "About ten weeks, maybe a week or two more. The camp always closes after summer and only opens during the summer school break."

Kevin frowned.

"So you've seen the campers get elected in The Choosing and sent to die, and you did nothing about it?"

He asked this with slight anger in his voice, intending on letting the groundskeeper hear his frustration.

"Don't be so quick to judge, son. I didn't know up until a week ago what exactly was going on – until I went into the woods the night Bill got sent. I couldn't do anything else even if I wanted to," Andy replied. "I'm alone here, and they have armed guards. Now, I'm not sure if they would harm your kids, but I know for sure that they wouldn't hesitate to shoot *me* if I proved to be untrustworthy. So, I had to lay low while figuring out what's going on."

"What *is* going on here?"

"Don't know. That's why I'm here. To find out what they're doing with the campers and find my son."

"Can't you just call your buddies at the force? Have them raid this place and rescue us?" Kevin asked.

The groundskeeper shook his head.

"Haven't you been listening to what I just said? Whoever these people are, they're in cahoots with the police. They're probably paying them some real good money to keep things quiet. But if I find evidence, they'll have no choice but to support me. Hell, with the right type of evidence, I can forward the case to the FBI, have all the corrupted policemen arrested."

A moment of silence filled the air while Kevin contemplated everything the groundskeeper just told him. A secret organization abducting kids and sending them in the woods to die. If Andy personally signed up his kid for Camp Firwood, that eliminated the possibility that the parents were willingly sending their kids to die. That still didn't answer one important question, though.

"What happens to the kids who are chosen for Departure?" Kevin asked.

"Like I said, I don't know. They don't tell me anything; I'm just the groundskeeper. I see them getting escorted by the director out of the camp, but that's all."

"You think they just let them go? To maintain the image of a somewhat functional camp?"

Andy didn't answer. He scratched his bushy beard and picked up the first aid kit.

"Do you think Owen is still alive?"

Even Kevin felt the sting of his own words. The groundskeeper looked at him. Kevin expected anger, but there was only insurmountable sadness on his face. He sighed and said, "I don't want to have my hopes high. But I pray to God that he is, son."

Kevin reached into his sock and felt the key. It was still there. He pulled it out and handed it to the groundskeeper, who snatched it and put it in his pocket, his facial expression suddenly changing back to the usual, frigid one. The weight of what the groundskeeper just told him started to dawn on Kevin. That boy was someone's son. And he had a bright future ahead of him until the camp took it away. The same went for the other countless campers who were snatched away.

But what happened to the ones who were chosen for Departure? The Choosing, the murderers in the woods, there was so much going on - and Kevin knew at that moment that this camp was way more dangerous than he initially ever could have thought. At the back of his mind, he somehow knew it all along ever since the day he arrived, but the rational part of him refused to admit it. He wondered how many times he had a close call getting into some serious trouble that would have the counselors organize Repentance for someone to get sent into the woods to die? The thought of it made him sick.

"So, what now?" Kevin abruptly asked to shake those morbid thoughts away.

"Now..." Andy said. "I need to go back to the cabin before they get suspicious."

He stood up and turned to the exit of the cave.

"Aren't you going to help us find a way out?" Kevin asked.

Andy shook his head.

"I'm working on it. But there's not much I can do. Besides, I need to find out what happened to Owen."

"But what about us? We could all end up like him," Kevin protested.

Andy frowned slightly, making Kevin regret saying what he did.

"I'm not leaving until I have closure and I see all the people responsible for Owen's disappearance rotting behind bars," he said sternly before calming his tone. "Besides, I don't have any means of contacting the outside world. Not without leaving the camp. They don't let me keep a phone, either. And I have no idea where exactly we are."

Just then, the groundskeeper raised a forefinger and maintained a focused gaze. Kevin listened and then heard it. The sound of footsteps at the entrance of the cave. The groundskeeper reached into the side leg pocket of his overalls, pulling out a handgun, which Kevin immediately recognized as a Beretta, thanks to his video game experience. The groundskeeper pointed the gun at the entrance with both hands, retaining a steady posture, which unexpectedly contrasted his usual groundskeeper-like hunched form. The light from the entrance was obscured and then gyrated left and right until a figure emerged inside the cave.

As soon as he did, Andy grabbed the figure with one hand and, with impressive speed, tackled him to the ground, pointing the gun at him.

"Hey, what gives?!" Bill squirmed on the floor.

Andy sighed and helped him up, putting the gun back into his pocket. The pocket was wide enough to easily conceal the handgun, so unless someone specifically touched the groundskeeper's leg on the exact spot, there was no way they'd see the sidearm. Kevin remembered seeing the groundskeeper the first time, wearing the same overalls. He shuddered at the thought that he was probably armed this whole time.

What a badass, he couldn't help but smile.

"I told you a million times not to sneak around, Bill," the groundskeeper said.

Bill dusted off his mud-caked clothes, to which Kevin raised an eyebrow. He noticed that Bill had a bow in his hand as well as a quiver full of arrows hanging off his belt. Kevin's first thought was how he wanted a bow for himself, even though he didn't know how to use it.

"Sorry, Mr. Andy," Bill said.

"And I told you not to go out there alone but wait for me so we could track him together."

"That's what I wanted to tell you, Mr. Andy!"

Bill looked at Kevin before turning to the groundskeeper and saying.

"I found him, sir. I found the second camper's tracks."

313

16
Ninja

"You what?" The groundskeeper asked, "Where?"

"Close by. We need to go look for him now!" Bill excitedly said.

"No, can't do, son. I have to get back before I become even more suspicious than I already am. Wait a few hours, and I'll come here so we can look for him."

"In a few hours, he could be dead!"

Kevin couldn't help but notice how Bill sounded exactly the way Kevin did a few hours ago.

"If I go with you now, they'll know something is up. And then we'll all be dead. Wait for me, and I'll come help you later. Okay?"

Bill hung his head down, apparently agreeing with the groundskeeper. Andy put a hand on his shoulder and said, "You kids stay put. Bill, if any adult comes in here, shoot 'em with your bow. Don't hesitate because they sure won't."

With that, he picked up the backpack he left in the corner of the cavern, stuffed the first aid kit inside, and left. Bill and Kevin sat in silence for a while, staring at nothing in particular. Kevin was starting to feel hungry by this time, so he ended up opening one can of baked beans and eating it with a plastic spoon Bill had stowed in the cave. Once he was done eating, which took only a few minutes, he gulped half a water bottle and wiped his mouth.

After what felt like minutes, Bill looked at Kevin and said, "So. Wanna go look for Ninja?"

Kevin was already starting to like Bill.

"Andy said we should stay put," he said sarcastically as he frowned.

"Yeah, you're right. You're right," Bill nodded and looked down.

"You got another bow around here?"

"No. Just the hatchet. I can give it to you if you want."

"Okay, sure, I'll take the hatchet."

"I want it back, though."

They had already stood up by then and were preparing to leave the cave. Bill's bow hung around his torso and shoulder diagonally, and he was handing Kevin the hatchet. Bill went through the passage first, shouting from the exit for Kevin to bring one bottle of water. Kevin stuffed a full bottle in his side leg pocket and followed Bill.

"So, what if we run into those killers again?" he asked.

"We won't. They only come out at night, I think," Bill said from the front without even bothering to look back.

"You're not sure?"

"I'm like, eighty percent sure that we're safe."

"Fair enough."

Bill pointed in a random direction and began leading the way through the woods. The day was bright, the beams of the midday sun piercing much more prominently through the trees and brightly illuminating the woods. Bill's stride was confident and long, and Kevin had to walk much faster than his natural walking pace to keep up with him. He wasn't sure if Bill's pace was like that naturally or if he got it from the camp, or if Kevin himself was simply slow in the woodland terrain. They went through dense and sparse thickets, climbing up and down hills, for what felt like twenty or so minutes in silence before Kevin finally spoke up.

"How did you form a partnership with the groundskeeper?"

"Oh, you mean Andy?" Bill asked.

"Is there another groundskeeper that I don't know about?"

The question was ironic, but Bill still answered with a brisk 'no' before continuing.

"He tracked me down. I found that cave, and he saw my tracks and found me on my second day in the woods. I was really lucky, too. I thought he was there to finish me off, but he brought a bunch of food and drinks and even this bow he took from the storage so I could defend myself."

"What a guy."

"Yeah. I would have died without his help here. I actually snuck back to the camp a few times during the night, but Andy warned me not to do that because it was too risky."

"Wait, you're the one who was making the sounds outside the cabins that the campers complained about?"

Bill sighed.

"Yeah. I wanted to see how Michael and the others were doing, but I accidentally made more noise than I was supposed to. One of the campers saw me, but he probably didn't recognize me in the dark."

Kevin groaned at the mention of Michael.

"I can't believe you were friends with a guy like Michael. That guy's a dick."

"No, he's not," Bill looked offended. "What's your problem with Michael?"

"I got no problem with him. He's got a problem with me. He's been nothing but hostile toward me since I arrived. Claims I'm in 'cahoots' with the counselors." Kevin made a quotation mark with his fingers. "Thinks I'm responsible for you being sent into the woods."

Bill made a grimace, which oddly reminded Kevin of a popular 'reaction image meme' which circulated the internet around that time. Bill shook his head and said, "Okay, I admit that he probably should have used better logic there, but given the current predicament we're all in, I don't blame him for being paranoid. We agreed to look for each other once this was all over, so I guess he thinks I died in the woods and probably blames you."

"Great. Well, why didn't you tell him you're alive?"

"I wanted to. And I tried waking him up by tapping on the window near his bed, but he never woke up."

"Instead, someone else did."

317

"Yep."

The rustling of their feet through the grass filled the air until they stepped onto the flat dirt ground, which muffled their footsteps. Kevin walked behind Bill, but at times, he was next to him, when the path was traversable enough for both of them.

"So, who were you friends with in the camp?" Bill asked.

Kevin looked at him, not sure if he should answer that question. He then realized that he wasn't talking to the counselors, so he didn't need to worry about Bill using that information against him.

"Mark."

"Barrel Mark? The most obedient camper in Camp Firwood?" Bill let out laughter.

"Why's that funny?" now it was Kevin's turn to feel offended.

Bill's smile dropped, and he suddenly looked uncomfortable.

"Sorry, I didn't mean it like that… it's just that you don't look like the type who would hang out with Barrel Mark."

"What's that supposed to mean?" Kevin asked with a frown.

He wanted to sound harsh, even though he wasn't offended anymore, now that he knew that Bill just misspoke. He still wanted to fuck with him, though, since he found his fumbling with words amusing.

"Nothing!" Bill nervously said. "I mean, you look like a person who doesn't really hang out with well-behaved people like Mark. I mean, you look like one of the cool kids and-"

"Oh, relax, man. I'm just messing with you."

Bill nervously laughed before he said, "Oh, haha. Fuck you."

Kevin chuckled, and they continued walking in silence for a few awkward minutes. Kevin felt that he might have offended Bill, so he decided to gauge him with another conversation.

"You know, I broke into Mr. Adams' office just before I got sent here."

"You what?!" Bill turned around with a complacent smile, his tone saying that he didn't believe Kevin.

He's not offended. That's good.

318

"Yeah. I actually stole the office key from Andy's cabin, and with the help of *Barrel Mark*..." he emphasized his name. "We managed to break in."

"Damn. Are we talking about the same Mark here?" Bill chuckled. "But why'd you do it?"

"I wanted to use the landline phone Mr. Adams has in his office."

"Oh, shit. I can't believe we never did that. Ninja suggested it once, but we were all too afraid to try it. One guy did try it, though. He got sent for Repentance, and we never saw him again. So you're either crazy or brave."

Kevin felt a proud smile creeping up on his face. It felt good to become so well-known amongst the campers as one of the most daring members in such a short time.

"Well, the campers did give me the name Cocky Kevin."

Bill looked back and produced a 'huh' sound before saying.

"Because you broke into the office?"

Kevin shook his head.

"No. Because I called Dwight a zit-faced douchebag."

Bill stopped this time and stared at Kevin. He had a half-smile on his face, and his eyes were wide.

"Come again?" Bill asked.

Kevin stopped as well, letting out a sigh-laugh.

"It was my first day. And he was ordering us around. I wasn't used to it, so I just called him that name."

Bill slapped his knees and let out a loud guffaw. Kevin felt uncomfortable at that, but only because he wasn't sure if anyone would hear them.

"You crazy bastard," Bill shook his head before continuing to lead the way.

Kevin was beginning to feel a little thirsty from the baked beans, so he uncapped his bottle and took a swig. He gave it to Bill, and he took one big sip before returning it to Kevin. Kevin thanked Bill for reminding him to bring a bottle. They were probably going to be out here for a while. They had gone a little quiet on their next

319

portion of the walk, and Bill suddenly got more attentive to the environment, glancing at the ground more often and pivoting his head left and right.

"We're close now?" Kevin asked.

"Yeah," Bill reticently said as he crouched down.

He touched the ground and looked ahead of him before saying, "This is it. Here are Ninja's tracks."

Kevin saw footprints on the muddy ground, disappearing into the grassy area in front.

"How can you tell they belong to Ninja?"

"It's the same type of shoes. It's either him or another camper. But these are still kinda fresh, so I'm gonna guess it's him."

He began walking forward, still crouching. Kevin followed closely behind but still gave Bill enough space to do his thing. Bill kept a focused gaze on the ground, swiveling his head in various directions. From time to time, he crouched and put his hand on the ground, staying still for a longer time at moments. Kevin tried to understand what Bill was doing, but all he could discern was that he focused on the footprints and random portions of the ground.

"Ninja went through here," Bill said. "He was walking normally for a while, but here he started running."

"How can you tell that?" Kevin asked.

"More distance between the footprints, and they're deeper. See over there? A different set of footprints."

Bill pointed to the right at more grass. Kevin couldn't see the other set of footprints until Bill took a few steps forward. He then saw a bigger, heavier set of what looked like boot imprints overlapping with Ninja's footprints, some mostly consuming them under their weight. A chill went down Kevin's spine at the thought of a masked person hunting Ninja. He couldn't help but wonder where he was right now and if he was okay. He thought about the last time he saw him, on that cliff when they were running from the masked guy, right before Kevin tumbled down. The pursuer continued chasing Ninja instead of Kevin. Were he and Bill close to that cliff right now? Kevin looked around in curiosity but saw only one not-so-steep elevation of the ground on the left—no cliffs. Then again, there was no way he'd be able to recognize the place even in broad daylight since they ran during the night and could barely see anything.

"These are pretty fresh," Bill said, as he swung the bow above his head and grabbed it with one hand. "Let's hurry, and keep your guard up."

Kevin gripped the hatchet a little firmer, glancing around. He honestly expected someone to jump at him or to see someone prowling around behind one of the trees, but he then remembered that the chances for that were pretty low. That's at least what the detective from a forensic documentary said – that the chances of encountering the criminal on the crime scene a few hours later were abysmal. Bill led on, now swerving in various directions, still focused on the ground and the footsteps in front of him.

"He was trying to zig-zag him. The killer was probably faster than him, so he had to outmaneuver him."

Kevin noticed something small and green out of place on one of the nearby trees. He squinted and got closer and realized he was staring at a piece of fabric. He bent over it and snatched it off the small, pointy piece of a broken branch protruding from the tree. Rubbing the fabric between his fingers, he felt its rough texture.

"This is his uniform," Kevin said, locking eyes with Bill.

Bill immediately stood up and squinted at the piece of cloth. He nodded and said, "Yeah, we're definitely on the right track here. Let's hurry."

Bill began following the tracks with more hurried steps, more frantically glancing at the ground, then intermittently running forward a few steps. Kevin bumped into him a few times, but Bill hadn't uttered a word about it. They turned right around a hill, and the sound of water murmuring filtered through the air, and Kevin realized there was a creek slithering like a snake along their pathway to the left. Bill led the way around the hill and through an area sparsely filled with trees.

"Oh, no," he said as he stared at the ground.

"What is it?" Kevin curiously looked over Bill's shoulder.

"See the footprints? They're uneven. Ninja either got tired here and couldn't run properly anymore or was hurt and started limping."

"Shit," Kevin said.

He looked at the footprints, which were much clearer here in the sparse area that had nothing but dirt, and realized Bill was right. The smaller footsteps were going in various directions and were random distances from each other, kind of like a drunk person walking. Whereas the boot prints looked composed and even – the distance between them was shorter, too, which probably meant that the killer was at this point walking.

They went forward some more, and that's when Bill scratched his cheek and said, "The trail ends here. It's hard to see among the leaves. Let's look around and see if we can find anything."

"Sure," Kevin said.

"Look for any footprints or disturbed ground or grass."

Kevin began walking forward, squinting at the ground as if he were looking for a lost key. He had no idea if he saw anything or if it was his eye playing tricks on him. In some moments, he felt like he saw something, but then he'd blink, and the imaginary trail would be gone. But then he saw something that definitely stuck out in the environment like a sore thumb.

"Hey Bill, get over here!" he called out to the camper, who immediately rushed to his side.

"Got something?" Bill asked.

"Yeah, look at this."

Kevin pointed at the ground where there were tiny wedges. The ground itself looked like something was dragged through it, but Kevin couldn't quite connect the dots until Bill said, "He must have fallen here. See? He was probably using his shoes to push himself back on the ground. Look, there's even dried blood here."

Kevin hadn't even noticed it until Bill pointed to it. A few small, dark-red dots spotted the ground next to the disturbed area. Kevin looked up, and his heart jumped into his throat. He then felt his legs cut off.

"Oh, no. Oh, shit," he said as he stood up, fixated on the sight in front of him.

A few dozen feet away, peeking from behind one of the trees, he saw a foot with a shoe facing upward – and not just any shoe. It was a Camp Firwood shoe. Bill's facial expression changed as well from indifferent to one of palpable fear. He slowly stood up and stared in the direction of the foot, pale as a ghost. Kevin glanced at him and then back at the foot. For a moment, he couldn't see it anymore, which made him think the person just up and left, but a second later, he saw it again, well-camouflaged among the trees. The two campers stared like that for what felt like hours, even though Kevin knew mere seconds had gone by. They couldn't delay the inevitable forever. It was time to check out the body.

Kevin took the first step forward, the rustling of the grass resounding beneath his foot. Each subsequent step he took was less hesitant until he was striding confidently toward the body. As he got closer, he was able to make out more and more features – the exposed shins that were bruised and scratched, probably from the running through the shrubberies, the dirtied socks and shoes, the wrinkled pants… The lower part of the body – up to the waist - was entirely visible now since Kevin was only a few feet away from it, but everything above the waist was hidden by the thick tree trunk. Bill's footsteps pounded behind Kevin, but unlike before, they sounded timid and tentative.

Kevin stopped.

He needed to brace himself. He couldn't shock himself by just jumping in front of the body. He had killed a person yesterday, so by all rights, he should not be afraid right now, and yet he felt cold sweat forming all over his body and his heart rate beginning to speed up.

Come on, just look at the body. Just look at it.

A part of him was screaming in his mind at the body to move, to show that the person behind the trunk is alive, that it wasn't a corpse after all... But of course, the chances of that happening were probably non-existent. He closed his eyes and took a deep breath. With his eyes still closed, he took a long step forward, facing the body. He couldn't will himself to open his eyes – moreover, he kept them firmly shut as if he was afraid that they would just shoot open on their own. His heart was beating so quickly that he felt it all the way up to his throat.

This was it.

He opened his eyes and looked at the face belonging to the body on the ground. The eyes were vacantly staring at the canopies of the firs above. The mouth was agape, and a single fly skittered around it, producing an occasional buzzing sound before flying onto a different part of the face, sometimes getting dangerously close to entering the nose. The color of the face was pale, ghostly even. The body had a slash from the chest all the way to the bottom of the stomach, leaving the Camp Firwood shirt cut in half from the chest down. The cut on the stomach was so deep that it revealed internal organs that the flies were massively feasting on.

Kevin put his hand over his mouth, feeling his breakfast climbing up. He turned around and vomited into the grass, pieces of undigested beans and bile and water spewing out of his mouth. He retched three times before the food stopped coming out. He spat and gasped, leaning on his knees, feeling wobbly.

"It's not Ninja," he said.

"Come again?" Bill asked from behind.

"The dead body isn't Ninja," Kevin repeated.

"What?!" Bill said.

Kevin got irritated when he thought he'd need to repeat what he said, but a moment later, he realized that Bill's question was more of a surprise than an actual question when he took two fervent steps forward and glanced in the direction of the body.

"Shit," he said. "I know him. It's camper Carlos."

Kevin stood up and spat one more time before wiping his mouth.

"He's from cabin five if I remember correctly. He was chosen for Repentance a few days ago. He was caught stashing meds from the infirmary."

"Caught? How?" Bill frowned.

"No idea. They searched his locker, or so I heard."

Bill's expression turned from shocked to stern. He said, "That can't be right. The counselors never search the campers' lockers."

"Well, that's what they said."

"*Unless...*" Bill emphasized the word before pausing for a long moment and staring at Kevin.

Kevin stared back, waiting for his response before saying, "Is there... a continuation of that statement, or...?"

"Unless someone ratted him out," Bill finished his thought.

They stared at each other in silence. Kevin shook his head and said, "No way. Why would anyone rat other campers out?"

"For better privileges. It's happened before. You really don't know how the camp's punishment and reward system works, do you?"

Kevin scratched his cheek.

"I do. You fuck up, you get punished, you rat someone out, you get rewarded. Right?" he asked.

"Yeah. You reduce your detention time, have fewer chores, stuff like that. I never tried it, so I don't know," Bill nodded.

"And you think someone back at the camp is doing that?"

"Not just someone at the camp. I think it's someone from the camper's cabin."

Another moment of silence filled the air, excluding the chirping of the birds and the breeze gently blowing through the woods.

325

Kevin pondered the sentence Bill just uttered. A traitor from cabin five?

"No, that can't be right. I mean, who could possibly do that?" Kevin asked.

Bill shrugged.

"Could be anyone. My suspicion is on Cowardly Adrian. He's been against everything we ever planned so far. He doesn't believe we're in any danger. I think he's bullshitting us."

"Maybe."

"Not to mention he's been spotted talking to Dwight and Mr. Adams privately a few times.

"Yeah. If he really ratted his cabin-mate out, then he is fucked in the head."

Kevin spent a moment thinking about that. Would anyone really go that far to alleviate their own stay in the camp? If anyone had Dwight's personality, then maybe... but they were the campers; they weren't Dwight. They were supposed to stick together.

"I guess we should get going," Bill said, finally breaking the silence a moment later.

"What about the camper?" Kevin motioned with his hand toward the body.

He happened to glance at the guts visible in the open wound and felt nauseous again. He averted his eyes to Bill in order to avoid vomiting again.

"Well, what do you wanna do with him? Bury him?" Bill asked.

"We can't just leave him here."

Bill glanced over his shoulder at the body momentarily with a disgusted look on his face before turning back to Kevin.

"Listen, his corpse is still fresh. He's been dead less than a day. That means whoever killed him may return to pick up his body, and if they see it's been moved around, they'll know someone else was here."

"So you plan to just leave him here to the flies?" Kevin frowned, motioning more furiously toward the body this time.

"Yes. He probably would have done the same. We have to think about our own survival right now, okay?"

Kevin looked down reticently before nodding. He knew that Bill was right. They had the upper hand by not letting the killers know that they were still alive. They had to use it to their advantage.

"Alright," Bill said, putting his bow over his head. "Then let's find a place to rest. And then I have something else to show you."

17
The Building

Kevin and Bill sat next to one another on a toppled tree trunk. Kevin drank a few sips of water from his bottle, which he offered then to Bill. Bill declined with a disgusted look on his face, after which Kevin remembered vomiting just earlier. Kevin wasn't feeling exhausted from the walking, but he was wobbly from the puking prior to sitting down. Now he felt his strength slowly returning and was just about ready to get going again. Bill stared in front of himself with a grievous expression on his face. It felt awkward, sitting in silence with him in the middle of the forest, but the forest sounds alleviated that awkwardness somewhat. Still, Kevin felt the need to strike up a conversation with him.

"So, they call you Caveman Bill, right?"

"Yep. Got it on the second day in the camp."

"Why?"

Bill shrugged and pursed his lips.

"Because of my survival skills, I guess. I told Baldwin that he was making snares the wrong way, and the name kinda stuck after that."

"Wait, you made a better snare than Baldwin?" Kevin chuckled.

Bill nodded.

"Yeah. He tried mouthing off and showing us the snares but was using the old method that isn't even used anymore. So when I told him that, he ordered me to come up in front of everyone and show them how a snare should be made. He wanted to embarrass me; I could see it on him right away. But I made the snare, and he couldn't show the campers where I was wrong."

Kevin laughed. He imagined Baldwin's glistening head-turning red from anger and him shouting at Bill to get back in line with a bulging vein on his neck while Bill complacently returned to the other campers.

"So, what did he do?" Kevin asked.

"Nothing. Told me the snare isn't bad but needs some work. Which is bullshit, of course; he just wanted to save face in front of the teenagers. But some teens laughed, and he gave them extra chores."

"What a loser," Kevin shook his head.

"So why were you sent to the camp in the first place?" Bill asked.

"Disobedience. I wrecked my parents' yacht. You?"

"Uh… something like socializing or whatever. They wanted me to gain more people skills."

"That's a first."

Bill continued staring in front of himself while tapping his foot on the ground. He then suddenly turned his head toward Kevin and asked, "So, how come you were friends with Barrel Mark? I mean, how did you two even get acquainted?"

Kevin thought for a moment with a frown. He remembered his first day in Camp Firwood, which seemed like a million years ago. Has it really only been one week? What day was it today, anyway?

"Well, the day I arrived, he was assigned to help me get my things and explain the basics to me – you know, the bed-making, the uniform-folding, all that shit," he finally said.

"Yep, Mark's a good guy. Well-behaved. Never got in any trouble, come to think of it. And everyone's been in trouble at least once as far as I know. I'm actually surprised they haven't let him leave the camp yet." Bill frowned as if contemplating what he just said.

"Yeah. Well, that's because they're probably not letting the campers go. But you're right. Mark is a good guy. Showed me all the ropes. We never got to talk too much, but we agreed to meet up after the camp and play some *Mortal Kombat*. I'm not sure if that's still happening, though."

330

"I sure hope not. *Mortal Kombat* sucks," Bill said with an entirely serious tone.

Kevin shot him a bemused glance before asking.

"Well, what fighting games do you play, wise-guy?"

Bill shrugged.

"*Tekken. Dead or Alive. Soul Calibur.* That kind of thing. But I don't play fighting games much."

"Wait, *Dead or Alive*? You mean the game with half-naked chicks that moan every time they get hit?"

Bill's face turned red, and he looked down.

"It's a good game," he said as he drew his shoe across the dirt back and forth, "It has realistic fighting moves."

"Sure, it does. Especially when the girls jump and their skirts flutter above so you can see their asses. Or when the fight is over, and you can watch the jiggle physics of the tits," Kevin winked.

"Well, how would you know about that?" Bill accusingly asked.

"I played it once. The game's shit."

Bill awkwardly chuckled and looked at the ground. He cleared his throat and stood up before saying, "We should get going."

Kevin stood up as well and asked, "What is it that you wanted to show me?"

"It's hard to explain. But trust me, you'll wanna see it."

He began walking down the grassy land, and Kevin followed behind.

"And what about Ninja?" he asked.

"I didn't see any tracks from him. If we run into a set of footprints, we'll follow them. Ninja is versatile. If we haven't run into his tracks yet, then he's probably alive."

"Got it."

Kevin didn't like leaving Ninja on his own in a place like this, but he knew that there was nothing they could do right now, so he instead opted to follow Bill and hope that whatever he had to show him was worth their time. They trekked for around fifteen minutes with a quick pace before Bill slowed down. He wasn't looking at the ground anymore, but Kevin did notice him pivoting his head left and right occasionally, at some moments even staring at certain spots for a longer time.

"What's wrong, Caveman?" Kevin asked,

Bill shot him a glance with a grimace before saying, "Nobody calls me that. And what do you mean, what's wrong?"

"Well, I see you looking around."

Bill produced a 'hmph' sound before saying.

"Just wanna make sure we're going in the right direction. Some areas in these woods can be hard to recognize from time to time."

"*Some*?" Kevin asked. "How do you recognize *any* of the areas? Hell, how do you not get lost in these woods completely?"

Bill lifted a branch above his face and gently lowered it while speaking.

"The area we're in is pretty easy to navigate for the most part. Either you have traversable areas, or you don't. Think of it like... like a sandbox video game."

"What do you mean?"

"I mean, you have like, paths to follow, but there's no way you can reach the area beyond the paths or the area outside of the map. At least, not with a huge amount of effort."

"Oh, I get it."

"Most of the areas we walk through over here are the same ones we'll be using in the future if we stay that long. Kinda makes me think that the camp staff deliberately chose this place... or made it that way to trap us."

That suddenly got Kevin thinking. He hadn't had the time to think about it so far, but how were they going to escape?

"Hey, so what is the plan, anyway? We just stay here and hope we don't die until it's safe to run?" he asked.

"I don't know," Bill said.

Kevin grinned sourly.

"You've been here a whole week, and you haven't devised a plan to escape?"

332

"Well, excuse me for focusing on trying not to starve to death in the woods while being hunted by a psychopathic killer."

"Fair enough. But once we're back in the cave, we should start working on a plan. Inform the other campers, do something."

Bill kept silent, and Kevin wasn't sure if that meant he agreed or if he wanted to avoid answering that question directly. They had climbed over a small hill where they used the trees for support, and as soon as they moved down, they were greeted by a rather flat, grassy area full of densely packed trees, moss, and rocks. Bill stopped by this point and crouched, darting his eyes in various directions ahead of him with much more scrutiny. Kevin had no idea if they should be aware of potential danger here, but just to be on the safe side, he crouched too and silently awaited Bill to give him the next sign.

"Okay," Bill spoke up. "We're close. Be very, *very* quiet here, and move slowly. If you see anything moving, don't scream. Just grab my shoulder, get down on the ground and stay as still as you can."

"What the fuck, Bill?"

"Don't ask me. We can't talk here, alright? Just follow me, be quiet, and keep a lookout."

Kevin nodded, now getting a little apprehensive. He instinctively scanned the horizon, expecting to see another masked killer just standing and staring at him with that mouthless face and a butcher's knife in his hand.

No, the killer (or killers) from last night didn't have any finesse that Michael Myers from Halloween possessed. We'd hear him before he attacked us.

That's at least what he tried telling himself. He didn't want to train his brain to constantly be aware of something lurking behind him. He was sure he'd lose his mind that way. Bill raised one index finger and pointed it in a random direction before leading the way. He took much more cautious steps this time, stepping gently on his heel first and then placing the rest of his sole down to produce as little noise as possible. Kevin mimicked his movement, doing his best to avoid any stray twigs on the ground.

The forest was much quieter over here, bringing with its stillness a sense of dread, which Kevin became increasingly aware of the more they moved forward. He hated not knowing what they were up against and wanted to stop Bill to ask him so that he could at least know, but they were too deep inside the thick woodland area to start speaking now. Before Kevin could even finish that thought, Bill stopped behind one of the firs and placed his hands around it. He peeked around the tree at something before looking back at Kevin.

"There. See it?" he whispered.

Kevin leaned forward so that he was even with Bill's face and squinted. He spotted it right away among the trees. A small, gray concrete building, sitting in the middle of the woods.

"What the f-" Kevin started but was interrupted by Bill's *shhh*.

Kevin stared at the building in awe. Just a plain concrete building with two windows visible on the side they were on and literally nothing else special about it. For a moment, he thought it was just an outdoor restroom like the one they had back at one of the parks in Portland because it fit the looks and size. But Bill wouldn't bring him here just to see an abandoned old restroom, would he?

"We have to be really careful from here on. Okay?" Bill whispered.

Kevin nodded as he held his breath. Bill nodded back in approval and stepped around the tree as he started leading the way, this time crouching while he moved. Kevin crouched behind him and followed as they went from tree to tree, slowly inching toward the building. It must have been around two hundred feet away, and whenever Kevin looked up at it, it seemed to barely move any closer.

It reminded him of the time his dad tried teaching him how to swim. He took him out into deeper waters with an inflatable air mattress for the beach and then threw him into the water. Kevin was only seven back then and panicked, desperately trying to get back onto the mattress, but his dad kept swimming away, just out of reach. Kevin's arms were getting tired, and water kept filling his mouth from the panicked breathing. He pleaded with his father to let him back onto the mattress, but his father ignored him and told him to keep going. Since he was facing the beach, he could see the shore getting closer with each passing second, but it was gruelingly slow progress. He felt that he wouldn't make it to the beach before his arms gave out. About halfway through, his father stopped swimming away and allowed Kevin to grab on.

Never before had resting in the middle of the deep waters felt so alleviating, despite him not being able to touch the ground with his feet. His father simply shot him a disgusted look before he took them back to the beach. When Kevin's mom asked how it went, his dad gave a comment down the line of 'pretty goddamn horrible.' His mother responded by telling Kevin to try harder next time while grinning from her sunbathing position. This repeated a few times, and Kevin quickly learned how to swim, albeit the wrong way. Now that he was older, he realized what horrible consequences such teaching methods could have had on him, even giving him thalassophobia. He was simply lucky it didn't happen.

The grey building was much closer now. Only a hundred feet away. Kevin even noticed what looked like a trail crossing in front from left to right. As they got closer, he realized that it was indeed a beaten path wide enough for two people to walk on, side by side. Kevin followed the trail with his gaze and realized that it ended on the right in front of the building, but on the left side, it disappeared among the trees, leading god-knows-where. What was this place?

"Get down," Bill said when they were around fifty feet away from the building.

They fell to the ground on their stomachs, staring at the building. They were lying on the grass, and hopefully, their shirts helped them blend in with the environment. Kevin still couldn't discern any more prominent details on the building. It was still just a concrete building, no bigger than a gas station restroom, with two dirty windows on the side that they faced. He couldn't see the entrance from here.

"Bill, what is this?" Kevin asked in a whisper.

Bill opened his mouth but then closed it, bringing his head down even lower as he stared at the building. Kevin instinctively jerked his head toward the building and saw a figure emerging from the right and stopping in front.

The security guard?

Kevin gasped when he saw one of the security guards from the camp standing in front of the concrete building. He was lighting a cigarette with a hung head, cupping the lighter with his hands. A moment later, he placed the lighter in his pocket and exhaled, plumes of smoke leaving his mouth and dispersing upward in the air. A moment later, a second guard came out of the building and stopped in front of the first one. They started talking, but Kevin couldn't make out what they were saying from here. They seemed to be engaged in small talk rather than a formal conversation since the guard whose face Kevin could see from here with his peripheral vision was laughing from time to time.

The guard looked in Kevin's direction while talking, and for a second, Kevin thought that they'd been spotted. However, the guard moved his gaze back to his coworker a moment later, confirming that he saw nothing. The two guards then turned in the opposite direction and stared over yonder. The second guard who came out of the building was gesturing something energetically while the first one stared at him and nodded every few seconds. A minute or so later, the first guard dropped his cigarette on the ground and crushed it under his boot before the two of them returned inside the building.

"We need to get closer," Kevin whispered to Bill.

His eyes had been focused on the guards, so when he looked at Bill, he saw the camper's eyes widen.

336

"They'll kill us if they see us," he said.

"How do you know that?"

Bill pressed his lips together, obviously hesitating to say something. He opened his mouth slightly and said, "Because that's how the camper who was with me died."

"What?" Kevin raised his eyebrows.

Bill sighed and looked at the ground, pretty near touching it with his nose. He took a deep breath, looked at the building, and then said, "That first night in the woods, Victor and I got attacked by two people. Different ones than the one from last night. They attacked us while we were walking through the woods, and we had to make a run for it. We actually wanted to talk to the people, ask them for directions, but then we saw their machetes, and we knew that talking to them would do no good."

Bill stared at the building intently, pausing for a second, before continuing his story.

"Somehow, while running through the dark, we saw some lights. We followed them and found this building. We managed to escape from the killers by then, but we were exhausted. We figured that someone helpful might be in there. But Victor had his suspicions. So he told me to stay here while he checked it out."

Kevin virtually held his breath the whole time. He knew that the ending of this story wasn't a happy one, but he was still on the edge of his seat while listening. Bill continued.

"So Victor knocked on the door. And the guard came outside. He pointed the gun at him, ordered him to get on his knees. Started asking him questions: how he found the building, where the other camper was... but he said he came alone, that he accidentally found the building. By then, the other two guards had come out to see what the commotion was all about. They started radioing someone, telling them that a camper found them, asking what they should do with him."

Bill looked at Kevin with a quivering lip.

"Victor looked scared shitless. And of course, he was, I'd be, too. Whoever they were talking to on the radio, ordered them to... 'dispose of the camper.'"

"What the fuck," Kevin said.

"The guard didn't look like he wanted to do it. He asked whoever was on the other end if that was really necessary if they should just send him back to the woods, but the person in charge started shouting over the radio, and in the end, he had no choice."

"He killed him? Just like that?"

Bill looked back at the building and sniffled.

"Victor looked in my direction with pleading eyes just before the guard shot him. I should have helped him. Should have distracted them or done something."

Kevin saw tears forming in Bill's eyes.

"There's nothing you could've done. They would have killed you, too," he said with as much compassion as he could muster.

Bill wiped his eyes. "I've been trying to find the building ever since, but I couldn't. Up until yesterday." He looked at Kevin with dreary eyes and said, "I'm gonna make those motherfuckers pay."

Kevin glanced at the building. It was quiet and still, but that didn't mean that the guards couldn't pop out any second. Walking up to the building would be too dangerous. Kevin looked at the bow on Bill's back and asked.

"How good are you with that bow and arrows?"

"Good enough. What have you got in mind?" Bill asked.

Kevin pushed himself with his elbow to get a little closer to Bill. He pointed to the right of the building. "Take up a position behind one of the bushes over there. I'll get closer to the building and see if I can't find out anything useful. Have your arrows ready, and in case they spot me, shoot them."

"Sounds like a plan. There are three guards in total. I think I could take two, maybe even all three of them if I hide well. But if you *do* get spotted, I don't think all three of them will run outside with their guns drawn. There'll probably be just one of them."

"Alright. I'll try not to get spotted. I'll wait here while you find a good spot."

Bill nodded and immediately propped himself up with his palms. He began loping to the right, keeping his body bowed low as he moved, carefully glancing at the building every second or so. His footsteps were nimble and silent, which was highly impressive, especially given the fact that there were lots of fallen, dry twigs that he had to avoid stepping on. Once Bill was behind one of the larger bushes, kneeling with his bow drawn and an arrow in his hand, he gave Kevin a thumbs-up. Kevin sent the thumbs-up back and slowly stood up. He wiped his dirty palms on his already-dirty shirt and slowly began moving toward the building in the same crouching position as Bill. He moved from tree to tree, prudently glancing at the windows and the right side of the building where the door was so he could quickly hit the floor if a guard came out. The building was getting closer now.

Thirty feet…

Twenty feet…

Kevin stood behind a tree that was right in front of the trail. He knew that crossing the path would expose him since it was stripped of any cover and that he would need to cross it quickly. He glanced at the windows and saw the tip of a figure's head moving from left to right. He realized that the building's interior was illuminated by a sickly yellow light, even though it was still light enough outside - the windows were too narrow and probably provided meager light inside. One of the windows facing the road was left open on the upper side in a tilt and turn style, and Kevin heard muffled, indecipherable voices inside.

He moved to the left along the treeline until he was out of direct sight from the windows. There was another smaller window on the left side of the building, but it was too high up for him to reach and peek inside it. He looked left and right down the small dirt road. The coast was clear. Laughter broke out inside the building a moment before the muffled speaking resumed. Kevin's heart jumped into his throat instantly, but then resumed its 'normal' elevated pace. He had to get across. He braced himself by putting one foot back and slightly crouching. He then propelled himself and, as quickly as he could without making noise, crossed the road and hugged the corner of the grey building.

He felt the cold concrete wall at the tips of his fingers and waited a moment to see if anything would happen while his heart rate went through the roof. He expected any moment to hear a voice from the inside say something like, 'Did you hear that?' Instead, the silence resumed, and then the muffled speaking continued, albeit much clearer now. Kevin still couldn't discern what the voices were saying. He strained to decipher some words, but the more he tried, the more difficult it became to understand. He just then became aware of the chirping of the crickets and cursed them for drowning out the voices inside the building so loudly.

Kevin reckoned he'd be able to make out some of the sentences if he got closer to the window, but he'd be too exposed facing the road. He would have to check the other side. He followed the building on the left until he reached the corner and then peeked to the right, which was the side opposite the road. Another two windows were here, both of them also open on a tilt and turn style. Kevin grabbed the hatchet with his left hand and then held his right palm on the concrete wall as he slowly made his way toward the windows, careful not to step on anything that might attract the guards' attention.

As he approached the window, he realized it wasn't high up at all. If he stood up straight, the bottom of it would easily reach down to his chest. He slowly stopped right under it, leaning his back against the wall, and squatted. The voices were much louder now, and he could discern a word or two here and there, but it was still impossible to understand anything more. He looked up at the window above him, staring at the light meagerly gleaming through the glass. Suddenly, the light in the window disappeared under a shadow, which began dancing left and right across the glass. A masculine voice came as clear as day, just above Kevin's head.

"Yeah, I told her not to do it. But she still does it."

Another voice responded indiscernibly. Kevin held his breath and pressed his back against the wall harder, feeling the surface of the concrete digging into his skin through his shirt. He felt his heart pounding a million miles an hour, but he remained still.

"Yeah, she still does it. And she got to-"

The voice faded away, and with it, the light returned to the window. Kevin breathed a sigh of relief as silently as he could. Ever so slowly, he used one hand for support and turned around to face the wall. He put his free hand just under the window and knelt on one knee as he held the hatchet in the other, hanging limply at his side. Holding his breath, he slowly raised his head, inch by inch as the interior of the building came into view. First, he saw the ceiling and the simple ceiling light dangling above. Then the windows on the opposite side came into view. Then, two tops of short-haired heads. One was moving around while the other was still.

Kevin didn't stop there. He continued raising his head until he realized he was staring at the group of guards. One was standing in front of a bunk bed on the right side of the room while the other sat on the bed itself. The third guard was on the left side of the room, sitting by a desk facing the wall. Overall, they seemed jovial in their conversations. The room seemed pretty small, barely enough to hold all three of them. But the size of the room was smaller than the entire building, so he assumed that there was at least one more small room, maybe a bathroom, on the right side where he had seen the higher window. One of the guards turned around to face the window, and Kevin immediately ducked down. The silence was so deafeningly that Kevin heard his own heart beating against his chest.

Oh, shit. He saw me.

"So, anyway..." One of the guards continued, and the conversation went on with its regular flow.

341

Kevin breathed a sigh of relief. But then another thought occurred to him. What if they had cameras around the building? He immediately looked up toward the top of the wall, scanning it from one end to another.

No surveillance cameras. He breathed another sigh of relief before deciding to continue moving alongside the wall. When he reached the corner of the opposite side, he peeked around toward the spot where the guards had come out from just before. He noticed a sturdy, metallic door that served as an entrance. He then returned behind the wall and scanned the treeline ahead of the door. It took him a moment, but as soon as Bill began waving, he saw him crouched behind a bush. Kevin assumed a more relaxed pose, and as if on cue, the sound of the door opening reached him where he was hiding. Kevin instinctively stuck his back and hands on the cold concrete wall and turned his head to the right to have a better view. He gripped the ax in his hand firmly but didn't raise it. The voices he heard before were no longer muffled but clear as day. Kevin remained as still as possible.

"Yeah, well, let's see how it's gonna go," one guard said.

Kevin saw Bill nocking his arrow. He hadn't pulled back the arrow yet, but he looked like he was ready to fire. Kevin slowly raised one hand toward him in a stop sign before putting it down. The sounds of rustling footsteps shuffled around the front of the building, and seconds later, Kevin saw the shoulder of one of the guards around the corner. He pressed harder against the wall but was too petrified to move. The guard shifted his weight from one foot to the other, intermittently getting closer and further. Kevin gripped his ax tighter.

Should he run? Should he lie down on the ground? He looked at the ground, attempting to assess whether was safe to move before he heard the guard's voice again, making him jerk his head back to the right.

"Any news on that new disposal yet?"

"Actually, yeah," another voice said. "The director radioed in today, said they'll organize another Choosing on Friday."

"So soon? Why?"

"They have a batch of campers arriving, a big one. And they wanna clean up the ones who have been here a while to make room."

"Well, if they send a bunch of them running into the woods, we might have more situations on our hands like the one from a week ago."

The guard whose arm was peeking around the corner took a crunching step to the right, moving farther out of sight. Bill was still at the ready, from what Kevin could see. It was difficult for even Kevin to spot him in the bushes, let alone the guards who were oblivious to the camper's presence.

"Yeah. Well, I sure hope not," one of the guards said. "I don't wanna shoot any kids."

"I hear ya," the other guard said. "That Eli is a cold son of a bitch. But I guess that's why they recruited him. Did you know that he worked as a mercenary before joining the camp?"

The first guard scoffed and then lowered his tone.

"Well, I'm not surprised. He does look the part with his constantly serious attitude. Let's just hope we don't get on his bad side."

He heard the sound of footsteps shuffling again, and then the door shut, silencing the voices once more. Kevin's heart was beating violently against his chest, and just then, he realized how hard he was pressing against the wall. The rough concrete imprinted into his hands (and his back, painfully reminding him of his injured side). He couldn't stay here any longer. This was a close call, and he wasn't sure if he was going to be so lucky next time. He looked in the direction where he assumed Bill was, taking a moment before he located him blended with the bushes' green environment.

Bill waved him over, but Kevin still made sure to peek around the corner toward the door. It was clear, and he wasted no time

343

running diagonally away from the building, using the trees for cover as much as he could, while glancing back at the door every few seconds. Reaching Bill felt as relieving as reaching the shore when his father took him swimming. He ducked behind the bush and stared at his friend breathlessly. Bill stared back, his wide eyes begging Kevin to start speaking.

"The Choosing!" Kevin said. "They're going to organize another Choosing!"

18

The Return

"So, now what?" Bill asked. "What are we gonna do about the Choosing?"

They were striding through the woods toward the cave. It was late afternoon, and Kevin was already starting to feel the exhaustion and the hunger getting to him so much that he couldn't think straight.

"Let's first find our way back," he said as he held onto the hatchet.

The thought of eating some of the canned goods like beans, tuna, or whatever else Bill had in the cave made his stomach growl in response, and his mouth began salivating. He estimated it would take them at least thirty minutes, up to an hour to reach the cave.

"So what did you hear from the guards?" Bill asked, somewhat out of breath from the quick strides.

The two of them must have been too adrenaline-pumped and were therefore walking really fast without even realizing it.

"They were talking about a disposal," Kevin said. "That's what the guards called it. They were referring to The Choosing. They said a new batch of campers is arriving soon, and the camp is going to organize a Choosing to make room for them."

"Holy shit. They plan to cull the camp?"

"Either that or they plan to let us go home earlier. But my bet is on the first one," Kevin sardonically said.

"What *does* happen to those campers who get chosen for Departure? They get to go home? Happy ending and rolling the credits?"

"Yeah, I don't think that's what happens. Somehow, I think whatever happens in Departure is probably way worse than The Trial or Repentance."

Bill maintained a focused gaze for a breath as if pondering what Kevin just said. A moment later, he shook his head and said, "I don't know how much worse than this it could be."

"You never know," Kevin retorted.

They walked in silence for the rest of the way back to the cave. As soon as they were inside the unpleasantly cold cave, Kevin slumped down on the sleeping bag with one of the cans of spaghetti in tomato sauce. He hoped it would at least be half as good as the mac and cheese MRE he had last night but still kept his expectations in check. He was right to do so because the canned spaghetti was essentially a watery puke-like food with over-salted tomato sauce and bland pasta. Whenever he speared the spaghetti with the fork, the tomato sauce would essentially slide off of it and back into the can to join the rest of its soupy liquid while leaving naked pasta on Kevin's fork.

After eating the spaghetti, he still felt hungry, so he tried drinking the sauce and narrowly escaped puking again. Feeling disgusted, he pushed the can full of tomato water away and washed it down with tons of bottled water. Bill, on the other hand, ate packaged oatmeal and a dry-looking brownie. At that moment, though, it looked to Kevin as the best brownie ever. Bill was generous enough to share a bite, and sure enough, even though it was dry and somewhat bland, the sugary taste felt heavenly.

They sat in silence for a while after eating, both of them probably too tired from the expedition and too sleepy from the food. Daylight was slowly burning, and with it, the dreadful dark approached, ominously reminding Kevin of last night. He looked at the entrance of the cave and wished he could barricade it somehow. Although the cave made him feel safe, it also made him uneasy, knowing that someone could just waltz inside. But then again, he knew that it would be hard – impossible even – for anyone outside to spot this particular place, even in broad daylight.

His thoughts wandered back to Ninja. He wondered if he was okay and if he had made it out alive and was now hiding somewhere in the woods like Kevin or Bill. Or if he was unlucky and his dead body was now rotting like Carlos. He hadn't even thought about it until now, but now that the image of the dead camper crept into his mind, he couldn't get it out. The vacant, staring eyes, the open mouth with the fly buzzing in the proximity of it, the gutted torso... Kevin momentarily felt pain in his own stomach as a placebo effect. He lay on his back and stared at the cave ceiling. As time went on, the image of the dead camper faded from his mind, and he instead found himself thinking about other things.

"I miss music," he suddenly said aloud, much to Bill's surprised glance.

Bill was splayed on his own sleeping mattress on the side as if he were on a beach. After a moment of silence, he said, "What kind of music do you listen to?"

"The loud, obnoxious kind. Punk rock, heavy metal, that kind of thing."

"You mean the really loud screaming into the microphone?" Bill asked.

"Sometimes."

Bill didn't respond.

"I miss coffee," he finally spoke up, to Kevin's surprise this time.

"You drink coffee?"

Bill nodded.

"I thought we would be getting it in the camp. Or at least some mild version of it. Or some tea would have been nice."

"I hate hot beverages. How do people even drink coffee? It tastes like shit."

"How do you survive *without* drinking it? Besides, I don't drink it for the taste, I drink it to wake up. The smell is also nice."

Kevin scoffed, dismissively waving his hand above himself. He started thinking about his cellphone and how he'd use it while lying in bed on his back, always firmly holding it to prevent it from falling on his face. When was the last time he held it in his hand? The last time he checked out a Facebook comment or a meme on Instagram on his newsfeed or responded to a message? How many messages did he have piled up in his inbox up until now? Did people even remember he existed?

"I miss technology," he finally said.

"Amen to that, brother." Bill nodded. "I didn't even realize how addicted I was to my phone until Mr. Adams took it away from me."

Kevin laughed.

"Well, I guess that's one thing you can thank the camp for."

"I miss video games," Bill said. "I was halfway through that new Zelda game before I was taken to the camp. I even brought my Nintendo Switch with me to play it here. But of course, those assholes took it. I wonder if it's still there. I'd hate to lose all my progress in the game..."

"I think losing your progress in Zelda is the least of your worries, man."

"It's debatable," Bill said, much to Kevin's amusement.

He continued thinking about the things he used to have and do in his life before all this happened. What was it that he had outside the camp that he enjoyed doing? The answer came surprisingly late in his mind.

Hang out with my friends, of course.

He thought about Amy. He thought about her every day. Not as much as he'd like to since the camp kept him pretty busy, but whatever happened in his daily life, he wished he could share it with Amy. He wondered if she thought about him as much as he thought about her or if she completely forgot about him and went about her normal life. That thought made him sad. He wanted to run all the way back to the camp, sneak inside the storage room, grab his phone, and call her. He just wanted to hear her voice, or if possible, see her face in a video call. Hell, even a message from her would do it. He closed his eyes and thought about her features. Her pretty, shoulder-length black hair. Her green eyes. The freckles on her face. The cute way she smiled and laughed – especially the way she laughed at Kevin's corny jokes.

He noticed that he had difficulty remembering her features clearly. Her face was in his mind's eye, but it was as if he couldn't recall all the features exactly as they were. Slight panic began brewing inside him. He focused harder and tried to remember her. He tried imagining her with various expressions – serious Amy, angry Amy, happy Amy. But none of the faces came as clearly as they should have. How long would it be until he completely forgot her face?

Amy... I wish I was with you right now...

And then another voice told him that he could be with her, but he needed to do something about it. Feeling a surge of adrenaline pumping inside him all of a sudden, he sat up and said, "We need to go back to Camp Firwood tonight."

"What? Why?" Bill asked with a frown.

"To warn the others," Kevin determinately said.

Bill stared at him with an unblinking gaze.

"But why tonight?" he asked finally after a moment of pause.

"To give them enough time to prepare. If we're going to attack Camp Firwood, we'll need to get some weapons."

"Whoa, whoa, slow down there, partner," Bill said before Kevin even finished his sentence. "Who said anything about attacking?"

"You got a better idea?" Kevin interjected.

Bill opened his mouth and then closed it. He scratched his chin, staring Kevin down.

"We could tell the campers to stash the hatchets and knives from the storage," Bill said.

"Won't they know that the items are missing?" Kevin frowned.

Bill shook his head.

"Not if they're careful. Here's how the item count works in Camp Firwood." He leaned forward and raised a hand as he started gesturing with it. "The only items accounted for are the ones taken out into the field during training or work. So let's say you have twenty campers who go setting up tents; that means twenty tents are brought out of the storage. All twenty of them have to be returned after the training is over, but the other tents in the storage all along-"

"Are not on the list," Kevin finished his sentence and immediately felt a smile creeping up on his face. "Caveman Bill, you should change your name to Genius Bill."

"Nerdy Van is the one who figured that one out."

Kevin's smile dropped along with his mood.

"Oh, right. Nerdy Van..." he said.

"What's wrong?" Bill asked.

"He got picked for Departure yesterday."

He frowned at the last word he said. Has it really been only one day since then? It felt like way longer.

"Shit. I can't believe they got him. Poor fucker," Bill shook his head.

"Well, who knows, maybe you're right. Maybe they let him go." Kevin shrugged.

They sat in silence for a short time before Kevin continued.

"Okay, so here's the deal. We sneak back into the camp, and we tell the campers to start stashing the weapons. But how exactly are they going to get into the storage and get the weapons is the real question."

"Andy can help them with that," Bill said.

"Help them with what?"

Both Bill and Kevin jerked their heads in the direction of the cave entrance. Groundskeeper Andy stood there in all his glory, staring down at the campers. His face looked even more sunken in the dim light inside the cave. Kevin was surprised at the groundskeeper's ability to sneak inside the cave so silently. It also made him question how safe they really were in there.

"Well?" Andy asked sternly.

Neither of the campers responded. Andy took a step closer to them and placed his hands on his hips, now towering above them threateningly.

"You went out looking for your friend, didn't you?" he asked.

"Mr. Andy, we had to look for him while the tracks were still fresh," Bill timidly said. "We couldn't let him die out there."

"And did you find him?" the groundskeeper asked in a tone that sounded like a parent scolding a child while staring down at Bill.

"We didn't find Ninja," Kevin interjected. "But we found another camper. He was already dead."

The groundskeeper's eyes shifted to Kevin. His gaze was so penetrating that Kevin felt compelled to look away. If he was reacting like this to the tracking, what would he say to the fact that they went over to the gray building?

"That's… not all," Kevin said.

"Okay," Andy nodded slightly.

"Kevin, no," Bill quietly said.

Kevin shot him a glance and said, "He has to know. If we're doing this, we have to tell him everything."

He looked back at the groundskeeper; he was still staring at Kevin with a stern and yet oddly patient stare.

"Mr. Andy, have you ever seen a building out here in the woods?" Bill asked.

The groundskeeper's gaze turned back to Bill, this time in slight curiosity from what Kevin could detect. Since he didn't respond to the question, Bill began telling him about the building and about camper Victor, how he got killed in front of the building. As Andy listened to the story, his eyes widened, and his expression went from curious, to confused, to angry.

"You went there, even though you *knew* armed guards were inside?! You could have been caught and killed!" he said with a higher tone.

Bill seemed taken aback by this but didn't back down.

"But we didn't! We were careful! And now we have valuable information."

"What kind of information?"

"Another batch of campers is coming. And they'll organize a huge Choosing to cull the herd," Kevin said.

Andy looked at him momentarily before turning back to Bill. He scratched his bushy beard. "You kids need to stay put until this is all over."

"You can't be serious!" Kevin said. "We can't stay here all summer and hope we don't get killed! And what about the other campers?!"

Andy kept quiet.

"Mr. Andy, we need to do something before more kids get killed!" Bill interjected confidently. "With each passing day, more and more campers are put in danger!"

"No," the groundskeeper sternly shook his head.

"If it were Owen, would your answer be the same?" Kevin asked.

Andy jerked his head to him with a bewildered look in his eye. Kevin expected the groundskeeper to slap him, but the old man simply stared at him for a long moment until Kevin looked down. The groundskeeper sat on the ground, forming a triangle with the other two campers. He inhaled deeply and said, "It's too dangerous."

That was all Kevin needed. He was going to agree if they presented him with a solution; he was sure of it. He jumped in and told the groundskeeper about their plan to inform the campers and tell them to stash weapons. He said that campers would need to all attack together to take over the camp, and once that was done, they could get their phones back and call the cops.

"That's why we need your help, Mr. Andy," Bill said, "We need you to leave the storage door unlocked so that the campers can start taking away items from there."

Kevin expected Andy to laugh or lose his temper, but instead, he just stared blankly in front of himself. The cave was filled with awkward silence as Bill and Kevin waited for the groundskeeper's reaction. Andy finally spoke up after a long moment of silence in a raspy voice, "I guess this has gone on far too long. But the camp staff need to be stopped. The campers will have to take weapons one by one. They can't take out too many items at once, it'll be suspicious."

"But you can help them?" Bill asked.

"I'll have to control them to make sure they don't overdo it and do something stupid that will get them in trouble, but yeah. I can do it. And so, what then? You just plan to take over the camp, just like that?"

"There's almost fifty of us. And around ten of them," Kevin said.

"Plus three armed guards," Andy interjected.

Kevin was left dumbfounded with no response to that. The groundskeeper seemed to be aware of this, so he said, "There are three guards who are always present during The Choosing, that much I can confirm. Whenever there's a Choosing, two guards join the director in the camp. But are they the same guards from that building in the woods?"

"Yes," Bill said.

"Then we need to take care of them as well," Andy scoffed.

"We can do it tonight," Kevin said.

Andy shook his head.

"You said they have a radio. If we do it now, they'll know something went down, and the plan goes to hell. What we need to do instead is wait for the two guards to leave the building when the director arrives."

"And then what?" Kevin impatiently asked.

"Then, I'll take care of the two guards once they are separated from the director. The director usually goes to talk to Mr. Adams alone."

"Why not take the director hostage instead?" Kevin quizzically raised his eyebrows.

"Like I said, the guards have radios. If we take the director hostage, they can probably call for backup – and trust me, they *do* have a backup. I'll take care of the guards in the camp while you take care of the guard in the building."

Bill and Kevin exchanged surprised glances.

"You want us to kill the guard?" Bill asked.

"No, not kill. Just tie him up or something. You're good with your bow, right? Do something to immobilize him. But even if you kill him, I'll honestly tell you 'no harm done.' I'm not in favor of turning you into killers, but I am in favor of keeping you alive."

"We'll figure that part out," Kevin said.

"Okay, so let's go over the plan one more time." Bill said, "We warn the campers about the situation. It has to be us since they may not believe you, Mr. Andy. No offense. You leave the storage open for them, and they take some weapons and slowly get ready for The Choosing. Then, when Friday comes, Kevin and I go to the building and take care of the guard once the other two leave. Meanwhile, you take care of the other two guards… speaking of which, are you sure you can take on two armed guards?"

Andy closed his eyes and nodded. Bill continued.

"Okay. Once the guards are taken care of, Kevin and I will join the Choosing Grounds. By then, the director will probably wonder where the guards are. But I suppose you can take him hostage from there, right?"

Andy nodded again.

"Alright. We force them to surrender, we get our phones, and we call the police. Simple as that."

"A flawed plan if you ask me," Andy said. "But right now, we got no other choice. If worse comes to worst, a couple of campers need to make a run for the director's car and drive away with it. Choose a good driver from the camp."

Bill and Kevin nodded. Kevin felt excitement surging through him. He felt like he could run for miles. He wanted to go to the secret building right now and take care of all the guards so that he could finally get out of this living nightmare. But that would have to wait. Tonight, he and Bill would return to the camp to warn the other campers of the real danger all of them were in, and they would start preparing for their attack. Having Groundskeeper Andy on their side was an immense relief, and Kevin felt like nothing could go wrong with him around.

***

Night fell much later than Kevin hoped it would, and he soon found himself surrounded by the inhospitable trees of the woods and the permeating darkness once again. The groundskeeper had escorted Kevin and Bill as close as he could to the campgrounds before he went his own way. The cave Bill and Kevin used for shelter was actually much closer than Kevin thought at first. He figured that it might take him and the groundskeeper hours to reach the camp, but they were there in less than ten minutes.

It was a strange sight, too, because one moment they were walking through the dense firs, and in the next, they were near the edge of the tree line. When he asked the groundskeeper how no other campers accidentally stumbled back upon the camp after being sent into the woods, the groundskeeper shrugged and said that this spot was probably chosen specifically for the camp because of those reasons.

Echoing Bill's words, the groundskeeper said that it was easy to navigate the woods because they had traversable pathways, but everything beyond that was hard to go through. That's how it was for the walk between the cave and the campgrounds. It first went forward normally for a while, climbing up and down gradients in between, but then, all of a sudden, they had a steep climb over a rock-covered hill, which then sharply descended. Anywhere else around the climb was covered in slippery, moss-covered rocks and densely packed fir trees, which didn't seem like a place anyone would want to traverse, therefore probably deterring any campers who may have come across it.

Kevin looked back at the inhospitable terrain and realized that he was sure he would have no trouble finding his way back to the cave even if he were on his own, due to the uniqueness of the path leading back. Now, enveloped in the darkness of the woods and surrounded by the chirping of the birds, Bill and Kevin stared at the lights coming from the main campgrounds. The cabin lights were off, their windows painted black, but strong light still emanated from the main lodge inside, acting like a beacon or a lighthouse in the middle of a stormy night. Kevin and Bill were at the edge of the woods behind the cabins, crouching behind a tree.

"So, what do we do?" Bill asked.

Kevin stared at the cabins intently, focusing his gaze on cabin four. It felt surreal standing there like an intruder, staring at what was his sleeping quarters for almost a whole week. He looked at Bill and said, "Let's check cabin four. See if everybody is sleeping. If they are, I'll go inside and wake Mark."

"Inside?"

Kevin glanced at the cabins again and then back at Bill, "Yeah. Knocking on the window might cause him to freak out."

"But what if the other campers wake up and see you?"

"They probably won't see me clearly in the dark. Besides, there's always someone coming back from watchtower duty, right? They might just confuse me for one of them."

Bill nodded. "Okay. Let's check out the cabins then."

Without another word, they stepped in front of the tree and onto the hostile and oddly familiar Camp Firwood grounds. Once they were close enough to the cabin, Kevin leaned closer to Bill and whispered, "I'll check out this side." He pointed to the left. "You check the other, make sure everyone is asleep. We'll meet in front of the entrance."

Bill nodded, and they immediately split up. Kevin stopped at the corner of the left side, between cabins four and five. He scanned the windows of cabin five, and once he was sure that there was no movement in the sleeping quarters, he approached the first window of cabin four. He peeked through the corner of the window. At first, he saw nothing. And then, his eyes started adjusting, and he saw rows of beds, with unmoving silhouettes in them. Most of them, anyway. Three of the beds were empty, and from what Kevin could see, the blankets had been removed as if the beds have never been used in the first place.

Those sons of bitches.

Kevin saw Bill's silhouette through the two opposite windows on the other side of the cabin before he disappeared. Kevin glanced down at the camper on bed number ten. Michael. He was lying on his back, fast asleep. In fact, all of the campers were on their backs because the beds were too small for them to sleep on their sides, but the pillow was too hard and tall to sleep on their stomachs. Kevin moved to the left toward bed number nine.

Empty.

He moved on until he checked all five beds on his side. Everyone seemed to be asleep, despite the occasional shifting coming from Javier. Kevin got to the front entrance with a confident stride and found Bill sitting at the steps leading to the door. Kevin glanced toward the main campgrounds before moving his gaze away from the blinding lights. He didn't want his eyes to get used to the light now that he had to move in the dark. No one seemed to be around – no patrolling counselors, no zit-faced Dwight, no annoying Mr. Adams. Bill stood up and moved closer to Kevin before whispering, "Everybody is asleep."

Kevin nodded. "I'm gonna wake up Mark and bring him outside. Do you wanna go talk to Michael?"

Bill looked like he was contemplating what Kevin said before nodding.

"You know what? Sure. I'll wake him up. But we gotta be real quiet."

"Let's go then. We can take off our shoes in the foyer."

Kevin was the first one to enter. He gently turned the knob and pushed the entrance door open. It slightly creaked before the sound of it stopped. Once they were inside, they took off their shoes. He hadn't even realized it until now, but taking off the shoes was an immense relief to his feet. He hadn't taken them off for over a day, and now his feet could breathe more easily. Kevin stopped himself from instinctively placing the shoes neatly at number nine on the shoe stand but then remembered that he had no obligation to do that.

Fuck Camp Firwood's rules.

He messily (and gently) kicked them to the side and looked at Bill to make sure he was ready as well. He was. Kevin gave him a nod of approval and turned to face the sleeping quarter's door. He grabbed the doorknob firmly, and as quietly as he could, turned it ever so slowly. Even as he pushed the door inward slowly, it produced no sound whatsoever, much to his relief. Within seconds, the steady sounds of snoring and breathing filled the air from both sides of the room where the beds were placed.

Kevin scanned the silhouettes of the campers under the blankets to make sure all of them were still asleep. It was late, around 1 a.m., since Bill and Kevin deliberately waited at the edge of the woods for close to two hours after splitting up with the groundskeeper to make sure everyone was asleep. Kevin looked to the left and tip-toed to bed number four where a somewhat bulkier silhouette protruded from under the blanket. The floorboards of the cabin were stable for the most part. However, one particular board creaked momentarily as he stepped on it.

Nothing alarming.

Bill went past Kevin and over to bed number ten where Michael slept. Kevin saw Bill leaning closer to Michael but focused on bed number four – on his friend Mark. He looked peaceful, worry-free

358

almost, as he slept with his mouth agape, snoring steadily. Kevin got as close as he could and put his hand on Mark's shoulder. He started shaking him gently. Mark continued snoring. He shook him harder. Mark inhaled a loud snore and then clicked with his mouth and swallowed.

"Mark," Kevin whispered, leaning as close to Mark's ear as he could.

Mark moaned briefly, indicating that he was woken up.

"Mark, it's me," Kevin repeated.

Mark opened his eyes and blinked confusedly. And then he sluggishly jumped back in his bed, propping himself up on his elbows, squinting in the dark.

"Kevin?" he asked loudly.

Kevin put a finger on his mouth and produced a *shhh* sound. He looked around to make sure no one else was awake. He noticed Michael getting up from his bed and Bill heading back toward the exit. Mark confusedly glanced at the two of them with wide eyes before looking back at Kevin. He must have thought that he was dreaming because he kept opening and closing his mouth as if unsuccessfully trying to say something.

"Don't wake the others. Let's go outside and talk. I'll tell you everything there."

He took a step back from Mark's bed and lingered long enough only to make sure Mark understood that this wasn't a dream. When he saw Mark swinging his blanket aside and jumping into his slippers, he knew that he wouldn't just go back to sleep. He allowed Mark to get past him, making sure Mark would not only move but be quiet enough in the process as well. Once Mark was in front of him, Kevin turned toward the foyer and made his way back to his shoes. He saw the three silhouettes of Mark, Bill, and Michael silently moving toward the open foyer. Kevin was half-sure that some of the other campers would wake up any second, but once the four campers were inside the foyer and the door shut behind them, he knew they were fairly safe.

359

Kevin silently motioned with his hand for the rest of them to follow. Even through the dark, he could see Mark's and Michael's dumbfounded facial expressions. They must have been confused as hell, being woken up in the middle of the night by two campers who they probably believed were dead. Kevin stepped through the front door and onto the beaten path created by the campers' daily stampeding shoes. He turned around and waited until the other three were outside. Michael gently closed the door behind him, and Kevin wasted no time gesturing again for them to follow.

"Let's get behind the cabins," he whispered. "We don't wanna be seen here."

They snuck between cabins four and five and made it all the way back to the tree line in silence, even though Kevin was sure that Michael and Mark were bursting at the seams with a million questions. Mark seemed a little hesitant to step near the treeline, but once they were close enough, they formed a circle and stared at each other for what felt like minutes, even though it was only seconds. And then Mark and Michael both started talking at the same time – Mark to Kevin, Michael to Bill. The words were mostly those of expressing surprise and shock, asking a ton of questions, just like Kevin predicted.

Once the initial excitement settled down, Bill started, "We are all royally fucked, Mike. We are all in far greater danger than we initially thought."

"You mean because of the Firwood Wraith?" Michael asked.

Bill shook his head.

"There's no wraith. It's people. Campers are getting killed by some people in the woods."

"People?" Mark interjected. "But... I hear sounds outside the cabin almost every night. Last night I saw someone moving around in the trees."

He pointed at the thick trees enveloped in the darkness behind Kevin. Kevin looked over his shoulder, feeling goosebumps on the back of his neck. He exchanged a glance with Bill before turning back toward Mark.

"It's people. Not wraiths. The counselors are eliminating us, one by one," Kevin said.

"Wait, you've been in the woods this whole time, Bill?" Michael asked.

Bill nodded.

"Groundskeeper Andy helped me. Listen, there's no time to explain the details. You guys need to get ready to attack the camp."

"What?" Michael exclaimed loudly, causing Bill to shush him.

"He's right," Kevin said. "Another Choosing is gonna happen on Friday. And they're bringing in a new batch of campers. They plan to eliminate a big number of the current campers."

"But... what about the ones who get picked for Departure?" Mark timidly asked.

"We don't know. But what we do know is that getting picked for Repentance or The Trial never ends well. That camper that got sent into the woods a few days ago... Carlos... we found him dead in the woods," Kevin said.

"And Victor got killed by the guards. They were stationed in a small building in the middle of the woods, and they... they shot him."

"Oh, man," Mark awkwardly scratched his shoulder. "What about Ninja? Is he still alive?"

"We don't know that, either. He and I split up the first night when one of the men attacked us. I haven't seen him since."

Silence ensued while the two campers in pajamas contemplated what they were just told. Finally, Michael intermittently glanced between Kevin and Bill and said, "So, what do we need to do?"

Bill raised one hand and began gesturing.

"The groundskeeper will help you guys get into the storage to get some weapons. Start slowly stashing the weapons somewhere. Maybe in the woods. You don't wanna take a lot of things at once.

But take some weapons, stash them, and on Friday, get them and be ready to attack."

"What do you have in mind, exactly?" Michael asked with a robotic tone.

Kevin jumped in for the first time that night, speaking directly to Michael.

"The groundskeeper is going to take care of the director's guards. Bill and I are going to take care of the one remaining guard in the woods and then join you. We're going to take the director hostage or just simply surround the counselors and force them all to surrender. Once that is done, we'll call for help and get the hell out of here."

Michael stared at him with a frigid expression on his face. Kevin couldn't tell what he was thinking, but he looked irked. Or maybe that was just his normal face. A moment later, he gave him a nod of approval.

"Okay, so it's settled," Bill said.

"It's settled," Michael repeated.

Kevin looked at Mark, who awkwardly stared in various directions.

"Mark? You good?" Kevin asked.

Mark looked at him with his lips pursed and nodded hesitantly.

"Yeah. I'm good. I'm ready to execute this plan," he said.

"Alright," Kevin said. "Okay, listen. Either Bill or myself will come back here every night until Friday to update you guys on the plan. Let's meet in the woods behind the cabins after dinner. Sound good?"

Michael and Mark nodded. Bill jumped in and said, "Oh, and one last thing. Be careful who you tell about our plan. You may have a snitch among you."

Michael and Mark exchanged a glance before Bill continued.

"Kevin told me that was the reason Carlos was sent into the woods for stashing meds in his locker. Michael, you and I both know what that means."

Michael nodded.

"Yeah. And it's happened before. With Tyler and the knife in his locker. Someone must have ratted him out."

The campers exchanged glares with each other. Mark's color seemed to drain from his face.

"B-but how do we know who to trust?" he asked.

"You don't," Kevin said. "The best thing you can do is try to stash the weapons without telling anyone. Also, don't tell anyone that we're still alive. And then, on Thursday night, we tell everyone about the plan. That will give everybody the time to prepare and not enough time to think about saying something to the counselors."

"You got it, Cocky Kevin," Mark said.

Kevin rolled his eyes at that name.

"Alright. You guys best head on back," Bill said. "We need to return to our shelter, too."

"Bill…" Michael started, a solicitous expression on his face. "I'm sorry I didn't look for you."

"It's a good thing you didn't. Otherwise, you probably would have been dead," Bill said.

The two of them firmly shook hands before Michael turned to Kevin. He outstretched his hand and said, "I was wrong about you, Kevin. Accept my apology."

Kevin looked at his hand before taking it and shaking it firmly.

"No apology needed. The real enemy is – and always has been - Camp Firwood."

They said goodbye to each other and went their separate ways. Kevin felt good. He felt like they actually had control over something, for the first time since he arrived. Although the plan was flawed, it was far better than the other ones they had thus far. And now, with the groundskeeper *and* two additional campers on their side, they had a far greater chance of succeeding.

He was sure that, no matter what happened next, this would be the last plan they would be concocting – they would either take down Camp Firwood and finally make it out of here alive, or they would fail and pay the ultimate price.

19
The Plan

Things were starting to fall into place. Kevin and Bill had gone to Camp Firwood every night after dinnertime (by the camp's standards) to meet up with Mark and Michael. Over the last two days, the campers managed to snatch a bunch of knives and folding spades. They stashed them in the woods behind the cabins, in a spot beneath a pile of leaves. Mark made sure to conceal all the weapons well enough and secure them with a couple of rocks in case the wind blew the leaves away.

The campers agreed that only the four of them should know the spot where the weapons were hidden, in case someone ratted them out. They did agree, however, not to talk even if the counselors put pressure on them. Mark claimed that there was no way they could know about their plans even if they saw him or Michael leaving the building with the tools - which they couldn't have because they were extremely careful.

There weren't nearly enough tools for every single one of the campers, but they couldn't risk stealing more since it would be noticeable. Mark told them that he saw a lot of MREs in the storage, too, in case they decided to walk out of the camp and needed food for longer periods of time. His suggestion was to send Bill and Kevin packed with MREs and water to look for help, but Bill disagreed. Any civilization was far away, and there was no guarantee that they'd be able to make it even with Caveman Bill's skills.

As the day of reckoning grew closer, Kevin became more and more anxious. The days seemed to be passing slowly, and since he didn't have too much to do during the day, he spent a lot of his time wracking himself with worry. As a result, he decided to occupy himself by getting ready for the plan. He asked Mark to get him binoculars from the storage, and as soon as he got his hands on them, he started sneaking close to the secret building in the woods daily. He'd observe the guards, trying to learn their patterns and routines.

Unfortunately, it was hard to tell if they even had patterns. They'd come out for a smoke break multiple times a day and sometimes walk around the woods near the vicinity of the building but never did anything more than that. Kevin hadn't even thought about it until the following Tuesday, but the trail in front of the building bothered him. He asked Bill where it led, and Bill confirmed that it simply went in a circle and merged with a tiny road that led directly to Camp Firwood. When Kevin asked Bill if they could simply use the road to walk out, Bill shook his head, stating – again – that it was too far from anything. And, according to him, Andy told him there were rumors of nearby outposts with guards inside, waiting to catch unsuspecting campers who tried escaping.

When not spying on the building, Kevin spent the rest of his day practicing with the hatchet. He'd swing it at various branches from multiple angles, trying to see what the best way to strike would be. He briefly tried learning how to toss the hatchet and have it embed itself in the tree, but that proved much more difficult than the heroes in movies in TV shows portrayed it to be. Not only would he miss the target most of the time, but on the rare occasions when he did hit it, it would bounce back because it hit the tree with the blunt end. Not to mention that tossing the hatchet and missing would effectively leave him without a weapon, so he'd no longer have the upper hand. A scene from the TV show *Spartacus* replayed in his mind over and over where the main character chucked the sword in the direction of his opponent, but his opponent deflected the attack. The slave trainer then sternly shouted.

"You hurl your sword in the arena – you are dead!"

You hurl your hatchet at the counselors - you are dead.

Eventually, he decided to just focus on striking from close quarters.

He'd imagine the trees and branches being Mr. Adams, the director, or Dwight, and he'd strike them from various angles. Unfortunately, whenever he'd think of that, the image of the man he killed would pop into his mind. He'd see his masked face, the hatchet embedded in his skull, the blood pouring out of it and soaking his mask, and then finally, his unmasked face. A normal-looking face that Kevin would never suspect to belong to a killer. The images were sometimes remarkably vivid, but in most cases, he managed to push them back and continue training.

Bill, on the other hand, practiced using his bow. He was a pretty good shot and was even able to shoot trees from a huge distance of over a hundred yards. He would then progressively practice nocking the arrows and releasing them faster as well as shooting multiple different targets Kevin would mark for him. Overall, they were confident that they would have no trouble taking down the guard at the building, provided nothing went South.

They had already devised how to get the guard out of the building and incapacitate him. Bill was confident that they would be safe from the others being alerted even if he happened to fire from his gun. However, if he radioed for help, the plan would go to hell. They revised the whole plan with Mark and Michael back in the camp and with Andy in the cave. They planned on doing exactly what they discussed with the groundskeeper, prior to returning to the camp, with no changes.

Andy would be in charge of taking down the guards escorting the director. Kevin and Bill would take down the guard in the building. The campers would hide their weapons in their side leg pockets and calmly go to the Choosing Grounds. Once everyone was there, Andy would come back and either sneak up to the director to take him hostage or simply pull his gun out and threaten him.

If he somehow failed to take down the guards, the campers would have to take the director hostage and get the counselors and guards to stand down. Once everyone was taken care of, they would call for help and escape. This is why Bill's bow would come in handy. If Andy did fail to take down the guards, Bill could threaten the director with the bow, while the rest of the campers, including Kevin, backed him up. They kept revising the plan to see if there was a better way to execute it, and they kept going back and forth over whether they should kidnap the director *before* taking care of the guards. Andy was adamantly against it because of the previous reason he stated – the guards could then call for backup.

***

It was Thursday morning, and Kevin had just finished his late breakfast. He had woken up earlier and was unable to fall asleep, so he snuck outside to train while Bill continued snoring. It was a miracle to Kevin that no one had discovered them so far due to the loud noises coming from the cave at night. The sun was already up, and it was a little colder that morning, but the cold felt good. It helped sober him up and get his mind off things. He'd had a bad dream, but he couldn't remember what it was exactly. He knew it was something about his friend Henry and that something bad was happening to him, but the harder he thought about it, the more the dream seemed to slip out of his memory.

He eventually let it go and focused on striking the tree in front of him. He was going to try to bring it down, but the more he managed to chip away at it, the more resistance the tree seemed to give. He was also worried that he might make the blade duller than it already was, so he decided to take a break. Bill had woken up by then and went to check out the snares he'd set up the previous days. When he came back, he looked as ecstatic as Mark was the day they were served burgers for lunch. He was carrying a dead rabbit in his hand, proudly showing it to Kevin.

Kevin couldn't say that he was indifferent about it because catching a rabbit with a snare in the middle of the woods was pretty damn impressive. Bill wasted no time preparing the rabbit and setting up a campfire and a makeshift grill to cook the catch. Kevin warned him about the fire making smoke, but Bill said that he knew how to avoid letting the fire smoke. Just to be on the safe side, they made the campfire a few hundred feet away from the cave in case they were discovered. And so, pretty soon, the rabbit was cooking, the smell of savory meat filling Kevin's nostrils. It'd been days since he tasted anything freshly cooked. The cans and packaging of the MREs were strewn about the cave, looking like a bunker of a person who hadn't been in civilization for a long time, and while the two campers had enough food from what the groundskeeper managed to bring them, Kevin wanted *roasted meat.*

Some time later, he and Bill were eating the cooked rabbit, moaning in pleasure at every bite they took, loudly smacking their lips. It was unsalted, but it was tender, and it was the best meal Kevin had had since the sinewy sausage and old bread Mark gave him on his second day in the camp.

"Bill, tell Lunch Lady Daisy to step aside because she's got some fearsome competition," Kevin exclaimed after finishing his meal and burping.

"I'll have to set up more snares," Bill said with excitement in his voice. "And in different locations. There may be more rabbits there!"

"Well, your snoring probably chases away the ones around the cave, so that makes sense." Kevin shrugged before standing up. "Listen. I'm gonna go scout out the building."

"Right. And I'll go do some archery. And set up the snares."

***

Kevin patiently lay on the ground on an elevation that overlooked the secret building. He felt like a soldier doing recon of the enemy base before an attack. Only, he knew that he wasn't the main hero of the movie here, and the odds of him getting killed were pretty high. As he lay on the ground, the solid dirt surface painfully digging into the formed scabs on his knees, he couldn't help but wonder how in the hell the movie heroes were able to just shrug off a bullet wound and continue fighting.

The building was quiet, for the most part — no one going out and no movement detected inside the building either. And then, after about an hour of patiently lying on the ground, the front door of the building opened. Two guards waltzed outside and closed the door behind them. They talked for the next five minutes or so while one of them smoked a cigarette.

I hope your lighter stops working and you have no others lying around, asshole, Kevin thought to himself.

He didn't know which one shot camper Victor, but it didn't matter. All three guards were equally evil for standing by and doing nothing. The guard dropped the stub of his cigarette and crushed it under his foot. They were about to head on inside.

No. No, they weren't.

Instead of going back inside the building, the guards climbed down on the trail in front of it and started following it. This was unexpected. Was another Choosing about to happen already? After days of observing the same boring routines, this sudden change got Kevin's blood pumping. He stood up from a prone to a crouching position and watched with his binoculars as the guards intermittently disappeared behind trees and then reappeared. Since they were moving farther away from his position, he decided he would need to follow them.

He went down the elevation and, from the cover of the trees, watched as they followed the road. Whenever they would get a little farther away, he'd run to the cover of a tree closer to them but still kept his distance. He knew he was well camouflaged in the woods, provided they didn't see him running like an idiot, but he also wanted to avoid alerting them in case he accidentally made some noise. The whole time, his heart kept pumping quickly, and he had to strain to push down the thoughts of what would happen if he got caught.

Just like Bill said, the path went in a sort of circle on the left, leading all the way around the camp. It took them about thirty minutes, but once the guards reached a portion of the trail, merging with a big dirt road, they turned left. Kevin waited for them to move ahead some distance and then got closer to the forking and looked to the left. He saw the guards walking down the path, and beyond that, sure enough, there it was – the big arc that said CAMP FIRWOOD. He suddenly remembered the day he arrived at camp. He remembered seeing the arc when his parents drove him to the camp, the first time he saw Mr. Adams, the cold demeanor of his father when they said goodbye, the nagging of his mother to behave well.

It was a painful memory. It felt like it was a lifetime ago and that the Kevin from that day was an entirely different person than who he was now. He wished that he could go back in time, to run away from his home before his parents could take him here, jump out of the car, anything just to avoid being taken to the camp. His innocence was destroyed, and he would never get that back. He was forced to kill a person, and he would probably be forced to kill again – or be killed.

Kevin looked left and right down the road. The guards were facing away from him on the left, and the right side was empty. There was no way he could tail the guard inside the camp, but he could get a better view from the tree line at the campers' cabins. He took the risk and sprinted across the road to the other side of the forest. From there, he freely ran through the woods all the way in a circle until he reached the area with the campers' cabins. He stayed at the edge of the woods, observing the main grounds. From this position, he saw the army of campers lined up in front of the mess hall, tiny ants from such a distance. The distinct figure of Mr. Adams stood in front of them, gesturing something, while the campers stood still. And then Kevin saw two figures coming from the left – from the direction of the main lodge.

The guards.

They stopped behind Mr. Adams while he continued to gesture. This lasted for a few minutes until one camper got in front of the line. And then another. Kevin couldn't see from here who the campers were. The guards approached the campers and began escorting them somewhere. Kevin couldn't see it clearly from here, but it looked like they were headed for the study hall.

What are they gonna do to them?

They disappeared inside the building (or behind it, Kevin couldn't tell), while Mr. Adams and the other campers went their own way, toward the meadow where Andy's cabin sat. Kevin quickly made his way back through the woods and to the road where it merged with the trail leading to the guards' building. There, he took up a position and observed the main grounds, past the arc. The guards would have to go back to the building in the woods. And he'd get to see if they were coming back with the campers or without them. He didn't have to wait long. Within the next thirty minutes or so, by his estimation, he saw the guards emerging under the CAMP FIRWOOD arc and making their way back.

Without any campers.

Kevin wasn't sure if it was a good sign or not. He followed the guards all the way back until he made sure they were back inside the building. But then, what happened to the campers? They had to still be in the camp, right? Unless the director made a surprise visit and took them away. No, that couldn't be the case; Kevin would have seen or heard the car. And they had a Choosing tomorrow. Why would they do it two days in a row? Or one day earlier?

Maybe they know about the plan.

Dread filled Kevin, and he immediately left the area with the secret building in the woods to make sure Bill was still okay. Upon returning to the cave, his nostrils were filled with the same juicy aroma of the cooked meat as before. He saw Bill complacently sitting on the ground and chewing on a roasted rabbit – a bigger one this time.

"It's our lucky day, Cocky Kevin!" he said.

"No, it's not," Kevin said.

He explained everything he saw just now, and Bill's face vascillated from confused to downright scared. He stood up, holding the half-cooked rabbit in his hand, and said, "We have to make sure tonight that the plan is not jeopardized."

"Agreed."

***

"They did what?" Kevin asked, dumbfounded.

He intermittently stared at Mark and Michael, who nodded. Bill had just arrived behind Kevin and was scratching the back of his head. Prior to meeting with the two campers, Kevin and Bill agreed that one of them should stay behind in case their plan was discovered and someone was waiting to ambush them. Once it was safe, Kevin signaled Bill to join him in the conversation with Mark and Michael. The four campers were in the woods behind the cabins. It was dusk, and it was approaching time for the two who were still in the camp to start getting ready for bed.

"Okay, so tell us the whole story again," Bill said.

Mark inhaled and started.

"The guards arrived at the camp after lunch. Mr. Adams picked two volunteers for an interview with the guards. It was supposedly similar to a 'healthy survey'," he made exclamation marks with his fingers. "No one volunteered, of course. So Mr. Adams picked Sneaky Rob and Michael."

Kevin and Bill looked at Michael with penetrating gazes that clearly demanded answers. Michael stared nowhere in particular.

"Mike?" Bill asked. "What did they do?"

Michael sighed before locking eyes with Bill.

"They took us into the study hall. Got us in two separate classrooms. Sat us down and interviewed us. They first asked me some mundane questions like: What do you think about Camp Firwood? How friendly are you with the other campers? How would you rate the counselors? That kinda thing. I didn't wanna seem suspicious by answering positively to everything, so I told them what irked me about Mr. Adams, Dwight, and so on. But then the questions got weirder."

"Weirder, how?" Kevin asked.

Michael scratched his chin and frowned and then continued.

"Well, they started asking me things like: Have you or your fellow campers ever planned on running away? Have you ever *tried* running away? Is anyone in the camp conspiring right now to run away? And so on. And then he told me about the reward program. Like, how reporting someone for acting in an undisciplined manner would get the camper who reported the incident a huge reward. He even knew who I was, said I only had one week left until I was out of here. Said that I could be out by tomorrow if I reported someone for bad behavior but that I would stay longer if I lied."

Silence hung in the air for a long moment between the campers.

"So, did you talk?" Kevin decided to ask the awkward question.

When he saw Michael looking at him in confusion (or enmity), he added, "In the interrogation."

"No. I didn't tell him anything," Michael sternly said.

"You guys think they know something about our plan?" Kevin asked. "I mean, why else would they interrogate us now? It seems too coincidental."

"Maybe just precaution." Mark shrugged. "Maybe a hunch. Maybe just a crazy coincidence."

"I don't like it. We'd better be even more careful," Bill said.

"Well, the plan execution is tomorrow," Kevin said. "I say Bill and I should introduce ourselves to the other campers and lay out the plan for them."

"I'll get the groundskeeper." Bill grinned complacently.

***

"You ready, Cocky Kevin?" Mark asked as he put his hand on the door of cabin four.

"Yeah. Just go on and assemble them."

374

Mark nodded. He had entered cabin four while Michael went inside cabin five. Kevin sat by one of the benches outside the cabins, trying to assume a 'cool guys don't give a shit' position by putting his legs up on the table. Within seconds, he heard Michael bellowing inside cabin five, saying something he couldn't understand. He heard nothing from Mark's cabin, but within seconds, the armies of campers began swarming through the entrance, some already in their pajamas, some in their uniforms. All of them had bewildered looks on their faces before even spotting Kevin. But then, when they saw him at the table, their eyes widened even more.

"Holy shit! It's Cocky Kevin!" Tough Norton pointed his finger.

"SHHHH!" Michael scolded Norton. "We can't let the counselors know, so everybody shut up!"

By the time the campers of cabin four and five gathered around Kevin at the bench, cabins one, two, and three had emptied as well, forming an ever-growing circle around Kevin. Excited murmurs filled the air, and Kevin raised his hands and stood up from the bench.

"Whoa, whoa. Slow down, everyone. I can give you all autographs, just one person at a time."

"Dude, how did you survive?"

"Did you see the wraith?!"

"I told you The Trial was safe!"

Various voices filled the air until Steve, the natural leader, silenced them all.

"Ryan, keep a lookout for any counselors or Dwight. You like to avoid crowds of sweaty, dirty men anyway."

"Fuck you, Steve," Ryan said but complied in looking over his shoulder to see if anyone was coming.

The good thing about the cabins was that they were separated from the rest of the campgrounds by a large open field, making it easy to see from afar when someone was approaching.

"Cocky Kevin, go on," Steve calmly said. "Tell us what the hell happened."

The crowd was quiet by now, giving Kevin the ability to talk at whichever tone he liked.

"The Firwood Wraith doesn't exist," he said.

"Ha! Told you!" Clean Ryan triumphantly exclaimed.

"There are people killing the campers sent on The Trial," Kevin added.

More murmurs filled the air until Steve silenced them once again. Kevin continued.

"I don't know who they are. But they killed the camper who got sent for Repentance. Carlos. And camper Victor who got chosen with Bill."

"What about Ninja? Is Ninja still alive?" Norton impatiently jumped in.

Kevin shrugged.

"We got separated the night we were attacked. I haven't seen him since then."

"Shit," Norton swore.

Kevin raised one hand and said, "Look, the details don't matter. What matters is that Bill and I are here to warn you all. And to tell you about our plan."

"Where is Bill, by the way?" one camper asked.

Other campers exchanged surprised remarks at Bill still being alive.

"Right here!" the voice came from the tree line next to cabin five.

Bill came waltzing down the grassy ground toward the campers, which produced sounds of awe and exclamations of surprise. Their surprise was short-lived because, in the next moment, Clean Ryan shouted.

"Guys! The groundskeeper is coming! We gotta split!"

Kevin looked down toward the grounds where the main lodge was and saw Andy's hunched-over figure coming over to them.

"Relax!" Bill said. "He's on our side!"

The group now formed in front of the two campers while they waited for the groundskeeper to arrive. He was a few dozen feet away from the group (which seemed to grow tighter, dodging the groundskeeper) when he said, "You kids are in serious danger."

Some of the campers widened their eyes and exchanged glances with each other as if unsure that the words had actually come out of the groundskeeper's mouth. The groundskeeper stopped in front of the group, opposite Kevin and Bill, and put his hands on his hips.

"There's a new batch of campers coming tomorrow. A whole bunch of 'em," the groundskeeper spoke up.

"There's not enough room for more campers," Steve dared to speak up, causing a few heads in the dark to turn in his direction.

"Exactly. That's why-" Andy scratched his unkempt beard. "-the director will be arriving with them."

It took the campers a moment to understand the gravity of what Andy had just said, and when it did, it hit like a ton of bricks.

"Shit. Shit, shit, shit!" Ryan said. "They're gonna have another Choosing, aren't they?"

Andy's silence was their answer.

"Mierda, what are we gonna do?" Javier asked.

A few panicked murmurs resounded in the group.

"We have to attack them now!" Norton shouted.

Others agreed or disagreed. Despite the loud arguing, as soon as Andy spoke up, the air went silent.

"Now, don't get so excited," he said, shifting his weight from one leg to another. "You can't go rushing like idiots now. Wait until morning when the director arrives. Your friends Kevin and Bill already have a plan."

The heads turned to Bill and Kevin. Bill took the effort to explain the entire plan to the campers, telling them to be ready to fight during the Choosing.

"But the guards, they're armed!" Javier shouted.

"It don't make no difference," Andy said as he scanned the group of campers. "I'll take care of two of them. Bill and Kevin will take down the last one. And then we can take over the camp."

"You can't just go against armed guards!" Steve said.

"I can, and I will. You just make sure you're ready to attack if something goes South. Because if it does and they manage to subdue all of us... we're all gonna die."

The weight of his words seemed to hang heavily in the air as the campers exchanged worried glances with each other.

"It's gonna get messy tomorrow. Don't do anything stupid unless I tell you to. That especially goes for you two, ya hear?" He was referring to Kevin and Bill.

With that, he turned around and began walking back the way he came. The group was left with flummoxed expressions on their faces, unsure of what they should do. Everyone looked scared, much more scared than Kevin had ever seen them before.

"I know none of you wanna do this," Kevin said. "I know some of you probably still don't believe any of this. But it's true. The fact that Bill and I are standing here right now, still alive after spending days in the woods, proves that this camp is fucking evil. And if we don't fight, they won't hesitate to kill us. Trust me, I know."

Some of the campers hung their heads down. Others stared at Kevin in silence. Kevin felt compelled to continue.

"Mark and Michael have already stashed the weapons in the woods. They'll give them to you in the morning. And then once we take the director down, the counselors will have no choice but to surrender. We do that, and we can all go home. But if we don't... if we keep waiting as we did so far..."

He didn't know how to finish the sentence without bluntly telling everyone that their lives would come to an end.

"You're right," Steve said as he stepped in front of the group next to the two campers. "He's right. We need to fight back. We sat idly, believing that the counselors would let us go if we behave. And instead, they rewarded us by killing us off one by one. That ends now!"

"Fuck yeah!" Norton shouted along with a few other campers cheering.

The other campers seemed to agree as well, nodding their heads and murmuring words of approval. Kevin smiled. He felt his strength increase tenfold. With the entire camp unified, there was no way they could fail.

"We're with you!" Sneaky Rob raised his fist.

Kevin scanned the faces of the campers. Everyone seemed to be in on the plan. Even the ones who seemed reluctant, like Cowardly Adrian, nodded their heads eventually, agreeing to the plan. The campers began breaking down into smaller groups and murmuring amongst each other, the spotlight no longer focusing on Kevin and Bill. Michael approached Bill to talk with him privately while Mark stopped next to Kevin.

"Good going, managing to get all of them assembled," Mark said. "No one has ever done anything like that for as long as I've been here."

"No one has ever tried," Kevin retorted.

"That's what makes you even cooler. Maybe a new name would suit you well. Cool Kevin. Survivor Kevin. Or maybe something more epic like Kevin, Bane of Camp Firwood."

Kevin laughed at that.

"Now that, I like. But you would need a name, too. Because let's face it, Barrel Mark won't suit you."

Mark's half-smile dropped, and he shrugged.

"Let's not jump into giving me heroic names before the battle."

"Are you kidding? You already deserve an epic heroic name."

Mark nodded with a somber look in his eye.

"We'll see tomorrow. For now, we should probably get back inside the cabins before Dwight shows up."

Mark was right. The talking had faded away, and the campers had to return to their cabins, since it was nearing time for roll call, while Bill and Kevin returned to the cave. The entire time on the way back, Kevin kept thinking about whether someone would spill the beans in front of Dwight, but campers like Steve and Norton reassured him that no one would talk.

This was it. It was almost time to execute their plan.

20
Ambush

"So, how do you feel about... well, everything?" Kevin asked Bill, amazed at how he was able to eat at a time like this.

Bill had a mouth full of rabbit in his mouth, sitting next to the flashlight pointed upward at the ceiling. The light cast ominous shadows across Bill's face, making him look old and gaunt. It was a late night, and they both should have been asleep, but it was evident that their energy level was high, and they would not be going to bed any time soon.

Bill shrugged, taking another bite of the rabbit.

"Are you serious?" Kevin chuckled.

"I mean, I'm not indifferent. I'm worried, yeah. But I think everything happens for a good reason. So whatever happens here happens. I believe we can't really change some outcomes, that it's a force higher and more powerful than all of us."

"God?"

"I'm thinking more like... fate."

Kevin smiled.

"Wish I could think like you."

"Don't worry, Kevin. Whatever happens in the morning, we'll end it one way or another."

"Hey, uh... if the guard manages to shoot me... don't be a hero. Just run. Don't even go back to the camp. Just stock up on supplies and go as far as you can."

Bill cocked an eyebrow.

"Why?"

"Because most likely the guard will have already alerted the others, and the campers are gonna be captured. And Andy will likely get killed, too. We'll need someone to inform the outside world of the horrors of Camp Firwood."

Bill stopped chewing his food, glowering at Kevin. After a moment of contemplation, he nodded. "Alright. Fine. But there won't be a need for that. We'll take down the guard... *safely*... and go help the other campers. And once all of that is done, we're all getting out of here. Everybody involved in this sick operation is gonna rot behind bars while we're hailed as heroes."

"Let's see if you're right," Kevin said as he slumped on the sleeping bag, staring at the ceiling of the cave.

He flicked off the flashlight, engulfing the cave in utter darkness. For a moment, he saw nothing. And then some features started getting discernible.

"Hey, Kev?" Bill asked after a moment of long silence.

"Yeah?"

"I have to tell you something."

Kevin waited, still staring at the ceiling. When no continuation came from Bill's side, he said, "Go on."

Bill sighed. "I lied to you. They didn't send me to the camp because they wanted me socializing."

Kevin pivoted his head so that he faced Bill, even though he couldn't see him in the dark. He frowned and asked, "Why did they send you, then?"

"Because... because I'm gay."

Kevin propped himself up until he was sitting. He stared at Bill, his silhouette barely discernible in the dark. He opened his mouth to say something but didn't know what to say.

"I just figured you should know that before... you know," Bill finished his thought.

"I, uh... I see. Well, that makes your parents assholes, sorry to say that."

"I know."

"So... did they like, hope to cure you here or something?" Kevin cleared his throat.

"Yeah. My dad wanted to, anyway. He thinks being gay is an illness."

"Your dad's a dipshit."

Bill laughed. Kevin lay back down and, as he stared at the ceiling, said, "Well, if it's worth anything, it doesn't change my opinion about you one bit."

"That... means a lot to me." Bill sounded hesitant and yet touched.

They lay in silence for a while. Kevin thought about everything Bill said. He felt like he should say something about it, but he honestly didn't know what to say.

"Well, we should try to sleep," he finally said awkwardly.

"Yeah." Bill yawned.

Despite having excitement surging through his entire body, Kevin felt his eyelids becoming heavy. He closed them, fantasizing about Amy before he drifted into sleep.

***

The morning anthem blared, startling Kevin awake. No, it wasn't the anthem. He must have dreamed about it. He could still hear the anthem of Camp Firwood in his mind so vividly that he thought for a moment that he was back at the camp. Daylight seeped inside the cave, illuminating Bill's figure. He was sitting with his hands huddled around his knees, and a half-eaten jerky sat on the ground next to him in its packaging.

Upon seeing Kevin stir, he said, "You're up. Good. We should get going soon. Here."

He snatched up an MRE pizza on his other side and tossed it to Kevin. Kevin managed to catch the pizza packaging, surprised that they even had pizza. He unpackaged it, and it looked exactly how he'd expect an MRE pizza to look. It was a block of dough with strips of cheese and little cube-shaped pieces of meat on top. The dough was hard and cold to the touch, and Kevin took a small bite first to see if it would make him gag. It wasn't great, but it wasn't terrible, either. The dough was better than the bread they served in the camp, and the meat wasn't hard and sinewy like Kevin expected it to be. He reckoned this slice of pizza would be good enough to keep him satiated until they were done with everything for the day.

"Well, let's go then," he said as he clambered up to his feet.

Bill mirrored his movement, and the two grabbed their hatchet and bow, ready to go. He hadn't even thought about it during breakfast, but now that they were out in the woods and heading to the building, it hit him. They were about to do something perilous. Kevin began feeling a little nauseous, and at that moment, he was thankful he didn't eat more food, even though he initially wanted to after finishing his pizza. He pushed the negative thoughts away and focused on what was ahead of him.

They wouldn't fail.

The walk through the woods to the area with the secret building was slow and uneventful. The only sound in the air was the rustling of Bill's and Kevin's shoes since they didn't speak the entire time. Bill kept staring at the ground a lot of the time, but he didn't seem distressed. Kevin wondered if he regretted telling him what he told him last night. The day was sunny and the weather too cold for what could be called summer, although it could have been the fear causing that sensation. Once they were on the elevation Kevin had used previously to scout out the building, they lay on the ground and observed the place with the binoculars.

For a long time, they saw nothing. And then, the door of the building swung open. A loud voice of one of the guards echoed in the area as he said something jokingly. Kevin clearly heard him say something down the line of, "Alright, see you later, man," before he and his partner went down the trail. The remaining guard closed the door of the building behind them.

"There they go," Kevin said as he put his binoculars down. "Right on schedule. I sure hope Andy gets them."

"I'm sure he'll do fine. Time for *us* to do *our* thing," Bill said.

"Okay," Kevin exhaled. "Get in a good shooting position. I'll grab the guard's attention."

Bill nodded and pulled the bow off his back. With hasty steps, he made his way toward the same bush as last time. Kevin, on the other hand, instead of going to the back of the building, made his way around the other way and to the front where the door was. He firmly held his hatchet as he approached the door, his heart drumming against his chest. He glanced back at Bill, who was in position and ready to nock an arrow. Just like last time, he was concealed really well, and it would take someone who has an eagle eye or thermal vision to spot him among the well-blended leaves and branches.

Kevin gave Bill one final nod of approval and turned to the door. He raised his free hand and loudly knocked three times. When he'd finished knocking, he retreated around the corner to the right (in case the other guards decided to come back down the road and he found himself cornered). Even before the door opened, he heard the guard's voice behind the door.

"What? Back already? What'd you forget?"

The sound of the metallic door squeaked as it opened.

"Hey," the guard said in what sounded like confusion.

Kevin gripped his hatchet firmly with both hands, with his back tightly against the cold concrete wall. He heard the guard taking tentative footsteps on the ground, enough to see his figure standing in front and swiveling his head left and right. Kevin saw him scratching his chin in confusion before putting his hand on the holster where his gun rested. He was about to turn around when an arrow whistled through the air and embedded itself in the back of his thigh. The guard shrieked in pain and fell onto his knees before toppling sideways. He strained to look at his wounded leg, placing a palm on the side of the thigh. Kevin knew he didn't have much time before the guard called for backup or drew his gun.

He jumped out from the corner and rushed him. The guard managed to jerk his head toward Kevin and put his hand on the holster before the blunt side of the hatchet struck him directly across the forehead. His head fell backward on the ground. In the midst of the commotion, he managed to draw his gun but had it pointed to Kevin's left, which confirmed that the hit disoriented him. Another arrow whistled through the air and struck him on the forearm that held the gun. The guard yelled again, instantly dropping the gun and groaning in pain as he cradled his arm.

"Son of a bitch!" he shouted.

Kevin dropped the hatchet and scrambled to pick up his gun. The Glock felt heavy, much heavier than he assumed it would be from what he'd seen in movies and video games. He had no idea how to use it, but he hoped that pointing it at the guard would be enough to intimidate him. The guard's groans and swearing stopped, and he raised his uninjured hand in a *stop* sign, his eyes wide with palpable fear.

"Wait. Just wait," he said in a surprisingly calm tone.

Kevin's hands were trembling, but it didn't matter. He got the effect he wanted. He heard the quickened footsteps on his left approaching and looked to see Bill coming toward him with his bow and another arrow ready.

"You okay?" Bill asked.

Kevin nodded.

The guard was now staring at Bill with a bewildered look on his face. He was probably starting to realize that he had been bamboozled. He reached with his uninjured hand for the radio, and Kevin pointed the gun more firmly at him, taking a step closer.

"Go on! Make my fucking day!" he said, shooting the guard the most glower he could muster while trying to hold his hands steady from shaking.

Bill had also nocked an arrow and pointed it at the guard from a two-foot range, waiting to see what he would do. The guard stared at Kevin silently with his hand on the radio before glancing over at Bill. As if realizing that he was outnumbered, he lowered his hand indignantly. The bluff worked.

"Good. Now let's go inside. We need to talk," Kevin said.

***

Five minutes later, they were inside the building with the guard tightly bound to a wooden chair with duct tape that Bill managed to find inside the desk. The building looked as cold on the inside as it did back when Kevin observed it from the outside. It was devoid of any life or soul with only the same grey concrete walls closing in on the room. The floor had cracked white tiles that looked like they were in need of a good scrubbing, and the three beds looked exactly like the ones the campers were using and were clustered together on the opposite end of the room like sardines in a can. Kevin noticed that the guards didn't have to bother making their beds like the campers as they were left messy, with the sheets all wrinkled up and the blankets thrown on top in a mess. The sight of it would make Dwight lose his shit for sure, Kevin thought.

There was a single desk in the room right next to the entrance and a dirty, rusted kitchen by the adjacent wall. A small refrigerator sat next to the kitchen, and perched on top of it were stacks of canned food – with a lot of empty cans tossed on top, the contents of the moldy food visible on the inside. On the other end of the room, past the third bed, was another door leading into a tiny bathroom.

The guard made grimaces in pain as he sat in the chair. His hands were bound behind his back, and his ankles were tied to the legs of the chair. Bill had carefully removed the arrow from the guard's leg but left the one in his forearm. Since the arrowheads were not made to kill but rather just to practice archery, the guard was at no risk of bleeding out – hopefully. Kevin placed the gun on the desk, still skeptical about holding it. He knew that keeping his finger off the trigger would make sure it didn't go off, but he still didn't like having such a dangerous thing around.

He turned to the guard, the hatchet limply dangling from his hand.

"Now. You're going to tell us everything we want to know. Got it?"

The guard had his head down but stared at Kevin from under his forehead with an expressionless face, like a subdued wild animal. He must have been no older than thirty, but he definitely looked like the cold-blooded type capable of committing murder.

"Start talking, or I'll shoot another arrow in your leg, asshole!" Bill commanded, waltzing over to the guard, towering above him.

The guard didn't budge. He stared at Bill and then at Kevin before smiling vaguely.

"You kids are so fucked," he said. "When the other guards find out about this, they're gonna ass-rape you with those fancy weapons of yours."

He let out a meager chuckle.

Kevin punched him in the face. The guard's smirk disappeared, but he didn't seem fazed by the punch. Kevin punched him again and again until the guard's mouth started bleeding. He continued punching over and over since he lost all control and anger took over. Anger over being taken to the camp. Anger over the innocent campers who got killed. Anger over the guard being a part of all of that and having the audacity to laugh.

"Kevin, that's enough," Bill put his hand on Kevin's shoulder and pushed him back.

Kevin took a deep breath and turned around, just then feeling the pain in his knuckles. Bill took over the interrogation.

"Tell us what's going on over here, and I promise we're not gonna kill you. But if you refuse or lie… then we're slowly going to torture you. We have more than enough time until The Choosing is finished. And when your buddies come back to find your mutilated corpse in here, we'll do the same to them."

Kevin turned around to see Bill staring the guard in the eye mere inches away from his face, impressed by his interrogation skills. No doubt, he watched a lot of action movies. The guard's bleeding mouth contorted into a spiteful grimace, his nose intermittently wrinkling up and down. A moment later, he looked away from Bill's intent gaze and locked eyes with Kevin.

"This isn't a summer camp," he said.

"Yeah, no shit," Kevin said.

"It's not a reeducation camp, either. That's the backup story the ones running the camp use in order to take suspicion off themselves."

"So, what is it then?" Bill asked.

The guard hesitated for a moment before he spoke up again.

"It's a game."

Both Bill and Kevin stared at the guard while he glanced back and forth from one camper to the other. When he realized that they demanded more answers, he continued, "It's a game where teens like you are brought into the camp and hunted by the rich."

"Excuse me?" Kevin chuckled at the absurdity of the guard's statement. "You expect us to believe that shit?"

"You've seen the people in the woods, right? They attacked you, chased you. They were hunting you for fun."

Kevin felt like he was in a dream. No, more like in a horror movie where he was the victim.

"Tell us everything from the beginning," Bill said.

The guard looked at Bill momentarily and then averted his gaze to the ground before saying, "Camp Firwood buys teens from parents who don't want them anymore. They get sent to the camp under the pretense of getting a reeducation, but in reality, the parents who send their kids to Camp Firwood simply want to get rid of them for a fee."

"Bullshit!" Kevin interjected.

"No, it's the truth." The guard looked at Kevin.

"Kev, let him finish," Bill calmly said.

The guard took a few breaths before continuing.

"The kids who get sent to the camp participate in a hunting game. The rich elite who have way too much money and way too much time on their hands pay to hunt the campers."

"So that's who those people are?" Kevin asked. "Some rich assholes who kill campers and then pose for photos that they post on some dark fucking web version of Instagram?"

"Pretty much, yeah."

"What about the one we killed a few nights ago?" Bill asked.

"We didn't even know anything went wrong there. The clients are not our problem. The director said that the clients pay, hunt, and then leave without a word. And it's our job to either kill any stray campers we come across on our patrols or escort the ones who get chosen for Disposal. "

"Disposal? You mean The Choosing?" Kevin asked.

"No. I think you guys call it Departure."

Bill and Kevin exchanged glances. They both knew that using the word Disposal instead of Departure was not good news.

"What happens to those campers?" Kevin looked at the guard.

"I don't know. We escort them to the director's car, and he drives them off somewhere."

"And he doesn't tell you guys where he takes the campers?" Bill asked.

"No."

"You goddamn liar," Kevin angrily retorted.

"I'm telling you the truth," the guard said. "We know about the clients paying for the hunt, but that's pretty much all they tell us. We're just as much pawns as you are."

"Oh yeah? Do you also get sent into the woods to get hunted by fucking knife-wielding, masked psychopaths?"

The guard remained silent.

"Tell us what they plan to do today," Bill said.

The guard looked up at him. "They'll bring a new batch of campers. And they plan to send some of them to the woods for The Trial, and others for Disposal."

"They plan to get rid of the ten surplus campers, right?" Kevin said.

The guard guffawed.

"Ten? No, no. All fifty."

"What?!" Bill and Kevin asked at the same time.

"Summer's almost over, kids. They're organizing a big fucking hunt. The grand finale. They're gonna choose the campers either for Disposal or to send them into the woods and then let the clients hunt them. They're gonna be competing for the most kills, and the winner takes a grand prize, whatever that is."

"That's too many campers. They'll disperse easily," Kevin said.

"No. They're bringing in more guards tonight to cordon off the area so that the campers can't go too far," he locked eyes with Kevin and grinned. "You're all gonna die."

Kevin felt a wave of panic surge through him. What if the guards were already there? What if Andy got in trouble? A crackling voice coming from the guard's radio snapped him back into reality.

"Hey, Travis, how are things on your end? Over."

The guard stared at Kevin in anticipation while Bill's eyes widened in palpable panic.

"Yo, Travis! You asleep there?" the voice repeated.

"If they realize something is wrong, they'll call for backup," the guard said.

Kevin gripped the hatchet firmly and put his other hand on the radio. He looked the guard dead in the eye with determination and said, "If you so much as say one wrong word, I'll kill you. Don't think I won't, because I've done it before. Got it?"

"Hellooo?" the voice over the radio called again, playfully this time.

Kevin pressed the button on the side of the hand microphone on the guard's shoulder and held his breath. The guard continued staring at Kevin with defiance.

"Yo, Travis? If you don't respond soon, I'm gonna have to report this," the voice said.

"Hey, sorry. I was taking a shit. All clear here," the guard finally said.

Kevin let go of the button and waited. There was silence for what felt like minutes before the radio crackled to life again. The voice on the radio laughed before saying, "Alright, man. No worries. We'll have to keep shit formal in front of the director, though, alright? So make sure to respond with that 'base' and 'patrol' and 'sit-rep' bullshit."

Kevin pressed the radio button again.

"Roger that," the guard said.

Once Kevin let go of the button and stepped back, Bill said with worry in his tone, "We gotta get back there and stop them before it's too late."

"Yeah. Let's do that." Kevin nodded before gesturing to the guard. "But what about him?"

Bill scratched his chin for a moment. "We can lock him up in here. But we have to take his radio away," he approached the guard with lightning steps and wrenched away the hand microphone on his shoulder. "We can simply toss this thing so-"

Bill failed to finish his sentence because the next thing Kevin knew, the guard swung one hand from behind his back and punched him across the face, instantly knocking him to the ground, still holding the hand microphone in his hand, with the wire dangling from it and across the guard's shoulder until it detached entirely.

"Bill!" Kevin shouted.

The guard had freed one hand and was now struggling against his restraints with full force and a furious expression on his face. His shoulder heaved up and down with each swing, and he was getting closer to yanking his hand free. Kevin charged at the guard with the hatchet above his head. He was ready to bring it down on him – with the sharp end of the blade this time. The guard grabbed Kevin by the arms, effectively stopping his strike. He was strong, preventing Kevin from moving in either direction. The guard grunted and pushed Kevin so hard that Kevin fell backward across the room on his back, dropping the hatchet from his hand.

He immediately raised his head to see the guard bending down and struggling to rip the duct tape off his ankles, the arrow still sticking out from his forearm. Bill had managed to stand up and was drawing an arrow from his quiver. The guard noticed this and jumped up from the chair, his feet still taped to the legs of the chair. He jumped on top of Bill, knocking the arrow and bow out of his hands. The guard then reached for the arrow on the ground, but Bill took hold of the arrow hanging from the guard's forearm and twisted it. The guard screamed in pain, his hand convulsing uncontrollably. The arrow broke with a loud snap, leaving only half of it embedded in the guard's forearm.

Kevin crawled toward the hatchet on the floor, lifting it and preparing to stand up and charge the guard again. The guard punched Bill in the face again and gripped the arrow in his forearm. With one yank, he pulled it out, causing blood to momentarily spurt out of the wound. He raised his hand, ready to stab Bill with the pointy part. Kevin didn't think. He swung his arm, releasing the hatchet. The hatchet flew toward the guard, and the distinctive words formed themselves in Kevin's mind.

You hurl your sword in the arena – you are dead.

The blade struck the guard across the shoulder, causing him to stumble backward with a loud yelp, along with the chair still stuck to his ankles. The hatchet didn't embed itself in the guard's shoulder, but it was a good enough hit to cause his shoulder to start bleeding. The guard grabbed at his shoulder, blood flowing between his fingers. His eyes fell on the hatchet on the floor, and he immediately began pushing himself with both hands to rotate his body toward it. Kevin clambered up to his feet, but the guard's fingertips had already grasped the hatchet.

And then his entire body twitched momentarily and he fell face down on the floor. It took Kevin a moment to realize that the guard had an arrow sticking out of his temple. Bill was standing above the guard, breathing heavily with the bow in his hand. Kevin took shallow breaths and asked, "Holy shit. You okay?"

Bill nodded.

"Fuck that guy," he said, wiping the blood off his lip.

Kevin glanced at the guard's now-lifeless body one more time. A trickle of blood poured from the spot in his head where the arrow was embedded while the guard's eyes vacantly stared at nothing in particular. Was he really a killer? Or was he simply doing his job?

Not able to withstand looking at the body anymore, Kevin tapped Bill on the shoulder and said, "We gotta get to the camp."

21
The Showdown

They practically ran through the woods toward Camp Firwood. For the first five minutes or so, Kevin couldn't get the image of the dead guard out of his mind. He also couldn't help but notice how much closer he was to feeling indifferent than when he killed the man in the woods. He remembered the words from a video game character he heard years ago.

Unfortunately, killing is one of those things that gets easier the more you do it.

And it was true. Kevin had no doubt that if he continued down this path, he'd become a ruthless, cold-blooded, desensitized killer in no time. He didn't want to consider himself a killer yet, though. Everything thus far was self-defense. When they got close enough to the camp, they slowed down to preserve their energy. They had to be ready – either to fight or to run. They walked all the way through until they reached the treeline near the groundskeeper's place.

"Think Andy's okay?" Kevin asked.

"Sure hope so. Our plan depends on him," Bill coldly said.

His jaw was starting to swell slightly from the guard's punches. They followed the treeline all the way to the left and went through the small portion of the woods that opened into the Choosing grounds. The campers were already there, seated on the stumps of the trees, anxiously waiting. A lot of them had wide, fearful eyes, shuffling left and right in their positions. Others, like Steve and Norton, looked calm and composed, but none of them were talking. However, that wasn't what caught Kevin's attention. What caught his attention were the new faces among the campers, already dressed in the Camp Firwood uniforms. He tried counting the ones he didn't know and realized ten new teens were sitting among the group.

They already integrated them into the camp. They could help us in the attack.

The counselors weren't there yet. Bill and Kevin took up positions near the edge of the woods, hiding behind tree trunks. Now they just needed to wait. Kevin repeatedly clenched and unclenched the hand, gripping the hatchet, more out of nervousness than anything else. He was itching to swing it. He tried imagining what the best way to swing it would be for a sure hit. He envisioned the director standing in front of him and blocking the blunt hit from above with his elbow or striking him over and over on the side until he keeled over, cowering under the campers.

The murmurs that suddenly came from the campers as they looked over each other's shoulders behind them told him that the counselors were coming. Mr. Adams and all the counselors came into view – Mr. Adams was giving some instructions to the others in passing while they followed him. Pretty soon, they got to the front of the group, all dozen or so of them, and then climbed onto the stage. The counselors stopped at the back of the stage while Mr. Adams stood at the front.

What few meager sounds had been coming from the campers prior to their arrival were now extinguished entirely, and all eyes focused on the orchestrator of the show – the head counselor. Mr. Adams motioned with one hand Dwight to get closer, while he held his notepad in the other. Dwight rushed over with thudding footsteps, glancing up at Mr. Adams' towering figure like a curious puppy. Mr. Adams explained something fervently to him before patting him on the shoulder and looking away from him. Dwight nodded and ran down the stage and through the meadow, out of sight. Mr. Adams faced the campers and looked down at his notepad before taking some notes. Even though Kevin couldn't hear it, he saw Mr. Adams clicking the pen multiple times.

"Good morning, campers!" he suddenly looked up and grinned at the campers.

"Good morning, Mr. Adams," the campers chanted, the new ones looking around in confusion.

He hadn't even realized how much he didn't miss the whole Camp Firwood obedience bullshit. Mr. Adams looked down at his notes and began a roll call. He called out name after name, looking up from his notepad with raised eyebrows, scanning the group until he found the camper that shouted 'me!' Once all was done, the head counselor started nervously pacing around, glancing over the heads of the campers. The director's arrival sure seemed to put him on edge every time. The ominous silence seemed oddly familiar but this time carried with it an overwhelming sense of dread that seemed to choke the air surrounding the campers and settle deep into their bones.

Any minute now.

The whirring of an engine started in the distance, from a location Kevin couldn't pinpoint. At first, it was barely audible, but slowly, it grew in intensity, and it became clear the sound was coming from the left where the main grounds of the camp were. Some of the campers tried turning their heads, but Mr. Adams reprimanded them for it. Kevin and Bill pivoted their heads to the left but couldn't see anything yet. Within seconds though, the front of a familiar, pristine, black car came into view, speeding toward the Choosing grounds, leaving a billowing cloud of dust behind itself before passing on to the grassy ground. More and more campers turned their heads, and Mr. Adams had to start shouting since his reprimands weren't working anymore.

The black car slowed down and came to a halt a few dozen feet to the right and a little bit behind the Choosing stage. The engine was barely audible now that the car was stopped, and within seconds, it ceased producing all noise entirely. He caught the sound of the door opening on the left, and out came the grey-headed, suited figure of the director. Only upon seeing him did Kevin feel relieved because it meant that the guards were telling the truth and that he was not paranoid. He feared that, had the director not arrived, the campers would not believe him and would potentially withdraw from the attack.

It also made panic brew further inside him because he knew it meant that the real attack was about to begin and that the campers were almost out of time. The director smiled and waved to the counselors while closing his car door as if he were a celebrity whose photos were being taken by the media. He walked up onto the stage where Mr. Adams stood wearing his usual ass-kissing grin.

"Mr. Director." Mr. Adams stuck out his hand and shook with the director.

The director gave him an aloof nod of the head, only briskly smiling.

"Campers, please give a warm welcome to the person responsible for making all of this happen – the director of the camp!" Mr. Adams jovially exclaimed.

"Good morning, Mr. Director," the campers chanted with much less enthusiasm than Mr. Adams.

The director only briefly raised his hand in a greeting. He nodded to Mr. Adams, and the head counselor went over to join the ranks of the other counselors at the back of the stage. The director took a few steps to his right so that he was in the middle of the stage. He inhaled deeply and said with an authoritative tone.

"Campers, recite the Camp Firwood core values."

The veteran campers began unanimously.

"Discipline is the mother of all values. Discipline is the bridge between goals and accomplishments. By following the rules of the camp, I will become a disciplined and better person. Discipline is the core value of Camp Firwood. Discipline is the core value of life."

Some of the new campers opened their mouths or swiveled their heads left and right but were taken aback by the recital. The director applauded complacently before spreading his arms welcomingly with a PR grin on his face.

"Welcome, new campers, to Camp Firwood!" he proclaimed theatrically.

Kevin couldn't help but conclude that no matter how much the director flashed his pearly teeth, he would still always look like he sucked the souls of innocent children to keep his hair slick.

He continued, "I am happy to see so many faces here. Camp Firwood has only been operating for three years, but we've had a success rate of over ninety-five percent satisfied clients! As you know, Camp Firwood values discipline over anything else, and in order to provide good quality to both the campers and clients, we need to continue to improve the education methods here."

He clapped his hands together and grinned as he exclaimed, "Ah, right on time!"

He was staring above the campers' heads, and upon realizing this, the campers began turning their heads around to see what the director was looking at. Kevin and Bill did the same but couldn't see anything from this position.

And then they saw who came into view, following the trail, and into the meadow.

The two guards from the secret building were striding side by side with furious steps, directly toward the Choosing Grounds. But they weren't alone. Between them, squeezed tightly under their arms and dragged across the ground, was Groundskeeper Andy.

"Oh, no. Shit, no," Kevin chanted quietly over and over when the gravity of the situation hit him.

He watched as the guards with the groundskeeper inched closer toward the stage, more and more features becoming prominent on them. Andy's face was red and bleeding like he'd been beaten pretty badly. His overalls were dirty, indicating that he was probably thrown on the ground in the fight. His feet dragged behind him across the grass while his head hung limply, his eyes staring at the ground. The guards ignored the curious and now-terrified campers' gazes as they made their way to their right and toward the stage. Kevin saw one of the new campers standing up from his seat to better see what was going on, and before he knew it, a few other campers joined in curiously peeking at the guards.

"Sit down!" the director's surprisingly sharp voice instantly caused the teens to return to their spots.

So many things happened at once. Kevin stared as the guards brought the beaten groundskeeper up on the stage and to the director's left side and dropped him to the ground. Andy groaned in pain and remained prone on the floor. The guards then drew their guns, one of them pointing it at Andy while the other guard stepped behind and around the director and to his other side, holding his gun firmly with both hands but pointing it downward.

"Campers! Toss away your weapons! Now!" the guard with the lowered gun shouted as the director calmly stood next to him with his hands behind his back.

The campers exchanged confused glares with each other before the guard raised his gun and loudly shouted, "RIGHT NOW!"

The campers – one by one – started obeying and unzipping their side leg pockets. Kevin watched in desperation as they brought out their foldable spades and knives and threw them on the ground in front of them.

"Now put your hands behind your heads!" the guard shouted.

This seemed to come as a surprise to the counselors as well because they exchanged wide-eyed glances, intermittently darting their eyes from the director to Andy, to their fellow staff members, to the head counselor. Mr. Adams was the only one who seemed composed and nonchalant, staring in front of himself with a bemused expression on his face.

The director looked at the campers and said with a smile, "As I said, discipline is extremely important. And unfortunately, someone here decided to disrespect that." He turned to the counselors. "Marvin, thank you for performing an outstanding job as always." He gave Mr. Adams a wide smile.

"My pleasure, Mr. Director." Mr. Adams slightly nodded with a complacent smile.

"You've proven to be a valuable asset to the company, and I believe you will do even better in higher positions. Let's discuss it in your office later." He then turned to face counselor Baldwin and said, "Mr. Baldwin, how does the position of head counselor sound to you?"

Baldwin stepped forward and nodded with his shiny head.

"I'm honored, Mr. Director, thank you," he said before returning to his place in line.

The director turned to his left toward the woods, staring just to the right of where Kevin and Bill were. He grinned as he raised a forefinger and slowly scanned the woods with his gaze. Kevin's heart jumped into his throat.

"Camper Kevin! Camper Bill!" the director called out. "Come out, or I will order the guard to shoot Groundskeeper Andy!"

The seated campers swiveled their heads left and right in confusion, their hands still stuck to the backs of their heads.

"Shit! Shit!" Bill swore, peeking at the director from behind a large tree trunk.

"Fuck, what do we do?" Kevin asked in a panic.

"Campers! I'm gonna count to three! If you're not out by then, my guard will shoot Andy!" the director ordered.

"Don't listen to them! Run!" Andy shouted.

He was on his knees when he shouted that, and the guard in front of him hit him over the face with the pistol. Andy fell on his palms with a yelp.

"One!" the director counted.

"We can't let him die!" Bill whispered to Kevin.

"If we show ourselves to them, we're as good as dead!" Kevin retorted.

"Two!" the director's voice reverberated.

"Fuck, what then?!" Bill asked.

There was no time. Kevin stood up and stepped out into the open.

"Alright, alright! Don't shoot!" he shouted, still holding the hatchet in his hand.

Bill followed his lead and stepped out as well. All the campers seated in front of the stage stared at Kevin and Bill, their hands still held on the backs of their heads. The director locked eyes with Kevin, smiling complacently.

"Well, well, well," he said. "The organizers of the great plan, correct? Come closer."

Kevin tentatively took the first step forward, to which the director said, "Oh, and… please be sure to drop your weapons there, will you?"

Kevin let the hatchet fall limply out of his hand. Bill hesitated but eventually threw his bow on the ground with force before unbuckling his quiver and letting it fall on the ground, too. As they slowly walked toward the stage, Kevin felt defeated. It was over. They were caught, and now they were going to be severely punished. Probably even killed. The panic that started building up in him when he first saw the guards dragging Andy had now reached a tipping point, and he contemplated whether he should simply take his chances and run back into the woods.

It still wasn't too late. He still had a chance to escape before the guard started shooting at him. But then he looked at the other terrified campers. Especially the new ones, who had no idea what was going on. Despite his urge to survive, he kept moving closer to the stage, each step diminishing his odds of successfully running away.

No more running. It's over.

Kevin and Bill stopped a dozen feet to the right of the stage, looking up at the director, who still had a grin plastered to his face.

"You two have caused us a lot of trouble, haven't you?" he asked.

He looked away from them, toward the seated campers, and raised a finger to his chin.

"Now, where is… Camper Mark! Where are you?"

He swiveled his head left and right, scanning the rows of campers. Kevin turned his head toward the campers and saw Mark standing up from his seat in the middle, his hands behind his head.

"You can put your hands down, camper. Come up here now; don't be shy," the director motioned with his hand.

Mark had a petrified look in his eye staring at the director, and his face was drained of all color. He tentatively put his hands down and made his way past the campers and onto the stage, stopping a few feet from Andy and the guard that had him at gunpoint. The director raised one hand from behind his back and curled his forefinger as if to motion Mark to come closer. Mark went around the groundskeeper's kneeling figure and stopped in front of the director, trembling violently from head to toe. Kevin's heart was beating a million beats a minute as he waited in anticipation and fear of what they would do to his friend.

"Don't hurt him! This was my plan all along. He had nothing to do with any of this!" Kevin rapidly recited.

The director looked over Mark's shoulder toward Kevin, still smiling. He gently put his hand on Mark's shoulder and spun him around so that they both faced Kevin.

"You misunderstand, camper," the director said. "I wish only to award Mark for his cooperation."

Kevin opened his mouth but had nothing to say. He wasn't sure if he understood the director's sentence clearly.

"I'm sorry, Kevin," Mark said. "They threatened to bring Sherry into the camp. I... I had to cooperate."

Kevin couldn't believe what he was hearing. Mark? His friend Barrel Mark? No, that couldn't possibly be true. But it was. The panic he felt up until then began morphing into a white-hot rage that blinded him to everything else.

"It was you all along, wasn't it? You're the one who ratted Carlos out about the meds! And us about the plan! That's why you were talking to Dwight that one time I saw you! That's' why you never got in any trouble! You sold us out, didn't you?!"

He took a menacing step forward, but the guard with the lowered gun shouted a loud 'HEY!' which caused him to stop.

"You double-crossing son of a bitch!" Norton shouted and stood up with his hands down, only to have the same guard point his gun at him, barking at him to sit back down and raise his hands.

Norton unwillingly listened to him and returned to the previous position.

"Now, now. Like we often said, disciplined campers are *rewarded* in Camp Firwood. Camper Mark here will be offered a position as an assistant counselor."

Mark was looking down at his feet the whole time, visibly feeling ashamed. Or faking it in front of the other campers to save face. Kevin didn't care how he felt. He wanted to strangle him alive. But then something else caught his attention. Just under the stage, through the supporting pillars, he saw some movement in the darkness. He couldn't tell what it was because it was so subtle, and he thought that his mind might have been playing tricks on him.

The director turned back to the campers, smiled sadistically, and said, "Now, as for you campers... We can't have you doing this again, can we? So starting today, these two guards will be present all day with the main group. You'll have roll calls four times a day. The tools will be kept in complete check. And of course..."

He knelt in front of Andy, who was still on his knees in front of the director while the guard held him by the shoulder.

The director continued. "We'll need a new groundskeeper." He looked at Andy with pity as he said, in a lower tone, "Andy. We know who you are. We've known who you are for a while now. We just wanted to see how long you'd keep up the act before we got rid of you.

He stood up and triumphantly spread his arms, giving a speech about the severe punishment that staff members suffer, calling the campers lucky not to be in their shoes, but Kevin wasn't listening. He was transfixed on the movement that once again subtly appeared under the stage. He stared at it as it slowly moved from directly below the director to a little bit to the left.

"And as for you, campers. I'm *very* disappointed. A lot of you could have gone home much earlier," the director finished.

"Liar! You've been killing campers all along!" Bill shouted defiantly.

Murmurs from the campers filled the air.

"You've been sending campers to be hunted like wild animals by your rich clients! The guard told us everything!" Bill continued.

More murmurs before the director ordered them to be quiet. He laughed and clapped his hands together while staring at Kevin.

"Well, you spoiled the surprise, camper. But it doesn't matter." A moment later, he turned to the guard standing above Groundskeeper Andy and said, "Do it."

Kevin's heart jumped into his throat. And then the other guard screamed. He fell on his side, holding his foot and wailing in pain while the counselors and the director stared at him in wide-eyed confusion. The shadow under the planks slinked toward the back of the stage and, with great finesse, jumped and scaled the stage, emerging into the light. The figure pushed its way between the rows of perplexed counselors and grabbed the director from behind, pulling him down on top of himself.

Ninja!

The guard who had Andy at gunpoint by then looked toward the director in confusion, his eyes wide in a *what the fuck* manner, not dissimilar to the expression the guard back at the building had when Kevin and Bill ambushed him.

That was all Andy needed.

With incomprehensible speed, he seized the gun from the guard in front of him and turned it on him. A loud bang caught them all by surprise, and the guard's head kicked back. Blood and pieces of his skull skyrocketed into the air before they toppled down along with his lifeless body. Andy turned to the other guard, who was already raising his gun. Another bang had everyone turning

405

toward Andy again, and the guard's head recoiled back, hitting the floor of the stage. Screams filled the air as confused campers and counselors stood in awe, not knowing what to do. The counselors were about to start running when Andy pointed his gun at them, swiveling it left and right.

"Don't move! Get on the fucking ground, now!" he shouted authoritatively.

Most of the counselors obeyed. They immediately started dropping on the stage floor. But counselor Baldwin refused to do that. He turned around and jumped off the stage, bolting toward the woods. He was fast. Andy took two quick steps forward and fired another shot. A scream pierced the air, and Kevin saw Baldwin falling forward to the ground and gripping his leg in pain. Andy made sure that all the counselors were on the ground and then turned to the director. Ninja was under him, holding a bloodstained knife to his neck. The director was panting, holding his hands up in the air, the smug smile gone from his face. Mark stood on the stage next to them, trembling like a leaf in the wind. The campers at the seats were now standing up, some of them grabbing the weapons they brought in apprehensive positions. Others were confusedly staring up at the stage, and a small number cowered on the ground.

"Is everybody okay?" Steve asked, glancing around himself. "Groundskeeper?"

"I'm fine, son. Drag Baldwin back here," Andy ordered.

Immediately, Steve and a few other campers rushed behind the stage toward the shot counselor. Andy strode toward the pinned director.

"I got this, son," he said to Ninja, pointing his gun at the director.

Ninja slithered out from under the director and jumped to his feet with as much finesse as he displayed when climbing the stage. The groundskeeper approached the director and hit him across the face with the butt of the gun. He kept hitting over and over before taking hold of him by the collar and pointing the gun to his forehead.

"What is this place?! What are you doing to the campers here?!" Andy asked.

The director panted as he shook his head. Kevin watched in relish as Andy punched him two more times. The director's nose was effectively bleeding now, and he coughed a few times, staining his once-pristine suit with red and uttering a few barely coherent words.

"Okay... Okay... I'll tell you..." he said.

"Talk!" Andy shouted angrily, and it looked like he was just about ready to pummel him to death.

"We take away children from parents who don't want them. We offer them a small fee, and they sell them. Then, we enlist them in our game, which the clients pay for. The ones who get sent into the woods are hunted."

"And the ones who are not?"

The director hesitated.

"TALK!" Andy bellowed.

"They're bought by the clients to be used however they see fit."

"What do you mean ' however they see fit'?" Andy pressed the gun against the director's head harder.

The campers were as still as statues, and complete and deafening silence filled the air, save for Baldwin's groaning, as he was dragged and tossed on the ground next to the stage.

"Answer me!" Andy requested.

"I mean exactly that," the director said. "Some clients want new organs, others want a child they can add to their family because they can't have their own... and some simply want... company."

"You sick fuck!" Kevin shouted.

"My son Owen. He disappeared from the camp last year. Now, you better remember his name, or I'm gonna blow your fucking head off," Andy hissed through his teeth.

The director held his hands up, panting and staring at Andy.

"He's dead," a voice said, but it wasn't the director.

All heads looked up at Mr. Adams, prone on his stomach, with his hands on the back of his head. The head counselor locked his eyes with the groundskeeper and huffed.

" The short, smart kid, right? He was chosen for Disposal. The director took him away after that."

"Shut up, Marvin!" the director retorted.

Andy's face contorted into a grimace of anger. He looked back down at the director, pressing the gun harder against his forehead.

"What did you do to him, you son of a bitch?!" he asked.

The director started laughing mildly, and soon that laughter broke into a cackle. Andy looked like he didn't know what he should do.

The director shook his head as his laughter reached a halt, and he said, "I remember your son, Andy. Your ex-wife had everything planned out. She didn't want a brat to interfere with her and her new boyfriend's life. But she also didn't want you to get the pleasure of having him back. So she sold your son for a meager three thousand dollars. Oh, Andy, Andy. You had no idea how *thrilled* the clients were to see a pretty little thing like your boy join the program. They were practically fighting each other over who was going to bid more for him."

He smiled complacently before Andy pushed the director down on the stage planks and gripped the gun with both hands firmly. The director's smile remained plastered over his face as he continued talking.

"He was the first one to go in The Choosing. The client who won him in the end was a plastic surgeon from Minnesota. He really, and I mean *really*, liked little boys, especially cute ones like yours."

Andy clenched his fist and the gun more tightly, bulging veins appearing on his hands and his chest heaving as he stared at the director. The director seemed unaware of this or simply chose to ignore it as he continued talking.

"Unfortunately, doctor Harris has one major flaw. He gets bored with his toys rather quickly. And when he does, he likes to experiment with them, push the boundaries of aesthetic surgeries. If I remember correctly, his specialization was facial reconstruction. I don't even wanna think about what your son had to go through in those last moments before he decided to recycle him like a used-up condom."

The director barely had the chance to finish his last sentence because before anyone knew it, Andy was on top of him, holding him by the collar and hitting him with the gun over the face. He ferociously pummeled the pretentious director's face over and over, the old man's smile now gone and replaced by a grimace of agony, and his arms hanging limply by on the floor. Droplets of blood flew in the air in various directions, and after a while, the only thing that could be heard was Andy's grunting with each punch he threw and the thud the gun would make upon contact with the director's face.

None of the campers wanted to intervene. Andy earned this. A whole year of unimaginable torment, only to find out it was all in vain. Andy finished off with one final punch before dropping the director, sobbing loudly. The director limply fell to the floor but was still alive. His face was swollen so much that one of his eyes was completely covered, and it looked like a few of his pearly teeth had been knocked loose. He coughed painfully, blood flying out of his mouth and on the side of his face, trickling to his ears. He raised his head as Andy pointed the gun at him, gripping it so feverishly that veins bulged on his forearms, and his hand shook violently.

"You... you killed... my son?" Andy sobbed, his voice sounding like it was a mix of immense rage and sorrow.

The director took a few shallow breaths, coughing and spitting more blood before speaking with a slur, "We... we could have killed you long ago, Andy. But... but we didn't."

"That was a mistake."

He put his finger on the trigger and took a deep, hissing breath.

"Andy!" Kevin shouted.

Instantly, the tension in the air seemed to ease up a little. Andy looked at Kevin with bloodshot, tear-riddled eyes, staring at the teen as if he were seeing something unfamiliar for the first time in life.

"Andy, don't do it," Kevin said. "That's what he wants you to do."

Andy looked back at the director. The old man laughed wheezily before coughing up more blood.

"Come on, you pussy. You don't even have the guts to finish off the man who murdered your son," he said.

Andy got closer to the director, pressing the gun to his bloodied forehead.

"Andy, please," Kevin begged.

A moment of intense silence hung in the air as Andy held the finger on the trigger, and then-

He lowered the gun. He placed it in the pocket of his overalls and grabbed the director by the collar. He picked him up like he was nothing until he was face to face with his mutilated face.

He said, "You have a daughter, right? She and the rest of the world are going to find out what kind of a monster you are. And you will rot in prison for the rest of your pathetic, worthless life."

With that, he dropped him on the ground. The director groaned in pain and then coughed up some more blood. A long moment of silence hung in the air before Andy looked at Bill and said, "Bill! Go get the ropes from my cabin! Go!" he tossed the keys with a jingle to Bill, who caught them graciously.

Bill immediately started running toward the woods, in the direction of the groundskeeper's cabin. Some of the campers began climbing onto the stage. Kevin stopped in front of Mark, who had a look of shame on his face. He was staring down, avoiding Kevin's glance. The eerie silence was pierced by Norton's voice behind Kevin.

"You fat son of a bitch!" he charged at Mark, but Ninja and Steve held him back.

Mark recoiled momentarily while Norton shouted profanities and threats at him.

"Enough! No more violence!" Andy shouted in a mix of authority and desperation. "Enough blood has been spilled here! It's over."

He was completely red in the face, and his eyes were swollen from tears. Norton immediately got defused by this. Andy's voice seemed to intimidate the entire group of campers, all fifty of them. Minutes passed, and most of the attention was divided by now, a lot of the campers displaying amazement at Ninja's ability to survive. He was as dirty as Kevin and Bill were but was in a much better condition than the two of them, looking like he just went on a stroll through a muddy park with no major scrapes or wounds on him. A lot of the other attention was focused on Andy and the director, some of it on the dead bodies of the guards, and only Kevin was undividedly staring at Mark.

"I can't believe you did that," Kevin said. "I trusted you. We were friends."

Mark didn't look up. It made Kevin want to hit him, and it took everything in him not to do so. He turned away from him, fearing that staring at him any longer might cause him to do something classless to Mark like punch him or spit in his face. He instead turned to Andy and the director. The groundskeeper had flipped the director onto his stomach and forced him to spread his legs and put his hands on the back of his head.

"Hey, did anyone see Dwight?" Steve asked.

Everybody exchanged glances, but no one gave an answer.

"Fuck! I was really looking forward to beating the shit out of him," Norton angrily retorted.

"Don't matter. He's got nowhere to go," Andy said. "Let's wait for Bill to return and tie up these bastards."

While waiting for Bill, Norton tried to attack Mark again, but the other campers held him back again. Only when Ninja tried talking to him did he calm down. Kevin observed the new campers, who

411

looked confused as hell. He sat on one of the tree stumps, doing his best not to look at Mark.

"Good to see you again, Cocky Kevin," Ninja said, tapping Kevin on the shoulder and sitting on the stump next to him.

Kevin smiled and stretched out his hand. They firmly shook hands, as Kevin said, "Bill and I went looking for you. We thought you were dead."

"Nah, not me," he said in his usual lethargic tone.

How someone could be so physically active and yet so dead while speaking baffled Kevin beyond words.

"What happened to you that night when we got separated?" he asked.

Ninja snorted and made a grimace before saying, "I managed to run away from the Firwood Wraith. I hid somewhere and waited until morning. From there, I looked for a way back into the camp, because fuck it. And at night, I caught one of the campers from cabin five when he was taking out the trash behind the mess hall. Told him to leave a window open, and he did."

Kevin heard too much information to process it at once. He talked step by step with Ninja about what they both did to survive in the woods since that night when they got separated. Soon, Bill returned with stacks of ropes hanging around his arms and neck. They bound the counselors' and the director's hands behind their backs, and as soon as they were done, Andy forced the director on his feet. The director's face was so swollen and messed up that it looked like an entirely different person.

"Line all of them up so we can get them to the detention center! Bill, get a group and round up Nurse Mary and Lunch Lady Daisy!" Andy said.

"You got it, Mr. Andy!" Bill obediently said.

Once all the prisoners were lined up, the campers formed a circle around them with their foldable spades and knives, in case any of them tried running away. Baldwin's leg was patched up, and he was carried by Ninja and Norton under his arms. Norton himself

412

seemed to be just waiting eagerly for the counselor to try something stupid.

Andy personally made sure to escort the director separately from the group.

22
Barrels Part 2

Andy pushed the director, not taking the barrel of the gun off his back. The director stumbled forward but regained his balance momentarily. Kevin quickly noted how the director's now-dirtied suit and shoes no longer looked as flawlessly clean as they did earlier when he arrived. He smiled at the irony of the tables turning so fast. The director stepped forward, stopping in front of the detention center door. All the campers – new and old – were there, still encroaching on the bound counselors. Nurse Mary and Lunch Lady Daisy were added to the number of prisoners, their wrists indiscriminately bound just like the others. Dwight was nowhere to be found.

Mary pleaded and cried, but the campers ignored her. When Andy threatened to put a gag in her mouth if she didn't shut up, her desperate pleas turned into quiet whimpers. The lunch lady, on the other hand, looked as indifferent – irritated even – as she usually did, as if getting kidnapped by a bunch of campers was the most normal everyday occurrence. The director stood in front of the door, his shoulders tense. Andy grabbed him from behind in a chokehold, using his other hand to point the gun to his temple.

"Open it!" he commanded.

The director submissively raised his hands but said nothing.

"I'm gonna give you to the count of three. And then I'm gonna blow off one of your knee caps. How does that sound?" Andy angrily commanded.

"Okay, okay! Calm down!" the director nervously said.

He probably knew that Andy meant business and that he was not gonna waste time asking. Andy released the grip and pushed the director toward the door. The director knocked three times. A familiar voice broke the silence from inside.

"Who is it?" the person behind the door asked.

"This is the director of Camp Firwood! Detention center counselors, open the door!"

"Right away, Mr. Director!" the voice said with more excitement this time.

Kevin recognized the voice as Jordan's. He suddenly remembered how he and Peter treated him when he was in the detention center. It still made him boil with rage. Andy caught the director by the shoulder and shoved him back toward the other prisoners. He then gripped the handgun with both hands. Kevin quickly strode over to Andy and looked up at him.

"Andy? Can us campers be the ones to take care of the counselors here?"

Andy stared down at him as if searching his face.

"You wanna kill 'em?" he asked.

"No. We won't kill them. We're done killing." Kevin shook his head.

Andy stared down at him for a few seconds before putting the gun back into his pocket and nodding. The tongue of the lock clicked in the next moment, and the door swung open. Kevin wasted no time. As soon as Jordan saw the army standing in front of the door, his eyes widened, but it was too late. Kevin used the momentum of his entire body to swing a punch. His fist connected with Jordan's jaw in a perfect blow, and the counselor fell on the ground, holding his face painfully.

"Payback, motherfucker!" Kevin triumphantly said as the other campers began storming in.

It felt great punching him and seeing him on the ground with a perplexed and scared look on his face. It took everything in him not to step closer and continue pummeling his ugly fucking face.

"What the fu-" was all Peter could utter before Norton's anvil-like punch connected with his nose. The counselor fell on the

416

ground, writhing and holding his face, repeating the phrases 'you broke my nose' over and over.

"Lock them up!" Andy ordered, and the campers got to work right away.

As soon as they opened the cellblock doors, Norton pointed at Mark and asked, "What do we do with him?"

"Lock him up with the rest of them. He betrayed us," Kevin said, shooting daggers at Mark.

The whole time, Mark was quiet and reticent, probably waiting for his sentence.

"No. We can't leave him in here," Andy interjected,

"What?" Kevin protested. "Andy, he sold us out! We almost died because of him!"

Murmurs of bickering campers filled the air until Andy cut them off.

"I said leave him be!" the groundskeeper snapped, causing the campers to recoil. "He's as much a victim as we are. It's over. Now, let's get the staff members inside the cells."

Kevin frowned at Mark before turning away from him. Andy inserted the key he'd taken from the detention center counselors into the first cell door, unlocking it. The door screeched in protest, and the groundskeeper shoved the director inside, causing him to stumble before he caught his balance. He locked him up and then gave the keys to Ninja to open the other cells. The campers took relish in opening the cells and shoving the staff members inside. They put them in pairs in each cell, save for the director, who was placed at the far front of the block near the entrance, alone. Ninja locked up all the cells and made sure they were nice and secure. He made a show to dangle the keys with a jingle in front of the director's face before giving them back to Andy.

"Think of this as your sneak peek for what's to come," Ninja jovially said, which caused a few campers to laugh out loud.

The counselors were nothing short of distraught and terrified.

Good. Let them feel a fraction of what the campers felt.

417

Nurse Mary was inconsolable and hysterical. She clutched the cell bars with a feverish grip, her face pressed against the metal.

"Please, you don't have to do this! I never wanted to do this! They made me do it!"

Andy stopped in front of her cell with visible resent in his eyes.

"How did they force you, Mary? Did they put a gun to your head and tell you that they'd kill you if you didn't obey? Or did they simply offer you a ton of money to stay quiet?"

Mary opened her mouth, a dry gasp escaping, before she shook her head, wiping away the tears on her face. "I'm sorry! I made a mistake! Please, let me out! I'll testify against them all! Andy, please!"

"Too late for that," Andy said and turned around to leave.

Mary got even more hysterical by that point, but he ignored her. He turned around to face the exit and then froze in place. Kevin jerked his head in the direction that the groundskeeper was facing and saw a figure standing at the door.

It was Dwight.

He was holding a pistol pointed in front of himself, randomly waving his hand with jerky motions at the various campers standing in his way.

"Don't move!" he shouted rapidly, "Hands up!"

He pointed the gun at Andy, and immediately, the groundskeeper raised his hands.

"Take it easy, son. Just take it easy," Andy said.

"You! This is all your fault!" Dwight said, pointing the gun directly at Kevin.

The campers around Kevin had dispersed to avoid getting shot, but Kevin remained still in the middle of the cellblock.

"Dwight! Put the gun down!" Andy commanded.

Dwight didn't seem to hear him. He had a crazy look in his eyes mixed with rage. Kevin couldn't help but notice how he was holding his finger on the trigger, and with such jerky movement, expected the gun to go off any moment.

"Shoot them, Dwight!" the director shouted from the back.

Kevin looked at the director's cell and saw his mangled face staring at Dwight with a voracious look in his eye. Dwight glanced at him momentarily before facing Kevin again.

"Don't do it, Dwight," Andy calmly said. "If you shoot, you'll kill an innocent person. You'll throw your life away if you do that. Do you really want that?"

Dwight looked indecisive about what he should do. Most of the unarmed campers had already retreated to the back of the block with Andy and Kevin at the front in a fierce standoff with Dwight.

"You can still make it out of here alive, son," Andy said with the tone of a compassionate father. "You didn't know what you were getting into. It's not your fault."

The director cackled like a movie villain before saying.

"Didn't know what he was getting into? He knew *exactly* what he was getting into." He looked in Andy's direction and said softly. "Unfortunately, he had no other choice. When I found him, he had just begun serving his twenty-five-year long sentence in prison for stabbing an autistic boy and leaving him to bleed out. All because he lost in a game of cards. Isn't that right, Dwight?"

"That's... shut up!" Dwight shouted, not looking in the director's direction.

The director got closer to the bars and gripped them gently. He said, "Dwight, you listen to me now. You shoot them both right where they stand, and you can walk free. No questions asked. But if you don't do as I say, you're going back to prison where you can rot until you are a middle-aged man."

"Shut the fuck up! Dwight, don't listen to him," Andy said as he took a step forward and slightly lowered his hands.

Dwight responded by jerking the gun hand toward Andy, making him recoil and raise his hands back up. There was no way they could jump him; it was too risky. Dwight looked at the director and then back at Kevin, shifting his weight from one leg to another.

"Shoot him," the director calmly said.

Dwight grimaced as tears streamed down his face.

"Shoot him!"

Dwight feverishly gripped the gun, staring at Kevin with what looked like pure agonizing rage.

"This is all *your* fault!"

It all happened so fast. Kevin felt someone pushing him to the side just in time for a loud bang to thunder in the cellblock, making Kevin's ears ring. Screams filled the cellblock, and when Kevin looked to the left, he saw Mark lying on his back, a red dot on his chest growing by the second.

"NO!" Kevin shouted and quickly rushed to Mark's side, falling to his knees.

Mark opened his mouth, and a trickle of blood ran down his cheek.

"Mark! Stay with me!" Kevin pleaded.

He instinctively pressed the wound on Mark's chest to stop the bleeding.

"Hold on, Mark. Hold on. You're gonna be okay!"

Mark gasped before looking at Kevin and smiling.

"You... you were right all along," Mark muttered.

"What? About what?" Kevin asked, letting a tear drop on the floor.

Mark coughed and took a shallow breath before saying, "We're not gonna be laughing at those barrels after all."

He let out a chuckle and then ceased all movement, his face frozen in a contorted smile.

"Mark! MARK!" Kevin started shaking his friend, but he wouldn't budge.

His eyes remained open, the smile still barely plastered to his face. Everything around Kevin seemed to fade into nothingness as he placed Mark's head on the floor and gently closed his eyes, stifling his whimpers. As if remembering just then, he looked up at Dwight. He was looking at Mark's lifeless body with wide eyes, pale in the face. Andy was slowly approaching Dwight with his gun drawn, uttering words of negotiation, but Dwight didn't seem to hear him as he was transfixed on Mark.

"You... you killed him!" Kevin hissed.

Dwight shook his head and, through tears, said, "I-I'm sorry... I didn't mean to... I..."

"Son, just put the gun down, alright? Andy politely said.

Dwight sobbed uncontrollably for a moment before calming down. He exhaled deeply and then calmly said, "I'm sorry. I can't go back."

He put the muzzle of the gun in his mouth, and a loud bang filled the room once again.

"No!" Andy shouted, but it was too late.

Blood painted the wall and door behind Dwight, and Dwight's lifeless body fell to the ground as more screams filled the air. His head was turned sideways, and Kevin saw a large hole at the back of his head. A pool of blood rapidly grew around the gunshot wound.

He was dead.

Everyone stared at his dead body in a trance for what felt like minutes, even though Kevin realized it must have only been seconds since Dwight stopped moving. He had never seen a dead body, let alone watched someone die before he joined Camp Firwood. After everything he's been through here, he knew that he would need years of therapy. As he stared at the assistant counselor's now lifeless body, he couldn't tell what he felt. Dwight was a victim turned killer just like him. A cackle filled the room, coming from the director's cell. He gripped the bars and said., "Looks like you can't protect any child, can you, Andy?"

He laughed some more, but Andy ignored him. He stared at Dwight's body before saying, "Kids, come on. We need to leave. We'll get your cellphones and call the police. Come on, move it."

The campers hesitantly started leaving the cellblock one by one, making their way around the dead bodies. Kevin looked down at Mark's lifeless body again. With his eyes closed, he looked like he might simply be peacefully sleeping. Kevin knelt next to the body and put a hand on Mark's already-cold wrist. He let out another sob before saying, "I'll protect Sherry for you. I promise."

Kevin felt a gentle hand on his shoulder.

"Son. We have to go," Andy said forlornly.

Kevin sniffled and nodded.

"Yeah. Yeah," he uttered.

As Andy slowly ushered Kevin outside, the director stared at them and hissed.

"This isn't over. You think you're doing something here, Andy, but you're not. This is only *one* camp. There are more of us all over the country. You can't stop us!"

For the first time today, there was spite in his voice. Kevin looked at him, but Andy muttered, "'Don't pay attention to him, son."

"You have no idea what you've gotten yourself into, you hear?!" the director continued more violently, now that Kevin and Andy were closer to the exit. "The Company will not let this slide!"

As soon as they were through, Andy grabbed the doorknob and slammed the door of the cellblock shut.

***

The campers went into the main lodge and retrieved their personal belongings. Most of them were feverish about getting their hands back on their cellphones. Kevin himself knew that he would have been, too, had he not felt numb after witnessing the tragic event just earlier. He expected to have the campers fight over who would charge their phone first, but they were instead woefully quiet.

Like a funeral.

Andy brought some power strips from the storage to let more campers charge their phones at once. Even with the five power strips, the campers still had to divide over who would charge their phone first. They split into two groups. Kevin was in the first group, and he impatiently waited like a drug addict, constantly checking

422

how much percentage he had – more to get his mind off things than for any other reasons. The glowing screen of his phone gave him slight comfort when he turned it on. There was still no signal, and connecting to his own internet proved useless. Despite that, he entered the last conversation he had with Amy in messenger and stared at their final exchange. It was a meme he sent her, and she replied with multiple emojis that expressed crying from laughter. He laughed at it, suppressing newly formed sobs in his throat.

That was about two weeks ago, but it felt like years. Would he receive some missed messages from Amy when he got a signal? Or would she have forgotten about him by now? Somehow, at this moment, he didn't care, even though he knew he would later.

Twenty-nine percent. Thirty percent. Thirty-one.

"Uh, Mr. Andy?" Bill said.

"What is it, son?" Andy asked.

"Look at this."

Kevin looked up with dreary eyes and saw Bill holding stacks of papers that he had pulled out from the desk in the storage room. He handed them to Andy and said, "This has the names of all the campers. And all the information about us. How much we were sold for and even what happened to us. Look!"

Andy took the papers and flipped through them with an expressionless face. The loud voices of the campers filled the air as they rushed to ask about their own names. Andy started reading the papers loudly and calmly, causing the campers to shut up.

"Samuel Taylors. Sold for nine thousand, five hundred, and thirty-four dollars. Status: disposal. Norton Macready. Sold for six thousand and five dollars. Status: blank."

"Son of a bitch!" Norton cursed.

The groundskeeper kept on reading, passing on to the campers the papers he was done with. And then he came to Kevin's name.

"Kevin Nilsen. Sold for eleven thousand, six hundred dollars. Status: trial."

Kevin couldn't believe what he was hearing. Andy handed him the paper, and he stared at his name at the bottom of the list. Eleven fucking thousand dollars. That's how much his parents valued his life. He was considered more expensive than the others. Mark, who was near the top of the page, was sold for meager four thousand dollars.

"I don't believe this," Kevin said. "The guard was telling the truth. Our parents sold us to be killed off or used like fucking toys."

Andy snatched the paper away from him.

"It's evidence. This is exactly what we need to bring down Camp Firwood. I need to make a call. Somebody give me a phone."

One of the campers gladly gave Andy his phone, and the groundskeeper nodded before dialing a number, putting the phone up to his ear, and going outside into the hallway. Kevin returned to his phone on the charger, staring at the screen but not seeing it. The gravity of the enormous discovery they just made began setting in with the entire group, as concerned murmurs filled the air. Kevin heard some of the campers trying to justify the evidence, stating that it may have been the camp's way of framing the parents, but there was no denying it – their parents wanted to get rid of them. Kevin looked at the battery percentage.

Thirty-nine. Forty.

Fuck it.

He detached the phone from the charger and clambered up to his feet, storming toward the exit.

"Where are you going?" Bill asked him.

He was in the minority that didn't sit glued to their cellphones while they were charging.

"The watchtower," Kevin said in passing and practically ran outside.

As soon as he was out, he sprinted across the grassy field, onto the shabby trail, and into the forest. Running felt good. The pain in his muscles and lungs reduced the mental pain. He couldn't keep up with the sprint the whole time, though, so he slowed down into a jog until he could speed up intermittently again. The wind stung his eyes – or maybe it was his own tears forming, he couldn't tell. He couldn't reach the tower soon enough, and when he did, the climb seemed like anything but bothersome this time. As much as he wanted to run up the stairs, he still had a slight fear of heights and didn't want to risk slipping.

That would be such a glorious way of dying. Taking down a pedophile, black-market, organ-stealing criminal organization and slipping, and falling to your death on a goddamn watchtower.

He pondered whether falling down and dying would really be so bad. With that thought, he slowed down. He had a mini heart attack when he put his hand on his right-side pocket and didn't feel his phone in there. He stopped and frantically dug through the pocket before he remembered that he actually put it in the opposite pocket. Relieved, he continued the ascend.

One day when we're out, we'll be laughing at those barrels.

The image of Mark came into his mind, encouraging him in his time of despair. And then another image of him happily eating a burger in the mess hall.

Oh boy! Kevin, look! Burgers!

Kevin had to stop. He leaned on his knees and exhaled steadily. He felt a weight on his chest, slowly and steadily causing him to have trouble breathing. His vision got blurry from the tears forming in his eyes, and he felt something getting caught in his throat.

"Mark, oh god… I'm… I'm so sorry."

He allowed himself to collapse so he was sitting on the stairs and let the flood gates open. He cried for his friend. He cried over the fact that they would never be able to meet outside the camp, to play *Mortal Kombat*, that he would never be able to introduce Mark to Amy and meet Sherry. And he cried over the way he behaved toward Mark just minutes before his death. The betrayal seemed like a million years away – an insignificant thing that would do nothing to taint their friendship. He just wanted his friend back.

Minutes later, when his tears had dried and he felt numb again, he was ready to continue climbing. He was eager to take out his phone right there and then and see if he had a signal, just to see if he could feel *something*, but the only thing stopping him was the fact that he could drop the phone, and that would leave him with two potential problems – going all the way back down, and assessing whether his phone had been shattered. By the time he made it to the top of the platform, he was panting, and his legs were burning. He wasn't aware of the pain until he stopped there. That wasn't important – what was important was seeing if he had a signal. Before he even reached into his pocket, he felt his phone buzzing.

And it wasn't just buzzing – it was going haywire. It was as if he was bombarded by message after message every second. He pulled out his phone, thrilled to see that he indeed had a signal and that his cellphone was rapidly collecting all the things his friends (and a few annoying marketing companies) had been sending him in his absence. Dozens of notifications for missed calls, dozens, if not hundreds of messages, some emails here and there, notifications from social media…

He kept swiping right, dismissing all of them. He saw a few messages from Rick, Luis, and Henry, asking how he was doing in the camp. Luis was frantic, sending a lot of question marks and asking if he was still alive. They still remembered him. They still cared, and it invigorated Kevin.

But they'd have to wait for his answer.

Right now, he had something more urgent to see. He entered his messenger, which was going crazy from the update. Icons of people on his list kept swapping places with each other like shuffling cards until the action finally halted, and he was left with a still screen of his unopened messages. He didn't even need to scroll down. Amy was on top, which meant that she was the last person who contacted him. He clicked her name, and the conversation opened to a bunch of missed messages and voice messages from her.

Hey Kev, you got any signal there?

I guess we probably won't be talking until you're back...

The next message was only one day later.

I spent some time with Rick and Henry today. Carla and Amanda were here, too. It's not the same without you here.

The following message was three days later.

Check out the kickass top I got today!

There was an image below. It was of Amy taking a picture in her bedroom mirror, wearing a black t-shirt that said *YES, I'M GOTH. NO, I'M NOT SATANIC.* Kevin smiled and couldn't stop smiling. The shirt was cool, yeah, but he smiled at Amy's face. Her disheveled black hair, her comically raised eyebrow, her provocatively pouted lips. Kevin zoomed in on her face.

That's her. That's her face. I remember her clearly now.

He let out a laugh, with newly formed tears in his eyes. He couldn't tell what kind of tears those were – of happiness and relief or of sadness over what he had witnessed in the camp. He stared at the picture, trying to absorb every detail about her as if he would go on another long period without seeing her. The next message was two days later.

I know you probably can't see these messages, but I'll just keep updating you, so you can read them when you're back online. Anyway, I went to the mall with Judy and Elizabeth today. There were some creeps hitting on us, but I threatened to kick their asses, so they left. You should have seen how I did it. Judy and Elizabeth said even they *got scared of me. :)*

Kevin felt a pang of jealousy, and at that moment, he was happy to feel anything. It meant that he was alive. He decided to scroll to the last message. It was two days ago.

I went to Barton Park today. The day was nice. It reminded me of the day when you and I went there and ended up running from the ranger. I know you can't see these messages, but I like to at least pretend I'm talking to you. I would never have the guts to tell you this if you were here or online, but... I miss you.

Kevin's heart jumped. That was Amy's last message. She probably felt embarrassed after sending that. Embarrassed, but hopefully not regretting it. No, she could have simply deleted the message. He exited the messenger and opened the dial. He input the first few numbers of Amy's number, which he still remembered, and pressed the call button. His heart raced as he placed the phone to his ear and listened to the first ring. He held his breath in anticipation. The second ring ended.

Click.

"Hello?" a confused, feminine voice stated on the other end.

Kevin opened his mouth, but no words came out.

"Hello?" the voice repeated with irritation this time.

Kevin realized that he was smiling dumbly to himself, but he didn't care. He didn't want to even try to contain the stupid grimace on his face. He heard Amy's voice, and right then, nothing else in the world mattered. Her voice was like a melody that dispersed all the bad around him.

"Amy?" he swallowed the invisible noodle in his throat and finally spoke up.

Her name felt sweet on his tongue, so much that he felt like he could say it over and over.

"Kevin? Kevin is that you?!" the way Amy raised her tone told Kevin that the excitement in her voice was tangible.

"Yes! Amy, it's me! I..." he found himself not knowing what to say.

Where would he even begin? How would he explain anything about Camp Firwood without causing her to think he was trying to mess with her? Luckily, Amy took over the reins.

"Kevin! Oh god, it's been two weeks; I thought you had forgotten about me!"

How could I ever forget you, Amy? he wanted to say in the flow of sudden emotions he had, but he decided to contain them.

He couldn't dump all his overwhelming emotions on her; it would probably creep her out.

"No, of course not," he said. "I thought *you* forgot about *me*."

Even *he* could hear how tired his voice sounded, like Ninja's when speaking normally, but he hoped Amy wouldn't notice it.

"Don't be ridiculous. You have no idea how empty it is without you here," she said through laughter.

Kevin felt butterflies in his stomach.

"Heh, okay. I'll probably be coming back home soon," he said.

"Really?" She asked, again with excitement in her voice. "Didn't you say you would be there much longer?"

"Yeah. But some things happened here, and, uh... we're all going home," he said as he stared at the endless firs over the horizon, feeling a sudden heartache again.

"Is something wrong, Kev? Are you okay over there? Do you need me to come to pick you up?"

Always so intuitive.

He didn't want to worry her, so he simply said, "No, no. Everything is okay. I mean..." he stopped mid-sentence to suppress a sob.

"Where is the camp? Tell me, and I'll come to get you."

Kevin cleared his throat and regained his composure.

"No, don't worry. Everything is fine now. Plus, you can't drive, Amy," his voice was shaky.

"What, you think I'm not ballsy enough to take Quentin's car and drive all the way out there?"

Kevin laughed. That's Amy, alright.

"Kevin, seriously, though. Li... I ca... pi... in..."

Amy's voice began breaking up, and Kevin frustratedly tried to catch bits and pieces of her speech. When he couldn't, he said, "Amy? Amy, you're breaking up. The signal is really bad over here. Amy?"

"Oh, no!" she said. "Liste... ust se... ge-"

"Amy!" the call ended.

It didn't matter because, in the next moment, a ping notified him of a message that arrived on his phone. It was from Amy.

Kev, are you really okay over there?

Kevin rapidly typed in a message.

Yes, I'm okay now. I'll be back soon, alright?

Okay :) Try to stay safe out there, alright? Amy wrote.

Don't worry about me. I'm as tough as a tank, he sent her a winking smiley face.

And Amy? he typed.

Yeah? she asked.

Kevin typed in the next message and hovered over the send button. He wanted to send it, but there was also something stopping him. He stared at his phone while his heart thudded more violently than any time he had been in a life or death situation in the camp.

Yeeeeees? Amy sent him a sardonic message when she probably saw in the chat that he was typing and then stopped.

Before he gave himself the chance to chicken out, he clicked on the send button.

I miss you too.

23
Six Years Later

Kevin was sitting in front of the cabins with the rest of the campers. Suddenly, an all-too-familiar voice boomed from the front.

"Campers! Line up!" it was Mr. Adams.

The campers hurriedly rushed to their respective spots. The whole commotion lasted only a dozen seconds or so before the air went entirely silent. Mr. Adams began a roll call, and once everyone was accounted for, he started giving the campers chores. He told Kevin to follow him so that he could show him to his own duty. Kevin felt that something was off, but he couldn't tell what. He went along with Mr. Adams all the way to the back of the mess hall, and only when he saw a bunch of rusted, worn-out barrels did he realize what it was.

He wasn't supposed to be here. When did he return to the camp? And how?

I can't do this anymore.

He would need to start planning an escape. This time it would be much harder to trick the counselors. Just the thought of going through the whole process demoralized him beyond words. He felt like crying. No time for tears, he had to fight. He was going to make it out of here. Even as Mr. Adams commanded him to clean the barrels, even as Kevin took the brushes and began scrubbing, he knew that he had to get out. The barrels remained tarnished, and no matter how hard he scrubbed them, no rust or stains came off. He rubbed harder, scraping his knuckles on the rust in the process. He felt no pain.

Scrub. Scrub. Scrub.

The rust refused to come off. It was going to take him at least two hours to finish all the barrels at this rate. And he had to hurry

431

because The Choosing was taking place soon. Someone would get sent into the woods.

I can't do this anymore.

Suddenly, a horn started blaring loudly. Was it the Camp Firwood anthem? No, it was something else. Maybe a warning for the campers to assemble for The Choosing? The sound got louder and louder at a rapid pace as if moving in Kevin's direction until it was all he could hear.

Kevin jolted his head up with a gasp. He looked around in confusion while his heart pounded heavily in his chest. It took him a long moment to realize that he wasn't back in Camp Firwood and couldn't have been. He was in his apartment. He rubbed his eyes, realizing that he must have fallen asleep at his desk. He stared at the messily strewn papers on top before getting up from the rickety old chair. A horn blared outside on the street again—a frustrated driver who was in a hurry, undoubtedly. Kevin approached the window on the left and peeked outside. It was still raining. The light drizzle was slowly turning into a downpour with droplets incessantly battering the window. The sky was grey, verging on black, making it look like it was verging on nighttime.

He glanced at his watch. It was only 3 p.m. He ran a hand through his greasy hair, contemplating whether he should get something to eat before getting back to work. He gave a once over to the desk with the messy pile of papers, cringing at the sight. Realizing that he had a lot of work to do for the day, he waltzed over to the foyer and put his coat on. He grabbed the umbrella and the apartment keys off the shelf next to the entrance, opened the door, and stepped outside. He lived on the fourth floor, but since the building had no elevator, he had to stroll down the staircase. He inadvertently glanced at the peeling walls of the apartment hallway. It was the first thing he noticed when he moved in, and it bothered the hell out of him, but now he barely even noticed them.

He saw the old lady from apartment number 21 slowly climbing the stairs up to the second floor. Kevin stopped and asked her if she

432

needed help climbing up, but she showed no indication that she heard him whatsoever. Kevin muttered an 'okay then' before continuing down the stairs. The drumming of the rain became audible as he approached the entrance, and as soon as he opened the door, the sounds of crunching upon the pavement got much louder. A car drove by with a swooshing sound down the street, much slower than it would on a normal, sunny day. Kevin opened his umbrella and raised it above his head before stepping outside.

As he walked down the street, he kept thinking about the dream he had earlier. He could vividly see Mr. Adams' face – his annoying grin, his grasshopper-like tall figure, his camp shorts that were pulled much higher than they should be, and the socks that were stretched so high up that they almost reached up to his knees. He could even hear the head counselor's voice in his head, greeting them and doing the roll call.

Good morning, campers. Camper Kevin. Camper Norton. Camper Mark.

Camper Mark...

Kevin felt a pang of pain in his heart as well as a wave of destructive emotions building up in him. He quickly tried to shift his thoughts to another topic to avoid causing his pain to resurface again. But whichever subject came to his mind, it wasn't a pleasant one.

I can't do this anymore.

He turned left around the corner and continued down the empty street. A car occasionally passed by, but other than that, there were no people outside. Kevin's mind inadvertently shifted onto the events directly after Camp Firwood. The final day at the camp felt so vivid and yet so blurry. He remembered everything up until he climbed the watchtower and contacted Amy in absolute clarity. But then the rest of the day...

The arrival of the choppers, the special police units that stormed the camp, the arresting of the Camp Firwood staff, the ushering of the campers inside the choppers, the three-hour-long flight over the endless woods, the arrival to the police station in Portland, the flashing of the news photographers' cameras, the 'polite' interrogation by the detectives...

Andy was with the campers the whole time, save for the moments when he was needed by some tough-looking police officials. They set up a temporary shelter for the campers inside the police station since they couldn't send them back to their homes. The evidence Andy brought in was more than enough to convict not just the staff of Camp Firwood but the outside operating staff and the parents. Kevin remembered it like it was yesterday. The entire process was quick. The campers, one by one, stepped up and talked in front of the courtroom about their grisly experience in Camp Firwood. The jury was appalled – if that word could even be used to begin describing their reaction. Kevin knew that the people involved in Camp Firwood were convicted before the judge even gave them their sentence.

On top of all that, Andy's evidence only further sealed their fates. The director wasn't smiling anymore when he was brought inside the courtroom, no longer wearing his fancy suit but orange prisoner attire. His face remained blank when the judge sentenced him to life in prison. Just like Mr. Adams. He never said a word even when the judge personally called him forward to present his own words of defense. It was clear that the judge wasn't convinced that the counselors were not coerced into collaborating with the director, and he wanted to give them a chance to explain their actions.

But when Mr. Adams said nothing, the judge simply frowned and sentenced him to one hundred and fifty years in prison. The rest of the counselors got between forty and sixty. Nurse Mary got only twenty-five. She presented a tear-jerking story to the judge about how hard her life was and how she didn't have enough money to feed her younger brother and was thus forced to join Camp Firwood.

It almost worked for her. Almost.

But when Andy presented the evidence pertaining to Mary's contract in the camp, which clearly explained that she was aware of basically everything that was going on in the camp, the judge's compassion disappeared instantaneously. Mary was dragged out of the courtroom kicking and screaming.

Next came all the parents involved in selling their children to the camp. Kevin watched in relish as his mother and father were sentenced to life in prison, and how their faces contorted into pure fear. Kevin's mother searched the crowd for her son, and once she found him, she began pleading and screaming for him to say something, to stop them from being taken to prison, swearing that they would never do that to their child. Kevin simply watched with an expressionless face, locking his eyes with his parents until the moment they were out of the courtroom. The satisfaction wasn't enough. He wished that he could watch them suffer in prison.

Mark's parents came about three days later. They were pompous-looking people with a look that pretty much matched that of a couple who would sell their child to a shady company. Kevin saw similarities between Mark and his parents in physical appearance, and it disgusted him. He didn't want to see anything of Mark in those horrible people. The campers were called on, one by one, to testify about Mark's death. Kevin spent the longest on the witness stand, talking about his and Mark's friendship, about the fact that they planned on escaping until he betrayed them in order to protect his little sister, and how, eventually… he tragically got shot by Dwight.

He broke down while talking about it but managed to regain his composure and tell the whole story. When he saw Mark's little sister Sherry climbing on top of the witness stand, clutching her teddy bear with swollen eyes, he felt sharp, knife-like pain in his heart. She looked devastated. But more than that, she looked frightened beyond words. She kept glancing at her parents in the courtroom until the judge ordered the police officials to escort them out. Sherry then tentatively opened up about how the parents verbally abused Mark, especially the dad, calling him a fat useless piece of shit and other names, telling him how he wished he was more like the other kids.

Kevin knew that Mark's parents were bad, but he didn't know to what extent that went. Mark only told him bits and pieces. They never had a chance to talk more about it after the camp. Mark's parents got the same sentence as Kevin's parents but were sent to a maximum-security prison. After the court, Kevin approached Sherry and introduced himself as Mark's friend. He said that he would be here whenever she needed something and that she should never hesitate to call him. She was placed in a foster home where Kevin made sure to visit her with every chance he got. He even sent her financial support as much as he could since he inherited a lot of money from his parents. He really didn't care about spending it on himself.

As for the campers – most of them were sent to either their closest families or put inside a foster care home. Kevin himself was adopted by his Aunt Kelly, his mother's sister. Aunt Kelly and Uncle Roy were more than happy to add Kevin to their family. His cousins Anna and Patrick were ecstatic to have a new sibling, although Kevin couldn't mirror their emotions – not then. The campers had a heartfelt goodbye before they were separated. Kevin felt especially connected to Bill due to their time in the woods. He later learned that that bond is something soldiers called 'brotherhood,' which was essentially a camaraderie they formed during their time on the battlefield together.

Steve created a group chat on Facebook called *Survivors of Camp Firwood*, and he invited all the campers to join. Only a small number of the new campers joined, and around thirty of the older ones. The chat didn't stay active for too long, though, because people began leaving one by one after a while. Kevin himself muted the chat's notifications since he couldn't bear to be constantly reminded of the traumatic events he endured in Camp Firwood. It was unfair. Mark was supposed to be alive. He was supposed to go back to his sister

436

and have a normal life with her until they both grew up. He and Kevin were supposed to play *Mortal Kombat* together and bond over something else, other than camp-related stuff.

"Hey, watch it!" a man on the street shouted when Kevin bumped into him with his shoulder.

"Sorry," Kevin muttered, his eyes filled with tears at the reminiscence of Mark.

I can't do this anymore.

He turned left and entered a small, inconspicuous burger place. The best one in town, in his opinion. He was going to take Mark here when they met up after the camp. As soon as he pushed the glass door open, the bell above chimed, and the lady behind the counter looked up at Kevin. Kevin gave her a slight nod of greeting as he closed his umbrella and made his way to her. The savory smells of the frying beef filled his nostrils, while the sizzling reached him from the back. He approached the counter where the woman was and scanned the menu pinned on the wall behind her.

"I'll uh… I'll have a regular burger," he said as he pointed at the nearest box.

He looked down at the woman to see her staring at him with a suspicious glare. It must have been the way he looked. His five o'clock shadow, his tired eyes, his dirty jacket. The lady was probably wondering if he could even afford the food.

"How much?" he asked.

"Three forty-five," the lady exclaimed, not looking away.

Kevin fumbled inside his pocket and pulled out a wrinkled five-dollar bill, and placed it on the counter above the stall. The lady reached out to take the bill and straightened it up with both hands before putting it into the cash register. She gave Kevin the change and then looked over her shoulder toward the kitchen and shouted.

"One regular!"

Kevin took a step back and glanced in various directions around the burger place. It was a nice, cozy place, overlooked by a lot of people in Portland. The staff were not that friendly, but that didn't matter, because their burgers were excellent. Five minutes later, the lady slapped Kevin's packaged burger on top of the counter. "Your burger."

"Thank you," Kevin said and grabbed the burger.

He saw the grease penetrating the paper, but that somehow made it even more appealing. There was something magical about unwrapping fast, greasy food that always had Kevin salivating. He opened the door and his umbrella before stepping outside. The beating of the rain was harder now, and Kevin saw the first lightning appearing in the sky momentarily before disappearing. A ten or so seconds later, thunder followed.

He remembered the day he was driven by his parents to the camp years ago. It rained, and he distinctly remembered thinking how the weather matched his mood. If that were the case, the rain today turning into a downpour was exactly what could explain how he felt now. As he walked down the street, he couldn't help but wonder how his parents were. He hoped that they were suffering in prison. He hoped that his father had a hole in his anus the size of a baseball and that his mother got shanked by her cellmate or other prisoners in the courtyard. But that would perhaps be too fast. Maybe a life of suffering in prison is precisely what was needed for a fragment of justice.

Kevin got a few letters from them at Aunt Kelly's address but refused to read any of them. Even though Aunt Kelly allowed him to make the choice on his own, he didn't want anything to do with them. He was afraid that if he read something from them, it might ignite him to feel some compassion, and he didn't want that. He wanted to continue hating them. He wanted that hate to fester and grow until it replaced the years of agony his parents inflicted on him. And so he never read their letters, and he never wrote back.

He managed to step inside his apartment building just in time for the rain to suddenly become stronger. The drumming turned into a waterfall-like sound, and Kevin quickly closed the building door behind him to prevent the splashing water from getting inside. He closed his umbrella and climbed up the stairs to his apartment. He unlocked the door, stepped inside, closed it, and locked it again with the deadbolt. He strode over to the living room (or as he called it, multipurpose room since it was a one-bedroom apartment) and sat on the bed.

Upon unwrapping the burger, the juicy aroma filled his nose once again, and he just then realized how hungry he was. He took the first bite, allowing the grease to flow down his chin. He knew that he was probably killing himself slowly with the kind of food he constantly ate, but he was too occupied with other things to care. Plus, he was still thin, which must have accounted for something. He'd go the entire day without eating and then have one meal similar to this one – that couldn't have possibly been so damaging to him. Not as much as the meds and the alcohol, anyway. As he swallowed the next bite of meat, onions, and lettuce, he wiped his greasy chin and glanced at his working desk. The piles of papers were still strewn on top of it, but he wasn't looking at that. His eyes were focused on the wall above the desk.

There were countless papers pinned on a huge board, some messily hanging, others pinned meticulously here and there. There was a map of The United States there, too, taking up the majority of the board, marked in various locations with little post-it notes and handwritten messages on them. Kevin dropped the burger onto the paper, suddenly no longer feeling hungry. He stood up and walked over to the wall of papers as he put his hands on his hips. He glanced at the map, at the area in Oregon near Portland. Mark's picture hung right above the spot where Camp Firwood's location was.

Mark looked happy in the picture, grinning a wide grin. It was the same grin he had the day the campers were served burgers. It felt strange sometimes to look at Mark's picture and see him as a teen. Kevin couldn't help but wonder what he would have been like as an adult. Would he and Kevin have been hanging out after getting out of the camp? Would they have played video games together or gone to all sorts of food places? Would they have gone to college and kept in touch? Would Kevin have introduced him to his friends and Amy? What would his girlfriend have thought about Mark?

Probably nothing good.

When he first got back to civilization, Amy was the first one to come to visit him. They embraced in a long, tight hug. She knew what Kevin had been through, and she simply ran her hand through his hair, consoling him, telling him that everything was going to be okay. Rick, Luis, and Henry arrived not long after her but didn't stay as long as Amy did. When Kevin moved in with his Aunt and Uncle, Amy spent every day with him. She got him to move out of the house and kicked him out of his bouts of depression by hanging out with him. Whenever he was with her, Kevin felt rehabilitated. It wasn't long until they went back to Barton Park and Kevin finally gained enough courage to kiss her.

Kevin picked up his phone and entered the messenger. He clicked on Amy's name and went into the search option. He typed in, 'I miss you, too.' Hundreds of search results popped up, but Kevin searched the first one he'd ever sent her.

Oh, and Amy?

Then Amy's message below.

Yeah? And then another. *Yeeeeees?*

I miss you, too, was Kevin's message.

He scrolled down through the old messages. They were constantly chatting with each other and sending all sorts of links, pictures, selfies, and stuff. Then when they kissed and started dating, they were all lovey-dovey with each other. Hundreds of *I love you, miss you, can't wait to see you* and heart icon messages, cuddling and kissing all the time. And then it gradually started to wane. The chatting became more sterile and formal, the *love you* and *miss you* messages less frequent until they were essentially non-existent, the meetups more formal. Kevin went down to the final exchange he and Amy had two days ago.

440

I'll be there around 5, she wrote.

Okay, he replied.

No new messages from her since then. It was expected. A part of him hoped that she would text him, but he knew it was just wishful thinking. Two days ago was when he last saw her. She came by to visit him and bring him some food. She was cold and distant, and by then, Kevin already knew what the right approach was. Whenever Amy was quiet, it usually meant she had a problem she was trying to resolve in her head, and approaching her then and trying to offer some attention would do no good. So he decided to do what worked best in the past –let her deal with her own shit until she was ready to talk about it. He thanked her for the food and offered to make her some coffee, but she politely declined. Then came the difficult part.

"We really need to think about where we are right now, Kev," Amy said.

She was sitting on the sofa while Kevin sat on the bed across from her. He nodded. He knew that's why she was here. She mentioned that they needed to have a serious conversation.

"We can't keep going like this. It's destroying us," she said.

Kevin kept silent as he stared at the dust-covered floor.

"Aren't you going to say anything?" she asked with concern in her voice.

"I don't know what to say," he said and looked up at her. "I can't stop now. I'm really, really close."

"Kevin, listen to yourself," Amy got more irked. "You sound like a crazy conspiracist. You have to let it go."

"They killed Mark, Amy. And countless other campers," Kevin hissed and furrowed his nose.

Amy stood up from the sofa and shouted.

"Mark sold all of you out, Kevin! He was gonna save his own life in exchange for yours! He pretended to be your friend while plotting behind your back!"

"No!" Kevin shot up from the bed with a furious shout. "He was doing what he thought was right to protect Sherry! I would have done the same if it were your life on the line!"

He pointed a finger at her and turned away, not able to face her. There was a long moment of stifling silence before Amy finally spoke up again.

"Kevin..." she started. He heard her sigh before she said through tears. "I can't do this anymore," her voice was quivering now, and she sniffled.

Kevin turned around to see her red in the face, with a hand across her mouth. She sniffled once more and said, this time completely calmly, "I love you, but... I'm sorry. I just can't do this anymore. I tried to help you. I tried to be supportive. But you just won't let go of the past. I can't fight your demons anymore. I can't... I can't keep letting you bring me down with you, as selfish as that sounds."

She wiped the tears off her face and sniffled one more time. She put her hands on her hips and stared at the ground, biting her lip. She then looked up at Kevin and said, "I don't wanna do this, but you're giving me no choice. You're going to have to choose. Either you forget about them, and you start living your life, or..." she stopped, newly formed tears glistening in her eyes. "Or you'll never see me again."

Kevin sat back down on the bed and stared at the floor again. He closed his eyes firmly, and after what felt like an eternity, responded "I'm sorry, Amy. I can't let it go."

Amy's face went slack, her eyebrows arching upward. She rubbed her shoulder and nodded before saying.

"Just like that, huh? Well... Well... I guess this is goodbye then."

Kevin kept staring at the floor silently. She went over to pick up her purse, sniffling along the way. She tromped across the room to the door and turned around one more time to face him.

"I wish you luck in your life, Kevin."

And with that, she turned around and stepped through the door quickly, slamming it shut behind her. Kevin had no doubt that Amy broke down even before the door closed properly. He thought about chasing after her, hugging her tightly, asking for her forgiveness, telling her that he'd change.

But he knew that was a lie. There was no escaping his past.

Kevin closed out of the messenger. He felt numb for the past two days. Being without Amy felt like losing a limb. And to have the burden that weighed on him on top of that didn't make things easier. He didn't have anyone else to talk to, either. Henry had gradually stopped hanging out with the gang. Luis had moved across the country for college, and Rick didn't really speak to Kevin that much anymore. The people with who he used to be able to share everything in the past were now complete strangers. His Aunt Kelly and Uncle Roy sent him messages from time to time, but he didn't want to bother them with such grave problems. And he definitely didn't want to bother Patrick and Anna with that, especially since they seemed to be having such good lives.

Andy wasn't there to help him anymore, either. Kevin looked up at the papers plastered to the wall. He glanced at a newspaper clipping on the left.

FORMER POLICE OFFICER KILLED IN PETTY ROBBERY.

It was dated two years ago. It probably wasn't a petty robbery, though. Just like the cause of Slow Ethan's death wasn't choking by food at his computer. Everybody knew he was snooping around the dark web, trying to find out more about The Company, and it was only a matter of time before they caught him.

Kevin's phone started buzzing. It was an unmemorized number. *It's her!*

He swiped the green button and put the phone to his ear.

"Hello?" he said with a croaky voice.

"Mr. Nilsen. It's Selena. We spoke a few days ago," a formal female voice greeted him.

443

"I remember," Kevin briskly retorted.

"Well, I'm happy to inform you that the background check went okay, and we are ready to proceed with the next steps. Are you okay with that?"

"Yeah," Kevin said as he leaned on the desk.

"Good. Now, I have to warn you that after you make the final decision and sign the papers, there is no way to effectively terminate the contract until it is over. Do you understand?"

"I do."

Good. Then before we proceed, I have to ask you one more time. Do you want to proceed with the next step?"

I can't do this anymore.

Kevin pulled away from the desk and stared at the papers on the wall. He looked at the picture of Mark smiling widely. The innocent smile that was forever extinguished by the mysterious company.

We aren't gonna be laughing at those barrels.

"Yes," Kevin responded before he could change his mind.

"Good. In that case, the company vehicle will pick you up this Friday at 5 a.m. You don't need to bring anything since you will get all you need at the site."

"Alright. Thank you," Kevin said coldly.

The woman's voice suddenly became much perkier. She raised her tone jovially and said, "Welcome to Camp Oakwood, Groundskeeper."

THE END

Final Notes

Huge thanks for reading my book. If you enjoyed it, I would appreciate it if you left a review on the **Product page**. Your reviews help small-time authors like me grow and allow us to continue expanding our careers.

Made in the USA
Middletown, DE
25 August 2022

72280315R00249